STOLEN
ANGELS

BOOKS BY RITA HERRON

STOLEN ANGELS

RITA HERRON

bookouture

Published by Bookouture in 2022

An imprint of Storyfire Ltd.
Carmelite House
50 Victoria Embankment
London EC4Y 0DZ

www.bookouture.com

ISBN: 978-1-80314-093-3
eBook ISBN: 978-1-80314-092-6

This book is a work of fiction. Names, characters, businesses, organizations, places
and events other than those clearly in the public domain, are either the product of
the author's imagination or are used fictitiously. Any resemblance to actual
persons, living or dead, events or locales is entirely coincidental.

To my wonderful, beautiful daughter Emily, who inspired the character Emily Nettles. She's a loving, caring daughter, mother and foster parent who leads by example and faith.
So proud of you and love you always,
Mom

PROLOGUE

SAVANNAH, GEORGIA

The police thought her little girl was dead. Worse, that *she* killed her.

Renee Wilkinson fidgeted in the metal chair and stared at the detective seated across from her in stunned shock.

His cold stare cut through her like a knife.

Twisting her hands together, she bit back a sob as she pictured her six-year-old daughter's bright green eyes lighting up with a smile. She could not believe Kaylee had been missing for seven days and the police had arrested *her*.

They'd already arraigned her and set bond at two hundred thousand. Worse, she didn't have money to pay bail. And no one was listening to her...

The detective, a barrel-chested man named Forrester, had already condemned her. His voice was even colder as he stood, towering over her. "I'm going to give you one more chance to make a deal before you go into lockup to await trial."

He laid Kaylee's fuzzy pink blanket on the table, the one she always slept with. Her daughter was so attached to it she hid it in her backpack when she went to school. Hot tears gathered in Renee's eyes, and she reached for the blanket, desperate to hold it and inhale Kaylee's sweet scent.

But he shook his head and snatched it away. Anger seized Renee at his cruelty, then he laid Kaylee's kindergarten school picture on the table. A lot of little girls wore frilly dresses for picture day, but Kaylee hated dresses, and Renee just wanted her to be happy. So Kaylee had chosen the yellow T-shirt with kitty cats on it, her favorite, and denim shorts. She'd added a purple barrette to her shoulder-length silky blond hair.

The detective tapped the picture. "If you love her as you say, then tell me what happened."

"I told you I don't know," Renee cried. "We had a picnic at the beach and made sandcastles and... then I must have fallen asleep." God help her, how had that happened? She always made it a point not to take her eyes off her daughter at the beach. She glanced at the public defender who fidgeted in his chair and looked at his manicured nails. So far, he'd been worthless. Did he believe she was guilty, too?

"Or did you just push her out to sea and let her drown and be eaten by the sharks?" Detective Forrester snapped.

Emotions clogged Renee's throat. "I did not hurt Kaylee. I would never. I *love* her." She gripped the edge of the chair with clammy hands, her stomach heaving. Terrifying scenarios tormented her, like they had for days. Where was her baby girl? Was she safe? Who had taken her?

"I don't believe you, Ms. Wilkinson." He pinned her with accusing eyes. "I understand you have a drinking problem."

Renee shifted uncomfortably. "No, I don't."

"You belong to AA," he said curtly.

She looked down at her own nails, which she'd chewed to the nubs. "I did join a couple of years ago, but I haven't had a drink since. You can ask my sponsor."

Damn him. He'd already tried and convicted her.

"I will be doing that. But for now, you're facing criminal negligence charges," he said bluntly.

Disbelief roiled through her. "Why aren't you looking for Kaylee instead of grilling me?"

"We're still searching for her." A muscle ticked in Forrester's wide jaw. "But I have no patience for anyone who hurts or neglects children. And neither will the fellow prisoners where you're going."

Renee gaped at him then angled her head toward the public defender, her heart hammering. But the scrawny young man simply looked away, his leg jiggling as if he had some place more important to go.

"Please listen to me," she said in a pained whisper. "I didn't hurt Kaylee. I love her with all my heart. Someone must have taken her, and they could be out of the state by now." If Kaylee was even alive. When she'd first insisted that her daughter had been kidnapped, the police had warned her that every day that passed diminished their chances of finding her.

Detective Forrester gestured to the guard at the door. "Get her out of my sight."

"Please find her! She must be so scared right now," she pleaded as the guard gripped her arm and hauled her through the door. Tears rained down her cheeks with every step they took. They passed through a hallway then another door to a block of cells. The nauseating stench of urine and mold swirled around her. The concrete walls were a faded pea-green, the floor cement, the toilet in the corner of the cell was rusty and stained with God knows what.

The guard's keys jangled as he unlocked the cell, unfastened her handcuffs and pushed her inside. The sound of the door slamming echoed, and she gripped the bars with white knuckled hands. "Please tell them to keep searching for Kaylee," she begged. "Whoever took her could be hurting her now."

He simply stared at her, his expression hard, then he strode away, his shoes squeaking on the floor as he disappeared.

Despair and shock crushed her, and she staggered to the cot against the wall, sank onto it and began to sob. Christmas was two weeks away. Kaylee had begged for a swing set, and she'd already put one on hold. She'd pictured her daughter's face when she saw it, Kaylee's hair blowing in the wind as she pumped her legs in the swing, and she choked on another sob. If the police were convinced she was guilty and that Kaylee was dead, they would give up looking for her.

She might never see her daughter again...

ONE

CROOKED CREEK

One year later

Detective Ellie Reeves was taking a night off from crime. Over the last few months, the cases in the small Georgian town of Crooked Creek had worn on her, but November had been blessedly quiet, just as her office was tonight. No files of dead women or children to sort through. No locals pounding at her door with complaints that if she'd only been faster to take down the last killer who'd stalked the town, she could have saved more lives.

She didn't need anyone telling her that. The voice of guilt nagged her all the time.

A sudden shiver rippled through her, and she thought of Ms. Eula, the old woman who lived on the hill and who insisted that she heard whispers of the dead. As Ms. Eula would say, it felt like the quiet before the storm.

Stop being paranoid. The town deserved a reprieve and so did she. She'd even tried to make peace with her parents, Vera and Randall, for lying to her about her adoption all her life. After months of frostiness, she'd shared turkey dinner with them on Thanksgiving.

Now the season of giving was upon them – six days till Christmas. Hopefully this month would be peaceful, bring the town closer together, and restore hope to those devastated by the wave of crime that had plagued the area.

Deputy Shondra Eastman, Ellie's coworker and friend, ducked her head into Ellie's office, her black braid wrapped into a bun on top of her head. "I'm heading over to the square—working security for the Christmas pageant tonight."

Ellie nodded. "I'm on my way. See you there."

As Shondra left, Ellie tied her shoulder-length ash-blond hair into a ponytail holder, added a touch of lip balm, then grabbed her winter coat and tugged it on. Shondra kept trying to convince her to spruce up with a little more makeup, some eye shadow to accentuate her blue eyes, but Ellie was more of a tomboy than a glam girl.

Special Agent Derrick Fox was waiting at the door, casually dressed tonight in jeans and a dark-blue shirt that accentuated his bronzed skin, and they walked outside together.

This was his first time experiencing the holiday in Crooked Creek and she tried to see the small-town festivities through his eyes. Twinkling lights adorned all the storefronts and you could see the town's Christmas tree lit up in the center of the square from the police department. Families strolled the sidewalks, where old fashioned decorations and a giant Santa sleigh added to the mountain charm.

Derrick worked out of the FBI's field office in Atlanta, but the governor had instigated a task force to handle crimes in the area of Bluff County, which encompassed the small towns of Crooked Creek and Stony Gap, a few miles apart. At the governor's insistence, Derrick was spearheading it, and Ellie and local ranger Cord McClain had worked with him. Last month Derrick had rented a cabin on the river here and traveled back and forth when needed.

In spite of the clear skies, a stiff wind ruffled her hair, hinting that rain might be on the way. Holiday music filled the air along with church bells as they crossed the street.

"Looks like a big turnout," Derrick said as they strolled toward the town square and the covered stage. Tonight, as they did every year, the kids in town presented a show to highlight the holiday. In lieu of buying tickets, a donation box had been set up by the tree to collect gifts for the needy.

"It usually is." She nodded at families and smiled at the children who were chattering about telling Santa the things on their Christmas wish list.

Last month, the tree had held prayer requests for Thanksgiving, cards collected by Emily Nettles, the thirty-something head of the local prayer group called the Porch Sitters. Now the tree sparkled with colorful Christmas tree lights that illuminated the paper angels on the limbs.

"What are the angels for?" Derrick asked.

"They hold requests from churches, charities and the foster system for toys and items to be donated to needy children and families, and to the children's hospital. It's a tradition in Crooked Creek."

This year, Ellie's mother Vera was coordinating efforts to ensure every child in need received a present.

Ellie spotted her near the stage talking to Emily, who'd organized the program tonight. In keeping with the theme, the kids were dressed in angel costumes, while the adults in the choir wore traditional caroler outfits. Ellie's father stood by Vera and threw up a hand to wave, and she waved back.

Chairs were set up in front of the stage and were already filling up. "My sister used to sing when she was little," Derrick said, his voice gruff.

Ellie squeezed his arm. "I'm sorry, Derrick. I know the holidays must be difficult when you've lost someone."

He shoved his hands in his pockets as the wind stirred again, rattling the limbs on the trees as if ghosts of the past were whispering through the pines. "After my sister disappeared, my mother used to buy presents for Kim each year and put them under the tree, hoping she'd come back to us." He cleared his throat, obviously still lost in the memory. "After we learned that she'd died, she donated them to a women's shelter."

Ellie swallowed hard.

A dark-haired little girl ran by, swinging hands with her friend. "I want a playhouse for Christmas," she squealed.

"I'm asking Santa for a puppy," the other child said.

Their excitement seemed to drag Derrick from his grief, and he smiled at the children as they giggled and pointed to Santa, who was taking his place on his throne. A photographer was set up nearby, preparing to capture the Santa visits, and two teens dressed as elves stood ready to hand out candy canes to the kids.

Emily stepped up to the microphone and tapped it to quiet the crowd. "Welcome to the Angel Pageant. Time for all our performers to meet in staging."

Children ran and squealed as they hurried to gather behind the stage.

A sudden stillness in the air made the hair on the back of Ellie's neck prickle, and she looked at the sky and saw the shadow of a storm on the horizon.

Across the street, she spotted Shondra and Crooked Creek's other deputy, Heath Landrum, combing the surroundings.

She'd never expected a serial killer to haunt the area, but she had dealt with more than one the past year. Her finger automatically stroked her chest where the maniac, the Hunter, had carved his name into her skin.

She'd had plastic surgery to repair the tissue, but she still woke up screaming sometimes, as if she could feel the blade carving into her.

She forced the memory away as the angels climbed the stage and began to sing. This evening was about having fun and celebrating.

Nothing bad could happen tonight.

TWO

He watched the little girls giggle and chatter as they gathered on the stage. Their glittery angel wings glowed beneath the white Christmas lights, their faces the most beautiful thing he'd ever seen.

His breath quickened. He knew he wasn't supposed to be here. It was dangerous for him. Dangerous for them.

But the draw was too strong. When he'd seen them practicing last week, he'd stood beneath the shade of a live oak and been mesmerized. On the stage now, a cherub-faced child's curly dark hair bounced as she grabbed a little blond's hand and they hugged excitedly. A cute redhead with freckles tugged at her angel wings, and the girl with the big red bow beside her waved at her mommy in the audience.

He knew the little girl with the brown curls. She lived down the street from him. He'd been watching her ever since he'd moved there. She was funny and precocious and had sky-blue eyes that lit up when she laughed.

During the summer, he'd watched her singing as she picked flowers in her backyard and ran through the sprinkler. Last week, through the window, he'd seen her skip into the den in her fuzzy red and white pajamas and gobble down a snowman sugar cookie as she hung the ornaments.

The woman on stage motioned that it was time to begin, and the girls quieted. Then 'Silent Night' began to play on the piano and the little angels started to sing, their soft voices heavenly to his ears.

He tugged his hat low over his head, staying behind the lamppost. So far no one here recognized him. Or knew what he'd done.

What he was.

He had to make sure they never did.

THREE

HONEYSUCKLE LANE, CROOKED CREEK

Friday, December 20

Lara Truman normally loved the holidays. But last night after the Christmas pageant, she'd had a migraine, and this morning her head was pounding so bad she felt nauseous. Still, she'd promised her five-year-old daughter she'd bake cupcakes for the school party today, and she couldn't let Ava down.

Being a single mom was challenging. But Ava deserved a supermom, especially since her so-called father had checked out to be with his new girlfriend. Yesterday, Lara had spent the afternoon sewing sequins on the angel wings for Ava's costume, and last night she let her daughter stay up a half hour later when they got home from the pageant because she was too excited to sleep.

She wanted a puppy this year, had been begging for it for months. Ava's father had refused to get a dog, but now that he no longer lived with them, she'd decided to honor her daughter's wishes. After all, the little girl had taken the separation hard.

"Mommy, mommy, mommy!" Ava sang as she skipped into the kitchen with her neon-green backpack slung over her shoulder. Her brown ponytail bobbed up and down, her red headband glittering with sequins. "Today's the party!" Ava squealed, her blue eyes full of joy. "We're having pizza!"

"I know, honey. Don't forget the book you're supposed to take for the children's hospital." Ava's teacher had asked each family who could afford it to donate a wrapped book.

Ava dunked her finger into the bowl where Lara had mixed the batter earlier, then licked it. "Are you bringing the cupcakes to school?"

"Yes, they're in the oven now." Lara rubbed her temple. Her migraine was slipping into full mode, her vision blurring. A quick check of the clock, and she realized it was time to walk to the bus. The aura that came with her migraine made her dizzy, reminding her to take her medication or she'd never make it through the day.

Ava ran her fingers over the shiny sparkles on her holiday sweatshirt, which boasted a felt tree with twinkling lights. Ava had wanted them to dress alike so Lara had handsewn the tree and added colorful felt ornaments. A smile curved her mouth, knowing that one day Ava would balk at the two of them wearing matching outfits. She'd secretly been tickled to do so.

"It's gonna be so much fun today!" Ava clutched her favorite stuffed bunny beneath her arm as she ran into the living room. "I can't wait to get to school."

Lara nodded, but the smoke alarm suddenly trilled as smoke seeped from the closed oven door.

"Mommy, we gotta go!" Ava shouted.

"Just a minute. Wait on me," Lara called as Ava ran to the front door.

Lara quickly grabbed a potholder and hurried to open the oven before the cupcakes burned. She yanked open the door and pulled them out, relieved they were just about okay, waving at the smoke as she set them on the counter.

"Ava," she called as she raced through the living room. But the door stood open, and Ava had already run outside. She must have raced to the bus stop, which was only a couple of blocks away.

Lara's heart stuttered, and she darted out, but the bus was rolling past by the time she reached the sidewalk.

For a moment, Lara stood and watched the bus, her heart in her throat. She thought she saw Ava's wavy brown hair as she huddled in the seat, so she waved to her and waited until the bus disappeared around the corner. Guilt nagged her for not walking with her daughter. For not kissing her goodbye. But her head spun again, and she staggered back to the house. Going inside, she was so dizzy she held on to the wall as she maneuvered the hall to her bedroom.

Fighting nausea, she snagged her medication from the bathroom counter, swallowed two pills and washed them down with water. Then she stretched out on the bed, pulled the blanket over her and closed her eyes.

She had plenty of time before the party later on, so she'd sleep a couple of hours then take the cupcakes to Ava's school.

Her daughter would be so happy to see how she decorated them.

FOUR

CROOKED CREEK POLICE STATION

Ellie's heart felt as heavy as the gray cloud that had come out of nowhere this morning. It hadn't yet rained, but she felt a fine mist in the air and knew it was coming.

Dr. Canton, her birth mother's psychiatrist, had left a message earlier asking Ellie to call her at Oak Grove Assisted Living. But Ellie needed a shower and coffee before she could handle the conversation, so she'd waited until she reached the station.

A mug of coffee in her hand, she closed her office door and rang the doctor's number. Dr. Canton answered with a friendly hello.

Relief filled Ellie. Her mother's condition was rocky at best. Mabel had been traumatized years ago by a sexual assault and then her baby—Ellie—was taken from her. Mabel's doctor, Ellie's birth father, had raped Mabel then kept her drugged for years to keep her from talking. The combination of the assault and the drugs had triggered a complete psychotic break and she'd lost touch with reality.

"Is everything okay?" Ellie asked.

"Your mother's condition hasn't changed much, but I wanted you to know I'm starting the TMR therapy we discussed."

Dr. Canton had explained that Traumatic Memory Recovery

was an intense treatment involving a mixture of hypnosis, drugs and therapy sessions. The goal was to help Mabel recover the traumatic events that had triggered her psyche to crack. In order to heal and move on, Mabel had to confront the past. But remembering the attack would be painful.

Emotions stirred inside Ellie. "Do you think she's ready?"

"I think it's time," the doctor said. "I'll send you updates regularly. But until she makes progress, it's best that you refrain from visiting for a while."

The twinkling Christmas tree that Shondra and Deputy Landrum had decorated in the bullpen area mocked her. She hated to think that her mother would be alone for the holiday. But Mabel didn't even know Ellie was the daughter she'd lost years ago.

Ellie's heart squeezed. Mabel might not ever return to reality.

FIVE

CROOKED CREEK ELEMENTARY

Lara woke up three hours later and sprang from bed. Her migraine had faded to a dull, low-grade headache that she knew would linger until the next day, but the painkillers had helped. She rushed into the shower and dressed in jeans and the holiday sweatshirt that matched Ava's, then hurried to the kitchen.

She decorated the cupcakes with white icing, added red and green sprinkles and a peppermint in the center for a festive touch. Dividing them into two boxes to separate the gluten free from the regular, she carried them to the car.

It had misted early this morning, but now a sliver of midday sunshine shimmered through the pines and oaks as she maneuvered the winding road to Crooked Creek Elementary. In the distance, above the towering mountains, thunderstorms brewed, casting a gloomy feel.

She didn't care if it rained or stormed today. Nothing was going to ruin the party for her daughter.

Lara smiled to herself. She'd already wrapped several presents for Ava and added a new one under the tree each day. "I wonder what this one is," Ava would whisper just before she shook the box and tried to guess what was inside.

With all the classes having holiday parties today, the school parking lot was almost full. Lara swung into a space, grabbed the cupcakes and hurried to the front entrance. She pressed the intercom and identified herself, then the lady at the front desk buzzed her inside.

Winter decorations adorned the school, with children's artwork displayed and paper snowflakes dangling from the ceiling. She signed in at the kiosk then walked down the corridor to Ava's kindergarten. A class was lined up in the hall, and an older grade was leaving the cafeteria. In spite of the teachers reminding the kids to be quiet, most of them couldn't contain their excitement over the upcoming winter break.

Their youthful exuberance was contagious, and Lara found herself with a spring in her step as she approached Ava's room. Her teacher, a twenty-something young brunette named Ms. Lovett, had decorated the door like a giant igloo, something Ava had talked about for weeks. Lara knocked, waiting until the teacher opened the door for her, and she stepped in. Two other mothers had already arrived and were setting up the refreshments on a long table in the back of the room. The children's handmade ornaments hung from the ceiling and red and green streamers draped the walls.

Lara scanned the room for Ava but didn't see her at her desk. She swept her gaze over the children on the floor building with blocks, then the art area, but she wasn't there either.

She turned to the teacher. "Where's Ava?"

Ms. Lovett arched a brow. "That's what I was going to ask you. I thought maybe she stayed home this morning and was coming to school with you."

Lara's pulse jumped. "What are you talking about? She caught the bus this morning."

Confusion clouded the teacher's face. "Ms. Truman, Ava never showed up at school today. They tried to call you from the office but said there was no answer, so I assumed you were bringing her."

She'd been in such a hurry to make it to the party she hadn't bothered to check her messages. Pure panic seized Lara and the cupcakes slid from her hand. Ms. Lovett caught them before they hit the floor and set them on the table. The other two mothers turned with questioning eyes, aware something was wrong.

"What do you mean she never showed up?" Lara asked. "She was so happy this morning, she ran out the door with her backpack and her book and..." *And you didn't walk her to the bus...*

Fear clawed at her, and she rushed over to Jenny Mathis, Ava's friend who she always shared a seat with. "Jenny, honey, did you see Ava this morning on the bus?"

Jenny's hazel eyes widened, and she shook her head. "She wasn't at the bus stop."

"What?" Lara gently took the little girl's arms. "Are you sure?"

Jenny bobbed her head up and down, her lip quivering. Lara realized she was scaring the child and released her, softening her tone. "I'm sorry, sweetie," Lara said. "I'm just worried. I thought she got on the bus."

"I saved her a seat but she didn't come." The other mothers exchanged worried looks, and Lara thought she was going to be sick.

She choked back a cry of panic and turned to Ms. Lovett. "Call the bus driver. See if she saw Ava."

Terror darkened the young woman's face, and she asked the other mothers to monitor the party. "I'll be back in a few minutes."

Lara was so terrified she could barely move, but the teacher nudged her arm. "Come with me, we need to talk to the principal and that driver."

The waver in Ms. Lovett's voice catapulted Lara from her stupor, and she found herself running down the hall behind Ava's teacher. As soon as they reached the principal's office, she gave a quick knock on the door but didn't bother to wait until Mrs. Remington answered. She burst into the room and told the principal what had happened.

"I thought she was here," Lara said in a strained voice. "That she got on the bus and was at school all morning."

"What bus does she ride?" Mrs. Remington asked, reaching for her phone.

"Number seventeen," Lara cried. "The driver is Terry Barker. I met her when school started."

Mrs. Remington gestured for her to wait a second, then she consulted her contact list and called the number. "Terry, this is the principal at Crooked Creek Elementary. Did Ava Truman get on the bus this morning? It would have been the stop nearest Honeysuckle Lane."

Lara's heart pounded as she waited. Then the principal looked up at her, shaking her head, and Lara's world completely crumbled.

SIX

Ellie clenched her hands together as she studied her boss, Captain Hale. Judging from the deep frown lines around his eyes and his furrowed brows, something was wrong.

"Five-year-old little girl, Ava Truman, is missing," he said. "Mother said she ran to the bus stop, but apparently never got on the bus."

Ellie's heart stuttered, and she stood, instantly alert. "Where's the mother now?"

"The school," he replied. "They were having a holiday party and she took cupcakes in for the kids. That's when she realized her daughter didn't make it to school." He wiped sweat from his forehead. "Principal made the call. The mom is terrified. Bus driver claims she didn't see the child at all this morning."

"What about the father?"

"Don't know yet," he said.

She pulled her keys from inside her desk. "If she disappeared this morning, that was hours ago. Issue an Amber Alert. I'll go talk to the mother. I'll get Deputy Eastwood to meet me at the school. Have Deputy Landrum start searching the area around where the Trumans live."

"On it," Captain Hale said. "I'll alert the sheriff too, and he can get his deputies looking around town. Although if someone took the child, he or she could be long gone by now."

Ellie nodded, a bad feeling pinching her gut as she raced from her office. *Dear God, don't let me fail this little girl. Especially at Christmas.*

Every second in a child abduction counted.

As she jumped in her Jeep, her mind clicked off steps she needed to take. Gather information. Get a picture of Ava Truman on the news. Set up a timeline. Question the parents and neighbors.

With a deep breath, she flipped on her siren and drove toward the elementary school, the same one she'd attended as a child. She phoned Shondra, explained the situation and asked her to meet her at the school, then she called Derrick and filled him in.

"I'm on my way back to Crooked Creek," he said. "I'll alert all train stations, airports, bus stations and make sure her picture is entered in NCEMC."

The National Center for Exploited and Missing Children would be helpful, Ellie agreed.

"What about the parents?" he asked.

"I don't know the whole story yet, but I'm on my way to talk to the mother. I'll keep you posted." She hung up and turned into the school parking lot.

The ancient red-brick building had undergone a facelift since she was little, and she knew security measures had since been instigated to protect the students. The guard met her at the front entrance and within moments Shondra rolled up behind her, jumped out and jogged to the door.

"Thanks for coming so quickly," the guard said. "The mother's hysterical."

"Understandable," Ellie said. "Let us talk to her."

He led them inside to the principal's office and knocked. A middle-aged woman named Mrs. Remington ushered them in. "This is Lara Truman," she said, although the introduction wasn't necessary.

The pure terror in the way the young woman was pacing and crying, told Ellie she was Ava's mother. She recognized her from the night before at the pageant, where she'd seen her smiling and waving to her child on stage.

A young brunette introduced herself as Ava's teacher, Yvonne Lovett.

"Ava didn't show up at all this morning?" Ellie asked.

Ms. Lovett shook her head. "Lara was supposed to bring cupcakes for the holiday party, so when the school didn't reach her, I didn't think much of it. I figured Ava wanted to ride to school with her mother."

Ellie glanced at Lara, who was pulling at her blond hair. "I... can't believe this is happening. You have to find her."

"I already have my captain issuing an Amber Alert, Ms. Truman," replied Ellie. "Do you have a photograph to circulate to the press and other law enforcement agencies?"

"Call me Lara. And yes... in my phone." She pulled her cell phone from her pocket with shaking hands, then accessed her photos and showed one to Ellie. "This was her kindergarten picture," she said, her breath rattling out.

Ellie took the woman's cell and texted the picture to her phone, then forwarded it to Derrick and her captain. "Lara, what was Ava wearing this morning?"

She swallowed hard. "A white sweatshirt with a green felt tree appliqued on it with a string of lights that lit up. It's like mine." Her voice warbled. "I made it for her. She... wanted us to dress alike..."

Ellie fought her own emotions. "What else?"

"Black leggings and a red headband with sequins. And she had her backpack with her."

"What color is the backpack?" Ellie asked.

Lara heaved a breath. "Neon green. It's her favorite color." She fidgeted. "It had bunnies on it. She's kind of obsessed with bunnies." She ran her fingers through her hair again. "Oh, and she took Bunny with her. She's so attached to him, she never leaves him behind."

"What color is the bunny?"

"Gray with white ears," Lara said.

"What about a coat? Hat? Gloves?"

Lara's face pinched with worry. "Yes, a bright orange puffy jacket and hat to match. I... don't know if she had her gloves." Her voice quivered. "Oh, God, her little hands will be so cold..."

Ellie patted her arm. "Her height and weight?"

Lara blinked away tears. "I don't know exactly. But last time we marked it on the wall, she was about three feet ten, maybe. And I think she weighed about forty-five pounds."

"Thanks, Lara, that's really helpful." Ellie texted the captain the description, then asked him to forward it to Angelica Gomez, her half-sister and the reporter who'd covered the recent cases she'd worked. The more people they had looking for Ava the better.

"I promise you we'll do everything we can to find Ava and bring her home," Ellie said softly. "Now let's sit down. I need to ask you a few more questions." She coaxed the mother onto a loveseat in the corner.

"You spoke with the bus driver?" Ellie asked Ms. Remington.

"Yes, she said Ava wasn't at the stop."

"And you're certain the bus driver didn't see Ava?" Ellie asked the principal.

The woman's eyes widened as if she was surprised Ellie would ask. "Our employees are vetted. And Terry has been driving for us for fifteen years. The kids all love her and so do the parents."

"Can you pull a list of all the children who rode that bus so we can talk to them?" Ellie asked. "I don't want to scare them, but maybe one of them saw something."

"Of course." Mrs. Remington went to her computer, clicked a few keys, then printed out a list.

Ellie turned to Shondra. "Walk Ms. Lovett to the classroom. And Ms. Lovett," she said, directing a look at her. "Please ask the children if they saw Ava this morning. Maybe she was on the street or wandered off."

"Her little friend Jenny said she wasn't at the bus stop," replied the teacher. "But I'll talk to the others."

Shondra exchanged a worried look with Ellie before following the teacher from the office.

The principal stood, a list in her hand. "I'll check with the students in other classes who ride that bus."

Ellie thanked her, hoping that one of them saw something as the principal left the room.

Knowing she had to explore every possibility, and that required using all the manpower they had, she texted her boss and asked if the sheriff could verify the bus driver's story.

Lara was rocking herself back and forth, tears streaming down her face as she mumbled her daughter's name over and over. She appeared to be going into shock. Ellie noticed bottled water on the credenza behind the principal's desk.

She offered one to Lara, but the woman only shook her head and glared at her.

"I don't want water, I want Ava," she said through her sobs.

Ellie placed a hand gently on her shoulder. "I know you're upset and worried, but I'm here to help," she assured her. "I need you to take a deep breath and talk to me. Tell me everything that happened this morning."

Lara clutched Ellie's hands, her fingernails digging into Ellie's arms. "She was so excited about the party. They were having pizza and I made cupcakes with sprinkles, and she had a book to donate to the children's hospital." Her voice broke off.

"Go on," Ellie said gently. "Any detail, no matter how small, might help."

She nodded, sniffing and wiping at her nose, then the words seem to spill from her. "It was time for the bus and Ava yelled she needed to go, but the smoke alarm went off and I had a migraine and ran to get the cupcakes out of the oven so they wouldn't burn. I... couldn't take burned cupcakes to the children!" Another sob was wrenched from deep within her gut and she doubled over, holding her stomach as if she physically needed to or she'd come apart. "I told her to wait... but by the time I put the cupcakes on the counter, she'd run out the door."

"How far is the bus stop from your house?" Ellie asked, keeping her voice neutral.

"Only a couple of blocks, but it's around the curve near the park," she choked out.

"Where is your house on her route?" Ellie asked. "First house? Last?"

"About midway," Lara said. "It's usually about half full when Ava gets on."

Ellie gave a little nod. "Has Ava walked to the bus stop by herself before?"

Lara shook her head. "No, I always go with her, but this morning she was in such a hurry... she couldn't contain herself..." She swiped at more tears. "Where is she? What if some crazy person took her?"

Ellie had dealt with enough depravity to know that was possible. But she didn't want to exacerbate the woman's fear by admitting it. "First, let's cover the basics. Would Ava have wandered off somewhere? Or have gotten into a car with a stranger?"

"No," Lara said. "We talked about that, about strangers and danger."

"What about Ava's father? Are you two together?" Ellie asked, squeezing the woman's hands, which were slick with sweat.

"No, we're separated," she said, a hint of bitterness in her tone.

Ellie snatched a tissue from the box on the principal's desk and handed it to Lara, her mind racing. A large percentage of child kidnappings were parental abductions, many involving custody disputes.

"How is your relationship?" she asked.

"Fine," Lara said, after blowing her nose on the tissue. "I mean, not great. But we're civil."

"Does he see Ava?"

"He did at first," Lara said, "then he started dating and he stopped showing up. Ava was so disappointed."

"But if he drove up and Ava saw him, she might go over to him? Or even get in the car with him?"

That suggestion seemed to settle Lara's nerves slightly. "Yes, she probably would." She gave Ellie a wide-eyed look. "Do you think that's what happened?"

"I don't know," Ellie said. She hoped it was. "Has he ever taken Ava without asking you before?"

"No, but he started making noises about seeing her more a few weeks ago. He even mentioned shared custody."

"How did you feel about that?" Ellie asked, her instincts kicked up.

Lara clamped her teeth over her bottom lip. "We argued."

It was looking more and more like the father had motive. "I need his contact information."

Fumbling with her phone again, Lara found it. "I'll call him."

"Put him on speaker."

Ellie held her breath as they listened to the phone ring over and over. But Ava's father didn't answer.

"Please pick up!" Lara screeched.

The phone rolled to voicemail. Lara's face wilted and she banged her hand against her head. "Jasper, it's Lara. Call me. It's an emergency. I need to know if you have Ava."

SEVEN

"Lara, I need to know where your husband lives and where he works," Ellie said, her stomach knotting in frustration. "If he doesn't call you back, I'll go find him."

The woman nodded. "I have all those details in his phone contact—since we separated, I've had to share them so often. Untangling our lives, you know...?"

Ellie smiled in understanding, and sympathy filled her as Lara tried to wrangle her phone with shaking hands. "Let me do it." She gently took the cell, found Jasper's contact information and forwarded it to herself. He worked for a construction company named Cato's Construction.

If he had Ava, she didn't want to give him a chance to run, so she decided to surprise him by just showing up. But she did phone the construction company to see if he was there first.

A friendly woman named Connie answered, and Ellie identified herself. "It's important I speak with Jasper Truman," she told the receptionist. "Is he working today?"

"Afraid not," the woman said. "He's taking off a couple of days."

Ellie's skin prickled. "Did he say where he was going?"

"No, just that he needed to take a trip." The receptionist hesitated. "Is Jasper in trouble or something?"

"It's actually about his daughter, Ava. She didn't show up at school today and her mother is frantic."

"Oh, my word. I would be, too," Connie said.

"We're hoping he has Ava," Ellie explained. She wanted to question Jasper's coworkers, but right now she had to divide up the tasks. "Please ask the other employees if Jasper mentioned where he was going and get back to me if they know."

"Sure thing," the woman replied.

"Did he ever talk about his wife or Ava?" Ellie asked.

Lara leaned forward, jiggling her leg nervously.

"Not to me," Connie said. "I don't cotton to men bashing their wives and the guys around here know it."

Good for you, Ellie thought. "Thanks, Connie. If you hear from him, try to find out where he is, then please give me a call."

"Of course," the receptionist said, her voice filled with concern. "I'll get on it right away. I know Lara must be going out of her mind."

After ending the call, Lara tried her husband's number again. This time, the phone went straight to voicemail, so Ellie texted Derrick and asked him to check out Jasper's residence. Derrick responded that he would and Ellie said a silent prayer that he would find Ava there safe and sound.

"Come on," Ellie said gently. "Let's go back to the class and see if Deputy Eastwood learned anything from the students."

Lara stood on wobbly legs, clutching a tissue in one hand and her phone in the other as they walked down the hall.

"Jasper has to have her, he has to," Lara whispered. "He just has to."

Ellie's chest squeezed with emotions. The alternatives were not a place she wanted to go.

As they reached the classroom, Shondra let them in. The holiday party was underway, the students chattering and laughing as they gobbled pizza. Lara walked over to the table and studied the display of glittery ornaments the kids had made. Her body shook silently as she picked up a silver and pink round ball that must have been Ava's.

Ms. Lovett curved an arm around Lara, quietly comforting her, while two other mothers roamed through the rows of desks handing out cupcakes and shooting furtive worried looks to each other. Once this story aired, all the parents in town would be panicking.

Ellie angled her head toward Shondra. "Did any of the students see Ava this morning?" she asked under her breath.

Shondra shook her head. "Afraid not."

"Lara and her husband Jasper are separated. We called Jasper to see if Ava was with him, but he didn't answer," Ellie said quietly. "According to the receptionist where he worked, he was taking a couple of days off."

"You think he took her?" Shondra's eyes narrowed.

Ellie shrugged. "We have to consider it. The principal is talking to other students who rode that bus. Wait here and check with her before you leave. Maybe one of them saw something." She gestured toward Lara. "I'm going to follow her home, take a look around the house and the neighborhood."

As she walked over to Lara, she kept her voice low. "Let's go back to your house. I want you to show me the exact route Ava takes to the bus stop."

Lara clutched the Christmas ornament in her hands and silently followed Ellie to the door. The other mothers gave her sympathetic looks, and a little dark-haired girl with brown eyes ran up and wrapped her arms around Lara's legs.

"I hope Ava isn't lost too long," she said. "I miss her."

Fresh tears filled Lara's eyes as she hugged the little girl.

Determination fueled Ellie. A missing child was every parent's worst nightmare. Ellie had a feeling every mother in town would be clinging to their own children tonight.

EIGHT

HONEYSUCKLE LANE

The moment they stepped into Lara's kitchen, the emptiness hit Lara like a fist in the gut. The kitchen was still a mess from where she'd hurriedly decorated the cupcakes. Sprinkles dotted the counter and the mixing bowl still sat in the sink along with Ava's cereal bowl and empty juice cup. The pieces of the snowman puzzle she and Ava had been working on were scattered across the table.

The detective glanced around the room, her eyes assessing. "Looks like you were busy this morning."

Lara rubbed her temple where her headache was starting to build again. The change in the barometric pressure always triggered her migraines. "Mornings usually are. But this morning I had a migraine and then the smoke alarm went off." She glanced out the window. "You know, we bought this house because of the honeysuckle along the back. When we first moved in, you could smell it all the way to the back porch. Ava loved it."

The detective frowned, and Lara realized she was lost at the moment, random thoughts and memories of her daughter jumping through her head.

"Do you take medication for your headache?"

Lara leaned against the kitchen bar. "Yes, but they make me sleepy so I waited until after Ava left."

The detective nodded and Lara wondered what she was thinking. That she was a bad mother? She was a bad mother. She should have run after Ava.

"Do you often have migraines?" the detective asked.

"Some, mostly when I'm stressed or overtired." Which had been a lot lately. "Or when the pressure drops, like it did this morning."

"So that was the trigger today? Or were you stressed too?"

"Do you have children, Detective?" Lara rubbed at the back of her neck where the tension was building.

The detective lifted her chin. "No, I don't."

Lara released a sigh. Sometimes she felt like the weight of the world had settled on her shoulders and she was bowing beneath it. "Being a single mother means everything falls on me. Getting Ava to school, helping her with homework, doing errands, meals, working."

"I imagine that is difficult," Detective Reeves said. "Do you have a job?"

"Part time at the Fabric Hut. I work the tables cutting and get discounts on fabric. They like for me to make clothes and curtains and placemats to display and when they sell, I get a commission." She ran her hand over the bar stool where cereal had been spilled, then gestured toward the corner table to a basket filled with colorful hairbows. "I make those and sell them at the craft fairs and the store. But I only work when Ava's at school so I can be home when she gets off the bus."

The silence echoing through the rooms mocked her. No Ava giggling, no rattling presents, no skipping around and singing Christmas carols and turning cartwheels in the family room.

Lara had always reminded her daughter to do her tumbling outside. Her throat burned with more tears. When she came home, she'd let her turn cartwheels all over the house.

God... she had to come home.

"You said you were in here when Ava ran outside." The detective pointed to the kitchen door. "Did she go out the back door here?"

Lara shook her head. "No, she ran into the living room. I yelled at her to wait, but when I got to the door, it was open and she was gone."

Detective Reeves walked around the kitchen looking at the table, the floor, and studying the back door. Then she went into the living room and glanced at the furniture and the Christmas tree.

Lara followed her, nerves bunching in her belly. The front door was still open.

Detective Reeves' gaze landed on the wrapped presents beneath the tree and the stocking with Ava's name embroidered on it. "What happened after you realized she'd run outside?" she asked.

"I raced to the door and ran out, but before I got to the sidewalk, the bus was driving past." She rubbed her temple again, replaying the morning in her mind. "I should have let the cupcakes burn and gone with her. Or I should have called the school to see if she made it. But I thought I caught a half-glimpse of her on the bus..."

Ellie patted her back. "You didn't know," she said softly. "You can't blame yourself. Now tell me about the rest of your morning."

"I was so dizzy from the headache that I had to lie down." She swallowed hard. "That's when I took my migraine medication. I was only going to sleep for an hour but woke up three hours later. Then I was in a hurry to get the cupcakes ready so I could make the party on time." Her voice was so brittle it sounded like glass shattering. "If something bad's happened to her it's my fault."

NINE

Ellie heard the guilt in Lara's voice and coaxed her toward the sofa. For a moment, Lara paused to stare at a picture of Ava on the mantle. "That was last year," she said in a tiny voice.

Ava was wearing a green velvet sweater and a red and white polka-dotted bow in her hair that Lara had obviously made.

"Is there anyone I can call to come and sit with you, Lara?" Ellie asked. "Do you have other family or a good friend that can come over?"

"My friend Emily Nettles. She'll come." Lara dropped her head into her hands and closed her eyes.

"I'm sorry this is happening," Ellie said, grateful Lara had a friend like Emily. Shondra had told her Emily was a godsend to the community. "Call Emily while I take a look around the house."

Lara nodded, and Ellie read it as a sign she wasn't hiding anything. She quickly checked the mother's room and noted the bed was still unmade, sheets tangled as if she'd rushed to get ready to leave as she'd said. She found a bottle of Sumatriptan on the bedside table, confirming Lara's story, too. The number of pills listed on the bottle was twelve, and Ellie checked the bottle. Ten remained.

So she hadn't overdone it on the pills.

The bathroom smelled of a floral-scented body wash, and a wet towel hung on a rack. She quickly moved on and found Ava's room. A white four-poster bed was draped in a neon-green comforter with a half dozen stuffed animals on top. Children's puzzles, a Barbie dollhouse and a shelf overflowing with books painted the picture of a happy child.

Ellie searched for signs of foul play but found nothing. Even the drawings on the child's desk were pictures of rainbows and sunshine and flowers. Daisies seemed to be a theme.

She went back downstairs and saw Lara hugging a rag doll to her, running her fingers through the red yarn hair.

Ellie paused beside the couch. "Lara, I need you to do one more thing for me."

The woman blinked at the tears and looked up at her through blurry eyes. "I'll do whatever it takes. Just find my baby."

Ellie nodded. "One of our deputies has been searching your neighborhood and talking to residents to see if any of them saw Ava this morning. I want you to show me the path your daughter takes to the bus stop."

Her soft tone seemed to help Lara pull herself together. Brushing at her wet cheeks with the back of her hand, she gestured for Ellie to follow her.

When they stepped outside, watery sunshine dappled the leaves on the trees. As they turned left onto the sidewalk and headed toward the bus stop, she sensed Lara's tension escalating with every step.

Ellie surveyed the street as they went, searching for anything that might be out of place. Lara Truman lived on a quaint street of starter homes that had been built about ten years ago to cater to young families. Evidence of that existed in the children's bikes and toys in the yards.

A stiff breeze stirred the trees as they neared a park, and two mothers strolling babies hurried from the gates as they passed, rushing to their cars before the clouds unleashed.

Lara paused at the bus stop, her face pained as she glanced at the empty sidewalk. "This is where the kids meet for the bus," she said in a haunted voice.

Ellie turned and scanned the area, realizing the park was almost directly across the way. A parking lot sat on the opposite side of the playground and the soccer field, which was empty now.

If Ava's father—or a kidnapper—took Ava, he or she could easily have gotten her across the park and no one would have suspected. The parking lot provided easy access for an escape.

"Go back to the house," Ellie told Lara. "I want to look around the park."

"I'll look with you," Lara offered.

"No, go home. If your husband calls or if somehow Ava just wandered off and finds her way back home, you should be there."

Hope lit Lara's eyes, and she turned and jogged back toward the house.

Ellie headed across the park, scanning for any signs Ava had been there. In the playground, the empty swings creaking back and forth in the breeze sounded eerie. A gray cloud gathered above the treetops.

She was parting bushes along the edge of the parking lot when she spotted something behind oak. She hurried to see what it was, her heart hammering. The fluffy white ears of a stuffed bunny rabbit poked through the weeds. Lara had mentioned that Ava carried her favorite bunny with her everywhere she went.

There was no way she would have thrown it in the bushes and left it there.

She must have lost it, possibly when someone forced her to go with them.

TEN

PINE STREET DUPLEXES, STONY GAP

Special Agent Derrick Fox hated missing-children cases. They always resurrected painful memories of when his sister Kim had disappeared. For over two decades, he and his mother had agonized over what had happened to her. Had prayed they'd find her alive.

But she'd been dead the entire time.

He hoped this situation would turn out differently.

He couldn't get the image of the smiling little brown-haired girl in the photo Ellie had sent out of his head. Big blue eyes. A button nose. A missing front tooth when she smiled. Freckles.

He fought the dark thoughts that came to him and latched on to the hope that the father had taken her. With the holidays upon them, maybe he'd just wanted to spend time with his daughter. It never ceased to amaze him how some parents used their kids to hurt each other.

The wintry breeze picked up, swirling leaves and twigs across the yard of the duplex where Jasper Truman lived. The wooden exterior of the building was rustic, the two units part of a complex of several that appeared to have been recently built. From the way the units sat on the property, he could see each one had a back deck which gave views of the mountains rising in the background.

According to Ellie's text, the father worked construction. Derrick wondered if he'd helped build these. When he'd stopped for coffee on the way back to Crooked Creek, he'd run a quick background search on the Trumans and learned they were recently separated and were financially in dire straits.

That meant if Ava had been abducted, she wasn't taken for ransom. But if the father didn't have her, he'd dig deeper in case someone had a vendetta against the family.

According to Truman's employer, Jasper was taking a couple of days off. Suspicious timing or coincidence?

The driveway was empty.

Derrick strode to the door and rang the bell, then pounded on the door. "FBI, anyone home?" No answer, so he knocked again, then jiggled the door, finding it locked. He looked through the front windows and could make out a living room that was open to the kitchen.

Frustration made him knot his hands. He didn't have a warrant.

But he could justify going inside by claiming exigent circumstances. After all, every hour that passed when a child was taken decreased the chances of finding her. And it had already been hours.

He examined the neighboring unit and property but didn't see anyone. Deciding to check the rear, he circled around the side and searched for any signs a child was here. No toys, balls or bikes. The small backyard had been landscaped but was empty.

He climbed the steps to the deck and jiggled the back door. Locked as well. Pulling a credit card from his pocket, he wedged it between the door and lock, jimmying it until the lock released. Then he slipped inside the small entryway.

The sun had disappeared behind the clouds, making the rooms seem darker, and he switched on the light in the kitchen. A stack of bills was piled in a basket on the granite counter and a coffee pot was near the stove. It was clean, with no signs that it had been used today. He checked the trash. Empty.

He moved down the hall, towards two bedrooms and a jack-and-jill bath. The first room held a single bed covered in a Trolls comforter, and a basket of toys and books.

The man's bedroom held an oak bed and dresser, and in the closet, he spotted work clothes stained with paint and with the name of the construction company on the shirt. Dusty work boots sat on the floor.

He looked for a suitcase but didn't find one. Had Jasper packed his things, picked up Ava and run off with her?

ELEVEN

HONEYSUCKLE LANE

Before Ellie returned to the Truman's house, she phoned Angelica. She and the tenacious reporter had gotten off to a rocky start when they'd first met, but during the last few months had built a trusting working relationship—especially since they learned they were half-sisters. Angelica was smart, a go-getter, and would do anything for a story.

She could also be discreet and patient, as long as Ellie gave her the exclusive.

"We have a missing child, six-year-old Ava Truman," Ellie said up front. "I need you to circulate her picture and name on the news ASAP."

Angelica cut straight to the point. "Do you think she was abducted?"

"I don't know yet. It's possible the father has her. We haven't been able to reach him. But we can't waste time. She's been missing since early this morning when she left for the bus stop. Her mother is hysterical."

"Understandable," Angelica said. "Details?"

"She left for the bus stop at the corner of Honeysuckle Lane and no one has seen her since. Weighs approximately forty-five pounds, and is about three foot ten. I'll text you a photo as soon as

we hang up." She paused, then filled Angelica in on the details of
her clothing and her backpack. "Post the number for the police
station and sheriff's department in case anyone has seen her or has
information on her whereabouts. Captain Hale is handling the
Amber Alert and Agent Fox has alerted the airport, train and bus
stations and borders."

They both knew that if a madman had taken Ava, he could be
hiding out doing God knows what to her. If he'd already killed her
and dumped her body, the miles and miles of forest and rugged
terrain would make it difficult if not almost impossible to find her.

TWELVE

Ellie was walking back to the Trumans' house when Deputy Landrum called.

"Hey," he said, "I've been talking to Ms. Truman's neighbors. Man across the street said he saw Ava run down the sidewalk this morning, but lost sight of her when she veered around the curve. Lady next door, Dottie Clark, said she didn't see her, but she did mention that the couple was having marital problems."

"I know. They were separated," Ellie replied.

"She said that, too. Said she heard them have some heated arguments. That the father accused Lara of not taking good care of Ava, of leaving her alone sometimes."

Ellie frowned. "That's odd. Lara told me she works part-time but was always home when Ava got off the bus."

"Neighbor was a little batty. Crazy cat lady, cats everywhere. She could have got mixed up," Heath said.

Ellie had heard the woman's name—some of the other women in town talked about her. Dottie Clark was trying to organize a neighborhood watch program. Of course, Carol Sue from the Beauty Barn—who fed the gossip mill—was doing the talking, and Ellie didn't put much stock in what she said.

"True." Or Lara could have lied. "Has the neighbor seen the father around lately?"

"She saw him drive by a few times," Heath said. "Once he stopped and went to the door, but the wife refused to let him come in. Screamed that he scared Ava when he got mad."

Ellie's stomach tightened. So Jasper had a temper. Maybe he'd snatched the little girl to get back at his wife. "Did any of the neighbors see anyone else watching Ava?"

"Three of the families work full-time and have no kids so they aren't home much. I have one more neighbor to check with."

Her phone buzzed with a call from Derrick, so she said thanks and clicked over.

"I'm at Jasper Truman's place," Derrick started, filling her in on what he'd found.

"Lara said he hadn't seen Ava much, but lately had hinted at wanting shared custody. They argued about that." Ellie hesitated. "Derrick, I found Ava's stuffed bunny at the park across from the bus stop. It was in the bushes as if she dropped it. It looks like she was taken."

Derrick cursed. "The father's suitcase is gone. He may have run off with her."

"Let's issue a bulletin for his vehicle and for him."

"I'll handle it. Don't know if it means anything, but it looks like the man was behind on his bills. After I checked the closet, I skimmed through them. He owed the children's hospital a big chunk. I'm going to dig into their financials and see if they owe anyone else, someone who might have kidnapped Ava to send a message to them."

"Definitely dig into the husband." Ellie sighed. "Lara didn't mention anything about Ava having been in the hospital," she said, wondering why. "I'm on my way back to the house. I'll find out the reason."

THIRTEEN

To cover all bases, Ellie called Ranger Cord McClain and asked him to bring his Search and Rescue dog to comb the neighborhood for Ava. Cord was the best tracker in the area. Every year hikers began the Appalachian Trail —2,200 miles of untamed wilderness from Georgia to Maine—with high aspirations. But many fell foul to the elements, had accidents on the sharp ridges and steep cliffs, and others got lost, keeping SAR busy.

Cord knew the AT like the back of his hand and had been instrumental in other cases. She and the tough, brooding ranger had been friends since she was in high school and she'd tagged along with him on several search missions.

"I'll organize a team and meet you at the Truman house," Cord said. "We'll need something with Ava's scent on it."

Ellie's gut clenched. "I know. I'll talk to the mother."

They hung up, and she made her way back to Lara's house. She knocked gently but there was no answer. Uneasy, she slipped inside and heard Lara's voice coming from the kitchen.

"Jasper, if you took Ava, call me right now!" Lara cried. "If you hurt one hair on her head, I'll kill you with my bare hands!"

Ellie went still, but the floor creaked and Lara turned and saw her. Her mouth opened in a gasp and she slammed the phone onto the table.

"I... I didn't mean that," she said, her voice hysterical. "I... just want my daughter home."

Ellie crossed the room, the bunny in her hands.

Lara spotted it immediately and panic seared her face. "That's Ava's. Where did you find it?"

"In the park, near the parking lot," Ellie said.

Confusion clouded Lara's eyes. "Not at the bus stop?"

"No, it was in the bushes."

A dozen emotions flickered in Lara's eyes as she realized the implications. "Ava would never leave Bunny behind. Never," she insisted. "I tried to get her to leave it at home when she went to school, and a couple of times she left it on her bed. But then she started crying for it at the bus stop and we wound up running back to the house to get it."

Ellie didn't like the scenario forming in her head.

"You think someone kidnapped Ava, don't you?" Lara's hand shook as she shoved a strand of hair from her face.

Ellie gave her a sympathetic look. "We're still looking at the possibility that your husband has her. You mentioned that the two of you argued about custody." She claimed the seat across from Lara. "One of the neighbors said that they overheard your husband accuse you of leaving Ava alone sometimes."

"That's not true," replied Lara, expression pained. "I mean, Jasper said it, but it's not true. I was always here."

"Then why would he accuse you of that?"

Lara shook her head. "Because he was angry and tired. He was working two jobs, and... and he was mad because we couldn't pay our bills."

"We've also had a report that Jasper showed up to see Ava one day and you wouldn't let him in. That you screamed at him that he scared Ava."

"When he got anxious, he yelled. And yes, that scared Ava." Perspiration beaded on Lara's forehead.

Ellie studied the woman for a reaction. "Do you think he would hurt your daughter?"

FOURTEEN

Lara's head spun with confusion. Nothing about this day made any sense to her. She thought back over the past two years and how her marriage had fallen apart. Sometimes she blamed Jasper and sometimes she blamed herself.

Both of them had felt the brunt of the bills, the threats of foreclosure on the house, their busy schedules and Ava's illness, to the point that their relationship crumbled. She'd never wanted a divorce, but she couldn't raise Ava in a volatile household.

"Lara, do you think Jasper would hurt Ava?" the detective asked again, slicing through her spiraling thoughts.

"I... don't know..." Lara's voice was shaky. "I mean, I don't think so. He loved her, but..."

"But what?"

"His temper got the best of him sometimes. That's why I asked him to move out. I wanted him to go to anger management."

The detective showed no reaction, making Lara wonder what exactly she was thinking.

"We're issuing a bulletin for him and his vehicle," Detective Reeves finally said. "Is there any place you can think of that he'd go? Does he have property somewhere? Or family he might visit, someone who'd help him hide out?"

"His parents are deceased," Lara said. "But he has a girlfriend."

"Do you know her name or where she lives?"

"Her name is Autumn," Lara said. "But I have no idea where she lives."

"How about her last name or how to reach her?"

Lara rolled her eyes. "Her last name is Juniper."

"Like juniper bushes?" the detective asked.

Lara nodded. "Jasper said her mother had a wicked sense of humor. I think it sounds like a stripper's name. She works at that bar by the cemetery."

"Haints," Ellie said. "I'll find her. Maybe she knows where Jasper is." The detective pulled her phone from her pocket. "There's something else. You mentioned having financial trouble. We sent an FBI agent to your husband's residence, but he wasn't home. When he searched inside, he said your husband was behind on bills. That he owed the hospital?"

Pain flashed in Lara's eyes. "Yes, we did," she admitted. "Ava had to have a liver transplant two years ago. We've been making payments ever since, but we still owe a lot."

"I'm sorry your daughter had to have surgery," the detective said. "Is she all right now?"

"She's been doing great. We had to give her anti-rejection medication for the first six months. And now she takes immuno-suppressive medication." Lara stood, her legs wobbly. "Oh, my God, if she doesn't take her meds, it could be dangerous for her. We've worked so hard to get her healthy again..."

The detective straightened and Lara saw the worry deepening on her face. "We'll add that to our description of her and alert hospitals and pharmacies to be on the lookout in case someone tries to steal or purchase those type of drugs." She paused. "But if your husband did take her, then he knows she needs the medication, right?"

Lara nodded and prayed that was the case.

"There's one more question I have to ask," the detective asked. "Was there a relative, or someone in the neighborhood or even a handyman or visitor, who showed special interest in Ava?"

Lara's hands trembled as she twisted them together. "No one that I've noticed. Do you think a stranger took my daughter?"

"I don't know, Lara," the detective said gently. "Hopefully Jasper has her. But I have to consider every possibility."

A knock sounded at the front door and Lara jumped, then the two of them walked to the door together.

"It's Emily," Lara said when she spotted the young woman on her porch.

Lara swung open the door. "Thanks for coming, Em."

Fear and worry flashed on Emily's face, then she pulled Lara into a hug. "I'm here, sweetie. I'll do whatever I can to help."

Lara felt her heart splintering, the floodgates opening all over again.

"Come on, I'll make us some tea," Emily said.

Lara nodded and leaned into her friend as they walked back to the kitchen.

"Do you want some too, Detective?" Emily asked.

"No, but thank you. I have work to do."

Reeves patted Lara's shoulder. "Keep your phone line open, Lara. Once the search teams are underway, I'll track down Jasper's girlfriend. Maybe she'll have some answers."

FIFTEEN

SOMEWHERE ON THE AT

Six-year-old Kaylee Wilkinson stared through the window of the upstairs bedroom, looking out into the dark woods behind the house. The trees looked like giant statues with arms that could reach out and grab you.

Just like last year, when the lady had brought her here, lately the lights had shone down the hill. She'd seen cars and knew there were people going to the farm to find a tree. If only she could have gotten to them, someone might have saved her and taken her home.

Except the lady said she didn't have a home to go to. That her mama was dead. She'd even showed her a picture of her mama's grave.

Fresh tears welled in her eyes and she blinked, searching for the lights down the hill again.

But tonight it was dark on the farm and the lights were all gone.

Kaylee pictured Mama singing to her at night, sewing her costume for the Christmas pageant and handing her reindeer antlers to wear when they decorated their tree.

Her heart hurt so bad she could barely catch her breath.

Even if her mama was dead, maybe Mama's sister would take

her to her house. She liked Aunt Priscilla—Prissy, she called her. When she smiled, her eyes looked sweet just like Mama's did.

She pulled out the picture of her mama she'd tucked beneath the mattress and looked at it. She missed her so much. Could hear the sound of her singing to her when she'd been sick. She'd made her grilled cheese sandwiches and tomato soup that she drunk from a coffee cup like she was a big girl.

"Feel better, my sweet girl," Mama had whispered as she tucked her in bed at night.

A few weeks later, when Kaylee got better, Mama took her to the beach. They packed sandwiches and beach toys and their water bottles and built sandcastles.

Her heart started drumming in her chest. Her chest heaved. The salty air smelled so good. She heard the waves crashing on the shore. Then Mama stretched out on the towel. Her water bottle tumbled over. She closed her eyes and Kaylee thought she was sleeping.

The sun was bright, even though it was nearly Christmas, and the wind was chilly. This morning they'd bundled up in jackets and hats to hunt for seashells.

Kaylee finished the grapes Mama packed and all her water. She'd wanted to play in the waves, but it was too cold today, so Mama said they'd come back in the summer. Mama said never to go in the ocean alone either. The big waves could grab you and throw you out to sea with the sharks.

The sun started to go down into the ocean and she hunched inside her jacket with a shiver. Fewer and fewer people were walking by or stopping with their own picnics. Suddenly scared, she shook her mama. "Wake up, Mama," she whispered.

But her mama didn't stir. Then the lady came along. At first Kaylee couldn't see her face for the baseball cap and sunglasses. She leaned down and touched her mama.

"She's gone, honey," the lady said. "Come on. We'll get help."

Kaylee yelled at her mama. But she didn't move or open her eyes. She shook her again, but the lady took her arm and pulled her away. Suddenly she was dragging her toward a van. Kaylee pushed back and yelled out but there was no one else around. Then she pushed Kaylee inside and locked the door.

"Shh, honey, it'll be all right," the lady said. "I'll call someone to take care of your mama."

Kaylee beat at the window and cried as the lady started the van and pulled away, leaving Mama behind.

SIXTEEN

HAINTS BAR

Twenty minutes after Emily had arrived, the silence in Lara's house was grating with tension. Jasper still had not returned Lara's call. Ellie read that as a bad sign.

While Emily busied herself making a pot of vegetable soup for Lara and Cord organized the search teams, Ellie put a trace on Lara's phone in case whoever took Ava called. The woman didn't argue, just seemed to slip into a quiet dazed shock. She'd gone into her daughter's room a dozen times, touching her pillow and the other stuffed toys and dolls lined up around her bed. "She pretended they were her friends and kept them all around her to keep her safe at night," Lara told her.

Ellie arched a brow. "Why didn't she feel safe?"

"Just kids' stuff. Some boy at school told her that monsters snuck in your windows at night and tried to snatch you. We used to play a game where I'd search the closet and under the bed and pull the curtains tight. I told her if they were closed, the monsters couldn't get in." Her voice wavered. "But now some real-life monster may have grabbed her in broad daylight." Another sob escaped her and she rushed to the bathroom and shut the door.

Her gut-wrenching cries tore at Ellie.

Finally, Cord and the search team rolled in, ready to start the hunt.

Cord's dark eyes met hers as she joined the men outside, a spark of pain in their depths as if he was remembering what had happened on the last case. Lola, the owner of the Corner Café, had been kidnapped and Ellie had gone after her. Both of them had been tortured by the Hunter, and Cord had been captured by the bastard as he was trying to save them.

Thankfully, Derrick had come to the rescue. The last month, she'd seen Cord around town with Lola and they seemed to be growing close. She was glad for Cord. He'd had a rough childhood and deserved some happiness.

"This is Ava's bunny," Ellie told Cord as she handed it to him.

He allowed Benji, his SAR dog, to sniff it then stuck it inside his pocket.

"She had a neon-green backpack with bunnies on it, too," Ellie said, before describing the little girl's outfit.

"I'll pass her description and photo to all the rangers in case whoever abducted her disappeared with her into the mountains."

Ellie shuddered at that possibility. There were hundreds of miles of off-grid areas where a predator could hide, places that even the seasoned hikers avoided.

As Cord and the team set out to search, she drove to Haints, the bar where Autumn Juniper worked.

The bar, overlooking a cemetery, had become a popular watering hole for law enforcement. Ellie's lungs tightened as she glanced at the small tombstones in the section of the graveyard reserved for children. This time of year, with all the presents and Christmas trees the parents brought to the cemetery, made it look even sadder. She'd do everything possible to make sure that Ava would not wind up there.

Country rock music blared from the speakers and loud voices and laughter boomed as she entered the bar. Sheriff Bryce Waters liked to hang out here, and she spotted him at the counter. Irritation shot through her as she crossed the room to him. She and

Bryce had a falling out in high school, and ever since he'd replaced her father as sheriff, he'd held his office—and his power—over her head.

But a little girl was missing, and she was determined to set aside her personal feelings.

"I thought you were looking around town for Ava Truman," she said as she stopped in front of him.

His eyes narrowed as he looked down at her, but she shot him a look of disapproval. "Bryce, how can you sit here drinking when a child is missing?"

"I know you're running the show," he snapped. "And I was out looking for her but stopped to pick up dinner."

Ellie shook her head. "I thought you might clean up your act now you discovered you have a daughter. Losing her mother has been hard for Mandy, Bryce. She needs security and a shoulder to lean on."

Something dangerous flashed in his eyes, and he heaved a breath then grabbed the bag of food the bartender set on the counter. "I am trying. And for your information, I haven't been drinking tonight."

Ellie opened her mouth to speak, but he strode from the bar in an angry gush of air. Ellie shrugged it off. She didn't have time to dwell on Bryce. Ava needed her.

She greeted the bartender. "Is Autumn working this evening?"

"No, yesterday she said she was taking off for a few days."

"Did she mention where she was going?"

"Nope. I figured she was hanging out with her boyfriend but didn't ask." He gestured toward another waitress in a short skirt and v-neck top that accentuated her large breasts. Her wavy hair was bleached blond and earrings that looked like feathers dangled to her shoulders. "Chanel might know."

Ellie murmured thanks, then wove through the crowded bar toward the woman. She waited until Chanel finished delivering the mugs of beer then cleared her throat.

"Chanel, I'm Detective Reeves."

The woman raked her gaze over Ellie and obviously found her appearance lacking. "You need a table?"

"No, just some information. I'm looking for Autumn. The bartender mentioned she was taking a few days off. Do you know where she is?"

The woman twirled a strand of hair around one finger. "She didn't say where she was going, just that she had a trip planned. She was hoping Jasper's wife would finally sign the divorce papers so he'd join her."

Ellie stiffened. "Did she mention anything about his little girl? Were they taking her with them?"

"I have no idea." Chanel shrugged. "But Autumn wasn't crazy about children. She said as long as the kid was around, they'd never be free of his wife."

Ellie's pulse jumped as an ugly thought slammed into her. Was Autumn capable of getting rid of little Ava?

SEVENTEEN

SHADY SPRINGS

After getting her phone number and address from the owner of Haints, Ellie tried calling Autumn, but there was no answer. Ellie left a message, then drove to Autumn's apartment complex in an area called Shady Springs.

With the mountains as a backdrop, the area was named after the dozens and dozens of live oaks bordering the property that the locals referred to as shade trees during the hot summer months. Birds nested in the Spanish moss which hung like spiderwebs to the ground, adding an almost sinister feel to the surroundings.

The older wooden units needed a fresh lick of paint and the grass was patchy and overrun with weeds. Three teens were hanging out smoking in the parking lot but cast their heads down as she drove past. A few pickup trucks and other vehicles were scattered around, but with the disrepair and cracked windows, many of the units looked vacant.

Two buildings over, though, a new section boasted nicer apartments framed in stone and brick with small yards that looked more well-kept. Autumn's place was on the end with a yellow door and ferns hanging from the small front porch. Hoping the rain held off, Ellie hurried up to the door.

Disturbed by the possibility that this woman had nefarious intentions towards Ava, Ellie peered through the front window. There was no movement or indication anyone was inside. She pounded the door and identified herself, but it was locked. *Damn.* She didn't have a warrant, but Ava's sweet face haunted her.

Ellie walked around the side of the building, checking windows and the back door. She finally found an unlocked window and looked inside. Seeing that it opened to the laundry room, she pushed it all the way open then hoisted herself up and crawled inside.

She crossed the small laundry room to the hall. A smoky odor of burned bacon wafted from the kitchenette.

She looked around the area, noting two plush bar stools facing a breakfast bar and a sophisticated coffee system occupying one corner. She looked inside the refrigerator for juice boxes or kid-friendly foods but only found a bottle of wine, cheese and a bagged salad.

She checked the one bedroom and found female clothing, silk blouses and designer jeans, stilettos and risqué underwear in the drawers. There were also several shopping bags overflowing with recent purchases and two unopened boxes. It struck Ellie how different Autumn's lifestyle was from Lara's, whose life revolved around her daughter.

Clothes and shoes had been tossed around as if Autumn had packed hastily, and Ellie didn't find a suitcase in the closet.

Because she'd decided to run off with Ava? Or Jasper?

Her phone buzzed. Cord. She quickly connected. "Please tell me you found Ava."

"I wish I could, but Benji lost track of the scent at the parking lot. I did find the backpack. It had been tossed in the ditch off the main highway at the edge of the park, a couple of miles from the bus stop."

Ellie squeezed her eyes closed as the possibilities hit her. If Jasper took Ava, why would he toss the backpack or the bunny?

Her gut clenched. The pieces didn't fit. He would have wanted Ava to have her beloved stuffed animal.

But if someone else had abducted Ava, they might have wanted to get rid of anything that would remind Ava of her home...

EIGHTEEN

CROOKED CREEK

On the way to the police station for a briefing on Ava's disappearance, Ellie stopped at the Corner Café for coffee and donuts to take to the meeting. God knows they were going to need fuel. They'd be working around the clock until they found Ava.

Rain drizzled down like teardrops from heaven as she parked and got out. Her parents were just leaving the café and paused when they saw her. Her mother's short brown hair looked tousled, as if she'd forgotten to comb it after being out in the wind. Ellie had never seen her wear jeans but she was today, as well as a dark green sweater. Randall had finally added back a few pounds that he'd lost when he'd been shot a few months ago. She missed seeing him in the sheriff's uniform.

"We heard about the little Truman girl, so scary," Vera said, worry lines fanning around her eyes. "I talked to Emily Nettles about organizing a prayer vigil."

"Thanks, I'm sure the family will appreciate that," Ellie said, surprised that her mother took the initiative.

"Let me know if I can help in any way," her father offered.

Ellie gave him an understanding smile, before thanking him. A string of jingle bells tinkled over the door as she entered and the scent of peppermint mocha and cinnamon apples filled the air. But as soon as she stepped in from the cold, the hushed whispers and stares started, the air charged with tension.

She stopped at the bar to place the to-go order and Lola, the owner, greeted her with worry in her eyes.

"Cord told me about Ava," Lola said. "I'm sure her parents are frantic."

"They're terrified," Ellie murmured. She didn't intend to air details of the case in public, especially around local busy-body Maude Hazelnut.

"I'm headed to the station to brief everyone," she said. "Can I get a dozen donuts and some hot coffees?"

"Sure. I'll pack it up. And I'm planning to take a meal to Lara in a while."

"That's really nice of you," Ellie said. "I doubt she's even thought about food."

"Can you believe it? Another child has gone missing in town," Maude muttered from her corner. She saw Ellie, gave her a disapproving look, then raised her voice. "I certainly hope Detective Reeves doesn't let another family suffer by falling down on the job."

The jab hit home and triggered Ellie's guilt over the victims who'd died on her watch. But she steeled herself from the rumors.

Carol Sue from the Beauty Barn, where gossip spread like wildfire, gasped next to Maude. "I heard that, too. One of the mothers who was at the Christmas party at school posted. Said Lara Truman is a mess, and police don't know what to make of it."

"I heard little Ava's daddy might have taken off with her," Bernice, who ran the bakery, said. "You know he's been running around on Lara for a while now."

The other women all chimed in, and Ellie forced herself to mute their voices. She had to focus on the case, not these women's opinions.

Two mothers entered with their little girls in tow, both clutching their hands tightly, eyes darting around as if they feared a predator was right behind them.

Moments later, Lola brought the coffees and donuts and Ellie paid her. As she headed toward the door, she almost ran into Winnie Bates, the owner of Books & Bites. "Detective, any word on little Ava?" Winnie asked.

"Not yet, but we're doing everything we can to find her," Ellie said.

"We're starting a prayer vigil by the angel tree tonight," Winnie said. "We're going to light candles and pray around the clock until you bring her home."

Ellie gave her a smile. "That's what my mother said and it's a lovely gesture. The Trumans could use everyone's support right now."

Anxious to get to the meeting and escape Maude's accusing eyes, Ellie rushed out the door. By the angel tree, she saw old Ms. Eula Frampton sitting on a bench, looking deep in thought. She'd once told Ellie she didn't actually commune with the dead, but she'd had a sixth sense when children and young women had passed.

Did she have the sense now that Ava was still alive? Or dead?

Just as she was wondering, a little girl went darting across the street toward the tree, and her mother and father screamed at her to stop. A car careened toward her, brakes squealing.

Ellie's breath stalled in her chest as the father grabbed the child's arm and yanked her to safety just in time. The car screeched to a stop and the woman driving jumped out, her voice hysterical.

"I'm so sorry, she just ran out in front of me!"

The mother of the child went to talk to her while the father scolded his daughter. "This town is not safe," the father yelled. "You have to stay by our side and hold our hand every minute."

Dear God, the panic had begun. Kids should be excited about Christmas like they were last night, when she'd seen them dressed, giggling and singing at the pageant, not living in terror that someone would snatch them from their families.

NINETEEN

Ellie was still shaken as she met Derrick, Captain Hale, Sheriff Waters, Shondra and Deputy Landrum at the station. She wanted to review what they had on the case before she addressed the media.

Every second counted.

"Thanks for coming, everybody," Ellie said. She attached Ava's photograph to the whiteboard. "Meet six-year-old Ava Truman, our missing little girl." She took a breath, then continued, "Ava disappeared this morning somewhere between her home on Honeysuckle Lane and the bus stop a couple of blocks away. Neighbors have been canvassed and no one seems to have seen her. I found the stuffed bunny she always carries with her in the bushes at the park, which is across from the bus stop." Ellie paused and studied the faces of her team who sat solemnly as the implications set in.

"As of now we haven't recovered Ava's body, so let's work on the theory that she's still alive. Ranger McClain found the girl's backpack a couple of miles from the park in a ditch off the highway, which suggests she was transported in a car instead of just wandering off. Her abductor tossed the backpack, which is being sent to the lab for fingerprinting, but given the timing, she could be anywhere by now, even across state lines."

Under Ava's photograph, she listed the information they'd gathered. "Parents are Lara and Jasper Truman." She reiterated Lara's account of the morning's events. "Midday Lara carried cupcakes to the school for the party. That's when she discovered her daughter hadn't gotten on the bus."

"That's a big time difference," Shondra said.

Ellie nodded. "Which means Ava's kidnapper had a four-hour jump on us."

That realization made them all shift uncomfortably.

"Parents are separated, and Jasper Truman has a girlfriend." She added the parents' pictures, then attached one of Autumn under the list of possible persons of interest.

"Girlfriend works at Haints. According to her friend Chanel, Autumn didn't like kids and wanted Jasper to leave his family for her."

Question marks went by Jasper and Autumn's names.

Sheriff Waters cleared his throat. "If the girlfriend didn't like kids, why would she take the child? That doesn't make sense."

"Maybe she wanted Jasper to leave his wife and child for her, and when he refused, she took the kid to get back at him," Shondra suggested.

Bryce didn't look convinced. "Sounds like you just want to blame the father," he cut in.

Ellie glared at him. "I'm exploring every possibility." Sensing he wanted to get a rise out of her, she moved on. "The Trumans had financial problems. Not sure if that plays into the situation, but their relationship was strained. Deputy Landrum interviewed one neighbor, Dottie Clark, who confirmed she'd heard the couple have some heated arguments. And Lara admitted Jasper had a temper, that she wanted him to go to anger management."

"Dottie Clark is the one putting up fliers about neighborhood watch programs all over town," Shondra interjected.

"And a little nutty," Bryce said. "She's supposedly working on starting a cat café."

Ellie didn't see how that was relevant. "The neighborhood watch is a good thing. Now, Special Agent Fox?"

Derrick cleared his throat. "So far, nothing suspicious on the couple's financials except they'd accrued some serious debt. Husband filed for bankruptcy after the hospital bills piled up."

"I talked to Lara about that," Ellie said. "Ava had a liver transplant two years ago. That's where the medical bills came from. Did the family have a life insurance policy on Ava?"

Derrick shook his head. "No life insurance at all, not on any of them."

"It looks like money was not a motive," Ellie replied. "Another problem we have is that Ava requires immunosuppressant medication daily. Whether our kidnapper knows this and can meet her needs is a major concern. I'm going to run with that on the news."

"Poor baby," Shondra murmured. "Even if the kidnapper doesn't plan to kill her, if she dies without that medication, we could be dealing with murder."

Ellie nodded. "Exactly. And all the more reason we work quickly." She aimed a look at Bryce. "And together."

He opened his mouth as if to say something, but Captain Hale backed her up. "Sheriff, we need your deputies on this ASAP."

"Of course," Bryce snapped.

Derrick gave Ellie a grim look, one she recognized from having worked with him before. He must have found something.

"What is it, Agent Fox?"

Derrick exhaled. "The dark web is full of predators. I dealt with a case a while back where a father was so desperate that he actually sold his child to pay off debt."

Ellie felt sick to her stomach at the thought. "I hate to have to say it, but let's look at that angle." She gestured around the table. "But do not leak that theory to the media."

Murmurs of agreement rumbled through the room, then

Derrick spoke again. "I also ran a list of the neighbors in that area. You're not going to like it, Detective."

Ellie's nails dug into her skin as she curled her fingers into her palms. "Go on."

A knock sounded at the door, cutting him off, and the station receptionist poked her head in. "Angelica Gomez is here, Detective Reeves. She says if you want to get an interview on the six o'clock news, you need to start now."

Ellie raised a questioning brow at Derrick, and he shrugged, his mocha eyes filled with worry. "We'll discuss this afterwards. It's not something we're ready to reveal to the press."

Ellie trusted Derrick. Discretion was of utmost importance, and he was a pro.

"Everyone keep working, and let's set up a tip line and alert hospitals and pharmacists about the immunosuppressive drugs Ava needs. We'll run her face on the news 24/7." She stood, her voice firm. "We have a little girl to find. And we want to bring her home before Christmas." *Alive*, she added silently.

She and Derrick headed to the room they set up for press interviews, the tension between them palpable as they faced the camera. Angelica's black hair was pulled into a fashionable chignon with a pearl clip, her coral suit accentuating her olive skin. She gave them a brief nod hello then got down to business.

"This is Angelica Gomez," started the reporter, "live for Channel Five news in Crooked Creek, where every parents' worst nightmare has happened. Six-year-old Ava Truman has gone missing." Angelica paused for drama, but Ellie knew her well enough to read the emotions underscoring her tough veneer.

As Angelica finished her intro and held out the mic to Ellie, she forced a steady voice. "This morning, Ava rushed out of her house to catch the bus for school, but according to the bus driver, she was not at the stop. Her mother had lost sight of her as she rounded the curve but thought her daughter made it when she saw the bus go by. Four hours later, when Mrs. Truman arrived at Crooked Creek Elementary for Ava's holiday party, she learned that her daughter never got on that bus." Ellie paused, maintaining a calm exterior. "She immediately phoned the police. When we arrived on the scene, we spoke with the teacher, students, and principal—none of whom saw Ava today." She paused again. "At this point, we are exploring all possibilities. As yet we have been unable to locate Ava's father, Jasper Truman, and his girlfriend Autumn Juniper—we urge them to get in touch with us. If you have any information regarding Ava's disappearance or these two individuals, please call the sheriff's office or Crooked Creek Police Department."

Angelica arched her brows. "Do you believe this is a parental kidnapping?"

"As I said," Ellie said calmly, "we don't know at this time. But we do need to speak to Mr. Truman ASAP." She addressed him specifically. "Mr. Truman, if your daughter is with you, please phone your wife and let her know Ava is safe."

Angelica turned to Derrick. "Special Agent Fox?"

He squared his shoulders. "We have issued an Amber Alert and notified all law enforcement across the country to be on the lookout for this child. Please help us find Ava and bring her home to her mother for the holidays."

Ellie spoke again. "There's one more thing, and this makes finding Ava even more urgent. Ava had a liver transplant and requires immunosuppressive medication daily. She cannot do without this treatment. I'm imploring whoever took her to return her home or to a medical facility immediately."

Sympathy flickered in Angelica's eyes. "We will keep you updated on this ongoing investigation as the story unfolds." The screen flipped to display photographs of Ava, her father and Autumn, along with the number for the tip line.

Anxious to hear what Derrick had uncovered, Ellie motioned for him to go into her office. When they were alone, she shut the door and breathed out.

TWENTY

AZALEA COURT

He stared at Ava's precious face on the television. He'd been watching the sweet little girl with the brown curls for weeks now. She had been the prettiest angel on stage last night.

He closed his eyes and remembered her face as she danced. Her eyes sparkled as she sang her heart out. And she'd tapped her patent leather shoes on the stage as if she couldn't be still when the music played.

"Once again, anyone with information regarding the disappearance of Ava Truman, please call the police ASAP," the reporter said, jerking him from his imagination running wild.

Sweat beaded on his neck and forehead, and he paced back and forth, then began to pound his head with his fists. No, no, no...

The police were looking for Ava. Everyone was looking for her.

Panic built inside him. He shouldn't have talked to her. Gone behind the stage.

Watched her this morning.

What if someone had seen him?

Footsteps shuffled outside his bedroom door, followed by a soft knock. His mama poked her head in. Her graying hair was piled on top of her head in a scraggly bun, her age lines prominent as she peered around the room.

When she saw the TV was on and that he'd paused it on the picture of Ava, she made a strangled sound. "Please tell me you didn't…"

TWENTY-ONE

CROOKED CREEK POLICE STATION

Ellie's stomach knotted at the dark look in Derrick's eyes. His jaw was set tight, every muscle in his body tense.

"I know this case triggers bad memories," she said softly.

"It does, but it's not that." Derrick ran his fingers through his hair, tousling the thick black strands.

Frowning, Ellie inhaled a deep breath. She had a bad feeling she wasn't going to like what he had to say. "Tell me."

He crossed her office and looked out the window, his body rigid. She wondered if he was thinking the same thing she was, that the gray skies looked dismal next to the festive red, green, silver and gold decorations adorning the town.

How quickly things had changed since last night's Angel Pageant, when families gathered excitedly to celebrate the season. Driving from the Corner Café to the station, she'd felt the difference, the fear, the silence shrouding the air, seen people scurrying to their cars and homes instead of lingering with each other.

No longer were the parents simply thinking about Santa and Christmas dinner. Instead, they were obsessing over protecting their children from another monster.

Derrick turned to face her, dragging her from her musings. "I ran a search for arrests of child predators and checked the registered sex offender list."

Ellie's breath stalled in her chest. "And you found one?"

He nodded gravely. "A young guy named Nolan Grueler." Derrick opened his laptop and accessed Grueler's arrest records. The man's mug shot made Ellie's skin crawl. Not because he looked scary, but because he looked normal. Nobody would have suspected him. The guy had short wavy brown hair, and his face was slender, clean-shaven. He was fine-boned, looked frail, harmless.

"He worked as a lifeguard at the community swimming pool in Savannah," Derrick said as he read the file. "Mother of a seven-year-old girl claims he was stalking her child at the pool, that he tried to convince her to sit on his lap, but she ran and told her mom. A couple of other mothers said they thought he was overly friendly to the little girls. Police investigated and found child pornography on his computer, and pictures of the children at the pool on his phone. He accepted a plea deal and served a year but is out now."

Bile rose to Ellie's throat. "Where does he live?"

She knew that registered sex offenders were restricted from living or working within 1,000 feet of a church, school, day care center, swimming pool, playground or any other place where children gathered. If he'd been at the park, he'd already violated that.

"According to his parole officer, he lives with his mother." Derrick's mouth tightened. "In the house that backs up to Ava Truman's."

TWENTY-TWO

Ellie cursed, then stood and snatched her keys. "Let's go have a chat with Mr. Grueler."

As they sped through town, lit candles flickered from the hands of those who'd joined the prayer vigil around the angel tree, the lights like beacons of hope flickering against the darkening sky. The town's Christmas carolers stood to the side, singing "Silent Night", as folks joined hands to pray.

Ellie spotted Lola passing out hot apple cider and cocoa to the crowd. As she left Main Street, the festive lights faded as the small town gave way to side streets of neighborhoods with homey bungalows, craftsman homes and old brick ranches where families felt safe.

Except tonight they did not.

The quaint family neighborhood where Lara lived, and the cul de sac where Mrs. Grueler resided, was only a few miles from town, but it felt like an eternity as sickening images taunted Ellie. She prayed and prayed they were wrong, that Jasper had Ava and not this man.

Not wanting to alert Grueler if he was home, she parked two doors down from the Grueler's house.

She and Derrick eased toward the property. With winter upon them, the dry grass was wilted, the trees bare of leaves, the path to the doorway cobbled with broken twigs and pinecones that had blown down in a recent storm.

A breeze rustled the leaves as she inched up to the front stoop. The wrought-iron rail wobbled as she clutched it and the windows desperately needed cleaning. She glanced back at the street as a black Mustang with tinted windows roared past.

Derrick punched the doorbell and knocked, and a minute later a gray-haired woman in a yellow printed housedress opened the door, her brows pinched as she peered at them over wire-rimmed glasses.

Ellie and Derrick identified themselves, and the woman fluttered a hand to her chest. "I figured you'd show up here."

"You did?" Ellie replied, schooling her reaction.

The woman nodded. "I went to get some more yarn today, I make Christmas pot holders for the church sale, and talked to Fanny Mae."

Fanny Mae was one half of the Stitchin' Sisters, who held a weekly knitting club.

"Anyway, Fanny Mae said something about the little girl in the neighborhood going missing. Everyone's talking about it."

Ellie and Derrick exchanged a look. "Ms. Grueler, may we come in?" Derrick asked.

Unease flickered across the woman's face. "I guess I don't have a choice."

Ellie and Derrick didn't respond. Instead, they followed the lady through the small entryway into an outdated living room with furnishings from the eighties. A green floral sofa and plaid chair occupied the room, which was attached to a small galley kitchen with avocado-colored appliances.

She scanned the living room for signs of Nolan but didn't see him. Knitting needles and yarn filled a basket by the sofa and a tabby cat lay curled on the braided rug.

"Is your son here?" Ellie asked.

Ms. Grueler pursed her lips. "We got into it a little while ago, and he tore out of here upset."

"What do you mean you got into it?" Ellie asked.

The woman heaved a wary breath. "You must know about my son or you wouldn't be here, right?"

Derrick's dark eyes were intense. "You mean that he's a convicted sex offender?"

She squeezed her eyes shut for a moment as if those words pained her, then opened them, her expression sad. "I don't know what happened to make him that way," she said in a raw whisper. "I don't. He seemed normal when he was little, although he liked to play with dolls."

"A lot of boys play with dolls," Ellie said gently.

The woman bit her lip. "I know that. It was... just the way he played with them." She lowered her voice. "You know he'd take off their clothes and... do things."

Ellie and Derrick both remained quiet, the silence thick with the implications.

The older woman sank into the chair, and twisted her gnarled hands together. Ellie and Derrick lowered themselves onto the couch.

"But he paid his debt, and he's been taking the medication like the doctor said and I thought he was doing okay, or I wouldn't have let him stay here." She cut her eyes sideways. As much as she defended her son, doubt crept into her voice. "He knew not to go near the school or park."

"You said you two got into it?" Ellie said, sensing the woman was engaged in a silent debate over how much to say. "Was it about Ava?"

Ms. Grueler rubbed a finger over a patch of age-spotted skin on her hand then gave a little nod. "After I saw Fanny Mae, I watched the news and went into Nolan's room, and he was watching it in there and..."

"And what?" Ellie prodded softly.

"He'd paused it on the picture they were showing of Ava, and I could see that look on his face... I confronted him, asked him if he'd been watching her, if he did something."

Ellie held her breath. "What did he say?"

"He started crying and screaming, saying he couldn't help himself, that he was trying but he knew when he saw the news that the police would come here, that they'd arrest him," her voice broke. "He said he couldn't go back to prison." Anguish tinged her voice when she spoke again, "They did terrible things to him in there. Terrible."

Ellie could imagine. Pedophiles were considered the lowest of the low in other inmate's eyes.

"What kind of car does he drive?" Derrick asked.

Ms. Grueler grabbed a tissue from the end table and dabbed at her eyes and nose. "A black Mustang. Belonged to his daddy but he left long time ago. He said he couldn't stand to be around Nolan." No doubt the same car that had torn out when they arrived.

Derrick pulled his phone from his belt. "I'll issue a bulletin for him and his car."

"Ms. Grueler," said Ellie, as she stood. "Do you think he kidnapped Ava this morning?"

Fear darted in the woman's eyes. "I... I honestly don't know."

"Would you cover for him if he did?" Ellie asked bluntly.

The color drained from the lady's face, and she shook her head. "I saw that little girl Ava running around in the backyard. She is a sweetheart. Her mama is, too."

"You said you watched her in the yard." Ellie glanced at the windows along the back wall. "You could see her from here?"

"Here and in the kitchen."

Ellie walked over to the window and looked out. She had a clear view of the Truman's backyard. There was a large grassy area with a small trampoline and a sandbox, along with a patio with a table and chairs.

Ellie's gaze focused on the patio, where she could still see the imprint of a chalk hopscotch board that Ava must have drawn.

If Ms. Grueler had seen Ava playing outside, her son had probably watched her, too.

TWENTY-THREE

"Did you notice your son watching her through the back?" Ellie asked, her heart thudding.

"When Ava was out there, and he was home, I closed the curtains."

"You were protecting him?"

"And the child, too." Her voice sounded slightly defensive. "If Nolan took Ava or did something to her, he needs help. I blamed myself before when he was arrested, had to listen to that mother crying and see her little girl scared. Broke my heart." She blew her nose.

"Is there some place where Nolan would go?" asked Ellie. "Some place with a special meaning to him or another property where he might hide out?"

The woman's hand shook as she rubbed her forehead. "Not that I can think of."

"Does he have a cell phone?" Ellie asked.

"He does."

"Then call him and tell him we want to talk to him."

The woman took her phone from the pocket of her housedress and made the call, leaving a message when Nolan didn't answer.

Derrick cleared his throat. "I'm going to step outside and call his parole officer."

Ellie gave a nod of agreement then asked, "Do you mind if we look around? I'd like to see Nolan's room."

Ms. Grueler stood, her legs wobbling, then she grabbed the chair edge to steady herself. Ellie couldn't imagine being in this woman's shoes.

The old woman hobbled down the hall and stopped at a room with a closed door. She opened it, stepping to the side allowing Ellie entry. At first glance, Ellie felt like she was in a teenage boy's room. A navy bedspread covered a twin bed and a poster of a popular pop band hung on the wall.

With a shaky hand, she pushed the curtain aside.

From Nolan's vantage point, he could see straight into Ava's bedroom window.

TWENTY-FOUR

Derrick didn't like the fact that the man had run. In his eyes, that made him look guilty.

He rang the parole officer's number. "Genesis Luttrell."

"Ms. Luttrell, this is Special Agent Fox again."

Her breathing sounded raspy. "Did you visit Nolan Grueler?"

"Yes," he replied. "I'm at his mother's house now. Nolan lives on a street behind the Truman house."

"Oh, dear heavens, that's not good," she muttered. "I thought he was managing his condition. He's checked in regularly and he's been seeing his therapist on schedule."

Maybe he'd learned to play the game, Derrick thought. Knew how to avoid being caught. Seasoned criminals could be cunning, even charming at times. "According to his mother, he saw the news report and she confronted him. Then he rushed out. Do you have any idea where he'd go?"

A tense second passed. "No. But I'll call his therapist and see if she has any ideas. If he was planning this, he may have talked to her about his feelings or gone off his medication."

"Ask her if he had a special place he might escape to. If he has Ava, we need to find him fast."

"I understand," she murmured worriedly. "I'll call her right now and get back to you."

After thanking her and hanging up, he decided to check around the outside of the house. Senses alert, he surveyed the side of the property then walked around to the backyard. The Grueler's yard was separated from the neighbor's by a fence. The yard held no patio furniture, although there was a flower bed that suggested Nolan's mother liked to garden. A magnolia tree and a few pines were scattered about but there was no outbuilding. Then he spotted a wooden crate wedged between a cluster of red tips, nearly hidden by the foliage. It looked big enough to hold a small animal, maybe a pet like a turtle or rabbit.

Curious, he crossed to it, knelt and used his flashlight to look inside. His pulse pounded when he spotted a small brown teddy bear, a rag doll and a stuffed panda inside.

Just the kind of toys a predator might use to lure a child.

Or had Nolan collected them from children he'd been watching?

His phone buzzed. The parole officer.

"It's Genesis," the woman said. "I spoke with the therapist. Although HIPAA prevents her from confiding personal medical information, she did say that Nolan was still taking his meds, but that he was struggling. He admitted fighting urges and that he hated himself for it."

He sucked in a breath. "Did he specifically mention Ava Truman?"

"No," Genesis replied. "But she said that sometimes he talked about going away and living off the grid. Said it would be easier not to be tempted daily." She sighed. "But he couldn't do that and keep his appointments with me and his therapist."

Frustration turned Derrick's stomach inside out as he considered the area. From this street, you could see the mountains in the distance, the jagged peaks rising to the heavens. The Appalachian Trail had become a hotbed of crime, with predators taking advantage of the wilderness, caves, old mine tunnels, and isolated areas as hiding places. Tangled vines, overgrown weeds, and thick tall trees created isolated areas and a sanctuary for those wanting to escape society.

Those hundreds of miles of forest might be refuge for another kidnapper now.

Miles and miles where Grueler could take Ava and dump her body, just as the man who'd abducted Derrick's own little sister had.

TWENTY-FIVE

"Ms. Grueler," Ellie said. "Did your son have a job?"

"No, with his record no one would hire him. He tried to do yardwork for neighbors, but this is a family neighborhood and no one wanted him near their children or in their homes."

"Just living so close to Ava was a violation of his parole," she pointed out.

"I know, but it was only temporary until he could find a place of his own. Though that was hard without an income. He needed something to do. Any job using computers was out. He couldn't even work at a grocery store."

Ellie gave her a sympathetic look. "That must have been difficult for you."

The woman looked down at her hands and picked at her fingers. "The whole mess ruined our lives. People gossip and whisper and say hateful things to me. I've already moved four times in the last two years."

"Did Nolan have a computer?" Ellie asked.

"No, it was part of his treatment plan. He wasn't allowed on the internet."

That made sense and again would have been a violation. Although he could have kept one hidden.

"How about a gun?" Ellie asked.

"That would also have violated parole, and I wouldn't have allowed it." She rubbed her hands together. "Besides, Nolan is not a violent man. He doesn't even like guns."

Ellie considered that comment. If he wasn't violent, then they might find Ava alive.

She searched the desk again, beneath his bed and then his closet. No laptop, tablet or weapon. But in his dresser drawer beneath his socks, she found a shoebox filled with hairbows. She examined them and realized the red and white polka-dotted one looked familiar. She'd seen a box of similar ones at Lara's that she'd handmade. Ava was also wearing this very one in a holiday photograph on Lara's mantel.

"Mrs. Grueler," she said. "Are you sure that there isn't any place your son might go if he was upset or scared?"

"Oh, my word, the cabins. I'd forgotten about that place," the woman said in a shaky voice.

"Where are they?" Ellie asked.

A tense second passed. "Blood Mountain. His daddy carried him up there to punish him once. He said he was going to get rid of the devil in his boy."

"Did they stay in one of the cabins?" Ellie asked.

"No. Some old, abandoned hunting shack before you got to the cabins on the creek. My husband was too cheap to rent something. But he knew the area and it was off season so he figured no one would be there."

"He might have taken Ava there," Ellie said.

His mother staggered backward, her face turning a sickly shade of green. Then she clutched her chest and collapsed onto the floor.

Ellie rushed forward, dropped to her knees and checked for a pulse. Low and thready. She pulled her phone to call for an ambulance, but Derrick strode in, took one look and called.

The next half hour was fraught with tension as the medics arrived and worked to revive Nolan's mother. They suspected a heart attack induced by stress and were transporting her to the hospital.

"I'll call Cord and ask him about Blood Mountain," Ellie told Derrick. "He may know where those cabins are."

Her stomach was in knots as she stepped back outside. Dusk had come and gone, and shadows from the thunder clouds created spidery patterns across the full moon. Ellie imagined Lara at home, pacing and worrying.

And little Ava terrified as night set in and she was missing her mommy.

TWENTY-SIX

BLOOD MOUNTAIN

Ranger Cord McClain parked at the entrance to the cabins where Ellie had asked him to meet her and Agent Fox. While he waited, painful memories bombarded him as his gaze encompassed the tall peaks and ridges of Blood Mountain.

With an elevation of over four thousand feet, it was the highest mountain on the Georgia section of the AT and a huge tourist draw for hunters and hikers. The smell of winter swirled through the air and the wind howled through the trees like a bear roaring, just as it had the first time he'd been here.

Any beauty of the mountain was tainted by his past. His foster father had dragged him here when he was barely a teenager.

"You got to either kill or be killed," the old man had said. "Now pick up that gun, follow the deer in your sights and shoot the damn thing."

"I'm not a killer," Cord had said, lifting his head to prove he was brave.

"You're a pussy," the man had snapped.

Then he'd raised his fist and beaten the shit out of him.

Cord had flung his arms in front of his face to protect himself, but the old man had hit him so hard he'd heard his wrist snap. Then his foster father had clobbered him in the face until he couldn't see for the blood in his eyes and the pain in his ribs sent him to his knees.

"I don't have time for a sorry worthless boy like you," the man had said, then kicked him in the stomach and left him in the wilderness.

For hours, Cord had lain there barely moving, bleeding and in agony. Hours later, when the blistering sun came up, he dragged himself to the creek and washed up. For days he'd stumbled through the forest, lost and hungry, with nothing but the ragged clothes on his back. Right then and there, he'd decided he had to toughen up. That he would survive no matter what he had to do.

The old man hadn't believed Cord would find his way through the miles of rugged forest. He'd gotten lost so many times in the dense woods that when he'd finally broken into a clearing, the light had burned his eyeballs. A rainstorm had flooded the creek and he'd been swept up in the current and dragged for miles, his body slamming into rocks, the sharp edges battering his skin. He'd lost consciousness for days and been dehydrated. He'd gotten sick and feverish, even hallucinated a couple of times and thought he'd died. He hadn't cared if he had.

But he had survived. Barely, but he had.

Only he'd never gone back to live with that sick bastard. Instead, he'd chosen to stay in the woods alone where he'd learned to survive with nothing.

And now, he was back at the mountain that held so many haunting memories. While he was at the café talking to Lola, Ellie had called and asked him to meet her here. He could never say no to Ellie. Especially when she was searching for a missing child.

He flipped on his radio and heard Angelica Gomez's briefing with Ellie airing, jarring him back to the reason he'd returned here tonight.

Little Ava Truman might be out here lost in these woods with a monster, just as he had been.

TWENTY-SEVEN

Nerves danced along Ellie's spine as she maneuvered the switchbacks and climbed the mountain. She could just imagine what Nolan's father had done to him when he'd gotten him alone.

"I came here with my dad," Derrick said, his voice faraway. "He said there was once a long gory battle between the Cherokee and Muscogee up here."

Ellie nodded. "There was so much bloodshed that the mountain turned crimson with blood. That's how the name originated— or so the legend goes."

The possibility that Grueler had brought Ava to a wilderness with its own set of dangers, sent a shudder through Ellie. The temperatures could drop well into the teens at night at the higher elevation and the dark foliage made it impossible to see.

Wild animals posed a threat, but a child left alone with no protection could more easily die of hypothermia. If she escaped Grueler, she'd easily get lost in the dense, never-ending miles of trees or slip and fall over a rocky overhang.

As she parked, Ellie spotted Cord's truck. If they didn't find Grueler, they'd need him to lead a search team to the more remote cabins. When he saw her, he got out and crossed to her Jeep. He acknowledged Derrick with a grunt. The two stubborn men had butted heads when they'd first met but had come to a kind of silent agreement to work together.

"Let me go in and see if the manager has seen Grueler." Ellie jumped out, leaving the men behind. She hurried into the office and found a silver-haired man with wire-rimmed glasses hunched behind the desk.

Ellie identified herself. "We're looking for this man." She flashed a picture of Grueler. "We have reason to believe he may have kidnapped a little girl and brought her here. Do you recognize him?"

The man squinted at the photograph. "Don't think so, but my eyes ain't so good anymore."

"Can you check your registry?"

He scratched his wiry hair. "Sure thing." He pulled a registration book from the desk and thumbed through it. "Got five cabins here. Couple named Anderson in one, family of four in the second, father and son in three, hunter in four and no one in five."

"You haven't seen a little girl?" Ellie asked.

He shook his head. "But there's another cabin further up on the trail that's been abandoned, near Dead Man's Bluff. You might want to check there."

"Thank you. Can I have a key to the vacant unit?"

He agreed and handed her one, then Ellie hurried back outside. "Let's check out that vacant one," she said as she started the engine. "Maybe you can knock on the others just to verify what he said, Cord."

"Copy that," he agreed.

He slid into the back seat, his jaw set firmly, and Ellie followed the GPS coordinates, turning onto a dirt road that crossed over an old railroad line. The pines and oaks seemed to close around them, the moon fading in the thick overhang of spiny branches and bare limbs that joined to form a natural tunnel.

A deer darted across the road and Ellie had to brake. Gravel and dirt spewed from her tires as they ground over the bumpy road.

Rounding another curve, she spotted a light seeping through a cluster of trees, coming from an area on the hill.

Cord noticed it at the same time. "There are the cottages on the creek."

Ellie slowed, maneuvered the winding road and pulled between an overhang of pines, parking on the shoulder. The three of them climbed out, gravel skittering beneath their boots, damp leaves clinging to their feet as they walked. "Start with one and two," Ellie told Cord.

"I'll check three and four," Derrick said.

"And I'll search the vacant one."

They divided up and Ellie checked her weapon as she approached cabin five. The lights were off, no car in sight. At first glance it appeared deserted, but she pulled her flashlight anyway.

When she reached the front porch, she shined her light through the dark windows. She fished the key from her pocket and unlocked the door, then eased it open. The silence was thick as she entered, and she called out.

Sweeping the flashlight across the rustic room, everything seemed to be in its place. No sign of anyone here.

Satisfied it was empty, she stepped back onto the porch, locked the door then met Derrick and Cord as they walked back to the Jeep. "No one in five," she said.

"One and two all checked out," Cord said.

Derrick heaved a sigh. "Same with three and four. Maybe we were wrong, and he didn't come here."

"We're not done yet," Ellie said. "The manager said there's an abandoned one further up the trail at Dead Man's Bluff." She turned to Cord. "Will you lead us?"

"Of course," Cord said as a thunder cloud rumbled above. "Let's go. If he has Ava, we need to hurry."

TWENTY-EIGHT

DEAD MAN'S BLUFF

Ellie followed Cord onto the dark trail with Derrick close behind. The cloud cover washed out the moon and stars, preventing them from using it as a guide and forcing them to move slowly and watch their footing.

Her father had once told her about Dead Man's Bluff, a steep ridge on Blood Mountain where some claimed they saw the ghostly spirits of Native Americans who'd died in the battles.

"I know that cabin," Cord said, his tone grim. "If he's there, he either came an alternate route or parked off road and hiked in. The road from this direction has been blocked by fallen trees for a while."

From his tone, Ellie sensed this area held traumatic memories for Cord, but she didn't push. Cord had his secrets, a dark past. And she knew better than to pry.

"Watch your step, the ground is slick from recent rain," Cord said as he led them through a labyrinth of trees and inclines. Weeds poked through the damp soil, the scent of moss hanging heavy in the air.

They passed clusters of hemlocks and tall pines as they followed the gurgling creek, stepping over loose rocks and slippery stones and around briar patches. Ellie had the sense that she would have been lost in a heartbeat without Cord's guidance, and Derrick seemed more brooding than usual.

Although missing child cases had to bother him more than any other.

Another mile, and Cord halted and gestured toward a section of forest cloaked in bushes and debris from a storm. A small shack was nestled in the middle of it, weeds climbing the walls.

They cut off their flashlights, and a shiver rippled through Ellie.

Shaking it off, she inched toward the hut, where a low light burned inside as if from a lantern. Derrick motioned that he'd go right and for her to go left, and she gestured for Cord to stay outside and check around the property.

Just as they neared the rotting place, she heard a low keening sound like an injured animal.

Or a crying child.

Ellie's pulse pounded, and she and Derrick took off running.

TWENTY-NINE

Ellie pulled her weapon at the ready and Derrick did the same as they paused at the door. Then he moved toward a tiny window to the right and peeked inside while she pressed her ear to the door.

Her heart thundered. The keening sound grew louder.

"Please don't have let him have hurt Ava," she whispered.

A quick glance at Derrick and he mouthed that he didn't see movement. Keeping her gun braced, she knocked on the door. "Nolan Grueler, police, open up!"

Derrick inched up beside her and she opened the door, peering into the dark space. The light from the lantern glowed across the room, slanting diagonal lines across the primitive wood flooring that had buckled in places from rain and water damage. A musty odor wafted toward her and she heard a rodent skitter into a corner.

She didn't see Ava. But her breath caught as she spotted Nolan Grueler on his knees, rocking back and forth. He was wailing as he gripped a .38 in his shaking hand.

Dammit, his mother claimed he didn't own a weapon.

She raised her weapon and slowly crept toward him. Derrick held behind her so as not to spook the man.

"Nolan, put the gun down," Ellie said softly.

He had his eyes squeezed tightly shut, his body curled forward as he lifted the barrel of the gun to his head.

"Don't do it, Nolan." Ellie leaned forward, her voice a whisper. "Put down the gun and we can talk this out."

He finally seemed to hear her and looked up with glazed eyes. His mother claimed he wasn't violent, but at the moment the desperation in his eyes said different. "Put down the weapon and talk to me."

The gun bobbed up and down, his body trembling. "It won't do any good. You don't believe me."

"Tell me the truth and I will," Ellie said. "That's all I want."

"I did, but you still think I took that little girl and so does Mama," he shouted. "It'll never stop."

"We found those toys you kept in the box outside your mother's house." Ellie said. "You watched her from your window, didn't you?"

He nodded, tears trailing down his cheeks, his thin face contorted in anguish. "I didn't mean to, but I couldn't help it. She was so pretty and sweet and always smiling..."

Ellie's stomach convulsed. "You said she *was* pretty," Ellie said. "Does that mean she's not anymore? That you did something to her?"

He shook his head, his hair sticking up wildly as he angled the gun toward her. "No, I didn't do anything," he screamed. "I wanted to, but I didn't. But it doesn't matter."

"It does matter," Ellie said. "If you took Ava, tell me where she is and I can help you."

"I told you I didn't!" he screeched. "But you're going to blame me anyway. And I can't take it anymore. I take the pills they give me and thought I could control my urges, but they come anyway." His voice broke off in defeat.

"We can help you," Ellie said. "Get you to a doctor."

"It won't do any good," he screamed. "I did watch Ava. Almost every day. But I did not kidnap her." He whirled the gun around toward himself. "It'll never stop. Every time a kid goes missing or something happens to one of them, you'll come knocking at my door. I can't live like this. I might as well be in prison."

Ellie swallowed hard. "Nolan, I talked to your mother," she said in an effort to distract him as Derrick inched into the room. "She knows you're troubled."

"She's ashamed of me," he cried. "She's better off if I'm dead."

"No," Ellie said firmly.

But Nolan choked on another sob and pulled the trigger. The whoosh of air and the click of the chamber as the bullet was released echoed in the air.

Ellie and Derrick dashed forward. The bullet had pierced Nolan's chest, his body bouncing backward and hitting the floor, blood gushing.

Running to him, Ellie shook him. "Dammit, don't you dare die, Nolan. Where's Ava?"

"I didn't do it," he rasped. His eyelids fluttering, he stared at her, his head lolling downward.

"Talk to me, please," Ellie whispered.

He stared into her eyes with a weak expression. "I wasn't the only one watching her. A lady, white van," he moaned. Before he could say anything else, his body convulsed, his voice died and the blood-soaked gun fell from his hand.

THIRTY

Ellie stared at him in stunned silence. Someone else was watching Ava?

"Who are you talking about?" she asked in a raw voice.

He coughed, his body jerking as he slipped into unconsciousness.

Derrick knelt to check for a pulse. "He's still alive. Call an ambulance."

Ellie lowered her gun while Derrick grabbed rags from the kitchen and pressed them to Nolan's chest. "I'll apply pressure. You search the place."

Ellie called for help and told the 911 operator to have the medics come the direct route as she opened the door to the cabin's only other room, which obviously served as the bedroom. It was bare apart from an old sleeping bag.

She shined her light into the closet but found nothing, so returned to the small living room and kitchen. Quickly checking the pantry, she saw an old bag of flour ripped open by critters, along with a metal tin of oil, bugs crawling along the empty shelves.

A small old-fashioned refrigerator sat in the corner, rusted and stained on the outside. A stench filled the space, mingling with the metallic tang of Nolan's blood pooling on the floor.

Holding her breath, she maneuvered around him and Derrick to the refrigerator. Shoulders tense, she pulled the door open, and was nearly knocked over by a fishy stench. She slammed it closed in a hurry.

"No sign of Ava," Ellie said. "I'll call an Evidence Response Team. Cord can lead the medics here. Then I'll check Grueler's vehicle."

"How did he drive up here if we couldn't make it?" Derrick asked.

"Like I said, there's an alternate route from the other side of the mountain," Cord said. "We took the short cut. But he might have come in that way so the caretaker of the cabins wouldn't see him."

Which meant he was hiding something. Ellie hurried outside. Maybe she'd find something inside his car to lead them to Ava.

THIRTY-ONE

Ellie rushed outside to search while Cord went to meet the medics. Inside, she found a Barbie doll and a My Little Pony, but nothing indicating Ava had been in the vehicle. Cord returned with the medics in tow and she showed them to Gruler. The medics took over, taking vitals and adding blood stoppers.

"He's a suspect in a kidnapping. Keep him alive," Ellie told them. If Grueler had seen Ava's kidnapper, she couldn't let him take his secrets to the grave.

"Did he say anything else, Derrick?" she asked.

"No, he just passed out," Derrick answered.

She turned to Cord. "Did you find anything outside?"

He shook his head. "I'll have a team search the woods and creek in case he left Ava close by."

"What about his car?" Derrick asked.

"A couple of toys, but nothing of Ava's. And no snacks he might have given her to keep her quiet, or rope to subdue her. We'll have ERT go over it though. If she was in there, they might find prints."

Derrick gestured toward Nolan, who still hadn't regained consciousness. "Do you believe him?"

"I don't know what to think," Ellie said. "He admitted to

watching Ava. If he decided to commit suicide, why not admit he kidnapped her and tell us where she was?"

Derrick twisted his mouth in thought. "Good question. Maybe his therapist can add some insight."

She glanced at Cord again. "Any outbuildings or a fallout shelter?"

"Nothing," Cord said.

Ellie scratched her head. "Nolan said a woman driving a white van was watching Ava."

"Could be a misdirect," Derrick suggested.

"True. Or maybe he didn't know who it was." Frustration clawed at her and she stepped aside and phoned his parole officer.

"I know he was tormented," the woman said, obviously disturbed by the news. "But I didn't realize he was suicidal."

Ellie had driven him over the edge, she thought. "He confessed to watching Ava. But if he abducted her, why not confess to that, too?"

A tense silence stretched between them. "That doesn't make sense," Genesis said. "When the accusations were made against Nolan before, he didn't bother to deny them. In fact, he admitted to what he'd done and to the plea deal without contesting it. I... think he wanted to be stopped."

"Do you think he shot himself because he lost control and abducted Ava?"

Another heartbeat passed. "I can't say for sure, but Nolan never lied about anything. If he abducted her, he wouldn't have hurt her. And if he was so guilt-stricken he was planning suicide, he would have left her some place where she'd be found."

But there was no sign of Ava anywhere.

THIRTY-TWO

Ellie got the therapist's number from the parole officer and phoned her while Cord organized search parties. Dr. Myers was in an appointment, so she left a message that it was urgent she speak with her.

"We'll divide up and start with a ten-mile search radius," Cord told her. "One of the men can drop me at my truck when we're finished."

Ellie addressed the team who'd gathered to help Cord. "Thanks for coming so quickly, you guys. We don't know if Ava's out there, but if she is, we need to find her." With winter on them, it was pitch dark already. "The wind is picking up and it's only going to get colder in the night. If Ava was here and somehow escaped from Grueler, she could have run into the woods and fallen over a ledge or in the creek. A wild animal could get her. And if she survived, she could be lying somewhere scared, cold and hungry."

"We won't stop until we've searched every inch for miles," Cord promised.

Ellie clapped her hands. "Then let's get to work."

Cord showed them the map and they divided up and set out, determination on the men's faces.

Derrick returned from talking to the medics and cleaning up his bloodstained hands. "They're leaving with Nolan," he said.

"Take my Jeep back." Ellie handed Derrick her keys. "I want to ride along with Grueler in case he comes to."

"Are you going to stop by and tell Ava's mother about Grueler?" Derrick asked.

"No. She's had a tough enough day. And so far we have no proof of Grueler's guilt. Let's wait, see if he survives that bullet wound."

He agreed and she rushed to the ambulance, where Grueler was pale and limp, hooked up to an IV. She climbed in the back beside him.

Siren wailing and lights flashing as they pulled away, Ellie phoned her captain to explain the situation. "We probably should have someone stand guard at his hospital room," she suggested. "He's too weak to try and escape. But if word leaks that we were questioning a registered sex offender as a person of interest..."

"We'll keep it quiet, but you're right," Captain Hale said. "That could be a problem. I'll talk to the sheriff."

Ellie sighed as the siren wailed into the night. Day one, fifteen hours after Ava disappeared, they were no closer to finding her than they were when Ellie first received the call.

THIRTY-THREE

HONEYSUCKLE LANE

Lara ran her finger over the glittered ornament Ava had made at school, her heart aching as she set it on the mantle. She wouldn't hang it on the tree until Ava came home and they could do it together.

Panic struck her. *What if she doesn't come home?*

She'd heard stories about kidnapped children who were never found. Ones who were raised by another person and brainwashed to the point that the child forgot her real parents.

And just last year all those bones of the little girls had been discovered on the AT.

Another sob caught in her throat and she dug the bag of gifts she'd bought for the twelve days of Christmas from her closet. She'd started the tradition when Ava was two. Each day she gave Ava a small, wrapped present leading up to Christmas Day. They were simple little presents, like a pack of cards or stickers or new markers.

She wrapped the giant box of crayons she'd planned to give her daughter today, then set the gift on the mantle beside the ornament. They would both be waiting for Ava.

Her little girl was not going to be one of those kids lost forever.

Jasper had to have her. If he did, at least she'd know Ava was safe.

But why would he run off without telling her? Didn't he realize she'd panic and call the police? Or didn't he care?

Was this a devious ploy to strong-arm her into signing?

Her heart hammered against her ribs, and she snatched her phone and called his number again. Three rings and it went to voicemail. "Jasper, it's Lara. Please call me. I need to know if Ava's safe. If you'll just bring her home, I'll sign the divorce papers. Please..."

Her voice wavered as tears filled her eyes and trickled down her cheeks. She hung up, then went to Ava's room and stared at her empty bed. The sheets were still tangled where the little girl had slept last night, her stuffed animals lined up against the wall like she always tidied them up at night. She liked to lie on her side, sing to them and whisper secrets.

Lara crawled into Ava's bed, pulled her pink blanket up to her cheek and sniffed it. With her daughter's sweet scent filling her nostrils, she rolled to her side and faced Ava's stuffed animals. Ava called the stuffed animals her friends and said they protected her while she slept.

Who was protecting her tonight?

THIRTY-FOUR

BLUFF COUNTY HOSPITAL

Anger at Grueler built inside Ellie as the ambulance swerved into the ER.

"I want an update on his condition as soon as you have one," she told the male nurse who'd met the medics at the door. "And I need to speak to him the minute he regains consciousness."

"Of course," the nurse replied. He turned and raced along beside the medics as they wheeled Grueler to an exam room.

Ellie walked to the vending machine and got a cup of coffee. Carrying it to the nurse's desk, she asked about Nolan's mother, who'd been brought in earlier.

"She's stable," the front desk nurse said. "But fragile."

"I need to tell her about her son," Ellie said.

"I'd wait until morning," she advised. "She's still fairly weak right now."

"I understand." Ellie dreaded that conversation anyway. Maybe by morning she could tell the woman whether her son had survived the night. Her phone buzzed, and she checked the number.

Dr. Myers, Nolan's psychologist. "Detective Reeves?" the doctor asked when Ellie answered.

"Yes, I hate to disturb you this late, but it's about Nolan Grueler. I'm at the hospital with him now."

The woman made a low sound in her throat. "What happened?"

"He's a person of interest in the missing child case I'm working. A little while ago, he attempted suicide."

"My word," Dr. Myers said. "Is he going to be all right?"

"I don't know," Ellie said. "Doctors are with him now. I did talk to him before he shot himself and he denied abducting Ava. But it makes me wonder why he would kill himself if he's innocent."

Ellie heard papers being shuffled at the other end of the line. "You know I can't divulge his medical information."

"We are talking about a child abduction," Ellie said bluntly. "Ava has been missing since this morning, and Nolan Grueler lived on the street behind her house." She paused, and when the woman still didn't reply, prompted her. "Tell me what you can."

Another heartbeat dragged by. "Nolan was deeply troubled and tormented about his condition," Dr. Myers said. "He claimed he didn't want to be the way he was and did talk about taking his life once but I thought he was stable."

"Do you think he could have given into his needs and abducted Ava?"

Her breathing sounded shaky. "If he did, I don't think he'd hurt her," she said. "His fantasies were never violent. In fact, quite the opposite."

Everyone kept saying he wasn't violent, but shooting himself had been an act of violence against himself. Maybe that spoke to the depth of self-hatred he possessed. "His parole officer believes that if he'd kidnapped her, he would have come clean," Ellie said.

"I would have to agree," Dr. Myers said. "He talked about wanting help, stopping himself and was open to more intensive therapy than what we've engaged in so far." She paused. "What hospital is he in?"

"Bluff County," Ellie answered. "I asked the nurse to inform me if or when he regains consciousness.

"Call me when he does, and I'll stop by and talk to him myself."

"Thank you," Ellie said. "He might open up to you before he would me."

Dr. Myers agreed and Ellie ended the call, then settled in the waiting room. Hopefully if Nolan came to, the psychologist could persuade Nolan to talk.

Although her instincts told her he was telling the truth. Which left them back at square one.

THIRTY-FIVE

Saturday, December 21

The next morning, Ellie jerked awake, stiff from falling asleep in the hard chair in the hospital waiting room. During the night, her boss had texted that the sheriff would either be by or send someone first thing to guard Grueler so she could keep exploring other leads.

She stood and stretched her aching muscles, then went to the nurse's station. "Any news on Nolan Grueler?"

"I'm sorry. He's stabilized, but in a coma," the nurse said. "Time will tell."

Frustration tightened every inch of Ellie's body. "Call me when he wakes up."

A heavy feeling weighed on her as she glanced at the wall clock again.

It was 8 a.m. Ava had officially been missing for twenty-four hours.

She stepped back into the waiting room just as the ER doors swished open. Bryce entered and stormed toward her. "What the hell, Ellie?" the sheriff boomed. "You chased down a possible child predator and I didn't know anything about it."

"I was going to fill you in," she said through gritted teeth. "But I didn't want the Trumans to know until I questioned him."

Bryce glared down at her. "They're going to find out. Especially now you're protecting the bastard."

Ellie crossed her arms. "What else can I do?" she said, her voice icy. "If he abducted Ava, which he denied just before he shot himself, he can't tell us where she is if he's dead."

Bryce's breathing echoed in the loaded silence. "If he hurts children, he doesn't deserve to live."

"Neither you nor I get to play God here, Bryce." Ellie pushed aside her own feelings. "Besides, Grueler claims a woman in a white van was watching Ava."

Bryce grunted. "He's probably just taking the heat off himself and you're so gullible you believe him."

"I'm banking on the system working," Ellie said.

"And I'm willing to bet that protecting him is going to bite you in the butt."

"It may," Ellie said. "But I have to abide by the law, Sheriff. And if you don't post a guard by his door, I will."

"I'll take care of it," Bryce said. "I want to talk to the guy myself."

Trembling with fatigue, Ellie rushed down the hall and outside. Already she couldn't breathe. And she had no doubt Bryce was right.

Some of the locals had turned on her father when they learned he'd kept information about Vera's son to himself. The town would probably crucify her for her decision to keep Nolan Grueler safe.

But she couldn't dwell on that now. Getting the job done sometimes meant stepping on toes.

Ava was worth crushing a few for.

THIRTY-SIX

CROOKED CREEK

With the doctor's permission, Ellie had explained to Nolan's mother what had happened. The poor woman looked distraught but resigned. "He's such a tormented soul," she'd murmured weakly. "Maybe it's better this way. He can finally be at peace."

Her comment echoed in Ellie's head as she drove home. Rays of morning sunshine splintered the clouds like shards of broken glass, the smell of winter hanging in the air.

She hurried inside her house and took a quick shower, dressing in layers for the day. With her fridge empty and knowing she needed fuel, she called in a to-go order at the Corner Café, noting fliers with Ava's kindergarten picture on them had been tacked all over town.

As she entered the café, the earthy comforting scent of ham and red-eyed gravy swirled around her, at odds with the sudden hushed silence that greeted her. The enthusiastic chatter about Christmas from two days ago had turned to worried whispers, and fear buzzed through the room.

A group of young women had gathered at a table, their children seated next to them. "Isn't it just horrible about Ava Truman disappearing?" a blond in a jogging suit asked.

"I joined the prayer vigil last night. So sad," a dark-haired woman with three kids in tow murmured.

A woman holding a baby on her lap spoke in a low voice. "They're asking everyone to keep a candle lit in their windows until Ava comes home."

"Whose child do you think will be next?" the blond said.

The baby's mother hugged her infant to her chest and rocked her, pulling her pig-tailed toddler closer to her. "I don't know, but I'm not letting my kids out of my sight."

The mother of three pressed her hand to her chest. "Can you imagine your daughter being snatched right outside your house?"

One of the little girls started crying. "Mama, I'm scared."

The child's mother pulled her in her lap to console her as Ellie's phone dinged with a text from Cord.

Searched ten-mile radius. Did not find Ava or any signs of her. Plan to do one more sweep, then heading back.

Ellie realized he'd been searching all night and texted him thanks. Footsteps clattered around her, and she saw Ms. Eula slide into the corner booth worrying the beads around her neck. While Lola retrieved Ellie's sausage biscuit, she stepped over to her table. Some of the women in town steered clear of Ms. Eula but Ellie knew the old woman meant no harm.

Ms. Eula's fingers fumbled with the beads as Ellie approached the table. "I've been wondering how you're managing."

Ellie shrugged. She wasn't sure Ms. Eula was talking about her personal life or the case. "I'm just worried about the missing little girl. I... don't want to be too late this time."

Ms. Eula squeezed her hand. "The people here are lucky to have you, Ellie girl."

Ellie wasn't so sure about that.

Someone cleared their throat behind her, and Ellie felt a hot breath on her neck. "What are you doing now, Detective? Asking advice on your case from a psychic?"

Ellie fisted her hands by her sides and turned to face Bryce's mother Edwina, the mayor's wife. Her judgmental tone already condemned Ellie as a failure.

"I'm just saying hello to this nice lady, then I'm headed to the station right now." Ellie and Ms. Eula exchanged looks, then Ellie straightened. "I have to go."

She returned to the counter to pick up her order, feeling stares burning into her as she paid.

The mayor's wife obviously thought Ms. Eula was unstable. Ellie knew different. The old woman might not talk to the dead, but she had grit and did have a sixth sense.

As she stepped outside, an icy wind whipped the tree branches and sent the only traffic light in town swinging back and forth, making fingers of apprehension dance up Ellie's spine. She turned in a wide arc, the sense that someone was watching washing over her. Clenching her hands by her sides, she searched the faces of the people rushing to their cars and inside the stores to finish their last-minute holiday shopping. Hunched in heavy winter coats, their faces were half-hidden by ski hats and scarves and no one seemed to be making eye contact.

Could one of them be a kidnapper?

THIRTY-SEVEN

Derrick was waiting as Ellie entered the station, his body rigid. "Did McClain and the dogs find anything?"

"Nothing." She rubbed her gritty eyes.

Angelica and her cameraman rushed in, the reporter signaling they needed an interview.

Ellie grimaced, but she knew she couldn't ignore the public.

Tom, Angelica's cameraman, set up and Ellie brushed a hand over her hair to smooth the strands escaping her haphazard ponytail. She always looked a mess next to Angelica.

The reporter gripped the microphone and began her introduction. "With the countdown to Christmas underway, the clock is ticking on finding six-year-old Ava Truman, who disappeared near her house yesterday morning. Police and the FBI are working around the clock to bring this child home to her parents before the holiday and are seeking your help. We are also trying to reach Ava's father, Jasper, so if you know his whereabouts, please contact the police."

Ellie tacked her professional mask in place.

"Is it true that a convicted sex offender lived in Ava's neighborhood?" Angelica asked.

Ellie bit the inside of her cheek to stifle a reaction. Had Bryce leaked it already?

Angelica cleared her throat. "Detective?"

She couldn't lie or people would totally lose faith in her. Besides, now Angelica had planted the thought in their heads, anyone could easily check public records and learn about Nolan. Better to get ahead of it.

She swallowed hard before she spoke. "Yes, that is true. We questioned him and he denied his involvement. At this time, we have found no evidence that he perpetrated a crime."

"Did you arrest him?" Angelica asked.

Ellie gritted her teeth. "No. The individual concerned shot himself and is in a coma." She paused. "But let me remind everyone. We are just beginning this investigation and at this point we have ruled no one out. If you have any information that could help us find this sweet child, please call us ASAP."

Angelica started to speak, but Ellie shook her head. "Now, excuse me, I need to get to work. Little Ava needs us." The Trumans would probably be showing up or calling any minute.

She rushed to her office, angry with Angelica, even though she knew that she was just doing her job. Now, not only was Nolan— the only real key they had to finding Ava so far—in danger, but his frail mother might bear the brunt of outrage toward her son.

A second later, Angelica knocked on the door and stepped inside, her expression dark.

"I wish you hadn't done that," Ellie said. "When Ava's mother sees it, she'll be even more upset than she already is."

"If I hadn't reported it, someone else would." Angelica gripped her phone. "Ellie, as soon as the interview was over, I received a text. You need to see it."

Ellie went still, her heart skipping a beat. "A tip on who took Ava?"

"Not exactly." Angelica worried her bottom lip with her teeth then angled the phone so Ellie could read the message.

There are other missing girls out there. Don't forget them.

A cold shudder ripped through Ellie.

THIRTY-EIGHT

WILLOW CIRCLE

Jan Hornsby struggled for a breath as the reporter on the TV finished interviewing the detective in Crooked Creek. Another child had gone missing. Six years old.

The same age as her Becky had been.

She'd been stolen on her birthday six months ago.

Her throat burned with unshed tears as she glanced at the Christmas tree that she couldn't bear to decorate. How could she celebrate the holiday when her baby girl was lost to her?

"Lordy, that poor family. What is the world coming to?" Jan's seventy-five-year-old mama said with a sad shake of her head.

"I don't know, Mama." Jan looked at her mother, saddened for the Trumans and tormented by her own memories. She'd come to live with her mother last month when she could no longer stand to be in the empty house that used to be alive with Becky's laughter. She'd thought being here would help with the loneliness, but she felt as if she'd abandoned Becky by leaving her home, as if one day her daughter would just show up and skip into the room begging for chocolate chip cookies.

Unable to pretend she wasn't thinking of her own daughter's disappearance, she wrapped a shawl around her, then stepped out onto the back deck of the house and looked into the gray skies, and the weeping willows that backed the yard. Some said the trees were no good, that they drew snakes, and at night she'd heard the eerie hoot of the owl that had made the trees its home. Its tiny eyes pierced the darkness as if it tracked evil around her.

The branches hung low, sagging, as if mourning the loss of their spear-shaped leaves just as she mourned the loss of her daughter.

Yet when spring came, they would be the first to leaf. Would Becky be here to see them?

Pain wrenched her gut, and she clutched her stomach to keep from wailing as her last day with Becky floated through her mind.

Her little girl had been so excited about the festival in Chattanooga along the Riverwalk. They had arts and crafts and music, a petting zoo, pony rides and face painting. In her mind, she saw Becky sitting still as the artisan painted a rainbow of colors on her cheek. Then she'd jumped up and squealed and raced to pet the goats in the petting zoo area.

She'd paid the artisan, then raced after Becky, but in the blink of an eye, Becky was gone.

Shivering now, she clenched the shawl around her shoulders, the terror she'd felt in that moment returning like a live beast inside her.

The police had investigated. Searched.

Found nothing.

She called them every week to see if they were still looking, but as each day passed, she sensed their drive fading, that soon her precious sweet child would be forgotten.

Some days the pain was so intense she didn't think she could go on. But she had to.

Becky was out there somewhere and needed her.

Despair overwhelming her, on her phone she signed onto the Facebook group she'd started as a support network. She'd called it *Mothers of Missing Children.*

Bonding with other mothers had opened her eyes to how the system sometimes failed and how easily lost children and their families got shoved aside for newer cases. And who else could possibly understand the unbearable agony of wondering where your child was, if they were hurt, hungry, being cared for?

If the mothers didn't fight for their lost children no one would.

She refused to let Becky be forgotten.

THIRTY-NINE
HONEYSUCKLE LANE

Ellie leaned over her desk and dragged in deep breaths to stem her rising anxiety.

Had Ava's kidnapper abducted other girls? Were they dealing with a serial child snatcher? Were they planning another abduction?

Derrick immediately attempted to trace the text Angelica had received, his expression bleak. "It was sent from a burner. No way to trace it."

Why was she not surprised? "Either the person who sent it is the kidnapper or he or she knows who is. And that the kidnapper has done this before."

Her captain poked his head into her office. "A domestic call just came in. The Truman house," he said. "Deputy Eastwood went home to shower. Get your butt over there now."

Adrenaline surged through her. "What happened?"

"Neighbor said they heard fighting," Captain Hale said. "That's all I know."

Ellie headed toward the door with Derrick close behind her, then they jumped in her Jeep and raced from the parking lot. Traffic was practically non-existent now the winter break had started and the threat of sleet along with fear was keeping people cowering inside. Leaves fluttered down to the ground, the wind swirling the brittle remains across the road. A huge dark cloud hung low in the sky, adding to the morose atmosphere.

As she drove, she noted lit candles in windows in support of the Trumans.

As she reached the Trumans' house, she saw a black pickup parked half in the grass, half in the drive, as if the driver had jumped the curb and stopped in a hurry.

Shouts echoed from inside as she and Derrick approached, and she heard a loud crash. She pulled her gun at the ready and gestured for Derrick to back her up. Then she knocked and called out.

"Lara, it's the police. Open up."

Through the front window, she spotted a man chasing Lara into the kitchen.

A quick look and she didn't see a weapon, but he'd knocked the lamp off onto the floor and was towering over Lara. He was around five-eleven, muscular, with dirty brown shaggy hair.

A tiny sliver of morning sunlight broke through the clouds and allowed her to see his face. "It's Jasper," she whispered to Derrick. "I don't think he's armed."

But he was angry, that much was clear.

She knocked once more, then pushed open the door and called Lara's name. "It's Detective Reeves and Agent Fox."

Gun at the ready, she crept past the entry until she and Derrick reached the doorway. Jasper must have heard her because he whipped his head around. His face was agitated, his hair spiked where he'd run his hands through it. His eyes looked wild and angry, and sweat coated his skin.

"You lost our daughter!" the man bellowed, then he raked his hand across the table, scattering the snowman puzzle pieces to the floor.

"Lara," Ellie said softly as she slowly moved toward the couple. "Are you okay?"

The woman looked up at Ellie with red-rimmed eyes overflowing with tears. Ellie raked her gaze over her, searching for injuries, and Derrick planted himself between Lara and her husband.

"Step away from your wife, Mr. Truman," he ordered Jasper.

The man threw his hands up as if to indicate that he wasn't armed, and Ellie approached Lara. "Are you hurt?"

Lara wrapped her arms around herself, her chin quivering. "He says he doesn't have Ava," she cried.

Ellie narrowed her eyes at the man, who fisted his hands by his sides. His face was red, stubble grazed his jaw, and his nostrils were flared. There were scars and scratches on his hands. From his work or from possibly burying Ava?

"I don't," he bellowed. "How could you let this happen, Lara?" He pivoted toward Ellie, tone accusatory. "And what are you people doing to find my daughter?"

Lara pressed her hands to her face, her body trembling, and Ellie slid onto the sofa beside her. Derrick nudged Jasper's arm. "Sit down, Mr. Truman."

He glared at Derrick with a shake of his head. Sweat droplets dripped from the side of his face. "I don't want to sit down. I want to know where my little girl is. Did that pervert take her?"

"What pervert?" Lara gasped.

"The one that lives behind us!" Jasper pointed to Ellie. "It's all over the damn news!"

Lara turned horrified eyes toward Ellie, and Ellie's stomach somersaulted. "Mr. Truman," Ellie said firmly. "I did question that man, but I don't think he took Ava. Not only did he deny it, but we found no evidence linking him to your daughter. In fact, we were hoping you could tell us where she is."

He pounded his fist into his palm. "How should I know? I went fishing and she was supposed to be here with her mother."

"She was," Lara said. "But she ran to the bus stop, and I just turned my head for a minute, and... she never made it there."

"Where were you fishing?" Ellie asked the husband.

"Up at Beaver Pond," he said. "What the hell is going on here?"

Derrick crossed his arms. "Your wife called you yesterday. Multiple times. If you're so worried about Ava, why wait until today to show up?"

"Because I didn't have cell service in the woods," Jasper snapped. "I didn't get my voicemail until this morning when I went to the bait shop." He grabbed his phone. "Last night Lara called and practically accused me of kidnapping my own little girl."

Ellie studied his body language. Rigid shoulders, jaw tensed, hands fisting and unfisting as if he wanted to hit something. His voice was a blend of fear and anger. Was the fear out of worry for Ava or that he'd gotten caught? "Was anyone fishing with you?" she asked.

Jasper's mouth tightened into a straight line. "Yes. A buddy of mine. Curtis Banks."

"We're going to need his contact information," she said.

He exhaled loudly, rage vibrating in the sound. But he pulled up the number. "He stayed this morning to fish, so he won't have service."

"Where were you staying?" Ellie asked.

"We set up a campsite at the pond."

"How far is the bait shop from your camp?" Ellie questioned.

Jasper slammed his fist into his hand again. "About a mile. Why are you grilling me instead of looking for Ava? And how do you know that sicko isn't hurting her right now?"

Lara paled and leaned her head into her hands as if she might faint. Ellie rubbed her back to soothe her.

"Because he tried to kill himself last night." Ellie cleared her throat. "Like I told you, we found no evidence that he had anything to do with her disappearance." Although he had been watching Ava, she reminded herself. "But we are keeping him under surveillance."

Lara jerked her head up. "I want to talk to him. Make him look at my face and tell me."

"I'm afraid that's not possible," Ellie said. "He's in a coma right now. But before he lost consciousness, he mentioned seeing a woman in a white van watching Ava."

"What?" Lara asked in a choked whisper. "Who was she?"

"I don't know. I'm hoping that when he regains consciousness he can tell us that." *If* he regains consciousness, Ellie thought. The doctor had not given him a good prognosis. "Lara, had you noticed a white van near the house or bus stop?"

Lara scrubbed a hand over face. "Not really. But I see white vans and trucks every day.

True, Ellie thought. *And Grueler hadn't been specific if it was commercial or a personal van.*

"Mr. Truman, we have to consider other possibilities," Derrick cut in. "To do that, we need your cooperation."

His eyes shifted nervously.

Derrick held out his hand. "Let me see your phone."

"Why?" Jasper grumbled.

"To verify your story," Ellie said.

She directed a look at Ava's father, searching for some indication he was lying.

He cursed but gave a resigned sigh and shoved it into Derrick's hands. "Look at whatever you want. You won't find anything." Then he turned to his wife, expression filled with contempt. "This is unreal, Lara. You lose our daughter and then you blame me."

"I'm just trying to find her," Lara said brokenly. "I thought you might have taken her to force me into signing the divorce papers."

"Well, I didn't!" he shouted. "So where is she?"

"I don't know," Lara said through her tears.

"Please, Mr. Truman, sit down and calm down," Ellie said.

He dropped into the chair. "How can I calm down with you accusing me of kidnapping my own daughter?"

FORTY

"We haven't accused you of anything," Ellie said. "We simply thought you might have Ava with you. And frankly, Mr. Truman, I think your wife was hoping you did because the other possibilities are more concerning." Terrifying in reality, but she needed to defuse the situation.

He clenched his jaw, his face turning ghastly white. She was sure his mind was going back to Grueler. In his state of mind, Jasper might go after him personally.

"Right now we've issued an Amber Alert and are circulating Ava's photograph and description across the country," she told Jasper. "We've also canvassed the neighbors and your wife has answered all of our questions. We need your cooperation as well."

He pulled a hand down his face. "I don't know anything, except that I was planning to see Ava for Christmas when I got back."

"Where is your girlfriend, Autumn?" Ellie asked, drumming her fingers on her leg.

He slanted his wife a dark look. "I don't know. We had an argument and broke things off. That's why I decided to get away for a couple of days."

Lara's eyes widened in surprise. "You broke up with her?"

He nodded, his anger fading slightly. "I... with the holidays coming, I wanted to be with Ava. And for maybe us to be a family, at least for the day."

Lara glanced down at her jagged nails then bit her lip.

Ellie's fingers went still on her leg. He sounded sincere, but she couldn't accept his word. "Is that what you and your girlfriend argued about?"

He shoved his scarred hand through his hair, drawing her gaze to the bruises there again. "Yes," he said. "She wanted me to finalize the divorce. But I... told her I wasn't ready."

"You did?" Lara whispered.

"Yeah." A muscle ticked in his jaw. "She was pretty mad. Said she was going on a trip herself."

"Did she mention where she was going?" Ellie asked.

He shook his head. "Probably shopping or the spa. Every couple of months she goes to Atlanta and stays in a hotel for a marathon shopping spree."

Ellie's mind raced. "Mr. Truman, do you think Autumn might have abducted Ava to get back at you?"

FORTY-ONE

A deep frown darkened Jasper's eyes. "I... don't think so, but... hell, I don't know. She didn't want kids. She told me to sign away my rights." His voice hardened. "I told her that was never going to happen."

Lara's mouth opened and closed in horror.

"How can I contact her?" Ellie asked.

He gestured to the phone Derrick was searching. "She's listed in my contacts."

Derrick tapped Jasper's cell in his hands. "Curtis didn't answer. I left a message for him to return my call ASAP."

Maybe Cord could go to Beaver Pond and find him. She turned to Jasper. "Is there anyone else who might want to hurt you by abducting Ava? Anyone you owe money who might ask for a ransom?"

"No," Jasper said. "And you can look at our financials. We were in debt, but I was slowly paying it off."

"Did you ever notice anyone watching Ava when you were with her?"

He shook his head. "No."

"No one in a white van?" Ellie asked.

"No."

Ellie gestured to his hands. "How did you get those scratches and bruises?"

Jasper lifted his hands and looked at them with a shrug. "I work construction."

Lara gasped. "Your construction company uses white vans. Did you loan one to your girlfriend?"

"No. But we leave a couple parked at the construction site sometimes." Anxiety radiated from him as he made the connection. "Let me call Autumn."

Ellie held up a finger. "Sure. But don't be confrontational. Just talk to her. Maybe suggest that you want to see her."

He heaved a labored breath, then murmured agreement and took his phone from Derrick.

"Put it on speaker," Ellie said.

He followed her instructions and rang Autumn. Ellie, not expecting her to answer, was surprised when she did.

"It's Jasper."

"I thought you were on a fishing trip," she said, her tone razor sharp.

Jasper sucked in a slow breath. "I was, but I came back early. I couldn't stop thinking about you and wanted us to talk. Where are you?"

"At the spa. What's going on, Jasper?" she asked. "Some detective left me a message asking me to call her."

Ellie chewed the inside of her cheek. So Autumn had received her message, but she hadn't bothered to return Ellie's call. Why?

"I know, I'm here with that detective now," Jasper admitted, his voice strained. "Autumn, we think someone kidnapped Ava."

A strained silence stretched between them for a second, then Autumn spoke, her voice edgy. "What do you mean? Someone took her?"

"Yesterday morning, on the way to the bus stop," he said. "Ava never made it to school, and we haven't heard from her since. I... thought you might know something."

Ellie heard Autumn tapping her nails on a table. "Why the hell would I know anything?" Autumn asked.

Another tense heartbeat. He glanced at his wife then Ellie then Derrick. "I thought you might have picked her up. Maybe to surprise me," he said, the lie rolling off his tongue.

"I told you I'm not into kids, Jasper. And if you're implying what I think you are, you can go to hell."

"Please, Autumn, if you took her, tell me," Jasper replied "I'll do anything to have Ava back."

"Then run back to Lara. Now, I need to get back to my massage."

The line went dead. Lara pressed her fist to her mouth as if to stifle a scream, and Jasper cursed.

Ellie considered Autumn's harsh tone. She certainly didn't have a soft spot for children.

But was she capable of kidnapping her to punish Jasper for choosing Ava over her?

FORTY-TWO

BEAVER POND

Shondra arrived to stay with the Trumans, and Ellie filled her in while Lara disappeared into Ava's room, crying. Jasper was pacing the living room, work boots clicking on the wood floor as he studied the photos of past Christmases that Lara had spread on the coffee table.

"What do you think?" Shondra asked.

"Not sure about Jasper. He seems truly upset but could be guilt kicking in if he hurt Ava." Ellie paused. "The girlfriend is one cold ice cube. Definitely keeping her on the list for the moment."

"I'll watch him carefully," Shondra said. "See if he changes his story."

"Monitor his phone in case Autumn calls him or he tries to sneak off and reach her."

"On it," Shondra said. "I've had plenty of experience reading weasels."

Ellie gave her a small smile. Shondra had been raised in an abusive situation.

"The desk clerk at the spa confirms that Autumn is there," Derrick said as he hung up. "She signed up for every spa treatment available."

Deciding to divide up manpower, Ellie dropped Derrick at the station to retrieve his car so he could search Autumn's apartment while she planned to meet Cord to hike to Beaver Pond.

Though the rain had held off for now, thick gray clouds still hovered on the horizon. Coupled with the shade of the pines and aspens, the chill in the air felt ten degrees colder as she parked and got out. Here, it had rained during the night and water droplets clung to the shivering trees, fallen leaves and the blades of grass and weeds.

"Are you okay?" Cord asked as they climbed along the narrow path.

"Just tired and worried about Ava," Ellie said, inhaling the scent of damp moss.

His deep brown eyes met hers. "I feel awful for the little girl, but I wasn't talking about that. You went through a lot with the Hunter."

Her cheeks heated. He reached out and touched her arm. "Ellie?"

She stiffened, fighting the urge to lean into him. "A few nightmares, but I survived. How's Lola?"

Pain and worry flared on his face. "Same. She doesn't want to talk about it though."

Ellie understood that. "She's lucky to have you there for support, Cord," she said softly.

He shrugged. "She deserves better."

"Don't sell yourself short." Uneasy with the tension between them, she strode deeper into the woods. Faint slivers of sun shone on the raindrops glistening on the trees, shimmering like clear pearls. Yet the smell of wet earth and the metallic scent of a dead animal negated the beauty.

They climbed another hill, then stopped at the bait shop where the owner verified that he'd seen Jasper with another man and pointed them in the direction of their camp.

Two miles in, and she sipped some water, her body achy from lack of sleep, but she pushed herself on and followed Cord along a narrow ledge. Rocks skittered down from the cliff, pinging down the side of the mountain. It was easy to lose your footing, especially when the ground was slippery and mud sucked at her boots. She felt hints of another shower coming in the misty air, and the scent of wild mushrooms and damp lichen.

Set in the valley, the pond was visible from the ridge. They reached the crest, then they cut across another path and wound downward, weaving through overgrown bushes and briars. As they descended the steep terrain, she held onto trees and limbs to keep from falling. Lungs straining, she breathed in the frigid air as they made it to the bottom.

Cord paused by an oak, examining the area with his binoculars. "Over there."

Ellie spotted a burly man hunched by the pond in a heavy overcoat and ball cap. She and Cord maneuvered their way through the trees and brush, noting the man seemed deep in thought as he fished.

The wind whistled, rippling the pond water, and birds soared overhead heading further south. Black crows dove down in search of food, and she could hear the rustles of other forest animals foraging through the woods.

The man must have heard them because he turned, his fishing rod in hand, and adjusted his hat. He wore overalls and boots, a cigarette dangled from the corner of his mouth.

The scent of the cigarette made Ellie's eyes water.

"Look around the campsite while I talk to Banks," Ellie told Cord. "Jasper could have brought Ava up here before Banks arrived."

"Copy that."

Sucking in a breath to ward off a cough, Ellie threw up a hand in greeting, introducing them.

"Are you Curtis Banks?" Ellie asked.

His thick brows bunched together in a question. "Yeah. Why?"

"We just spoke with Jasper Truman. He said he was here with you yesterday and the night before. Is that right?"

Banks flicked ash from his cigarette onto the ground, confusion crossing his face, and Cord walked along the pond bank searching for signs of Ava. "Yeah, we been buddies for a while. Said he was having girlfriend troubles, so we met up to fish."

"Did you two ride together?"

"Naw, he got here a little while before me. Left this morning to pick up more bait and hasn't come back." He took another drag of his cigarette. "What's going on? Something happen to him?"

Ellie studied his body language for indicators he was lying, but he genuinely looked concerned about his buddy. "His daughter Ava disappeared yesterday morning. His wife thought Jasper might have taken her from the bus stop."

His eyes widened in surprise. "Little Ava's missing?"

"Yes," Ellie said. "Do you know anything about that?"

He shook his head. "No, hell no. Cell service is spotty here and we didn't bring a radio. Whole idea is to get away to unwind."

"Did Jasper talk about his daughter?" Ellie asked.

The man tossed his cigarette butt into the dirt and smashed it with his muddy boot. "Just that he was missing her and was going to see her at Christmas. Said he might cave and buy her the puppy she's been wanting."

"He was here with you the entire time?" Ellie asked.

"Yeah, until this morning." He shoved his hat back and wiped sweat from his forehead. He dug his phone from his pocket then accessed a photo of Jasper holding up a trout he'd caught. "Made his day, catching this big one."

Ellie glanced at Cord, who was leaning against a tree listening. Banks sounded convincing, and the time stamp on the photo confirmed he'd been there, which meant Jasper had an alibi for the time Ava disappeared. "Do you know Jasper's girlfriend?"

The big man shrugged. "Met her a couple of times. Don't know what Jasper saw in her. He said he broke it off, that she was demanding and wasn't good with Ava."

"Do you think she'd take Ava to hurt him or force him into seeing her again?"

The man worked his mouth from side to side as if thinking. "I doubt it. Don't think she cared that much about him. Money was all that mattered to her." He rubbed his beer belly. "Jasper said she got knocked up a while back and talked about selling the baby. Got a pretty penny for it."

Ellie went still, sweat beading on her skin. If Autumn had borrowed one of Jasper's vans and had been driving it, Ava might have thought it was her father and climbed inside it with her.

But what would she have done with her?

FORTY-THREE

RAVEN LANDING

Priscilla Wilkinson couldn't shake the news story about the missing child in Crooked Creek from her mind as she did her annual hike to Raven Landing, her favorite scenic attraction near Raven Cliff Falls. She and her sister Renee used to bring Renee's little girl Kaylee here every year to look for the ravens who usually traveled in pairs, their wide black wings flapping as they soared across the clear blue sky. Some dipped and landed, then perched on the overhang as if to look down at the world with watchful eyes.

"What's the difference between crows and ravens?" Kaylee had asked.

"Ravens are larger than crows, the size of a Red-tailed Hawk," Renee had explained.

"They're beautiful, Mama," Kaylee said as she skipped rocks across the creek water.

Grief clumped in Priscilla's throat. *Dear God, it's been a year since little Kaylee disappeared.* She understood the horror of what the Truman family was going through. She'd lived it herself with her sister. Worse, the cop who'd investigated had arrested Renee and accused her of criminal negligence that had led to her daughter's death.

They never found a body.

Priscilla hung onto that and the hope that Kaylee was still alive. Renee had hung onto it, too.

Then two weeks after her sister was locked up, the call had come from the prison. Priscilla closed her eyes against the shocking agony the message had brought. "We're sorry to inform you that your sister Renee killed herself."

"No!" Priscilla had screamed, an animalistic sound tearing from her. "She wouldn't have. She wanted to find her daughter..."

But Renee was gone.

Now Priscilla was alone with her anguish. And all her questions.

She didn't believe for a minute that Renee would commit suicide, not without knowing what had happened to Kaylee.

"You have to investigate," she'd told the warden and the police. "Renee would not take her own life."

But they hadn't believed her just as they hadn't believed Renee.

And now both she and Kaylee were gone.

Reeling from the memory, Priscilla leaned against a tall pine, her breathing erratic as she spotted two ravens soaring above.

Renewed determination made her grit her teeth and she set the sunflowers she'd brought to honor Renee on the landing, the yellow flowers brightening up the dead weeds and grass, a symbol of hope. "I'm going to find the truth, Renee. I swear to it. And if Kaylee is alive, I'll find her, too."

FORTY-FOUR

CROOKED CREEK

By the time Ellie reached the police station, her muscles ached with tension. She checked in with Shondra. "Any developments with the Trumans?"

"Nothing new. Jasper's still sticking to his story. But they're arguing again. Jasper blames his wife for not walking Ava to the bus stop, and she claimed if he'd been around more she wouldn't have been so stressed she'd had a migraine."

That thought gave her pause, and she slid behind her laptop at her desk. She'd heard stories about babies being snatched from hospitals because a mother had lost a child or couldn't conceive and was so desperate she was driven to steal someone else's. There were also kidnapping rings who took children and sold them to couples wanting to adopt.

And then there was Banks's comment about Autumn. She'd messaged Derrick with that information, adding: *If Autumn would take money for her own baby, would she sell Ava?*

He sent a return text: *On my way to Atlanta to question her. Nothing at her apartment.*

Deciding to explore the possibility of a mother in the area who'd lost a child recently, Ellie accessed death certificates of children from the last six months. She spent the next hour combing through the records for Bluff County, and sadly found four children under the age of one. Two were stillborn, one had a heart defect and the other died in a car accident.

Sympathy for those families swelled inside her, but for now she eliminated them. If a person or family wanted to replace a baby, they would probably have chosen a child of a similar age.

She continued and discovered a seven-year-old who'd been struck by a car while riding his bike. A four-year-old who'd had a brain tumor. And an eight-year-old with leukemia.

She wiped at a tear she didn't even realize she'd shed.

None of the kids were Ava's age, and as she finished the search, she didn't find any children close to her age in or around the area.

Often times criminals chose a certain type of victim based on age, appearance, body type, or, in the case of adults, their job. Considering the victim profile here, she dug deeper and found pictures of the four and the eight-year-old, but neither even remotely resembled Ava.

Frustration gnawing at her, she stood and stretched, walking to the window and looking out at the gray gloomy sky. Another day was passing, thunder rumbling, an icy rain beginning to fall. The clock ticked away the seconds in the background, each hour her fears mounting.

Poor little Ava must be terrified now.

Wherever you are, don't give up, Ava. I'm coming for you.

FORTY-FIVE

ATLANTA

When Derrick arrived at the luxury hotel an hour after he'd checked Autumn's apartment, she was in the middle of a deep-tissue massage, which he interrupted by showing her the warrant he'd obtained. She grabbed a robe and pulled it on, irritation flaring in her eyes. "I can't believe this," she snapped. "Why are you treating me like a criminal? I told you I don't know where Ava is. Jasper wants to be with that woman and his brat, let him have them."

Derrick liked her less and less every minute. Did the woman not have a loving bone in her body? He could see why some men might have been entranced with her D cups and young face, but to Derrick she looked as plastic and phony as she sounded.

He escorted her back to her room, the manager waiting at the door while he searched it.

Her suitcase was open on the luggage rack, a complimentary basket of fresh fruit, Perrier, cucumber water, bath products and lotions on the credenza. Champagne sat in an ice bucket chilling, ready to be uncorked beside a charcuterie board.

Judging from the fact that Autumn worked at Haints, which was not a high-end establishment, Derrick guessed the woman had another income source. Maybe another business or even a sugar daddy.

Spotting her laptop on the floor, he picked it up.

"You won't find anything," she shouted. "I don't care enough about Jasper to do what you think." Her eyes lit up.

Disgust filled Derrick. She certainly didn't seem concerned about Ava or her family. Which meant if she didn't care, she wouldn't risk kidnapping charges just to hurt Jasper. She'd simply move onto greener pastures.

"Why are you doing this to me?" she asked, voice raised. "This is my vacation!"

"A little girl is missing," Derrick said, his anger mounting. "Her parents are frantic to find her and if you had nothing to do with it, then I can eliminate you and move on. Now be quiet or I'm going to charge you with impeding a felony investigation."

"You can't do that," she stuttered.

"I can and I will." He pinned her with his dark eyes. "I know how you feel about kids, that when you got pregnant you talked about selling the baby. Is that what you did with Ava? Took her and sold her to support your expensive lifestyle?"

FORTY-SIX

"What are you talking about? And what are you doing with my computer?" Autumn asked.

"Confiscating it," Derrick replied. "I need your phone, too."

She planted her hands on her hips, angry. "Why? There's nothing on there that's illegal."

"It's procedure in a kidnapping case to review everything and everyone that might be connected to the missing child." He took secret pleasure in the discomfort on her face. "Now, your phone?"

Her hand shook as she clutched it to her chest. "You can't take that. It's the latest iPhone."

He bit back a chuckle at her entitled attitude, then removed the warrant from his pocket and handed it to her. "This says I can."

She blinked rapidly, then skimmed the warrant, and clamped her mouth shut.

"I need to call a lawyer."

"Do you?" he gave her a questioning look. "Because if you don't have anything to hide and want to help us find your boyfriend's little girl, you should be eager to cooperate."

She bit her lip. "I'm not hiding anything," she said. "But this is a violation of my rights."

He ignored her, then held out his hand for the phone. "You'll get it back when we're finished. Now I'd appreciate it if you'd come with me."

Fear flitted through her eyes. "Do I have to?"

"You can come willingly or I can arrest you," he said. "Either way, you're coming."

She stared at him for a long minute, then huffed and stood. "At least let me collect my things and tell the desk so I can reschedule my spa treatments." She paused, hands on her hips. "And if they charge me extra, then it's coming out of your pocket."

Derrick bit back a curse. For God's sake, she was so selfish he wanted to lock her up for just being a bad human. If she had something to do with Ava's disappearance, he'd make sure the only massage she'd be receiving in the near future would be from a cell mate.

FORTY-SEVEN
CROOKED CREEK

Ellie looked up from her desk when she heard a commotion in the bullpen. Derrick was escorting an irate Autumn inside.

"I'm not saying anything until I have an attorney present," she insisted.

"Fine." Derrick hauled her through the double doors to an interrogation room and Ellie followed. The woman might be pretty on the outside, but the inside was clearly like sour candy.

"I have her computer and phone," he told Ellie as he locked Autumn inside the room to wait on her lawyer. "I convinced her to hand over her computer and phone passwords."

"That's a start," Elie said. "What did she have to say?"

"She claims she was at the spa and the employees there confirmed it." He set her laptop on the table in the corner. "But she's hiding something. Whether it's about Ava or she's into something illegal, I don't know."

"Let's look at her correspondence," Ellie said.

He passed her Autumn's phone, and he opened the laptop, booted it up and began to search.

Ellie entered Autumn's passcode and clicked on her text messages. She scrolled through, noting several to a man named Walton.

"Looks like she was doing private parties on the side," Ellie said. "Exotic dancing. I wonder if Jasper knew it."

"Hell, that may be how he got involved with her," Derrick replied. "It explains the extra cash at her disposal, anyway."

Ellie gave a little nod, then skimmed more texts. Some to the owner of Haints; a few, judging from the context and wording, to other dancers.

"This is odd," she murmured. "There are no texts to Jasper."

Interest sparked in Derrick's eyes. "Check for deleted messages."

Ellie's own suspicions mounted. The only reason to delete them was if they held something incriminating.

It took a few minutes for her to figure out how to reclaim the deleted texts, but eventually she found several to Jasper over the last couple of months. The first few were flirtatious, suggesting they'd just started seeing each other, times they were going to hook up, and phone sex.

She rolled her eyes and skated past them, then saw that the tune of their exchange began to become more terse.

Jasper: *Can't meet today. Supposed to see Ava.*

Autumn: *Ditch the kid, lover boy.*

Jasper: *Not again. Lara is already up my butt for money and threatening to not let me see her at all.*

Autumn: *Come or it's over.*

The texts picked up a couple of days later.

Autumn: *Will be waiting at our place. Midnight.*

Jasper: *Can't come. Have to make it up to Ava for missing last time.*

Autumn: *You want to fix your money problems and get your freedom. I have an idea.*

Jasper: *What are you talking about?*

Autumn: *Meet me and I'll tell you.*

Ellie's pulse jumped, and she read the text aloud. "We need to find out what that plan was." She scrolled for more messages.

Autumn: *Did you think about my idea? If you let me take Ava off her hands, you can solve your money problems and be single again.*

It seemed Jasper hadn't responded.

Ellie stood, appalled at Autumn's suggestion. "I'm going to have a talk with Autumn." If she had to, she'd ring the truth out of the conniving woman.

FORTY-EIGHT

Phone in hand, Ellie stormed into the interrogation room where Autumn had been left, barely controlling her rage.

The woman looked up at her as she twirled a strand of her hair around a finger. "It's about time. Can I go now?"

Ellie crossed the room, feet pounding the floor. "Not yet." Maybe never. If she discovered she'd hurt one hair on Ava's sweet head, the woman would never see the light of day again. "We have to talk, Autumn."

"Where's my lawyer?" she demanded.

Ellie sucked in a breath. "On his way. But if you know where Ava is, I can help you now."

"This is ridiculous," Autumn said, her voice edgy. "I told that fed I don't know anything."

"I don't believe you," Ellie said, setting Autumn's phone on the table in front of the woman. "Not after the texts I recovered." She raised a brow. "There's this one in particular—'If you let me take Ava off your hands, you can solve your money problems and be single again.'"

The woman clamped her lips tight. "Not another word until my lawyer is present."

Ellie folded her arms to keep from shaking Autumn. "Fine. But that tells me a lot about you, Miss Juniper. You care more about hiding behind an attorney than a missing six-year-old girl."

Autumn flinched, then said nothing.

FORTY-NINE

HONEYSUCKLE LANE

Ellie wanted to force the truth out of Autumn, but her hands were tied. While Deputy Landrum stayed with the woman and waited for her attorney to arrive, she called Shondra.

"Is Jasper still there?"

"Yes," Shondra said. "But it's really tense here. He's been pacing like a mad animal while Lara just stares at the Christmas tree looking heartbroken."

"Keep him there," Ellie said. "I found some incriminating texts between him and his girlfriend. Special Agent Fox and I are on our way to talk to him."

Shondra agreed, and Ellie and Derrick hurried to her Jeep. Except for the people gathered for the prayer vigil around the Angel Tree, the streets were empty now, giving Crooked Creek a ghost town feel.

Dread curled inside Ellie as she turned onto Honeysuckle Lane and swung into the Truman driveway. Unfortunately, she was about to make Lara's day worse with her accusations.

"How do you play this?" Ellie asked.

"Take the lead," Derrick said. "I'll stay to the side and examine Autumn's laptop for anything to back up our theory."

Ellie reached for the door handle. "That sounds like a plan," she said, as they walked up to the house. She rang the bell and Shondra let them in. "Emily Nettles just left," Shondra said. "But she said she'll be back. At least she got Jasper and Lara to stop shouting blame at each other."

Ellie gave Shondra's arm a squeeze. "Did either of them add anything to their original stories?"

The deputy shook her head and they followed her to the living room where Jasper was walking back and forth, looking out the window as if he expected Ava to run through the door any minute and throw her little arms around him. Just as Shondra described, Lara looked desolate and sat tracing a finger over a reindeer ornament that Ava must have made.

Ellie's heart ached. But she remembered Autumn's texts to Jasper and straightened.

He jerked his head up to look at her, and Lara dropped her hands to her lap. "Did you find her?"

Ellie gave her a sympathetic look. "I'm sorry, but not yet. We're not giving up though." She glanced at Jasper. "We need to talk to you, Mr. Truman."

He went totally still, his gaze wary. Meanwhile, Derrick seated himself at the desk in the corner and booted up Autumn's laptop. While he scrolled, he angled himself so he could watch their interaction.

"Sit down," Ellie told Jasper.

He dropped onto the couch and Lara sank back into the chair, the fear in her eyes tearing at Ellie.

"Why haven't you found her yet?" Jasper asked gruffly.

Ellie, Derrick and Shondra exchanged looks, then Ellie cleared her throat. "We're pursuing every possible lead. That's the reason we're here."

Ellie angled her head toward Jasper. "We've spoken with Autumn, Mr. Truman," she said.

He folded his hands together, his leg bouncing nervously. "She's not my girlfriend anymore. I told you that. Why?" His eyes narrowed. "Did she tell you we were still together?"

"No, as a matter of fact she's not saying much," Ellie said. "She requested an attorney."

Lara gaped at him, wringing her hands together.

A war raged in Jasper's eyes and he looked away from his wife.

Ellie retrieved Autumn's phone from her pocket, then read the text. "'If you let me take Ava off your hands, you can solve your money problems and be single again.'"

Lara groaned, and Jasper's skin turned a sallow color.

"What did you two have planned?" Ellie asked.

"N-nothing," he ground out. "I broke it off."

Ellie gripped the phone with sweaty hands. "That's not what it says in the texts between you two."

His steely gaze met Ellie's, a vein bulging in his neck.

Lara made a strangled sound. "What is she talking about, Jasper? What did that text mean?" When he rubbed his hand over his eyes, Lara threw up her hands. "For God's sake, Jasper, if you know where Ava is, tell us."

"I don't know where she is," Jasper said in a gruff voice. "Autumn probably deleted those texts because I was done with her."

Ellie's patience snapped. "Really? Because according to these texts, you two planned to meet to talk about getting rid of Ava, so you could get Lara out of your life permanently and you'd finally be free."

His wife staggered sideways then stormed toward him, gripped his arms and shook him. "Oh, my god, Jasper. What have you done?"

"Nothing," he stuttered as he tried to pry her hands off him.

Ellie and Shondra exchanged another look and Derrick stood, but Ellie motioned for him to wait. She felt for Lara. The fact that Jasper had had that conversation with Autumn gave his wife a right to slap the shit out of him.

But she had to uncover the truth, find out if he followed through.

"Tell me where she is!" Lara screamed. "What did you do with my baby?"

Jasper was sputtering and trying to talk, and Shondra stepped in to pull Lara away as she tried to pummel her husband with her fists.

Ellie gently touched Lara's back. "I understand you're upset, Lara, but please, let me handle this."

While Shondra led Lara back to the chair, Ellie confronted Jasper.

"Tell me what she meant," Ellie said between clenched teeth.

Jasper scrubbed a hand down his face, his skin mottled now, fear and confusion flaring in his eyes. "I deleted those damn texts because they were horrible," he finally said. "I told Autumn I would never let Ava go, but she said... said..." Emotions choked his voice as he glanced at his wife, who was staring at him in shock.

"Said what?" Ellie asked, her tone no nonsense.

"Said if we got rid of Ava, we could be together."

FIFTY

Ellie shuddered. It seemed Autumn saw Ava as an ill-fitting shoe that she wanted to toss, not a precious little child. "What did you tell her?"

His eyes shot to Lara's, panicked. "I told her no, of course." He inhaled a deep breath. "Let me see her. If she knows something, I'll make her talk."

Ellie mulled over the suggestion, but as she did so her mind went to another dark place. His job. A construction site would be the perfect place to dispose of a body. And if Autumn had borrowed one of the vans no one would have thought anything about it being at the construction site.

"Mr. Truman," Ellie said. "You mentioned you worked construction."

Confusion clouded his face, as if he didn't understand the change in her line of questioning. "Yes."

Ellie examined his body language. His shoulders were slumped, his hands clasped, scarred from manual labor he'd said, knee bouncing up and down. "And Autumn knew this?"

"Well, yeah. She met me at the site a couple of times."

Then she probably knew about the vans being parked there. "I need a list of all the sites where you're currently working."

Jasper shifted restlessly. "What does that have to do with finding my daughter?"

Ellie shoved a notepad and pen in front of him. "Just make the list." She'd verify the names with the construction company to see if he omitted anything. That would tell her more about his innocence or guilt than a conversation.

Her mind raced with the sickening possibility of what she might find.

Lara was rocking herself back and forth, her face void of color. Shondra walked to the kitchen, filled a glass with water and carried it to her. While Truman made the list, Ellie stepped into the kitchen to talk to Derrick.

"Maybe we should let Jasper speak with Autumn," Ellie said. "We could have him wear a wire."

Derrick grunted. "Forget the wire. If neither of them knows we're listening, they'll be more open."

True. And Ellie would do anything to get to the truth.

"I'll call the construction company and confirm his list of sites," Derrick offered.

Ellie nodded, then they returned to the living room. Ellie snatched the list Jasper had made.

"Are you going to let me see Autumn?" Jasper asked.

Ellie maintained a neutral expression. "I am. If you're innocent, maybe she'll tell you if she followed through on her plan."

Lara pushed to her feet. "I'm going, too. I want to look in her face and confront her."

That could turn volatile, Ellie thought. But if Autumn was involved, it might be the fastest way to find Ava.

FIFTY-ONE

Thirty minutes later, Ellie, Derrick and Lara settled into the observation room adjoining the interrogation room where Jasper was meeting Autumn.

Jasper was squirming slightly, his leg bouncing up and down again. But when the door opened and Deputy Landrum led Autumn in, he straightened, his eyes turning steely.

"Jasper," Autumn said in a throaty whisper. "What are you doing here?"

He curled his hands into fists on the table. "We have to talk."

Heath left the room as planned, giving Autumn the impression the conversation was private. Her gaze darted around the room, the chair rattling as she sank into it. "I can't believe they brought me in here," she trilled. "They're treating me like some kind of criminal."

She went straight to thinking about herself, Ellie thought in disgust.

Lara fiddled with the end of her messy ponytail. She still wore the same holiday sweatshirt she had on when Ellie had first met her yesterday.

Autumn was the opposite type. Probably ten years younger than Lara, with striking dark hair and alluring eyes that seemed to change between blue and green. But forget the face. The men would zero in on her cleavage. Ellie had always opted not to draw attention to hers. If a man wanted her for her boobs, he was the wrong man.

Jasper's jaw tightened. "Autumn, this is serious. Someone kidnapped Ava. I'm worried sick about her. And Lara's going out of her mind."

"Then she should have watched her own kid better," Autumn hissed between her teeth.

At the woman's crude words, Lara clutched her chest, as if she'd had the breath knocked out of her.

"I always watched her," Lara whispered miserably.

"I know." Ellie laid a hand over Lara's to comfort her, and sympathy registered on Derrick's face.

"I know you were angry at me," Jasper said, his voice surprisingly calm. "Did you take Ava?"

The young woman straightened a wrinkle in her silk blouse. "For God's sake, Jasper. I can't believe you'd ask me that."

"You mentioned getting rid of her," Jasper countered.

Autumn rolled her eyes, dismissing the comment as nothing. "I only suggested that because you were always so freaked out about money."

Jasper lunged at her and practically dragged her across the table. "Tell me," he shouted. "Did you take her to punish me for breaking up with you?"

Derrick rushed from the room, the door slamming shut behind him. Before Ellie could stop Lara, she'd run after him. Ellie followed, calling for her to stop, but she was too late—Lara had already caught up.

"Let her go, Jasper," Derrick ordered.

"Get him off me!" Autumn cried.

Jasper tightened his hands around Autumn's throat, squeezing hard. "Where's my little girl? What did you do with her?"

Ellie grabbed Lara to hold her back while Derrick yanked Jasper off Autumn and pushed him against the wall. "Calm down," Derrick hissed.

Autumn rubbed her throat with inch-long acrylic nails. The red imprint of Jasper's fingers lingered, but Ellie found little sympathy for this selfish woman.

"Arrest him now," Autumn said shrilly. "He assaulted me."

"You bitch!" Jasper lunged at her again, but Derrick gripped his arms and held him back.

Tears streamed down Lara's pale cheeks, "Please tell me where my baby is," she pleaded. "Please. She must be so scared."

Autumn glanced back and forth between all of them, her eyes as brittle as ice. "What the hell is this? Where's my attorney?"

A knock sounded at the door, and Captain Hale entered the room, his face set in a scowl as he took in the scene. "The attorney is here," he said, before addressing the rest of them. "Agent Fox, I suggest you escort Mr. Truman somewhere to calm down." Then he motioned for Ellie to step outside with him.

"I'll be back in a minute," she told Lara. "I'm sorry that got out of hand, Captain," she said once they were alone.

He shrugged. "It backfired, but it was worth a shot. That Ms. Juniper is a cold one."

"No argument there, sir," Ellie agreed. "I'll have Deputy East-wood drive Lara back home and stay with her."

"Good." He patted his pocket then handed her an envelope. "I have the warrants. And the ground-penetrating radar to search the construction sites is all set. We just need to tell them where to go."

FIFTY-TWO

LAZY DAYS DEVELOPMENT, CHATTAHOOCHEE RIVER

Ellie and Derrick spent the next hour comparing the sites Jasper had provided with the list from Cato Construction, the firm he worked for. They matched, which at least confirmed that Jasper had been upfront. Ellie sent Deputy Landrum to the construction site office to dust for prints on vans parked there and would have forensics do the same with each van at the various construction sites.

Thankfully, the list was short. There was only one site where the land had been dug to pour a foundation in the last forty-eight hours—a pool at a clubhouse for a new development on the Chattahoochee River called Lazy Days. It catered to retirees wanting to settle into a relaxing community with riverfront views, a pool, and daily planned activities.

She coordinated with the captain and the team set up to run the GPR equipment, and she called Cord and asked him to bring search dogs for the development. If Autumn or Jasper had killed little Ava and dumped her body, she could be on the property or buried beneath the pool that had been poured in the last twenty-four hours.

Her stomach lurched at the thought. Another one took root in her mind, equally as disturbing. Autumn worked at Haints, which overlooked White Lilies cemetery. What if she'd taken Ava and dumped her there?

Dear God, she hoped she was wrong...

Still, she relayed her suspicions to Derrick. His whole body tensed as he considered her theory. "You're right, Ellie, we should check out that cemetery. Maybe we should divide up."

Ellie agreed. If Ava was alive, she might be running out of time.

FIFTY-THREE

WHITE LILIES CEMETERY

Derrick offered to search the cemetery but considering it had only been months since he'd buried his own little sister's remains, Ellie insisted on going instead while he handled the construction site.

Her own nerves were on edge as she met with the caretaker of the cemetery, an older bald man named Floyd. The sight of the tiny burial plots, some so small they were for infants, others three to four feet long for older children, was the saddest thing Ellie had ever seen. Markers engraved with angels, doves, prayer hands, and baby shoes, and beautiful sentiments etched in the stone. Small vases held seasonal flowers, but this time of year tiny Christmas trees and poinsettias filled them. Families had left wrapped presents on the small graves, presents their child would never get to open.

Some folks said the ground stayed green here all year long from the tears the parents shed. Others said it rained more often because the angels were crying in heaven.

Floyd rubbed a hand over his thick beard. "Lordy, I saw that story about the missing girl on the news." He gestured around the pristinely kept lawn. "Why do you think she'd be here?"

"We're pursuing every possible angle," Ellie said. "Have you seen anything suspicious?"

His sagging cheeks bunched as he frowned. "What you mean?"

"Like someone digging a grave," Ellie said.

He shook his head. "Nothing like that. Mostly families visiting. A real sad time for them."

"Do you have security cameras?"

He nodded. "Put them in last year after someone started stealing the gifts and toys the parents left." He rubbed his beard again. "Damn low thing to do."

"I agree," Ellie said. She'd even heard that some older women stole fresh flowers from graves to carry home for their tables, or to put on their own loved one's graves.

"Let me walk around, then I want to view the security tapes," Ellie said. "Can you pull last week's footage?"

"All right," Floyd said. "But I hope that little girl ain't here."

"So do I," Ellie murmured.

Her pulse clamored as she began to comb through the rows of graves. The names and dates on the tombstones revealed lives cut short bringing a wave of sadness over her. The sight of the toys was heartbreaking. A blue teddy bear, a toy train, a truck, plastic cars, a baby doll wrapped in a blanket...

She passed grave after grave, searching for disturbed ground or a mound suggesting it had been recently dug. But the grounds were well kept and she found nothing suspicious.

She released a relieved breath, then followed the cobblestone path to the caretaker's building. When she entered, Floyd waved her into a small room set up with security monitors.

"Pulled up last week's like you asked," Floyd said. "You see anything out there?"

Ellie shook her head then thanked him for giving her access to the footage. She claimed a chair to watch and Floyd rolled the film.

Her heart dipped as she watched families—mothers, fathers, children and grandparents— visit the graves, crying and praying, their grief a palpable force.

Ellie had always been too dedicated to her career in law

enforcement to consider having a child of her own, but she imagined that the holidays intensified their grief.

As the footage scrolled past, she carefully scrutinized the visitor's faces. She didn't see Autumn.

But the hair on her neck prickled as a woman wearing a black coat and scarf ran through the rows of graves, her body movements agitated. She kept her eyes downcast, face away from the camera, and she dropped to her knees on the ground in front of a marker engraved with entwined hands of a mother and child, her body shaking with sobs. A tall broad-shouldered man in a dark green coat moved up beside her and put his arm around her, but the woman shoved him away. Ellie saw the shock and pain on his face as he looked at her.

Then the woman turned and shouted something at him. Ellie could have sworn she'd said, "You killed our daughter."

Her detective instincts sharpened. She didn't know if the woman meant it literally or figuratively. But either way, she blamed the man for her daughter's death.

She squinted, zeroing in on the name on the tombstone, but couldn't quite read it.

"Do you know who's buried there?" Ellie asked Floyd.

He studied the frame with squinted eyes. "A little girl died in an accident. Last name's Gooding. Mama took it real hard."

That was tragic. The family was obviously deep in mourning.

But she steeled herself to move on. She had to focus on Ava.

FIFTY-FOUR

LAZY DAYS DEVELOPMENT, CHATTAHOOCHEE RIVER

At the construction site for Lazy Days, the wind picked up, the temperature predicted to drop to freezing tonight. If they didn't find Ava and she was lost somewhere in the woods, she could freeze to death.

Derrick met the owner of the construction company, David Cato, in the parking lot for the community clubhouse and pool. The company overseeing the GPR was also waiting, a tall man in jeans and a shirt with the company logo printed on the front. His name was Eddie Beacon, and he was talking to Cato, who had curly sandy blond hair and a linebacker's body.

The men introduced themselves, and Cato led them around the side of the clubhouse to the newly poured foundation, where the owner of the development was waiting. With winter upon them, the pool wouldn't be filled with water until spring, but the owner explained that having it underway would motivate buyers to invest in the cabins.

Derrick scanned the pines and oaks flanking the Chattahooche River, which rippled alongside the development. There were miles and miles of untamed forest where Truman or Autumn could have left Ava. The river itself started in Jacks Gap in the Blue Ridge

Mountains, flowed south all the way through Atlanta, then from ridges that formed the Tennessee Valley Divide. If Ava had been dumped in the water, with its rapids and strong currents, she would have swept downstream and they might never find her.

FIFTY-FIVE

As Ellie arrived at the construction site, she saw a muscular guy talking to Derrick and another man running the GPR equipment across the base of the pool. At least the freezing rain had held off, although the gray clouds promised it was on the way.

Derrick looked up, a question in his eyes.

She shook her head, silently relaying that she hadn't found anything, then Derrick introduced her. "How deep can the equipment detect something?" Ellie asked the GPR engineer.

"About three feet," Beacon answered.

Three feet was enough to bury a body if you were in a hurry.

"Mr. Cato," Derrick said. "Jasper's girlfriend hinted that he should get rid of Ava. Do you think Jasper is capable of hurting Ava or that he'd go along with a plan like that?"

Shock flared on Cato's face, and he jammed his hands in the pockets of his work jeans. "I don't know about the girlfriend. But Jasper would never hurt Ava. He told me he was over that woman, and that he wanted to get back together with his wife and kid."

Ellie glanced at Derrick. Cato had confirmed Jasper's story.

They spent the next half hour watching Eddie Beacon scan the pool foundation with the GPR equipment. At one point, he paused, his expression indicating he'd found something, and Ellie held her breath while they scrutinized his findings.

He ran the machine over the area again, and they studied the screen. "Sorry," Beacon said. "It looks like a small animal. Maybe racoon or possum."

Ellie breathed out, looking out at the raging river. If Ava had fallen in, she could drown in minutes. The jagged rocks would batter her body and if she didn't drown, she could have suffered injuries or hypothermia could kill her.

Thirty minutes later, as the storm brewed, Cord and his SAR dog and a team of three men arrived.

"Ava Truman's father worked for this construction company," she explained, and filled Cord in on Autumn's suggestion.

A darkness crept over Cord's face. "I wish I could say I didn't believe people possible of doing that, but I know different."

So did Ellie. That was what worried her.

Cord clenched his jaw. "We'll be thorough," he assured her. "If she's out there we'll find her."

FIFTY-SIX

BIG BOULDER

Priscilla Wilkinson stood outside the door to her cottage, the grief weighing her down like the thick layers of blankets her mother used to pile on top of her and Renee at night when the heat went out in their house. They'd been poor, and home was a white clapboard house with only an oil heater in the living room.

"Let me come in tonight," Raymond, the architect she'd been dating for the last few months, said as he squeezed her shoulder.

"Not tonight," Priscilla said. "I... can't, Raymond. It's been a year since Kaylee and Renee—"

"You're obsessed with their deaths," Raymond said, impatience tainting his voice. "I know it's hard, but you have to move on with your life and stop living in the past."

He didn't understand. How could he?

"I need to be alone. Go home, Raymond."

His jaw hardened. "Is that what you want? To be alone forever?"

"No, I want my family back," she said heatedly. "You just want me to forget about them."

"I want you to face reality," he said, his voice rising an octave. "Let them go so we can have a life together."

Anger made her skin feel hot all over. "I can't forget them," she snapped. "Not when Kaylee might still be out there. When I might be able to bring her home." She pushed his hands away when he reached for her. "Now, good night." *And goodbye.*

She rushed inside and closed the door, her breath panting out. Raymond would never get it. And she would never give up looking for her niece.

Needing to talk to someone who'd understand, she signed onto the Facebook support group she'd found for mothers of missing children. Although she wasn't Kaylee's mother, she felt a comradery with the women that you could only understand if you'd had a child taken from you.

Some of the posts were from mothers of runaway teens, others involved child abductions, and three were custody battles. A lady named Jan Hornsby had started the group after her child disappeared on her sixth birthday.

Pulling her gaze from her laptop, Priscilla looked through the window at the giant rock formations that could be seen in the distance, rocks so big they looked like boulders, inspiring the subdivision's name. One reminded her of a bear, while three stood together, creating a cluster that Kaylee had said looked like a teepee the Cherokees might have lived in years ago when they inhabited the mountains.

Fresh pain squeezed her lungs. Kaylee, sweet Kaylee... even though she'd been sick for a while, she'd been so full of life. She loved the hiking trips and wading in the creek and singing to the moon at night. But she'd always wanted to see the ocean, so when she'd felt better, Renee had planned that trip to the beach.

The vacation was supposed to be the beginning of a new future for Kaylee.

Instead, it had been the end.

Don't give up. You have to find her.

Needing to vent, she began to write: *It's been a year since my niece Kaylee went missing. The police gave up when they arrested my sister. Now she's dead, they won't even take my calls.*

Jan was online and posted, *It's been six months for me. I called* the detective who investigated Becky's disappearance today, but he says there's no new leads. Frankly, I think he's given up.

I know how that feels, a woman named Julie posted. *My husband took little Ronnie and who knows where they are. The police say it's not kidnapping since he's Ronnie's father.*

Jan: *I used to love the holidays. I always went overboard and put up a tree in every room. This year, I don't have the energy to decorate even one.*

Priscilla responded: *Me neither. Seeing the lights and decorations only makes me miss my family more.*

Jan: *Did you hear about that little girl who was kidnapped in Crooked Creek?*

Priscilla shivered. *Yes. Ava Truman. The odd thing is that she was abducted December 20. That's the same day last year that Kaylee disappeared.*

For a minute, no one responded.

Jan: *That does sound odd.*

Priscilla looked out at the rain streaming down the windowpane and wiped her damp cheeks where she'd been crying.

Jan: *It could mean something. Maybe you should call that detective in Crooked Creek.*

The photo of Renee and Kaylee taunted Priscilla from the kitchen counter. It hadn't occurred to her before that Kaylee's disappearance and the Truman child's might be connected. But what if they were?

It wouldn't hurt to call the police, she supposed. Maybe this detective would listen to her.

Only she didn't trust the cops. The one assigned to Kaylee's case hadn't listened. Instead, he'd arrested her sister and crucified her. Then she'd died in prison.

Priscilla still thought she'd been murdered.

FIFTY-SEVEN

HONEYSUCKLE LANE

Lara wrapped another present, today's gift, a snow globe with a miniature version of the North Pole inside. Ever since she was two, when Ava saw a snow globe in a store she squealed with excitement, picked it up and shook it. She was mesmerized as the snow swirled around and around like a blizzard. Seeing her delight, Lara had started a tradition, and each year added a new one to her collection.

On the first year, a polar bear stood beside a sign for the North Pole. The next year's held a Christmas tree lit with colored lights. The third held miniature figurines depicting a family of three opening presents beneath a tree. Carolers were in the next one. Then a Santa sleigh and Santa's village.

She set the present on the mantle with the others, her throat thick. They would wait there for Ava to come home and open them. Her little girl *would* come home, she told herself. She had to.

The doorbell rang, and the deputy went to answer it. At the sound of her neighbor Dottie's voice, Lara stepped into the living room. Dottie had half a dozen cats and constantly watched everything everyone did in the neighborhood. Lara hadn't decided if she was a caring lonely woman or a busybody. She expected the neighbors who'd reported her and Jasper's arguments to the police were, in reality, all Dottie, so Lara was leaning toward the latter.

"I brought some chicken soup by," Dottie said with a sympathetic expression. "Thought you might need some comfort food."

Lara wasn't hungry but murmured thanks anyway.

"I'm so sorry to hear about Ava," Dottie said. "I'm praying for you, hon."

Lara felt suddenly moved, and found she couldn't speak. Dottie didn't seem to expect it. She just handed the soup to Lara. "Please let me know if there's anything I can do to help."

Lara nodded, battling the lump in her throat while Deputy Eastwood saw the old lady to the door. Maybe she was caring and lonely after all, rather than just nosy.

"She's right, you need to eat something," the deputy said when she returned. "Keep up your strength for when Ava comes home."

If she comes home, Lara thought, struggling with the fear consuming her.

"I'll heat this up and make some tea," the deputy offered, then she took the pot from Lara.

Lara simply nodded and followed her to the kitchen, her calendar on the table mocking her. Each day of winter break, she'd planned a special holiday activity with her daughter.

Her lungs strained for air. Yesterday was popcorn day. They were supposed to make popcorn balls and string popcorn for the tree. She'd also planned for them to fill bags, and hand them out to the neighbors.

Emotions choked her as she glanced at the supplies she'd purchased for today.

Graham crackers, assorted candies, sprinkles, and icing to decorate gingerbread houses. The candy canes were Ava's favorite. She always placed a Hershey's Kiss in the middle of the door for the doorknob and lined candy canes along the wall, then added M & M's on the roof.

Despair overcame Lara, and she laid her head down on the

table and closed her eyes. *Where are you, Ava, baby?* she silently asked. *Hang in there and don't worry. Mommy will keep everything waiting on you so we can decorate the gingerbread houses together when you come home.*

FIFTY-EIGHT

SOMEWHERE ON THE AT

"Come on, Ava, we're going to make gingerbread houses today. Won't that be fun?"

Ava looked up at the tall skinny woman with the messy dark hair and sank back against the wall. "I wanna go home. Mommy and I make the gingerbread houses together. She's waiting on me."

"No, she's not, Ava. I'm your mommy now," the woman said, her voice sharp, like when the teacher got onto the boys at school for throwing rocks. "And we're going to be a family."

Ava shook her head back and forth, tears blurring her eyes. "You're not my family. My mommy is." Her chin wobbled and she brushed at her cheeks. Her throat hurt so much from crying that her voice sounded like a frog's.

The woman stroked Ava's hair and straightened the sash on her dress. "Now, now, I know this is hard. But your mommy asked me to take care of you," she said. "She's so tired and doesn't have the money now to be a good mommy. And I'm going to love you forever and ever."

Ava pictured her real mommy in the kitchen making the cupcakes for her school party. A party she'd missed. Mommy had been tired and had a headache and was too busy to go with her to the bus stop.

Her chest hurt so bad she could barely breathe. She couldn't believe her mommy didn't want her anymore. All mommies got tired, didn't they?

"We have a big house and you'll have a nice playroom with lots of toys and an art easel and I can buy you pretty clothes and bows for your hair."

"I don't wanna wear bows except the ones Mommy makes. And you're a liar. Mommy wants me." Ava bit her lip. "We make sugar cookies and give popcorn bags to the neighbors."

The woman lifted Ava's chin and looked into her eyes. "We can string popcorn and make popcorn bags, too," the woman said. "And your daddy will be here soon."

Ava bunched her hands in the awful crinkly dress and tried not to blubber. Her daddy was coming for her? "Where's Daddy? He'll take me home. I know he will."

The woman's mouth tightened. "This is your home now. We're going to be a family and you're going to love it here. You even have a sister now. Do you want to meet her?"

Ava pouted. "I wanna go home with my real mama and sleep in my room with Bunny."

The woman took her by the arms and gripped her so hard her fingers pinched Ava's skin. "You *are* home, Ava. And the sooner you stop fussing, the better everything's going to be."

"Where's my backpack and Bunny?" she whimpered.

"I'm afraid they're gone. You'll have new toys and stuffed animals here to love," the woman said.

"But I love Bunny mostest, and he's gonna become real like the velveteen rabbit."

"Shh, we're not going to talk about Bunny anymore." The woman pulled her closer and wrapped her arms around her. Ava tried to push back, but the woman held her so tight she couldn't move. Her sweater was scratchy and her perfume stunk and made Ava feel sick to her tummy.

"I have all the candies to make the gingerbread houses," the woman whispered. "And I want you to help add more decorations for the tree, and we'll write Santa a letter. You can tell him everything you want for Christmas."

Ava bit her tongue to keep from screaming. All she wanted was to go home.

But it was like the lady had cotton in her ears and didn't hear her.

She closed her eyes and more tears came. But knowing her daddy would be here soon made her feel better. He would take her back to Mommy!

Then she remembered her mommy and daddy arguing about how much money it cost to take care of her, and how the debt people were calling, and how they might have to sell the house, and her mommy yelling at her daddy because he liked another woman, and her stomach jumped.

What if this lady was Daddy's girlfriend? And what if she was telling the truth and Mommy didn't want her anymore?

FIFTY-NINE

CROOKED CREEK

Night had fallen by the time Ellie, Derrick and Cord's team finished searching the construction site and property. Clouds rippled like turbulent ocean waves in the gray skies as the search teams dispersed. So far they had no proof that Autumn had done anything to Ava and were going to have to release her. Heath had phoned that Autumn's fingerprints had not been on any of the vans belonging to Cato Construction.

Hopefully Derrick would find something on her computer.

Ellie swung by the Burger Barn, picked up burgers and fries and drove toward her house. In spite of the dreary weather, the prayer vigil was still underway in town, with candles in the windows of homes and people gathering in the square in front of the Angel Tree.

By the time she reached her bungalow, the storm clouds obliterated any evidence of the stars and moon and lightning zigzagged across the sky. The clouds opened up and unleased their fury and she raced into her bungalow, getting drenched along the way. Derrick parked behind her and followed her in. She ducked in her bedroom to change and tossed Derrick a towel to dry off.

By the time she threw on a clean sweatshirt and sweatpants and returned to the kitchen, she had a voice message from Bryce.

"*The town is in an uproar over Grueler,*" Bryce bellowed. "*My office has been flooded with complaints. This is the last thing we need right now, Detective.*"

Ellie deleted the message, nerves climbing her neck. Let Bryce rant all he wanted. She was not a cold-blooded killer. And they needed Grueler alive to describe that woman.

"What's wrong?" Derrick asked.

"Bryce venting about the town being upset about Grueler."

"Don't sweat what Bryce thinks," Derrick said. "You put Ava first and went by the law. That's being a smart cop, not acting on emotions and playing judge and jury."

Ellie shrugged and poured herself a vodka. Derrick accepted the bourbon she offered him, and they carried the food and drink to the table, where Derrick had already set up his laptop with Autumn's beside it.

Yawning, Ellie felt brain-dead and exhausted with worry, but realized she needed fuel so she nibbled on the burger and fries, then forced herself to slowly sip the vodka. One drink was her limit tonight. She needed a clear head. She couldn't imagine how Lara was managing.

Derrick inhaled his food as if he hadn't eaten in days, then tossed his wrappers in the trash and returned to search Autumn's computer. His expression grew darker and darker as he searched, then he rocked back in his chair with a labored sigh.

"What did you find?"

He tapped the table with his knuckles. "Autumn looked at a brokerage site for children on the dark web. It's called MWC."

Goosebumps skated over Ellie's skin. "MWC?"

He nodded grimly. "Mother Wants Child."

Ellie went cold all over.

SIXTY

SOMEWHERE ON THE AT

Ava had been petulant and pouty all afternoon, but the girl would learn. It would just take patience. One day she'd accept that her mommy was gone, and she'd learn to love her. Kaylee had taken a while and then Becky... although Becky was the sickly one.

She didn't know what she was going to do about that.

Now, her husband was in there giving Becky her medicine. She'd made Kaylee and Ava take theirs, and they were watching *Rudolph the Red-nosed Reindeer.* That would occupy them for a while. It was *her* favorite movie!

Silas came out of Becky's room, his hair disheveled, his brows pinched together. "For God's sake, I can't believe you brought Ava here. Have you seen the news?"

She shook her head. "No, and I won't allow you to ruin this holiday for me."

"For you?" he barked. "You can't just keep collecting children. It's illegal."

Her eyes bore into his. "So what are you going to do? Tell on me?" She poked him in the chest. "You'll lose everything then because I'll tell everyone it was your idea."

A vein throbbed in his neck, then his anger melted like snow on a hot day. Guilt replaced it, making his eyes look flat and lifeless.

Guilt he deserved, she reminded herself.

For a tense heartbeat, he stared at her as if he didn't know who she was anymore, but she ignored him, made herself a cup of hot tea, then slipped over to her desk and opened her computer. If Ava's disappearance was all over the news, the police would be looking for her.

Although no one knew where they were. They were far away from town and other people, and it would stay that way. She didn't need other people anyway.

Just her family.

Still, she had to check on Kaylee's aunt Priscilla and Becky's mother. Last month, she'd discovered that Jan Hornsby organized a Facebook group for mothers of missing children, and she'd checked it out.

Kaylee's aunt had joined it and the two women had become chummy.

She didn't like that one little bit. But as long as all they did was bitch and moan, she'd leave them alone. She'd already taken too many chances and couldn't risk bringing attention to herself. She never chimed in, just kept an eye on them.

She skimmed the posts today, her hands shaking as she read the exchange. Priscilla had made the connection that Kaylee and Ava had disappeared on the same day.

Then Jan's comment: It could mean something. Maybe you should call that detective in Crooked Creek.

She gripped the table edge. Her chest hurt as she gasped and struggled for air. Those two women were trouble. If they started piecing things together, she'd have to put a stop to it.

An image of Renee's trusting face just before she'd died taunted her. She hadn't let Renee interfere. She wouldn't let Priscilla or Jan either.

SIXTY-ONE

CROOKED CREEK

Revulsion filled Derrick at the very thought of selling a child. Ellie rushed from the table and into her bedroom, and he let her go. This case was getting to both of them.

If Ava had been sold on the dark web, locating and recovering her would be more difficult than a parental kidnapping. They could be talking international exchanges.

Or it could be as simple as a desperate woman wanting a child. She could be hiding right here in the Appalachian Mountains.

Perspiration beaded his neck as he phoned his partner at the Bureau and explained what he'd found. He'd known Bennett ever since they were in the military together. They'd gone through a hell so bad that they'd made a pact never to talk about it. But sometimes at night the memories haunted him. The endless screams. The explosions. The smell of burned flesh. The bones of the dead scattered all over.

Shaking himself from the past he couldn't escape, he focused on the case. Work was all that helped him block out the darkness that sometimes threatened. Helped him forget what they'd done...

"Fox?" Bennett said. "You still there."

Hardly. "Yeah. Have our cyber team do a deep dive into this group," he said. "Find out whose spearheading it and their physical location. Also look for chatter about anyone seeking a child around Ava's age."

"I'll do it myself," Bennett said. "These sick bastards need to be stopped."

As Derrick glanced out at the dreary skies and heard the rain pounding the roof, he couldn't help but think about how frightened Ava must be.

If she was still alive.

Ellie emerged from her bedroom looking pale and wiped out. He stood and crossed the room to her. "Go to bed, Ellie," he said gruffly. "Hopefully my partner will have more on that group in the morning. Tonight, get some rest so we can hit the ground running tomorrow."

Ellie lifted her chin in a show of bravado but her tormented eyes told a different story. "You do the same." Then she turned and walked back to her room. When the door closed, he returned to his computer.

He couldn't rest right now. Not with Ava's little face haunting him.

They had to save her from whatever kind of monster had stolen her from her mother.

SIXTY-TWO

HONEYSUCKLE LANE

The wind blew strands of Lara's hair in her face as she stumbled forward in the dark. The woods were thick with trees so tall and close together she couldn't see two feet in front of her. But she could hear Ava crying somewhere ahead.

"I'm coming for you, baby girl, I'm coming," Lara cried.

Her calves ached from running, her breathing was nothing but a pant, and overgrown brush and weeds clawed at her arms and legs.

"Mommy!"

A sob welled from deep in her gut as she broke through a small clearing and spotted the monster dragging her daughter deeper into the forest, up a hill and into the wilderness. She picked up her pace, her lungs straining to breathe as she climbed higher into the mountains.

The acrid odor of a dead animal swirled around her, and rain began to slash the ground, turning into sleet-like pelts that stung her cheeks and eyes.

"Ava!"

The figure on the hill suddenly paused and looked down at her from the ridge above where she stood. The big winter coat and hat shadowed his face and body, but she heard his sinister voice.

"She's mine now. You'll never get her back."

"No," Lara screamed. "Ava!"

But suddenly the dark clouds unleashed a heavy torrent of rain and sleet, blurring her vision as the figure disappeared into the oaks and pines.

She ran faster, climbing higher and higher, but the trees were bending in the storm, dead leaves hurling at her feet, and limbs cracking and breaking. Her foot caught on something, a tree root maybe, then she felt the vines wrapping themselves around her like snakes, trapping her. She couldn't get up. The darkness swelled above her, and she fought at the tangle of vines, but they were alive and holding her down and choking her, and she couldn't find her way out and Ava was gone...

"You'll never get her back."

His words boomeranged off the mountain, and she screamed and screamed Ava's name, but her voice was lost in the thick forest just as her daughter was.

Suddenly someone gripped her arms, shaking her and calling her name. She opened her eyes, terrified to see his face, to find that he'd hurt Ava.

"Shh, Lara, it's me."

The deep voice bled through the haze and she beat at the man with her fists. But he wrapped his arms around her tightly and held her, rocking her back and forth. "Shh, it's Jasper. I'm here. You were having a nightmare."

Lara sobbed against him, hating him for leaving her, for sleeping with that vile woman, but grateful the police had released him tonight. That he was here.

She blinked back tears and looked up at him. Through the dim light pouring into her window, she saw the tears sliding down his cheeks.

Then she remembered the texts between him and Autumn and rage resurfaced. With as much force as she could muster, she pushed him away.

His breathing was erratic, his voice pained. "I swear to you, Lara, I didn't make that plan with Autumn," he said in a choked voice. "You have to believe me. I wanted to be with you and Ava for Christmas."

Maybe he was telling the truth. Or maybe he'd gone along with the plan at first then changed his mind. Maybe he was crying because he loved Ava. Or maybe because he'd gotten caught. The maybes were piling up.

She didn't know what to believe.

Except that she feared the monster in her nightmare was real and that she might never see her little girl again.

SIXTY-THREE

CROOKED CREEK

Sunday, December 22

The next morning, Ellie woke, worry pricking at her. It was three days until Christmas. She had no doubt that Lara and Ava would have been counting down the days and minutes until Santa came, if the little girl was home.

Dragging herself from bed, she quickly showered then stumbled to the kitchen for coffee. The blanket on her couch looked rumpled and she realized Derrick had spent the night there. She supposed she should be surprised, but he'd slept there before, and knowing him he'd worked half the night.

She found a note by the coffee pot, which he'd brewed for her, saying he'd gone back to his cabin to shower and that he'd meet her at the station in an hour.

Her cell phone buzzed as she poured herself a mug and breathed in the rich pecan scent. She glanced at the caller ID screen. Her father.

She answered but would make it quick. "Hi, Dad."

"Ellie, I just wanted to check on you," he said. "I know you're swamped looking for that missing girl. And I've heard about the locals being upset that you're providing protection for that man Grueler."

"If you called to lecture me, Dad, don't bother. Grueler definitely has a problem," she said. "But he's innocent until proven guilty, and I had no evidence that he abducted Ava. Instead, he claimed to have seen a woman watching Ava. If he comes to, maybe he can describe her."

An awkward pause fell between them. "Sometimes doing the right thing is the hardest of all," he said gruffly.

Ellie wondered if he was talking about her or himself and the secrets he'd kept to protect her. His had come at a cost.

She hoped hers didn't.

"I'm proud of you for standing up for your convictions and for being level-headed," her father said.

Ellie felt a blush climb her neck. "Thanks, Dad. I'm about to go to work now."

"Is there anything I can do to help?" he asked.

Ellie grabbed her service weapon from her nightstand. "Thanks, but I don't think so."

He cleared his throat. "Your mom wants you to come to dinner on Christmas Eve, and for lunch on Christmas Day."

Ellie clenched her teeth as a moment of nostalgia swept over her. As a little girl, she'd been too excited to sleep the night before Santa. She usually woke up at 4 a.m. to open presents. She'd tear into them and play in her pajamas while Vera made waffles, then by lunchtime her mother was already working on her famous prime rib dinner.

"It all depends on if we find Ava, Dad. We're working around the clock to bring her home before the holiday."

She had to put her own family on hold. At the moment, Lara's took priority.

SIXTY-FOUR

SOMEWHERE ON THE AT

Ava shivered as the stinky-smelling lady led her from the dark room into another one that was bigger with twin beds. She pinched her nose to keep from breathing in the yucky smell. It was like when she and Mommy walked past the perfume counter at the mall, and all the perfumes mixed together. It gave Mommy sick headaches so she rushed them past. It was giving her a headache now.

"Isn't the room pretty?" the lady said it in a sing-song voice. "Just look at the sun trying to break through the rain."

Ava blinked. The sun came in little streaks but wasn't bright like the walls. They were so yellow they looked like they'd been painted with butter.

"See, I told you you'd have books and toys here!" The woman pointed to a corner that was filled with a bookcase, table, blocks, an easel and games.

Then Ava saw the calendar on the corkboard, and her throat felt wet with tears again.

At home she and Mommy had an advent calendar where you plucked a piece of candy from the wooden tree to mark off the days until Santa came.

There were three days left. Was Mommy eating the candy today without her?

"Come on, don't dawdle," the lady said as she pushed her farther into the room.

A humming sound came from the corner, and Ava saw another girl sitting at the table drawing with markers, her blond hair in pigtails held with bright-red ribbons. Ava bit her lip as the woman nudged her forward, her feet so heavy they stuck to the floor as if she'd stepped in glue.

"This is the beautiful room I told you about, Ava. You'll have your own bed and lots of toys, and look, a sister." The woman had a weird smile on her face as she walked over and gave the little girl a hug. "This is Kaylee."

Kaylee looked at Ava with big eyes then back down at her drawing.

Goosebumps skated up Ava's arms. "I wanna go home," Ava said in a whisper. "Back to my house with my real mommy."

The woman stooped down and tilted Ava's chin up with her thumb. "Look at me, I told you that your mommy doesn't want you anymore. You're going to live here and we're going to be a family."

Ava's lip quivered, and she shook her head. "No, Mommy wouldn't get rid of me. She l-loves me."

The woman cupped Ava's face in her hands. They felt cold and clammy, not soft and warm like Mommy's. "You don't under-stand yet, but you will." Her eyes bore into hers like the skinny black and white cat's that lived at Ms. Dottie's house.

Then she stroked Ava's hair and whispered, "I've missed you so much, Piper."

Ava's stomach lurched. "My name is not Piper," she whis-pered. "It's Ava."

The woman suddenly let her arms go and stood. A frown pulled at her mouth, and Ava's legs wobbled. "I'll leave you to get to know your new sister," she said.

She turned, clasped her hands together and looked between the two girls. "While you play, I'll set up everything for us to make the gingerbread houses." She clapped as if they were celebrating then turned and left the room. Ava heard the door lock after she shut it.

Butterflies danced in her stomach. She turned and looked at Kaylee. Kaylee pushed the empty chair at the table toward Ava. "Sit by me, Ava."

Her legs felt shaky as she shuffled over to the table. Kaylee pushed another sketchpad in front of Ava and set the basket of markers in the middle. "You'll get used to it here," Kaylee said, her voice tired.

Ava swiped at her face, picked up a marker and began drawing Bunny. She didn't want to get used to it.

If Mommy wasn't coming, maybe Bunny would become real and save her.

SIXTY-FIVE

CROOKED CREEK

Ellie grabbed coffee for her and Derrick on the way to the office, the scent of the dark brew jumpstarting her fatigued brain. When he looked up from his laptop, his coal-black eyes glimmered with a mixture of worry and anger.

"I've been digging into that group MWC," he said. "It claims to bring families together by pairing a child in need with a mother who, for one reason or another, can't conceive one of her own."

"There are dozens of legal services for personal adoptions," Ellie said. "If it's legit, why advertise on the dark web?"

"Exactly." Derrick leaned back in the chair and gestured toward the IP address. "I've made contact."

Ellie's pulse hammered. "You did?"

"I have a plan. At least that is, if you agree."

Curious, she sank into her chair. "Okay, run it by me."

"I think we should pose as a couple looking for a child." His expression was solemn as he let his suggestion linger in the air.

"Us?" She crossed her legs, her brows arching.

"What better way to get information than to go undercover?" He rocked back in his chair. "If you don't want to do it, I'll ask another agent to."

"No, if there's a chance Autumn was involved in this and it has to do with Ava, I'll do it," Ellie agreed.

"I picked up a laptop this morning on my way that can't be traced back to the FBI or us."

Ellie tapped her fingers on her thigh. "All right, what's our story?"

A small smile twinkled in Derrick's eyes, and Ellie felt a flush along her neck. "You knew I'd agree, didn't you?"

He chuckled. "Yes," he admitted. "You're a go-getter, Ellie. I trust you'll do whatever it takes to rescue this child."

Ellie nodded. "Then let's get to work. If these people have Ava, they could pass her to someone else and we might never find her."

Worse, if they had international ties, Ava could be on a plane halfway around the world by now.

SIXTY-SIX

HONEYSUCKLE LANE

Lara felt limp with exhaustion and worry. Jasper seemed to be reacting the opposite way—he was jittery and couldn't sit still. She'd heard him pacing the floors all night.

Before she'd finally collapsed around midnight, she'd watched the news and seen that reporter asking Detective Reeves about Nolan Grueler. She'd gotten so angry she wanted to scream. How dare the detective protect that son of a bitch while her little girl was lost.

She'd laid in bed and thought of a hundred ways to kill him herself. All painful and final.

God help her, she was losing her mind. If he knew something about Ava, he had to regain consciousness and tell them.

The phone buzzed and she saw it was Emily. Although Emily's voice was almost melodic it was so calming, Lara didn't have the strength to talk right now, so she let it go to voicemail then listened to the message.

"*Hey, Lara, it's Em. I'm just checking to see how you're holding up.*" Compassion softened her words. "*There's a support group on Facebook I thought you might be interested in. It's called Mothers of Missing Children. I'm going to send you the link.*" She hesitated. "*Anyway, it might help to talk to some other mothers. If you want me to come later, please call or text me anytime, day or night. I'm here for you."*

Emily was definitely a godsend. She was there for everybody.

But Lara pushed the idea of joining the group away. How could listening to horrible stories from other mothers who'd lost their children possibly help her?

Dragging on her robe, she staggered down the stairs and found Jasper sitting at the kitchen table thumbing through the photo albums she'd compiled. Most people these days kept a library of their photos online. But she was old fashioned and she and her daughter had made scrapbooks of Ava's art, and she'd printed her favorite photos to chronicle Ava's childhood.

She hadn't wanted to forget the sweet special moments and her daughter's exuberance for life. Jasper's body shook with emotion, and as she passed him to get coffee, she realized he was looking at the picture of the day they'd brought Ava home.

Her chest squeezed with tenderness. That day she and Jasper had been so close, both excited and nervous. After thirty-six hours in labor, they'd been thrilled when Ava had popped out, all pink and wiggling and crying. Lara remembered the midwife pulling her gown away for her to nurse her baby and how Jasper had watched in awe. Two days later, they'd dressed their newborn in a tiny pink and white onesie and a hot pink bow, wrapped her in a blanket, settled her in her car seat and brought her back to the nursery Lara had designed herself. Jasper had carried her inside, holding her so carefully, as if she was a delicate piece of glass that might break.

Her gaze went to the box of glass ornaments she planned to paint with Ava today, then the set of watercolors she planned to wrap for her countdown to Christmas gifts, and her chest throbbed so bad she almost doubled over.

Ellie and Derrick began to compose a cover story that sounded plausible. "Let's use names that we won't forget," Derrick said. "It's important to base your story on things close to the truth and to keep it simple."

They tossed around suggestions and decided on a variation of Derrick's name by using Erikson as their last name.

"I'll use Mae, since that was my given birth name," Ellie said.

"I'll use my father's name, Jared," Derrick replied.

Derrick jotted the names down. "Good. Now if we're going to pay for a child, we need to present ourselves as having money. I'll be a financial planner with my own consulting firm."

"And I can work as your accountant," Ellie said, although truthfully math was not her strong suit.

"That'll work. Then we can set up a fake work site with clients and financial information."

Ellie nodded. "We should live in a trendy area with people our age who are more upper class."

"That would be Buckhead," Derrick said. "There's a lot of old money there. In fact, we could divulge that one of our families established a trust fund for us."

"Let that be you," Ellie suggested. "Now for the reason we're seeking a child this way. Let's say that we've been married five years and have tried to conceive. We finally resorted to IVF, but it failed." She paused, then took a breath. "I've been desperate since then and obsessed with becoming a mother."

"Why aren't we seeking an infant instead of an older child?" Derrick asked.

Ellie rubbed her forehead in thought. "Let's use my story. I was adopted when I was four and I know how difficult it is for older children to be placed in forever homes."

Derrick searched her face. "Are you sure you're okay with that? I know learning about your past has been difficult."

Emotions threatened, but Ellie squashed them. She didn't have time to let her messy personal life interfere with finding Ava. "I'm fine, let's just do this," she continued. "Since we both work, we want a school-aged child, preferably five to six years old, so we don't need childcare during the day. Being the accountant gives me flexibility, though, so I can work at home if necessary and be there when the child gets home from school."

"Sounds good," Derrick agreed. "We could throw in there that we plan to adopt a dog. Kids love dogs."

Ellie's chest clenched. "Lara said Ava wanted a puppy for Christmas."

Their gazes locked, tension building. The clock ticked in the background. Another hour into the third day Ava was gone.

Derrick gave a small smile. "I don't know if they'll ask. It depends on if these people are selling children for money or if they truly are trying to find good homes for needy kids. But we should have a background story for how we met."

"Like you said, let's stick to as many truths as possible. We can say we met during a freak snowstorm where we were both on vacation in the mountains."

"Not here," Derrick said. "That could draw suspicion."

"Then we lived in the same condo building at the time and there was a blackout. All the neighbors congregated in the common room, and we hit it off there."

"We married six months later," Derrick said. "At a resort hotel on St. Simon's Island."

That sounded wonderful, Ellie thought. Far away from murder and crime. The ocean crystal blue, sun shimmering off the water, waves lapping gently at the shore.

She shook herself back to reality. This was no vacation. Ava's life was at stake.

SIXTY-EIGHT

SOMEWHERE ON THE AT

Five-year-old Becky Hornsby rolled into a ball, clenching the sheets to her chest and burying her face in the covers.

She was sick again.

Her body shook with chills, and she ached all over. She pressed her hand to her mouth to keep from heaving, but she couldn't stop crying.

Ever since the lady had brought her here, she'd started feeling bad again. At first, she yelled at the woman to take her home, but the woman said Becky's mama didn't want her anymore, that she was too much trouble.

And she had been trouble.

Tears trickled from her eyes and spilled onto the pillowcase, soaking it. She hadn't meant to be such a mess, especially since her daddy died and Mama was alone and working two jobs and even then she couldn't pay the bills.

No wonder the lady had taken her. Her mama had had too much on her plate, the lady said. Becky had to be a good girl and stay here and be her daughter now.

"You should be grateful we're giving you a home," the woman had told her the night she'd put her in the room with the other girl,

Kaylee, and the twin beds and the toys. Kaylee was her age and
hugged her and told her everything would be all right.

But Becky got a weird tickle in her belly when the woman
looked at her. When the lady's eyes glazed over and she wanted
Becky to call her Mommy.

Suddenly she was sweating all over and shivering at the same
time. Her throat hurt like she'd swallowed sand. She wanted to go
back to the room with Kaylee, but her new mommy said no, that
she had to stay in here until she was better.

She'd fed her chicken soup and wiped her forehead with a cool
cloth. But she'd heard her fighting with the man she was supposed
to call daddy, and Becky didn't think it was all right at all.

Now, the man's voice boomed from behind the door. "Becky is
going to die if we don't do something."

The woman started crying and Becky dug her face into the
pillow and blubbered. She was only a kid. But she knew some
things. Like they put you in a hole in the ground when you died
like they had her daddy.

And then you went away forever.

Ellie called a meeting to fill everyone in while Derrick set up their cover. He was creating a fake website for Erikson's Financial Firm along with biographies for them and banking information, as he assumed the MWC would run background checks.

He also set up individual profiles on LinkedIn and was establishing a customer list with reviews the clients had posted after using their company's services. According to her bio, she'd attended the University of Georgia while he'd earned a Masters from Georgia Tech.

She glanced at the whiteboard from their initial conference while she waited on her captain, Deputy Landrum, and the sheriff to arrive. Shondra had driven back to the Trumans to keep watch.

Bryce gave a quick knock then stepped into the room, the first to arrive. He looked stone serious, his jaw rigid as he crossed the room to her. "Any word on the little girl?"

Ellie shook her head. "Any more tips come in?"

"Nothing that panned out. A couple more sightings of kids that resembled Ava, but in between checking in with my deputies—who are taking shifts protecting your child sex offender—I'm covering the tips." His tone reeked of disapproval.

"Is that it?" Ellie asked, her stomach plummeting. She'd been hoping someone had seen something.

"Oh, some nutcase called and said her niece went missing a year ago, but I looked into her story. Turns out the mother was a drunk, let the little girl wander off at the beach. The kid's thought to have drowned. Mom was arrested for criminal negligence and then killed herself." He rubbed the back of his neck. "My father is breathing down my neck about this, Detective Reeves. You'd better come through."

Ellie met his gaze head on, battling self-doubt. She and Mayor Waters had butted heads before and probably would again.

"Let's stick to updating everyone," she said curtly.

His hiss echoed in the air, and he backed away from her as Captain Hale, Deputy Landrum and Derrick joined them. But she caught the warning look in Derrick's eyes as he pinned Bryce with a cold stare.

Not willing to engage in a pissing contest with Bryce, Ellie stepped to the front and jotted down the new information they'd uncovered: the interviews with Jasper and Autumn, who still remained suspects. Under motive, she listed: Autumn suggested a plan to get rid of Ava. Then she wrote the acronym MWC.

"Autumn was linked to this site. They arrange private adoptions, but it doesn't seem legit," she added.

Derrick rapped his knuckles on the table. "We think they could be brokering children."

"The text Angelica received said there were others missing." Ellie's pulse clamored. "We still haven't been able to trace the origin of the message."

The room fell into silence as everyone contemplated the meaning.

Ellie continued, "Agent Fox has established a cover for the two of us to make contact with this group."

"What can we do to help?" Deputy Landrum asked.

"The sheriff is working the tips that come in and his people are searching vacant properties in the county," Ellie said. "Deputy

Eastwood is monitoring activity at the Trumans. Just be ready if we call for backup."

Captain Hale raised a finger. "Ms. Juniper's lawyer arranged for her to be released."

Bryce cleared his throat. "I'll have one of my deputies tail her," he said. "If she had something to do with a child kidnapping ring, we'll nail her ass."

Ellie was surprised at the adamant tone of his voice and that he'd said *we*. Was it possible he was becoming a team player?

He didn't smell like whiskey today either. Maybe learning he had a daughter was making a difference in his life.

"Time to get back to work, everyone," Ellie said. "It's only three days until Christmas. Let's bring Ava home in time to see Santa."

SEVENTY

SOMEWHERE ON THE AT

She arranged all the Santas around the living room, lining them on the fireplace mantle and on the corner table. She and Piper had started collecting the Santas when the little girl was one and she'd seen her first one in the store. Piper had giggled every time she talked about Santa's big belly. Once she'd even stuffed a pillow under her pajama top and run around belting out, "Ho, ho, ho." Another time she'd sketched him getting stuck in the chimney.

A lot of young kids were scared of Santa, but Piper was trusting and raced to have her turn, climbing up and giggling as she listed all the gifts she wanted.

Today, when she'd looked into Ava's eyes, she'd seen a little bit of Piper there and had wanted to wrap her in her arms and rock her like a baby. But Ava was as skittish as the colt she'd tried to ride when she was small herself.

She would get used to life here, though, just as Kaylee and Becky had. Soon she'd come to call her Mommy and laugh as they decorated cookies together and turn to her for help with her schoolwork.

She should have taken her sooner. Waiting till so close to the holiday made the transition harder. But she'd been watching Ava for weeks and that woman Lara was always around, practically clinging to her. She'd heard Lara and her useless husband arguing and yelling about who would watch Ava.

They didn't deserve to have Ava. Especially when she belonged to *her*.

She hung the girls' stockings, then decided Ava should decorate her own, so she laid it on the craft table for her.

She placed the three-foot Santa by the fireplace, then went to the girls' room. She'd made Piper's favorite lunch, macaroni and cheese, and couldn't wait to see Ava's face light up when she saw it.

She unlocked the door and found Kaylee at the table still drawing while Ava watched, hugging Kaylee's stuffed dog to her chest.

"Lunch is ready, girls, I made your favorite." She beamed at them. "Then you can decorate your stocking, Ava, to add to the family mantle and both of you can work on the gingerbread houses."

Kaylee stood and took Ava's hand and led her to the door. Ava looked up at her with those big serious eyes, the windows to the soul, and she brushed her hand over the little girl's hair. Her hair was all wrong but in time she would fix that. Soon Ava would forget all about her other life and learn to love her just the way Piper did.

SEVENTY-ONE

Ava didn't want to go with the lady, but her stomach growled, and she hadn't eaten since she got to this place. Kaylee tugged at her hand. "Come on, it'll be fun."

Ava's body stiffened, her legs like wood as she let Kaylee pull her along into the hall and down the stairs. The walls were bare, and it seemed like the walk lasted forever and ever, just like the drive into the mountains when the woman had brought her here. Finally, Ava stepped into a big kitchen next to the living room, where a fake Christmas tree stood with silver and red and blue ornaments.

"Isn't this the most perfect tree?" The lady's voice sounded like a bird chirping.

Ava blinked hard. No. It was all wrong. It looked fancy, like something you'd see in the store when Mommy told her not to touch things. "See the sign, sweetie," Mommy had said. "It says if you break it you buy it." Ava had hung onto Mommy's hand then, careful not to touch the glass balls.

She'd been so glad when they got home. They'd painted reindeer ornaments with a silly squiggly nose and button eyes. She lost one of the tiny buttons, but Mommy had said it didn't matter, and let her dig in her button box and she picked a bigger one. It didn't match the other eye, but Mommy said that was okay. "He's the most special reindeer because he's different," Mommy said. Then Mommy hugged her.

"See, I have everything ready," the lady said.

Ava gave a tiny nod. There were Graham crackers, candies, sprinkles and icing for the gingerbread houses on the counter. Tears burned Ava's throat. She was not a crybaby. But she'd cried and cried ever since she got here.

She dug her heels in. She didn't want to make a gingerbread house here, that was something special she did with Mommy. She could hear Mommy laughing and singing "Jingle Bell Rock" while they added M & Ms to the top of the house and spread icing on the Graham crackers. "We can do a whole village if you want," Mommy had said. "We'll make all different colors of houses."

Ava's legs wobbled beneath her as she pictured the row of rainbow houses, then the last one, one made of all chocolate. Late one night they picked that one apart and gobbled it down with big glasses of milk while they watched *Frosty the Snowman* on TV.

Kaylee tugged at her hand and Ava managed to unfreeze her legs and move again. She led her to a round table in front of some windows. Ava glanced at the sliding glass doors to the side and saw light spilling through. She wished she could run out those doors and run and run until she got home.

But the wind was howling, tree branches were swaying like when it stormed, and snow began fluttering down, making it hard to see. She usually liked the snow but that meant it was really cold outside and foggy and if she went outside she might freeze to death.

All she saw were trees and trees and more trees. If it snowed hard like it did last year, she might get lost and then the bears would eat her.

Shaking all over, she clamped her lips together as she sat down beside Kaylee and stared into her macaroni and cheese. Then she looked over at the giant Christmas tree with all the decorations and the mantle where three stockings hung. She'd learned to read this year. Piper. Kaylee. Becky. Then she saw the plain one on a table in the corner waiting for her to add her own name.

Her stomach heaved and tears caught in her throat. She had a stocking at home. She didn't need one here, because when Daddy got here, he'd take her back to Mommy.

"Go ahead, honey, and eat up, it's your favorite," the woman said, tapping her spoon on the table.

Ava shook her head. "No, it's not. Pizza's my favorite."

Kaylee went still beside her, and the woman's smile slipped off her face. "We'll have pizza for dinner then."

The woman acted like that made everything okay, but it didn't. With a frown, she stood, went to the refrigerator and poured milk into two glasses.

"I hate milk," Ava lied under her breath. The milk made her think of the chocolate gingerbread house. "I don't want it."

"Don't be silly, Ava, drink it. It's good for you," the woman said as she set the glasses down. The phone on the counter rang, and the lady picked it up and talked in a low voice.

Kaylee nudged her leg below the table then whispered, "Be nice, Ava, or Mommy will send you to the timeout room." Her nose scrunched into a frown. "You don't want to go there."

Fear tickled Ava's tummy. She pointed to the two empty plates at the table. "Who are those for?"

"Piper and Becky," Kaylee whispered.

Ava looked around for them. "Where are they?"

"I don't know, I've never seen Piper," Kaylee said in a low voice. "Becky stayed in our room for a while, but then something happened, and she was crying real hard one night. Mommy came in and got upset and she took her..." Kaylee's eyes looked big, like flying saucers on the space cartoons.

Ava wanted to ask more, but the lady came back to the table, sat down and stared at her. This time she wasn't smiling. Her green eyes looked mad and scary.

Terrified about where the woman took that girl Becky, Ava

wiped at a tear, then picked up the glass of milk and took a swallow.

SEVENTY-TWO
CROOKED CREEK

While a lot of girls played with baby dolls as kids, Ellie had always chosen to be outside, climbing trees, building forts, hunting for treasures in the woods, and digging for worms to go fishing. Later, she'd been so focused on proving she was fit to be a cop like her father that she'd never considered marriage. For as long as she could remember, she and Vera had butted heads. Ellie had been afraid of having a child, afraid she wouldn't be a good mother herself.

Deciding she needed to understand more to play the part, Ellie searched online and found several blogs where mothers posted about their yearning for a family, fertility problems and struggles.

Each one was heartbreaking.

I've wanted a baby ever since I got married when I was twenty-five. I'm thirty now and we've been trying. All my college friends are having families, and it hurts to be around them. All they talk about is their pregnancies and nurseries and baby names. Every month I get my hopes up and then... it doesn't happen.

My husband says I'm obsessed with having a child, but we've tried for seven years now and I've had two miscarriages. I feel like I'm failing him. And I want to be a mommy so bad. Sometimes I go to the park and watch the children play and then I cry and cry and cry.

I grew up in a family of seven children. Some people thought it was chaos at our house, but we had game night every week and I loved taking care of the little ones when they came along. But my doctor told me today that I can't carry a baby to term. When I told my husband, he left without a word. Now I'm all alone and I don't know what to do.

I tried to talk to my husband last night about IVF, but he says it's too expensive. I don't know where we'd get the money either, but I want a child so bad I cry myself to sleep every night. Some days it's hard for me to even get out of bed I'm so depressed.

Ellie sensed someone at her office door, then looked up to see Derrick watching her. Out of the corner of her eye, she saw the tiny Christmas tree she'd put up. It looked sadder and sadder with every day that passed.

"Are you okay, Ellie?"

She closed her laptop and wiped at her eyes as he crossed the room to her. She hadn't realized she'd been crying. "I'm fine," she said with a lift of her chin. "Just doing some research. There are some heartbreaking blogs."

Derrick's eyes flickered with questions. "Have you thought about having a family?"

His tender voice sent a lightning bolt of emotions through her. And a streak of panic. "I just want to play the part," she said, deflecting.

His gaze met hers for a loaded minute, then he released a sigh. "I hope you're ready. We made contact."

Ellie's breath caught. "That was fast."

"If they're holding kidnapped children, they want to turn them around quickly."

"Just a business to them, huh?" Ellie asked with a shudder.

"That's what we're going to find out."

SEVENTY-THREE

STONY GAP

Ellie and Derrick planned to dress her bungalow as if the Eriksons were ready to adopt a child immediately—right down to having a bedroom ready. If MWC turned out to be legit, which seemed unlikely, then they'd pass it off as giving the agency an idea of how the child's home would look. If they wanted a quick transaction, then the Eriksons were ready to go.

Right now Ellie had nothing at her bungalow that was kid friendly, so she drove to Vera's.

This year Vera had decorated the new farmhouse with white lights and her father had strung icicle lights along the roofline of the porch. She knew Vera wanted a snowy holiday, as did the locals who advertised, *Visit the Mountains for a White Christmas!*. But this year the weather was not cooperating.

Now, with a child missing, the mountains seemed macabre, the steep ridges and jutting cliffs ominous and echoing with the whispers of death.

She hurried up to the door, knocked, then for the first time since she and parents had become estranged, she entered their house without waiting for them to invite her in.

She called Vera's name and her mother came running. Gone was her usual coiffured hair and silk pantsuits. She wore a velour jogging suit and sneakers, with an apron tied around her waist. Somehow, she looked more approachable and softer in the casual outfit and flour on her apron.

"Ellie, is everything all right?" Vera asked.

"Not really. Ava Truman is still missing." Ellie's breath puffed out. "Do you still have some of my childhood things?"

Vera looked surprised. "There's a couple of boxes of toys and books," she said.

"I need to borrow them," Ellie said as she backed toward the door.

"Whatever for?" Vera asked with a raised eyebrow.

Ellie really didn't want to explain and considered a lie, that she was donating them to charity. But she'd insisted on truth in the family and she had to reciprocate. "It's about Ava's case," she said. "I don't have time to explain. But I'll bring the items back."

Concern darkened her mother's eyes. "If it helps find that little girl, then take them Ellie and keep them. They're in the attic."

"Thanks, Mom."

Ellie ran up the stairs. By the time she reached the door to the attic, she realized that for the first time since Vera and Randall had divulged the truth about who she was, she'd called Vera Mom.

SEVENTY-FOUR

CROOKED CREEK

When Ellie arrived at her bungalow, the wind had turned frigid and the temperature was dropping rapidly. She hoped to God that Ava was inside some place warm, not left out on the trail.

As she climbed out of her car and glanced at her front door, she shuddered. Someone had spray-painted her front door with a message in blood red.

Ellie Reeves doesn't protect our children.

Tears immediately rushed to her eyes. The box of children's things she'd brought from her mother's house mocked her as they dropped to the ground. People in town didn't realize how much it hurt her to lose a victim, much less a young one. Or how much the guilt ate at her.

For a moment, she considered issuing a statement in her defense but dismissed the idea immediately. People were going to think what they would. If she came out with verbal guns drawn, she'd only fuel their anger. Besides, she didn't have time for that.

She had to keep her head down and do her job. She had to save Ava.

Instincts alert, she scanned the property. The front lawn,

driveway and sides of the house were clear. Pulling her gun, she walked up to the door. The door was still locked, windows as well. No sign of a break-in and her security system would have alerted her if it had been breached. Walking around the side, she checked all the windows and then climbed the steps to the back deck which overlooked the river. The room was empty and just as she'd left it.

Breathing out a sigh of relief, she headed back around the front just as Derrick pulled up. He wore a disapproving scowl as he climbed out.

"Dammit to hell, Ellie. People in this town sure can be judgmental."

"With all the crime that's happened the last couple of years and now another missing child, who can blame them? They want their children to feel safe."

He gestured toward the door. "Do you have extra paint? I'll fix that."

"I can do it," Ellie said. "I picked up some of my childhood things to put in the house to make it look homey, as if we're prepared to adopt a child immediately."

"We have an online appointment in an hour and a half," Derrick said. "You set up the interior and I'll work on covering the door. I also want to put a fake number up in case these people track down where the house is."

Ellie hadn't thought of that. "Thanks. There's an extra can of blue paint in the garage and some brushes there, too."

Derrick nodded and she opened the garage, hurrying to retrieve the box of items she'd brought from her mother's house. Setting the box inside the foyer, she quickly surveyed her den and was pleased it looked cozy. Then she cleared a shelf and displayed some of her favorite childhood books. Next, she added three board games and stacked them so they would be visible. Her fuzzy bean bag chair went in the corner and she draped it with a kid's blanket boasting cartoon characters.

In her kitchen, she set out superhero plates and colorful plastic cups on the breakfast bar. Satisfied with the main living area, she moved to the guest room, pulled off the dark blue comforter and spread out the one Vera had bought her when she was ten—a pink comforter with white kitty cats. Pink had never been Ellie's color, but Vera loved it.

She added her favorite fuzzy pillow, a stuffed bear, and a doll that Vera had bought but she'd never played with.

In the adjoining bath, she set a basket with a hairbrush, bows and barrettes. On the tub, she put kids' bubble bath and shampoo and hung colorful towels on the rack.

A tiny seed of longing hit her as she surveyed the space. It looked like it was ready for a child.

Her heart squeezed. One she would probably never have.

One she'd never thought she wanted.

SEVENTY-FIVE

Thirty minutes later, Ellie and Derrick positioned themselves at the breakfast bar for their meeting. Ellie's face had been in the news too much lately to go into the meeting looking like herself, so she was wearing a disguise. The auburn wig and thick-framed glasses looked natural enough. Derrick had tended to stay in the background when they'd handled the press, so they calculated he didn't need to alter his appearance too much although he wore a baseball cap, Braves t-shirt and jeans to make him look approachable, not like a federal agent.

Nerves fluttered in Ellie's stomach as they connected. A woman sat behind a desk with a file open before her, the lighting poor as if to obscure details of the room. Her jet-black hair was secured in a neat bun on top of her head, her pale skin stretched so tightly her eyes looked squinted, her lips a dark coral. She looked to be in her mid-fifties, with dark brown eyes focused on them.

"Mr. and Mrs. Erikson," she began. "I'm Serena. It's nice to make your acquaintance."

Ellie was still adjusting to being referred to as a couple. "Hi," she said. "Please call me Mae."

"And I'm Jared." Derrick pulled Ellie close, his arm around her shoulders with a squeeze. "We're so excited. My wife and I have been trying to have a child for so long we'd almost given up."

Ellie cleared her throat. "It's all I've thought about for months now. But we both work hard, and we decided instead of a baby, an older child would be a better fit."

"Really?" Serena asked.

Ellie's heart thundered. "Well, I was adopted myself. And I'm grateful for the couple who gave me a home." She felt tension radiating from Derrick and wondered if she should have kept to the script. But her own feelings were rising to the surface.

"I'm glad it worked out for you, Mae," Serena said. "A lot of people want babies, but older children can be loving and rewarding."

She wasn't sure how rewarding she'd been to Vera.

Even though you had differences, she loved you anyway.

"I agree," Ellie said. "And I can't wait to welcome a child into our home." She gestured to the cups and plates on the counter. "As you can see, we're ready right now." She pressed a hand to her chest. "We can't wait to fill the void in a child's life and in ours."

Derrick's eyes brimmed with an intensity Ellie didn't know how to read. "Just tell us what to do and how soon we can start the process."

A silence fell between them, and Ellie realized Serena was looking at the photos of the house and the financial information Derrick had provided.

With a pummeling heart, Ellie leaned into Derrick. He hugged her tighter, although she sensed he was on edge just as she was. Their performance might mean the difference between finding Ava and losing her forever.

SEVENTY-SIX

Serena's response was quicker than Ellie expected. "Actually," she said, "I've reviewed your file and you're in luck. We can get started right away."

Had she run background checks on them or was she simply in a hurry to make a deal?

Serena tapped the folder on her desk. "According to your application, you prefer a girl around five to six years old. I may have the perfect one for you."

Alarm bells clanged in Ellie's head. "You do?"

Serena's lips curled into a smile. "It doesn't always happen this way, but your timing is spot on. She was in foster care for a while and is looking for her forever home."

Derrick's fingers curled around hers. "That sounds wonderful."

"Oh, my gosh," Ellie gushed. "Just think, we might have a little girl by Christmas!"

Serena folded her hands on her desk. "I'm glad you're excited. I need a retainer then I'll send you a photo."

Ellie felt sick to her stomach. This woman was presenting the child as if she was merchandise in a catalog.

"I suppose we need to discuss costs," Derrick said.

"Of course," Serena said, all business. "The retainer is ten thousand dollars, and the remaining fee, a hundred thousand, must be paid at the time you pick up the child. Does that sound agreeable?"

Ellie forced herself not to react.

"Money is not an object," Derrick said with confidence. "After all, you can't put a price on the love of a child."

"I so agree," Serena said cheerfully, as if she'd just closed a major sale.

"Will we need to hire a private attorney?" Derrick asked.

"No, no, that won't be necessary. Our fee covers everything, including the attorney that we use and all the paperwork that needs to be filed."

Ellie feigned a smile although her lips felt tight. "Perfect. I can't wait to meet her."

Derrick wrapped his arm around her shoulders and pulled her into a conspiratorial hug. "My wife is going to make a wonderful mother."

Ellie planted a kiss on his cheek for show and felt his quick intake of breath. *He just said that as part of the act.*

When she pulled back, he gave her a doting smile before turning back to Serena. "Where do I send the retainer?"

"I'll forward our bank information and you can wire the money directly into it. Then we'll make arrangements to meet and transfer the little girl to you." Serena's smile broadened. "Considering that your information is in order, you can spend Christmas Eve with your new daughter!"

Ellie clapped softly, and Derrick asked the woman to expedite the process, that they would anxiously be awaiting the next steps.

As they disconnected, Derrick grimaced. "Major red flags. They didn't ask a single question about the house, or education plans, or physicals. No mention of parent-training classes or home visits, nothing like the legitimate adoption agencies require."

Disgust filled Ellie. "You're right. Even pet adoption centers conduct more thorough background searches and interviews than this woman." Ellie scratched her head. "What are we dealing with here, Derrick? A lone kidnapping, or are these people running a trafficking ring?"

SEVENTY-SEVEN

Checking her phone, which had been on silent during the meeting, Ellie had several messages.

While Derrick phoned Bennett to arrange the wire transfer from a bogus account, she listened to the voicemails, mostly anonymous.

"What the hell are you doing, Detective Reeves? You should protect our kids, not known sex offenders."

"You've got your priorities all wrong, spending our tax money and manpower guarding that vile man instead of using it to find Ava Truman."

The last one was from Meddlin' Maude. Her granddaughter had died at the hands of a recent serial killer and she blamed Ellie for it. *"I hope you don't let Lara Truman down like you did me. That mama deserves to have her baby home for the holiday."*

Ellie pinched the bridge of her nose. She agreed with Meddlin' Maude. But it would do no good to return her call. She needed her line open in case they received a tip about Ava.

Derrick rocked back in his chair. "It's done. The money has been sent." His gaze settled on her. "What's wrong? I saw you on the phone."

Ellie stood, walking to the glass door overlooking her back

deck. Rain drizzled down in a steady rhythm, streaking the windowpanes and blurring the image of the mountains beyond.

Derrick stepped up behind her. "Ellie?"

Her shoulders sagged. "I had several messages about the way I've handled this case and about Grueler. People are not happy with me."

Derrick rubbed her arms. "You're doing everything humanly possible to find Ava."

As Derrick's laptop dinged, they locked gazes for a heartbeat before rushing over.

There was an email from Serena. The photograph was on the way, along with the little girl's profile.

SEVENTY-EIGHT

Derrick squeezed Ellie's hand. He wanted to assure her everything was all right, but nothing about the situation, the kidnapping, or MWC was anywhere near all right.

He'd had a knot in the pit of his stomach as hard as a baseball when they'd talked to Serena. The only thing that vulture cared about was money.

If she was legitimate, she would have insisted on personally checking out the house and arranged for a social worker or guardian ad litem to conduct home visits. Adoptions just didn't happen this quickly.

The first photograph appeared, jarring him back to the case, and he heard Ellie's raspy breathing beside him.

"It's not Ava," Ellie whispered.

No, but it was a small blond girl with pigtails dressed in a frilly Christmas dress. She looked doe-eyed and innocent. He wondered how she'd ended up in Serena's brokerage house for children.

Ellie read the description. "Daisy is six years old and loves to color, read stories, and play with her American Dream Girl doll named Sasha. Her father died in Afghanistan and her mother was homeless, so she turned her over to us to find a loving home. Daisy asked Santa for a mommy and daddy and we want to make that wish come true."

That last sentence got to Derrick. "What do you want to bet that half of that is a lie?"

Ellie nodded, emotions bubbling in her chest. "Do you think she was abducted?"

He shrugged. "It's possible. Also possible that one or both parents sold the child to the group out of desperation for money."

"It's hard to believe anyone could abandon a precious little girl like her. Or any child for that matter."

Derrick murmured agreement. "I'm going to compare the photo to missing persons reports in NCMEC. But first, let's respond to Serena."

Ellie clenched her hands by her sides. "Tell her to give us the time and place," she said. "No matter how they got her, I don't want to leave the child with her or that group another day."

"Don't worry. We're going to bust their operation wide open." Derrick sent the message, asking if they could meet in the morning. When he finished, he said, "I'll send Daisy's picture to the tech team to verify her identity and make sure this is not a stock picture they photoshopped."

"You think it could be fake?"

"We can't dismiss any possibility right now. For all we know, they could be running a con game. They take the money, then never show up with the children."

Ellie shook her head at the thought, then muttered that she saw his point. "Or they could have lined up multiple interested parties and promised them the same child."

"And sold her to the highest bidder."

She watched the angels dance across the stage, wings fluttering as they flapped their arms and formed a circle amidst the golden halo shining down as if from heaven. Tiny pinpoints of white lights flickered across the performers like stars, and a hand-painted mural of a snow scene served as a backdrop for the show.

One, two, three... ten in all. All beautiful little girls with shiny red bows in their hair and ballerina shoes, the dance choreographed by the local instructor.

But the star of the show was her very own daughter. Piper, with long golden hair that looked like corn silk and a smile that lit up a room like a sunburst. Piper, who was so beautiful people stopped her on the street to compliment her.

Piper, her sweet little angel.

The little girls whirled around, spinning and dancing on their tippy toes as they sang "We Wish You a Merry Christmas". Their voices taunted her with such precious memories, and then Piper stepped up in front of the microphone for her solo, singing "Here Comes Santa Claus".

The audience began to clap as Piper spread joy with her lyrical voice and mesmerizing sky-blue eyes.

Her heart sang along, emotions overcoming her, and she

reached out and touched the TV as if she could somehow touch Piper again, pull her from the video, and wrap her in her arms.

But the screen was cold and slick and Piper disappeared, floating away from her just like a feather in the wind.

Choking back a sob, she closed her eyes and imagined waking up and chasing Piper into the living room to find Santa's toys on Christmas morning. She would squeal in delight as she ripped open the packages and they'd make hot cocoa and blueberry waffles for breakfast and stay in their pajamas and play with her toys all day long.

Taking a deep breath, she opened her eyes, went to the closet in her craft room and pulled out her sewing kit, white fabric and glittery ribbon. Tonight, she'd make all the girls angel costumes and in the morning they could perform a show just like the one the little angels performed at Crooked Creek.

The girls would love it...

The sound of crying in the other room yanked her from her thoughts, and a seed of fear sprouted inside her. Becky.

Knowing the child needed her, she filled a kids' water bottle, then hurried down the hall to the room where she'd moved her. Panic seized her as she stepped inside and saw her thrashing at the covers. The little girl was growing weaker every day. Becky coughed and clenched the covers as she shivered, her complexion as milky-white as the bedsheets.

"Mommy..." Becky's voice was so weak and low it sounded a mile away.

She took a damp cloth from the nightstand and brushed it over the girl's clammy skin, then sat down beside her and buried her head against her. Becky had to be all right.

She couldn't lose her all over again...

EIGHTY

Silas gave Becky the injection, his thoughts as turbulent as the gathering storm clouds outside. She did not look well right now. She needed a hospital.

He wanted to save her. He wanted to save them all.

But he hadn't been able to save the one he loved the most.

His wife hated him for it. He hated himself.

The sound of Becky's labored breathing rattled in the air, and he closed his eyes. Instead of Becky's face though, his little girl's blond hair and bright eyes flashed in his mind.

"Come on, Daddy," she sang. "You promised we'd see the cattails."

He took her hand. He had promised. "I don't know if we'll find them today," he said. "The ground is frozen."

"But you promised, and we drove all the way up here to Cattail Cove," she said with a tug of his hand. "You said they're in the marshy parts. There's a pond over there."

She took off running, and his wife yelled at her to come back as she raced after her. "Stop her, Silas! The pond is frozen over!"

He jogged after her, slipping and sliding on the icy path weaving from their campsite to Jacks Rock Falls. He'd only wanted a day out with her, to have some family time after the hundred hours he'd worked this last week. The cases had piled up. The nursing staff was overworked and exhausted. He'd lost a patient.

He'd begun to feel helpless.

Ice crackled and popped from the trees and the ground as he ran and he saw Piper skate onto the pond, her ponytail swinging in the wind gusts that rolled off the mountain, arms waving excitedly. His wife reached the water before him and jogged onto the icy surface. "Stop, honey!" she called.

But his daughter danced across the surface, twirling and spinning as she belted out "Frosty the Snowman".

He reached the edge and suddenly heard the ice cracking. He looked down to see the frozen surface splintering like shards of glass.

"Get off the ice now!" he yelled.

But Piper was oblivious and flew into a dancer's leap, and his wife screamed in panic as the ice split and the force of the cold water below sucked his precious girl under.

EIGHTY-ONE

CROOKED CREEK

A pounding on her front door interrupted Ellie and Derrick. It was already 9 p.m. but the knock came again, this time louder, more impatient.

She opened the door and found Angelica waiting on the stoop, her chignon slightly disheveled, her teeth chattering. "Ellie, locals are calling the station complaining about that man Grueler. They're demanding we give them updates on what you're doing to find the Truman child."

Resigned, Ellie ushered Angelica inside. The reporter rushed to the fire to warm her hands, rain dripping from her coat. At the sight of Derrick, curiosity flared in her eyes.

Derrick nodded in greeting, but remained seated, his attention on their undercover operation.

Angelica crossed her arms. "What's going on, Ellie? I have to report something. People are panicking. They're even talking about canceling the Christmas Eve parade for fear there's a stalker hunting children."

Ellie pinched the bridge of her nose. "I wish I had good news. All I can say is that we're working a lead."

"That's not enough," Angelica pressed. "Everyone is scared,

Ellie. And when you say nothing, it makes them think you aren't doing anything to find Ava."

Ellie hated it, but Angelica was probably right. "Listen," she said. "Okay, but this is between us. We're looking at Jasper Truman's girlfriend and her affiliation with a group that sells children. Agent Fox and I are working under cover and setting up a meeting with them to determine if the girlfriend gave them Ava in exchange for money. But I can't have that leaked or it could compromise the investigation."

Angelica rubbed her hands together. "Oh my god, that's horrible."

"I know," Ellie agreed. "The Trumans can't hear about this. And if you think that people are in an uproar now, imagine how they'd react if they thought a child trafficking ring was operating in the area."

Angelica tapped her fingers on her arm. "All right, I see your point. But if this pans out, I want to be the first to know. Did you trace that message I received?"

"No, it came from a burner phone," Ellie said. "Obviously someone knows something, but they want to remain anonymous."

Angelica gave a decisive nod. "Understood. For now, I'll just report that you are actively working a lead and that you may be close to cracking the case."

Ellie hesitated. She didn't want to mislead the people. But with only two days until Christmas, they needed at least a breadcrumb of hope.

EIGHTY-TWO

SOMEWHERE ON THE AT

Ava's stomach hurt. She wanted to tell the lady that she felt sick, that when she'd looked in the glass of milk, she saw her Mommy making the chocolate gingerbread houses and the icing they'd smeared on their mouths and a gob on her cheek. Then them washing the gooey frosting down with tall tumblers of milk in bear-shaped mugs.

Kaylee crawled over onto the bed and put her arm around her. "It's okay, we're sisters now."

"I don't have sisters," Ava whimpered. "I hate it here."

"You'll get used to it," the girl said.

"I'll tell when I go to school," Ava mumbled.

"Mommy homeschools us," Kaylee whispered. "We never leave the farm except to go out and play when she's with us."

"Then I'll run away," Ava cried.

"I tried that when I first came here. But there's no place to run. There's just trees and the scary woods out there."

Ava hunkered into Kaylee, so mad and scared she was shaking, just like Ms. Dottie's orange cat did the day it got stuck out in the rain.

"Come on, let's look for Becky." Kaylee tugged Ava's hand, pulled her to the door.

Ava's stomach churned, the milk threatening to come up as they stepped into the dark hall. Kaylee felt her way through the shadows, and Ava held onto her, crouching low like a dog and sneaking around the corner.

"Where are we going?" Ava whispered.

"Shh." Kaylee turned around and clamped her hand over Ava's mouth. "Don't make a sound. If they hear us, we'll get in big trouble."

Ava went still and pressed her lips together. She didn't want to know what that meant.

They tiptoed around another corner, then paused at a door. From under the cracks, there was a weak light, and Kaylee leaned her ear against the door. Ava did the same and they both listened, even though she had no idea what she was listening for.

Then she heard the woman's voice. "Come on, you have to stay with me, baby. I love you."

Kaylee went still, and Ava clutched her arm.

"We have to let her go," a man's voice echoed from the other side of the wall. "We can't go on like this, sweetheart."

"You're her daddy now. You have to save her. I need her," the woman sobbed. "She has to be here for Christmas."

Ava dug her nails into the floor. The lady said her daddy was coming to get her.

But that was not her daddy's voice.

EIGHTY-THREE
CROOKED CREEK

Ellie rubbed her bleary eyes.

She and Derrick agreed that MWC could have changed the little girl's name. Some kidnappers even changed their victims' hair color and forced them to dress in opposite gender clothing so as not to be spotted. Daisy had been dressed picture perfect to pull at heartstrings.

Derrick entered her photo in the NCEMC data base, and they waited and waited while it ran, but it yielded nothing.

Had no one reported her missing?

Derrick rolled his shoulders as another message from Serena came through. He read out loud: "Deposit the remaining balance in the morning. Once it clears, we'll meet to make the exchange at Bear Mountain. Will send you the time and location."

Ellie twitched. This was happening so quickly her head was spinning.

"They want money first," Derrick said.

"It's despicable," Ellie said. "They're exploiting innocent women and couples who desperately want a child. And with the storm system brewing, the park will probably be deserted."

His jaw tightened. "Let's get some rest. Authorization from the

Bureau for the money is complete. I'll make the transfer in the morning, then we'll head toward the park."

Ellie nodded, her determination fueled by concern for the children. "If they have Ava, why not include her picture?"

"Because her face is all over the news. They'd want to keep her for a while before offering her up." He turned back to his laptop, where he had a message from Bennett that he also read out loud. "Child has not been photoshopped. Tech is analyzing the site and IP address to determine the location of the company headquarters."

Ellie gritted her teeth. "Hopefully they'll show up tomorrow and we can get some answers."

EIGHTY-FOUR

SOMEWHERE ON THE AT

Monday, December 23

Ava clung to Kaylee's hand as she led her into the kitchen the next morning. Last night after they'd run back to their room, she'd hidden under the covers and willed her real daddy to show up. She'd heard scratches on the window and thought she'd seen her mommy's face looking in.

Then it was gone and there was a monster there and a big fat grizzly bear and she'd pulled the covers up over her head so he couldn't see her.

Daddy had a temper sometimes and she hated it when he got mad. But right now, she wished he was here and he'd tell this lady that she belonged to him and that she couldn't keep her.

"Be good this morning," Kaylee whispered to her now. "Last night I heard Daddy say Becky couldn't stay here anymore."

Ava sniffed. "I don't wanna stay here either."

"You don't get it," Kaylee said, her voice hoarse like she had popcorn stuck in her throat. "We don't know where they'll take her. They might give her to some bad people or leave her out in the woods alone."

Ava pushed her fist against her mouth to keep from crying.

Bears and bobcats and snakes and other wild animals lived out there. And it was cold. So cold and windy the trees were shaking like she did when she went to the spooky house at the school during the fall festival. Outside, she could freeze to death.

She heard the lady humming "Here Comes Santa Claus" as she came into the kitchen, setting plates of bananas and pancakes on the table. Two pill cups sat by the juice cups, one for each of them. "Good morning, girls," she said with a big smile. "After you take your medication and eat breakfast, we have special plans." She stepped into the small room attached to the kitchen then returned with two angel costumes. "We're going to perform our own angel pageant in front of the beautiful tree." She clapped her hands. "Won't that be fun?!"

Ava hated that tree. She stared at the angel costume, her heart thumping. The night before this lady took her, she was at the pageant with her mommy and her mommy kissed her right before she went on stage. When Ava looked out into the crowd, Mommy blew kisses at her and waved. And when they got home, they had cookie dough ice cream and Mommy danced around the living room with her and whispered how much she loved her.

"That sounds good," Kaylee said obediently.

Ava shook her head. "I don't wanna wear that costume. I want the one Mommy made me."

The woman pointed to the glitter on the wings. "I made this one for you. And you will wear it."

Ava shook her head. "You lied about my daddy. Where is he?"

The lady looked into her eyes. "Your family is here. Now don't be a brat."

"Mommy never called me a brat," Ava shouted.

The woman's eyes grew so wide and mad that Ava thought she might hit her. She heard Kaylee's voice in her head, telling her to be good or they might send her away.

The lady stooped down in front of her. "Listen to me, Ava. You're my little girl. We're going to dance and sing and have a great day together."

Tears clogged her throat. "Liar, liar, pants on fire. You lied about Mommy not wanting me. And you lied about my daddy coming."

The lady's eyes went crazy mad again.

But Ava didn't care. She clenched her hands in fists. "You said Daddy was coming. Where is he?"

"You have a new daddy," the lady said.

"I don't want a new daddy or you. I want my old mommy and daddy." She stomped her foot, then turned and ran back to the stairs and up them. She flung the door open and threw herself on the bed. The tears came fast and hard and she looked out the window at all the trees that seemed to go on forever and forever.

On the tops of the mountain, it was raining little pieces of ice right now. When it snowed at home, the white hills reminded her of her snow globes. Only they were magical and pretty. It didn't look pretty outside now. It looked cold and ugly and not at all like her home.

She heard footsteps echoing, then the lady walked over to her bed. "Listen to me," she said in a hard voice, "I'm your mommy now. And I say we're going to have an angel pageant today. And we're going to."

Ava wanted to run but she remembered what Kaylee said about the lady getting rid of Becky or leaving her outside. Fear bubbled in her stomach as the mean lady took her arm and pulled her off the bed.

"Come on, now. Kaylee is already in her angel costume waiting."

Ava wanted to scream again, but her voice wouldn't work, and she looked out at the woods again. Her legs wobbled as the lady led her back to the living room.

Her breakfast was gone now. Kaylee stood by the Christmas tree in the angel costume and black shiny leather shoes with a big red bow in her hair. The lady dragged the other angel costume over Ava's head and pajamas then straightened the wings.

She brushed Ava's hair and clipped the bow in place.

Ava felt tears running into her mouth, but stood still, too afraid to do anything.

"You're on stage now," the lady said as she gently pushed Ava toward Kaylee. Then she started the music and Ava wanted to cry all over again. It was the same music from the Angel Pageant. Kaylee gave her an odd look then took her hand. She began to dance and sing "We Wish You a Merry Christmas", nudging Ava to join in.

She didn't feel like singing or dancing but the lady pointed a finger at her and gave her a look like Mommy did when she meant business. Ava closed her eyes and pretended she was dancing for her real mommy, and that when she spread her angel wings, she could fly back home, way high over the forest and the wild animals until she was back in her bed with Bunny.

EIGHTY-FIVE

BIG BOULDER

Priscilla had lain awake all night thinking about that phone call with the sheriff. She should have known the police wouldn't help her.

Over her morning chamomile tea, she flipped on the TV to watch the morning news.

"*Angelica Gomez, Channel Five News, coming to you from Crooked Creek again,*" said the local reporter on the screen. "*Folks, it's day three that six-year-old Ava Truman has been missing and her parents are desperate for answers.*

"*While Detective Ellie Reeves has no new updates that she can share at the moment, she had this to say. 'I want to assure the public that we are doing everything within our power to find Ava Truman. At this point, we are working a substantial lead and hope to have more information on this development soon. Again, anyone with information regarding Ava's disappearance or her whereabouts, please call the police ASAP.'*"

Priscilla's phone dinged, signaling a Facebook post. Checking it, she saw it was from Jan.

Did you decide to call that detective?

Her fingers flew over the keys: *I did but he brushed me off.*

Jan: *People think I'm crazy, too, because I haven't given up looking for my Becky. But I'll never give up.*

Priscilla inhaled a deep breath and glanced back at the reporter on the news. *I'll call Angelica Gomez. If the police won't listen, maybe she will.*

EIGHTY-SIX

SOMEWHERE ON THE AT

All she'd ever wanted was a child.

As a little girl she'd played with baby dolls, pretending to feed them and rock them and cuddle them. She'd dreamed of a big family with lots of children running around laughing and playing. And for a second in time, she'd thought that dream would come true.

Then... that awful, horrible day had happened...

And she'd lost everything.

She closed her eyes. God help her, she wished she'd died in place of Piper.

"We can have another child," Silas had said.

But that hadn't happened. She couldn't get pregnant.

"We'll pay for a private adoption," Silas promised. "I'll make the arrangements."

But she couldn't bring herself to do that either.

The sound of Kaylee and Ava's low whispers jarred her back to reality. They were making cards for the children's hospital with markers and glitter, although Ava had clammed up and wasn't talking again.

All night she'd worried about Becky and that conversation

between Priscilla and Jan on that stupid Facebook site. While the girls worked at the table, she checked it again.

More postings from Priscilla and Jan.

Jan: *People think I'm crazy, too, because I haven't given up looking for my Becky. But I'll never give up.*

Priscilla: *I'll call Angelica Gomez. If the police won't listen, maybe she will.*

Every nerve in her body zinged with panic. The police had ignored Priscilla, but she'd seen that nosy reporter and she was like a dog digging in the dirt for a ham bone. If she started asking questions, she might get the police's attention.

She cursed beneath her breath. She knew what she had to do.

She slipped to the closet, took her .22 from the shoebox on the top shelf and slipped it in her coat pocket. Then she went to tell her husband she had to run an errand and ask him to keep an eye on the girls.

No one was going to take her family away from her. Not now. Not again. Not ever.

EIGHTY-SEVEN

CROOKED CREEK

Ellie woke to a message from Angelica wanting another update. The message also said that the Trumans wanted to go on camera and make a plea for their daughter.

She called Angelica, a lump in her throat. "Hey. I'll text Shondra and ask her to arrange the interview."

"Do you think you're getting close?" Angelica asked.

Did she? "I hope so," Ellie said. "I'll keep you posted." She disconnected, turning her attention to her disguise. It had done the job on a video call, but now it had to stand up to in-person scrutiny, and suddenly it looked less convincing.

Just then, the doorbell rang. Answering it, she found Derrick in a Braves jersey and hat. They'd already planned to drive separately in case they were walking into an ambush and had to split up.

"Any word?" Ellie asked.

"The meet is confirmed for ten at Bear Mountain Park. Are you ready?"

"As ready as I'll ever be," Ellie answered. "Do you want coffee for the road?"

"That would be great. Thanks."

She hurried to the kitchen and poured two cups in travel mugs.

Grabbing her holster and weapon, as well as her coat and hat, she hurried outside with Derrick.

"I'll follow you and we'll park my car a mile from the meet spot," Derrick suggested. "Once we get Daisy, you can drop me and take her to safety. I'll follow whoever is at the meeting."

She climbed in her Jeep, then used her hands-free to call Shondra to set up the Trumans' interview with Angelica. As the steep ridges of the mountain road rose around her and rain began to pound the car roof, the wind beating at the vehicle, she wondered if they were going to make it in time.

Or if they would be too late for Ava.

EIGHTY-EIGHT

BEAR MOUNTAIN

The gray sky swirled, rain clouds morphing into full-fledged hail clouds, as Ellie maneuvered the winding switchbacks which were slick with ice. They'd dropped Derrick's car as planned, but her nerves were crawling.

Scanning the parking lot, she pulled into a spot and cut the engine, noting no other cars were in sight. The area was known to draw tourists who wanted to enjoy the scenic ridges, waterfalls and hike the trails. Not today, with the temperature below freezing and winter weather in full swing. In fact, the area was virtually deserted. This was definitely not a legitimate adoption.

As they waited, she debated if they'd made the right decision to forgo backup and plant undercover officers around the park. But with the park empty, she still feared that whoever was delivering Daisy would have spotted any undercover officers and run.

That would endanger the child.

She just prayed they weren't being conned and that MWC actually showed up.

Derrick rested his hand on his leg, his body tense. A second later a text came through on the burner phone.

"Go to the pavilion by the creek. Will be waiting for you," he read out loud.

Inhaling a deep breath, Ellie checked to make sure her weapon was well hidden beneath her heavy coat, and Derrick did the same.

She grabbed the stuffed unicorn she'd brought with her as a gift for Daisy as she climbed from the vehicle. The pavilion was on the opposite side of the park, and as she and Derrick walked past the swing set and jungle gym, chill bumps skittered over her body.

Charcoal clouds tumbled across the sky, shrouding out the sun trying to slice through the icy rain, and adding to the grisly gray.

Derrick took her hand in his and squeezed it. "Remember our cover."

Thankful for the reminder, she forced a smile and leaned into Derrick, playing the happy couple in case they were being watched. "Yes, I'm so excited! We're finally going to have the family we've always wanted."

"And just in time for the holidays," Derrick said, his voice loud. "We still have two days until Christmas," he said. "Let's take Daisy for lunch and then shopping and to see Santa."

"That's a great idea," Ellie said, her breath catching as they neared the pavilion and she spotted a white utility van parked close by.

Her heart skittered as they rounded a giant oak beside the pavilion, and she saw a small girl huddled inside a navy winter coat, her knees pulled to her chest. She looked so tiny and frail and scared that Ellie wanted to strangle the people who'd taken her.

A husky man in a black coat and hood sat with her, his eyes darting around, ham hock hands resting on the side of the bench.

Ellie's first instinct was to run as fast as she could to rescue the sweet little darling. But Derrick touched her arm, calming her.

Maintaining their act until they had Daisy safe, they held hands and crossed to the pavilion, but she was so worried about the child that she couldn't help but walk faster and faster until they reached them.

The man stood, one hand over the pocket of his coat, and Derrick halted. "We're the Eriksons," he said. "We came to bring our daughter home."

The big man had a thick beard, muddy brown eyes, and his ski cap pulled low over his forehead. Daisy looked up at Ellie with a terrified quiver in her eyes that broke her heart.

"Hi, sweetheart," she said softly. "My name is Mae and this is Jared."

The big man scrutinized her and Derrick with an intensity that made her stomach roil, but she concentrated on the little girl, stooping in front of her. "I brought you a present."

She started to pull the unicorn from inside her jacket but the guy shook his head and grunted.

"I just brought her a gift," Ellie said softly. "A stuffed animal."

"Slowly," the man said in a gruff voice.

Ellie nodded and eased the unicorn from her jacket. "Here you are, Daisy. I didn't name her. I thought you might want to choose her name."

Tears glittered on Daisy's pale cheeks as she stared at Ellie with a wide-eyed, wary look.

But she grabbed the unicorn and hugged it to her.

Ellie gently brushed hair from Daisy's forehead. "Can we carry her home now? We have everything ready."

A vein pulsed in the man's jaw, and for a moment Ellie thought he was going to refuse. But he gave a clipped nod.

"That's wonderful. Is Serena here with the paperwork?"

"She'll send it on. You shouldn't contact us again," he said harshly. "Unless you want another child, that is."

Ellie reached out her arms. "Come on, Daisy. Let's go home where it's warm and we can have cookies."

Even though Daisy bit her lip, she allowed Ellie to pick her up. Derrick offered the man his hand, but when he received a shake of his head, he brushed the side of the man's heavy coat instead.

Daisy shivered against her as she ran with her to the Jeep and Ellie helped her into the back seat.

"It's okay, sweetie," whispered Ellie. "I'm here to help you." She crawled in the back and pulled the girl to her, hugging her, then held her breath as she waited on Derrick. He jogged toward the jeep, then jumped inside.

"Let's get out of here."

"What about him?" Ellie said.

Derrick shot her a sideways look. "I planted a tracker in his pocket."

Ellie gave him a relieved look, grateful he'd had a plan, then he pressed the accelerator and sped from the parking lot. All she wanted to do right now was to get Daisy away from that monster.

Then they'd figure out if the group had Ava.

Priscilla reread Jan's text as she parked at the overhang overlooking one of the steep drop-offs near Blood Mountain.

> *It's Jan. I thought I'd text to make sure you got it. Meet me at Hangman's Dome, and we'll visit that reporter together.*

Priscilla had posted her number in the Facebook group a while back, but all the members usually communicated through Facebook and its Messenger app. Jan had been right, though—Priscilla didn't always pick up Facebook notifications quickly, and appreciated her friend's thoughtfulness. Priscilla had already been anxious about being treated like a crazy person again, just like with Detective Forrester and that sheriff, so had jumped at Jan's offer.

Jan had become her support system, and she needed a friend, especially during the holiday season when all she could think about was family. Despite the circumstances, she felt a little excited to meet her friend in person for the first time. The group was a godsend, but Priscilla could use the face-to-face connection right now.

The wind had died down as she cut the engine, the air still and listless, filled with the scent of pine and rain. The overhang lookout was deserted, the outline of soaring vultures barely visible through the thick cloud cover.

Hangman's Dome had been named for the rock structures that formed a dome-like shape above the creek which flowed into the Chattahoochee. Years ago, a group of teens high on drugs had hanged themselves here in a mass suicide that had haunted the area with stories. Some claimed the lost souls of those kids cried out for help, their voices boomeranging off the rocks with pleas for forgiveness, while some rumors claimed they begged others to join them. It was common for local parents to forbid their children from visiting the dome, afraid they would succumb to the mysterious lure of death.

She looked up as a vehicle approached. A van pulled up opposite her and flashed its lights. As Priscilla got out of her car, she waved, but something seemed off. Jan worked in an office, so it seemed a little odd she drove a van. Jan's windscreen was a little foggy, but even from here Priscilla saw a short dark bob under her ski hat, not the auburn hair she remembered from Facebook.

She guessed it was natural for people to look a little different in person, though. Maybe she'd changed her hair for the holidays. Priscilla grabbed her purse, locked her car and walked toward the van. Riding with Jan would give her time to sort through her feelings, bolster her courage and prepare exactly what she wanted to say to Ms. Gomez.

Jan hopped out and walked around the front of the vehicle, her face lost in the bright headlights, but Priscilla noticed something shiny in her hand. She froze, squinting to see what it was.

Her heart skipped a beat when she realized it was a gun.

"Wh-what are you doing, Jan?"

"I'm not Jan," the woman hissed. "And you're not going to talk to the cops or that reporter. Now turn around slowly and walk back to your car."

Priscilla turned and began to walk, wondering if this woman

was going to make her drive somewhere. Could she get her car started before the woman got in? She quickened her pace, fumbling with her keys as she drew closer to the car. She heard pounding footsteps behind her, and then realized why the woman had sent her back towards her parking spot by the ridge. She tried to brace herself, but a moment later, two hands shoved her violently in the back and she felt herself falling.

"It's all right now, you're safe," Ellie murmured as she rocked Daisy in her arms.

Derrick clamped his jaw tight. "We're being followed."

The sound of an engine roaring made Ellie jerk her head over her shoulder. He was right. A dark sedan was closing on their tail.

"They must have had someone watching," Derrick said.

He sped up, but the roads were icy, and she heard the tires grinding ice and spewing sludge. They rounded another curve as the sedan grew closer. The brakes squealed, and the Jeep skidded sideways toward the ravine.

"Hang on, Daisy," Ellie said as he clutched the steering wheel and struggled to maintain control.

But the sedan suddenly sped up, ramming into their rear. Daisy screamed as the Jeep slipped forward, and Derrick jerked the wheel to the right to keep from running into the ditch. A second later, the sedan banged into them again and the Jeep flew into a spin.

As Daisy screamed, Ellie covered the girl her with her body.

Shifting the gear, Derrick bumped backward into the sedan, sending it sliding. He took advantage of the moment, then propelled forward, gaining momentum as the driver of the sedan raced after them again. She spotted Derrick's car which they'd parked earlier, and he careened to a stop beside it.

"Get Daisy out of here," Derrick shouted as he jumped out, weapon drawn.

"I can't leave you."

"Just do it, Ellie."

Ellie didn't take orders well, but Daisy's life was at stake so she relented. "It'll be okay, honey," she murmured to Daisy. Then she crawled from the back seat, ran to the driver's side, and took the wheel.

The sedan roared to a stop behind her, the driver throwing open the door. A gunshot pinged her back fender.

"Stay down," Ellie shouted to Daisy.

Daisy ducked down and clapped her hands over her ears.

"Go!" Derrick shouted.

Ellie gripped the steering wheel with clammy hands, veering sideways as Derrick sought cover behind his car. Stepping on the gas, she pulled the Jeep back onto the road. Through the rearview mirror, she saw Derrick raise his gun and fire at the shooter.

Fear for him nearly choked her. But Daisy's sobs wrenched her heart and she sped away.

NINETY-ONE

Derrick hunkered behind his sedan's open door as the shooter fired at him. He quickly released a round, ejected the magazine from his weapon and reloaded. The man's face appeared, and he realized it was the same man who'd had Daisy.

Either MWC had figured out he and Ellie were cops or they'd meant to double-cross them from the beginning. Maybe that was part of their game. Sell the children, get the money, then kill the buyers to cover for themselves and sell the girls all over again.

Another bullet whizzed by his head, and he ducked, then inched to the edge of his vehicle. Creeping behind a group of boulders, he snuck up on the man. His foot hit ice though, crunching it, and the shooter pivoted, firing a bullet. It grazed Derrick's arm, and Derrick released another round, shattering the shooter's car window. When the man darted toward the pine trees, Derrick gave chase, stooping behind another rock then firing again.

The man vaulted up and shot again, but Derrick was fast and fired a bullet into the man's gut. His eyes widened beneath his ski cap, his body bouncing backward. Blood gushed from his belly, and he bellowed, dropping his gun as he collapsed into the slushy ground. A crimson stream pooled beneath him as his body convulsed.

Derrick kept his gun trained on the man, then rushed forward and kicked his weapon out of reach. Then he pointed his own at the bastard's head.

"Do you have Ava Truman?"

The man's eyes glazed over, his body shook and blood seeped from his mouth as it went slack. Derrick cursed as the perpetrator drew his last breath.

As much as Ellie wanted to pull over and comfort Daisy, MWC might have put a tail on her, so she kept driving.

Thankfully, after a few minutes, the motion and warmth of the vehicle lulled Daisy to sleep, as she hugged the unicorn to her.

Questions ticked through her mind. How long had the little girl been with those people? Had they taken care of her? At first glance, she hadn't noticed any visible injuries, but she needed to be examined by doctors.

While Daisy slept, she fended off images of Derrick being harmed and phoned her captain to fill him in.

"I don't think I was followed, but I can't be sure our cover wasn't blown. I'm driving Daisy straight to the hospital," she said. "Hopefully Agent Fox will catch this guy and bring him in."

"The sheriff just called for an update. He can meet you at the hospital. Deputy Eastwood and the Trumans are here for the interview with Gomez."

"Do me a favor and don't tell Angelica what happened yet. I don't want it leaked that we recovered Daisy until we've verified her ID and investigated her family situation."

"Understood. Let me know if you need anything."

Ellie thanked him, then disconnected and focused on the road.

Rain turned to sleet, pebble-like ice pelting her windshield. She flipped on the wipers and defroster, scanning the highway for black ice as she maneuvered the narrow country road and wound down the mountain.

Twenty minutes later, she veered into the parking lot for Bluff County Hospital's emergency room. She opened the back door then scooped Daisy into her arms.

"Oh, my gosh," a nurse gasped as Ellie ran inside with the child.

"Her name is Daisy," Ellie said. "No visible injuries but she's traumatized. I need a child psychologist and a pediatrician down here ASAP."

"Of course," said the nurse, pulling her phone from her pocket and making a call.

She disappeared inside, and Ellie looked up to see blue lights twirling in the darkness. The sheriff's car roared into the parking lot, then Bryce climbed out and jogged inside. His gaze swept the waiting room then he rushed toward her. "Captain Hale called."

Ellie nodded, grateful Bryce looked clear-eyed. She adjusted Daisy on her hip. She couldn't stand to think about that awful group selling children like cattle.

"Where's Agent Fox?"

"Chasing the man who delivered Daisy."

Protective instincts she'd never seen before flickered in his eyes as his gaze fell on Daisy. "Is she okay?"

"I think so but waiting on the doctors."

The nurse reappeared. "Follow me. The child psychologist and pediatrician are on their way."

"Thank you." Carrying Daisy, Ellie followed the nurse through a set of double doors to an ER room. Daisy stirred and looked up at her as she eased her onto the bed. "It's okay, sweetie," hushed Ellie. "You're safe now."

Bryce stood at the door watching quietly, while Daisy pressed the unicorn to her cheek, a tear streaming down her face.

"My name is Ellie," she said softly. "I'm with the police and I'm here to help you. Is your name Daisy?"

Big doe eyes stared at her, then the girl gave a weak nod. "Yes."

"What's your last name, sweetie?

Daisy licked her lips, then whispered, "Pridgen."

The child psychologist, a thirty-something woman with white-blond hair, a friendly smile and soft blue eyes, entered and introduced herself as Dr. Beth Laurens. "Hello, Detective. Nurse Nancy explained to me what happened."

Ellie nodded, then spoke in a low voice. "Her name is Daisy Pridgen. I was told her mother was homeless and her father was deceased. I found her with a group called MWC who deal in trafficking children, and I think she was abducted. But I don't know details."

"I understand," Dr. Laurens said. "I'll talk to her. But this is going to take time. Why don't you step outside and give us a few minutes?"

Ellie hated to leave Daisy, but the doctor knew best so she gave the little girl a hug. "I'll be right outside. And don't be scared. You're safe now."

Choking back emotions, Ellie slipped outside the curtained room, grateful to have saved Daisy. But where was Ava?

NINETY-THREE

NEAR BEAR MOUNTAIN

Dammit, he should have been able to take the bastard alive.

The Evidence Response Team showed up and Derrick explained what had happened, then a medic cleaned his wound where the bullet had grazed him.

The ME, Dr. Laney Whitefeather, also arrived. She'd worked for them on previous cases—she was a professional and cool in times of crisis.

"I need his ID ASAP." Derrick showed one of the ERT investigators the wallet he'd found in the man's vehicle. "I'll have my colleagues at the Bureau verify this is his real name. He's with a group selling children. Ellie and I suspected they might have abducted Ava so we were working undercover."

Laney adjusted her kit in her hand. "Did they have her?"

"I don't know yet. They offered us another child. Ellie rescued her and drove her to the hospital to be examined."

"Was she injured or abused?" Laney asked, her mouth drawn with worry.

"I didn't see any apparent bruises or injuries, but she's traumatized. No telling how long these people were holding her or what the conditions."

The ERT investigator bagged the wallet, and Laney turned her attention to the body where it lay in a pool of blood. "Get them, Agent Fox. Make them pay."

"I intend to." Derrick texted his partner with the ID on the man's driver's license, along with the phone number attached to it. *Dig into this guy. He made the drop with the child. Any word on the address for the group's headquarters?*

Bennett responded: *Not yet but we're getting closer. Will work on that trace.*

While the team gathered forensics and bagged the man's gun, Derrick searched the contacts on the man's phone. There were a couple of restaurants, a body shop, and the number for an urgent care facility.

He checked the recent call history and found an unlisted number, but no name. Then a text that had come through a few minutes ago.

Sweat beaded his neck as he read the message.

Is it done?

Derrick stabbed his thumbs at the phone in a return text. *Job complete. Where do I drop the girl?*

Ellie paced the waiting room while Daisy was examined, and Bryce went to check on the deputy guarding Grueler. A group of women had shown up outside the hospital to protest, and he had to defuse the situation.

Better Bryce go than her, especially since he admitted that his own mother was one of the protestors.

A commotion sounded at the ER entrance, and the doors swished open. Cord and the medics pushed in a gurney with a bleeding unconscious woman lying on it. "Possible concussion, broken wrist, cuts and abrasions. Pulse low and thready..."

The voices faded around Ellie as the doctor rushed to the woman's side. "Car accident?"

"No, some teenagers found her at Hangman's Dome and called the rangers," Cord said. "Smashed her head into some rocks. Police are there investigating."

The doctor started barking orders about which tests to run as they pushed the injured woman through the double doors to an exam room.

Cord's eyes lifted when he saw Ellie. "Did you find Ava?"

Ellie shook her head and relayed their investigation into MWC. "What happened with the woman?"

"Not sure yet if it was an accident, attempted suicide, or if she was pushed. I saw scuff marks as if someone else was there though. One of the sheriff's deputies is checking it out."

The pediatrician, a young woman with red hair and a warm smile, appeared. Her name tag read Dr. Norah Samuels, and a tiny stuffed panda bear was attached to her stethoscope.

"Can we speak in private?" the doctor asked with a look at Ellie.

"Sure."

"See you later, Ellie," Cord said. "Call me if you need me."

She murmured she would then turned to the pediatrician. "How's Daisy?"

"Physically okay. It looks like she's been fed and taken care of. I didn't find any signs of physical or sexual abuse."

"Thank God," Ellie whispered, her shoulders slumping with relief.

"The emotional ramifications of what she's been through may have long-lasting effects, though. I'm certain Dr. Laurens will suggest counseling once her family is located."

"I'm not sure if she has a family to go back to, but we'll look." Ellie explained about MWC and the information they'd provided. "Much of that could have been lies, though. We'll do everything possible to locate relatives."

Concern laced the pediatrician's voice when she spoke. "Good. Meanwhile, we'll arrange foster care. A local woman Emily Nettles has fostered in the past and hopefully will take her. I'll give her a call myself."

Ellie's heart ached for the frightened little girl. Part of her was tempted to take her home herself but her job wasn't conducive for that.

And right now that job was to find Ava.

"I know Emily. Thank you, placing her there would be perfect," Ellie agreed.

Dr. Samuels nodded, then headed down the hall and the psychologist stepped out of the room.

"Can I talk to her now?" Ellie asked.

"In a minute," Dr. Laurens said. "According to Daisy, her mother got sick and lost her job and they were living in their car. Her mother mentioned getting them to a shelter, but they never made it. The mother passed out and a lady came by, told her she was with social services and took Daisy."

So that part of the story was somewhat true. But Ava hadn't been homeless.

"Did she mention the woman's name?"

Dr. Laurens shook her head. "No, but she was kept in a basement for a while. She has no idea where, except she saw a lot of trees everywhere she looked."

Damn, that could be anywhere. "We're searching for another girl who was abducted, Ava Truman," Ellie said.

"Yes. I saw the news." The doctor dug her hands in the deep pockets of her cardigan. "Do you think this is connected?"

"That's what I'm trying to determine." She pulled her phone from her belt. "Is it all right if I show Daisy Ava's picture?"

The doctor breathed out a sigh. "If it'll help find Ava. But please, Detective, be gentle. She's been through a lot."

Ellie nodded and headed into the room with Dr. Samuels. Daisy was squeezing the unicorn and rubbing its ears as she entered.

"Hi, Daisy," Ellie said softly. "How are you feeling?"

The little girl shrugged.

"I know it's been a rough day and you're frightened," Ellie said. "But I'm your friend. And so is Dr. Samuels. We want to keep you safe."

Daisy gave a timid nod. "You won't make me go back to that basement?"

Ellie shook her head. "No, we're going to find out what happened with your parents. Until then you'll stay in a nice home with a really sweet lady named Ms. Emily."

The doctor chimed in. "You'll love her. She has four kids of her own and loves children. Her house has a big playroom with toys and games and art supplies and a play yard outside."

Daisy seemed to relax into the covers.

"I know you've answered a lot of questions, and you're tired," Ellie said. "But I need to ask you a couple more. Were you the only child at this house?"

Daisy shook her head. "The boys stayed in a different room."

Ellie's stomach clenched. There *were* more children. She turned her phone around to show them Ava's photograph. "I've been looking for this little girl. Her name is Ava. Was she at the house with you?"

Daisy's pug nose wrinkled. "I didn't see her. But I heard the lady saying they were getting a new girl."

Ellie's pulse spiked. The new little girl could be Ava.

NINETY-FIVE

LONGNECK CREEK

Derrick left Dr. Whitefeather with the shooter and ERT to process the scene then phoned Ellie and filled her in. Anxious to find Ava, she hurried outside the hospital and climbed in his car.

"The meetup is at a place called Longneck Creek," Derrick said. "Do you know it?"

"I think so." Ellie accessed a topographical map on her phone. "There it is. It's in a remote stretch that once housed warehouses for trucking supplies. Those warehouses have been torn down and now it looks like acres of undeveloped farmland." She consulted her GPS and directed him as he maneuvered onto the country road that led into the hills. The sleet intensified, adding to the hazardous conditions with strong wind gusts hurling branches across the road, rattling the car and pushing it sideways.

"This group either figured out who we were," Ellie said, "or they're con artists working both sides."

"That's what I figured too," Derrick replied.

The road veered around a steep incline then wound downhill to a flatter area with a thin creek running through the land. It looked as if they were in the middle of nowhere.

"This is off-the-grid," Ellie said. "There's no way these people are living out here, not unless they have a house hidden in the hills."

"If anything, it's a drop spot," Derrick said. "Or—"

"A trap," Ellie said, finishing his sentence.

"Most likely," Derrick agreed. "Right before I picked you up, Bennett called. He traced MCW's headquarters to a house in the Atlanta suburbs."

"Close to the airport, bus and train stations," Ellie said with a grimace.

Derrick parked beneath a cluster of thin pines, his gaze scanning the area, while Ellie surveyed the property with her binoculars. "Look—there's a dirt road leading into the woods."

Derrick started the engine again and drove onto the narrow dirt drive. Giant oaks and hemlocks surrounded them on all sides, the limbs low and closing in on them. Icy rain slashed the windshield, wet leaves clinging to it as he parked.

They pulled on ski hats and coats then climbed out, guns concealed and ready as they hiked into the woods. Afternoon shadows filtered through the rows of trees, the gray skies threatening even worse weather. Icy sludge crunched beneath Ellie's boots as she trekked around one fork and then another.

A vulture circled in the distance, and she ducked her head as the rain and sleet dripped off her hood. Maneuvering the cut-throughs and rocky terrain slowed them, but finally they reached the crest where the road ended at a cabin. She spotted the white utility van that had been at Bear Mountain. A black Cadillac sat next to it.

Ellie motioned to Derrick in confirmation, and they crept forward, weaving along the edge of the road and staying low until they were near enough to see that the car was empty. She inched up to the van and peeked through the windows. Van was empty, too.

But a light was burning inside the log cabin ahead.

Was Ava in there?

NINETY-SIX

SOMEWHERE ON THE AT

The sleet sounded like baseballs slamming against the tin roof of the house as she rushed back inside. She was still wired from meeting Priscilla, but hopefully her problem was solved now. Priscilla wouldn't be going to the cops or that damn reporter.

She wouldn't be going anywhere. And if that Jan woman caused trouble, she'd end up just like her friend.

She stopped at the sink to catch her breath, washed her hands, then forced herself to act normal.

Hoping to distract Kaylee, who was terrified of storms, she set the box of wooden ornaments on the table along with paints, then went to fetch the girls. While her husband sat with Becky, Kaylee and Ava were watching *The Grinch Who Stole Christmas*.

"Come on, girls," she said as she paused the movie. "We're going to decorate ornaments!"

Kaylee stood and clasped Ava's hand and coaxed her to follow. Kaylee was such a sweet, docile child, but Ava had a fierce stubborn streak.

Piper had never been stubborn or talked back. She was the perfect angel.

Ava would be, too. One day. She had to be patient. Give her

time to adjust. She would learn it was better to have a family than be alone.

Fresh pain stabbed through her chest where the hollow ache never seemed to cease. She knew all about being alone and the heartbreak of losing a loved one.

Kaylee smiled as she found the ornaments on the table, then selected a snowflake to paint. Ava chose a plain round ball.

While they began to dabble with the colors, she accessed the photographs she'd snapped of the next child on her list.

Sarah was her name.

The date on the calendar taunted her. Two days until Christmas. Her lungs clawed for air. In her mind, she could see Piper racing to the tree to find the presents Santa had left her, ripping open packages and tossing the bows in the air like confetti.

Her family had to be complete this year. She couldn't live without her baby girl any longer.

"I'll be right back, girls. Those look beautiful." She hurried to the living room then heard Silas leave Becky's room and go into his home office. He'd been locking himself in there more and more this month, sullen and silent, not spending time with the family. It was almost as if the more she wanted them all together, the more he withdrew.

She eased open the door to tell him she had another errand to do and ask him to watch the girls but found him looking at the news on his computer.

"Look at this," he said, his tone guarded. "Ava's parents are on TV pleading for whoever kidnapped their daughter to bring her back."

She turned away as the couple clung to each other crying. She didn't care what those people had to say. She wasn't a kidnapper. She just took what was rightfully hers.

They were not getting Ava back.

"I have to go out for a while."

"Again?" He stood and grabbed her arms, the frown lines around his eyes deepening as he scowled at her. "Where to this time? To steal someone else's daughter? For God's sake, look at those people's faces."

"What about *our* family?" she spat. "Or don't you care? You just let our baby die—"

Pain tore through his eyes. "This has to stop," he said, his teeth clenched. "You have to get some help. Go back to that counselor Emily and talk to her."

"I don't need help," she screeched. "I need my baby back and you killed her."

He shook her hard, but suddenly she heard Kaylee shouting, "Mommy, Mommy!"

The shrill sound of Kaylee's voice sent a jolt of fear through her, and she shoved at her husband, turned and ran back to the kitchen.

"What's wrong?" she said as she bolted into the room.

"Ava's gone."

Heart hammering, she looked up and saw the back door was open, frigid air swirling inside, rain running like a river across the backyard, reminding her of the awful night when her husband had killed her daughter. The world blurred and she was catapulted back to that horrible day.

NINETY-SEVEN
CATTAIL COVE

"Why did we have to come tonight?" she grumbled as she followed Silas and Piper along the path toward Cattail Cove. "It's too cold to be out here."

"I promised Piper I'd show her the cattails," her husband said. "It's rare to find them up here in the winter. But the climate here is odd right now, a mix of warm humidity with the trees shrouding the murky pond water. And Piper is so excited."

Their daughter was definitely excited. She'd been bouncing all over the place all day. But she had a bad feeling that it wasn't safe in these woods. All around her, wild animals scuttled about, and on the drive here, the weatherman had warned a freak tornado might strike in the mountains. Last year one had ripped through, tearing ancient trees from the ground and demolishing homes and trailers like a bulldozer.

"I think I see them, Daddy!" Piper burst into a sprint, singing at the top of her lungs.

Silas yelled at Piper to wait, but she skipped ahead. Pure panic ripped through her and she darted forward, jogging to catch her daughter. She jumped over a patch of briars and a fallen log, sweat trickling down her neck as she shouted. Suddenly Piper hit the icy pond at full run, skating across it, arms flying around her to keep her balance.

"Piper, stop!" she called.

"It may not be completely frozen," Silas yelled.

She stepped onto the pond. Oblivious, Piper was twirling and dancing and leaping like a ballerina.

The sound of ice splintering rent the air and sent her heart pounding so loud she heard the blood roaring in her ears.

A faint sliver of moonlight illuminated the slip of her little girl crashing through the ice and plunging below. Her puffy pink jacket... the bob of her ski cap, one pink-gloved hand clawing at the ice and air and disappearing.

The shrill scream of Piper's tiny voice boomeranging off the ridges filled her ears as she flew across the thin sheet of ice, grabbing and screaming and flailing to reach her. Ice popped and broke beneath her, and her boots hit the cold water, the freezing sludge swallowing her.

The light dimmed and dark surrounded her, but she kicked and pummeled her arms and hands, searching for her baby. But the cold and dark had trapped her, and Piper was lost as the frigid, swirling water dragged her away.

NINETY-EIGHT

SOMEWHERE ON THE AT

Ava ran as fast as her legs could carry her. Down the steps and across the big backyard and into the scary woods. But the ground was damp, and she kept sliding, her sneakers sinking into the mud. Big balls of sleet stung her cheeks.

Tears burned her throat and she blinked, wiping at the rain running into her eyes.

She ducked beneath the cover of a giant tree. Then she peered down the hill to the place she'd seen through the upstairs window. She thought she'd seen a light down there in the middle of the trees out back. If she could make it there, maybe someone would help her. She hated the lady who lied to her and made her sing and smile for pictures and wear stupid dresses and drink her milk.

The cold wind just about knocked her over, and she wanted to scream. But if she did the lady might hear her and drag her back to the house. And she didn't want to go back there. She wanted to go home.

She'd seen the calendar counting down the days until Christmas. Two more days and Santa would come. She had to be home or he wouldn't know where to find her. And she'd never get her puppy.

A sob clogged her throat. On Christmas Eve, she and Mommy

always set out a plate of sugar cookies and milk for Santa, and carrots for the reindeer. They would starve if she didn't feed them.

What was Mommy doing now? Did she miss her?

She shivered as the wind cut into her, her breath puffing out in a big cloud as she stumbled forward.

The ground was slick, and she fell and skidded down a hill, bumping over bushes and thorns. But she couldn't stop herself. She clawed at the ground and a tree as she whizzed by it on her bottom.

What if there was a bear? Or a mountain lion?

Weeds scratched at her arms and legs as she kept sliding, past a briar patch then finally skidding into a muddy hole and stopping. Tears pricked her eyes as her hand scraped the bark. She wished she had gloves and a coat. But the lady had taken them. She was a bad mommy.

Her real mommy always bundled her up before she went out in the snow.

She had to get back to her.

A light flickered through the trees. A voice yelling her name.

Run, Ava, run.

She pushed up to her feet, wiping her muddy hands on her pants, and took off again. She rubbed her side where a stitch grabbed at her. The big trees stood as tall as towers. She couldn't push past them. Rain and sleet burned her eyes. She couldn't see where she was going.

A noise boomed through the woods, and she ducked behind a big bush looking for the light. Down the hill somewhere. Where?

She heard the voices again. "Ava! Come back, Ava!"

Her feet dug into the slushy ground. Cold water and ice soaked into her socks. Her toes tingled. Holding onto the trees to keep from getting stuck, she pushed ahead. She couldn't go back to that place. Not to the lady.

The wind knocked at her and made it hard to stand. Clumps of ice fell from the trees and hit her shoulders. Tears streaked her cheeks, freezing on her skin, and she finally found the light again. She darted toward it, down another hill and around a curve, then stopped. She knew where she was—Spruce Tree Farm, where they grew the Christmas trees. She and mommy had come here to cut down their tree a couple of weeks ago! Maybe there would be people here to help her!

Ava remembered a hut where they sold Christmas wreaths and garlands. And they'd had hot chocolate with the little marshmallows floating on top. There were kids and mommies and daddies picking their trees. She and Mommy took silly pictures by the big sleigh. Then they'd cut down the biggest tree ever and carried it home. It was so tall they had to lay it sideways to get it in the house and Mommy laughed and laughed and so did Ava.

Wiping blood from her scratched hands on her shirt, she ran down the hill toward the shack. But she looked around and the parking lot was empty. There weren't any people here tonight. Where was everybody?

Tears filled her throat. They were home with their families. She wanted that too.

Her feet hurt and her arms ached as she ducked underneath the roof of the shack. Hay was stacked in one corner. She huddled behind it for a minute to get warm, then looked out at the miles of trees and the empty road. Closing her eyes, she tried to remember which way was home. When she and Mommy came here, they drove a long way. She remembered farms and old houses and a barn that had burned. And a few houses, but they were far, far, far away.

Her feet and hands were numb. Her eyes felt heavy, and she was so tired, she couldn't run anymore.

She pressed her hands over her eyes and tried to think. Even if she ran down that road, it would take her forever to find another house. It was dark, too, the wind colder. Night-time.

Mommy always said prayers at night. Shaking all over, she buried her head against her raised knees and prayed the lady wouldn't find her.

NINETY-NINE

LONGNECK CREEK

Derrick and Ellie crept up to the house and he peered through the window. A tall man with a goatee and angular face stood arguing with a rail-thin woman who wore her hair in an austere bun. Serena. Her cheekbones were so stark the bones practically poked through her pale skin. The black pants and black jacket made her look even more imposing, as she shook her finger at the man.

"I told you I had a bad feeling about that couple," Serena said. "I thought I'd seen that woman before."

Dammit, in spite of the wig Ellie had worn, the woman must have recognized her from the news.

Ellie nudged his arm. "The man is armed."

Derrick gave a quick nod.

"Where's Daisy?" the woman asked.

"Buck went to retrieve them. I received a text. He should be here soon."

"I don't like this." The woman paced back and forth, her heels tapping on the old oak floor. "We're going to have to lie low for a few days until the dust settles." She tapped her phone. "I'll call Yates about changing our security and delete recent correspondence with potential clients."

Derrick gestured to Ellie that they should move before the

woman had the chance. Releasing his weapon, he eased open the door then stormed inside, gun drawn. "FBI," he shouted.

The man spun around, reaching for the weapon on his hip.

"Don't do it," Ellie snarled. "Raise your hands."

Serena startled, then started to run toward the back, Derrick shook his head, eyes piercing her. "I won't hesitate to shoot," he said coldly.

Serena halted with a grunt, and the man's fingers wiggled as if he was going to make a play for his gun. "Put your hands in the air," Ellie ordered, her Glock trained directly on him.

Serena raised her hands and the man went still, before he slowly lifted them.

Ellie removed handcuffs from her pocket, crossed the room in two angry strides, and grabbed the woman's arms.

"I didn't do anything," Serena said shrilly.

"You're selling children," Ellie growled, then shoved the picture of Ava in front of the woman's face. "Have you seen her?"

"No. She's not one of ours."

Ellie flashed Autumn's picture next. "How about this woman?"

Serena's lips compressed into a thin line.

Ellie jerked her again. "Do you know her?"

"Yes," Serena said. "She brought us Daisy. I told her we only accepted homeless kids," she admitted. "We were trying to help them. Give them real families."

"Don't pretend like you care. You took homeless kids because no one would look for them. And so you could make a profit." Ellie jerked her around to face her, seething.

Derrick was going to throw the book at her and Autumn. But for now he kept his attention on the man who looked like he was going to run.

"You have the right to remain silent..." Ellie began.

While she read the woman her Miranda rights, the man suddenly bolted. Derrick sprinted after him, his boots pounding the floor, cold air slapping him in the face as he made it to the kitchen. The back door flew open and the man barreled down the steps.

"Stop!" Derrick yelled as he raced after him. But the bastard kept running around the side of the house, heading to his van. Derrick's shoes dripped with thick sludge as he ran to the front. The man jerked the van door open and started to climb inside, but Derrick shouted at him, then fired his gun at the car tire.

The man spun around, raised his weapon and released a bullet. Cursing, Derrick ducked behind the side of the house, then fired a shot in return. The bullet pinged by the man's head, and he dove into the front seat. Staying low, Derrick crept toward the driver's door, then aimed his weapon at the man's head. "Drop the gun or you're dead," Derrick ordered.

He dropped it with a loud curse. Breath heaving, Derrick dragged him from the car and handcuffed his hands behind his back. When he looked up, Ellie was shoving the woman, who held her head high, toward them.

"Call an ERT, and I'll search the house," Ellie said. "If she's lying and Ava's here, I'll find her."

ONE HUNDRED

CROOKED CREEK

Ava wasn't at the cabin.

Ellie sighed in frustration as she and Derrick escorted Serena and her accomplice into the police station. The sheriff met them there with Autumn, who took one look at Serena and asked for a deal.

"I'll question Autumn," Derrick said. "Then we're going to throw the book at her."

Bryce's glare scalded Ellie. "Once again, you should have called me to be in on this, Detective."

"We had information and had to act quickly," Ellie said, unwilling to take the bait. "But you're here now—if you want to question Serena's partner and see if he'll give up details of MWC, I'll push the woman." After all, she was the one in charge. Let Bryce feel like he was going head-to-head with the brawn.

Serena lawyered up the moment they'd arrived.

Ellie didn't bother to hide her disgust as she entered the interrogation room and faced her.

After seeing the fear in Daisy's eyes and knowing what Lara was going through, she despised this woman with every fiber of her being.

"I'm Detective Reeves," she said curtly as she dropped into the chair and faced the woman and the lawyer, Wyatt Humphries, she was hiding behind. She'd already planned her strategy. Derrick might not approve, but right now she didn't care. "I have just come from the hospital with a very frightened little girl who has been severely traumatized by your efforts to sell her on the black market."

Serena's unflinching steely gaze met hers, but Ellie met her with equal animosity.

"Whether you realize it or not, Ms. Morino, we already have enough evidence to put you away on charges of child kidnapping, child endangerment, trafficking children, and... I don't know, a half dozen other charges."

"You're bluffing, Detective," Humphries said. "You can't possibly make all those charges stick."

Ellie cleared her throat. "Actually, we can. The FBI has already tracked information on the dark web for the group called MWC that your client runs, and special agents and a SWAT team are storming their primary location now." The evidence bag holding Serena's cell phone crinkled as she waved it in front of the attorney's face. "Amazing how much information our phones hold, isn't it?" she said with a challenging look.

"I told you we're providing a service, arranging adoptions for needy children and helping parents who are desperate to have children," Serena insisted.

"At the bargain price of a hundred K," Ellie snapped.

The lawyer shifted. "Come on, Detective," he said. "You're just blustering now. That's entrapment."

Ellie saw red. She stood and placed both hands on the table. "Maybe a judge will see it that way. Maybe not. Frankly, Ms. Morino, you're in my jurisdiction now and the only thing I care about is finding this little girl." She slapped a picture of Ava onto the table. "You see, Ava had surgery a year ago and she needs immunosuppressive medication for a transplant she had and could die without it. If you have endangered her life in any way this is not going to go well for you, even with your pricey attorney."

The attorney shuffled in his seat, his eyes flashing with nerves.

The woman's seething look settled on Ellie, but then she gave a quick glance at the picture.

"Did you take her?" Ellie hit the table with her fist for emphasis.

The lawyer leaned toward his client, using his hand to shield his mouth as he whispered something to her. Serena listened, then gave a little nod and lifted her chin, a gleam in her eyes. "I told you no, that we only took homeless kids because we were doing them a service." She tilted her head, "Besides, if she had health conditions, it would be harder to place her."

"Now, my client answered your question, Detective," the attorney said. "She is not responsible for that little girl's disappearance." He stood with a dramatic flare. "Let's go, Serena."

Ellie folded her arms. "Not so quickly."

"You said all you were interested in was knowing whether she abducted Ava," he said with a snap to his eyes. "And she didn't."

Ellie stepped away. "I did. And I am done with her. But the FBI is not." She gestured toward Derrick as he entered. "She's all yours, Special Agent Fox."

ONE HUNDRED ONE

Derrick decided to let Serena stew in a cell for a while, hoping a big dose of reality would encourage her to talk. Bennett had called, saying he found an offshore account with half a million in it in Autumn's name.

"If you expect any kind of deal, then you'd better cooperate," he said tersely. Using that information, he spent the next half hour grilling Autumn, who spilled the beans quickly.

"I was only trying to help those poor kids," Autumn said. "They were starving and living in cardboard boxes."

"How many did you take?"

Autumn worried her bottom lip with her teeth. "Just three."

"Are you sure?"

"Yes," Autumn said.

"You kidnapped them for money," Derrick said in disgust. "And you're going to jail for it." He shoved a pad of paper in front of her. "Make a list of their names, where you found them and the dates."

The lawyer nudged her with a hand, indicating she should cooperate.

Bennett was calling as Derrick made it back to Ellie's office. "We found three other children at the headquarters," his partner said after they'd searched the house. "All boys. No Ava. We'll have them examined, determine their IDs and notify next of kin."

"Good. Ms. Juniper is making a list of the children she abducted so we can compare. How about evidence on the group and how widespread their operation is?"

"We're confiscating all the computers and will have the cyber team analyze them. But judging from the evidence I found here, they mainly deal in the States. Hopefully, we'll find contacts for all those involved in the laptop and have arrested two men who were here manning the phone and monitoring the boys." He sighed. "We should have enough to bust this group wide open and shut them down," Bennett said.

"And track down the children they sold," Derrick replied. "Even if they were all homeless as Morino insisted, some may have families looking for them."

"We'll organize a task force to look into each case," Bennett said.

"Good work," Derrick said. Although as he disconnected, his gut pinched. He should feel victorious after tracking down this group.

But Ava's name wasn't on the list, and Serena and Autumn had denied taking her. If they hadn't abducted Ava, who had?

ONE HUNDRED TWO

In the conference room, Ellie studied the whiteboard, her head starting to throb again. Another night was setting in and she still had no good news to report to the Trumans.

A commotion sounded from the front area, and she went to the bullpen, finding Angelica and her cameraman talking to the sheriff.

Angelica began the interview right away. "We're coming to you live from Crooked Creek's Police Station where Sheriff Waters is prepared to make a statement."

Ellie glared at Bryce, but he seemed unfazed. "This evening, in conjunction with the FBI, Bluff County Sheriff's Department and Crooked Creek PD busted a child kidnapping and trafficking group who called themselves MWC, an acronym for Mother Wants Child." He paused. "Detective Ellie Reeves was instrumental in rescuing a little girl from the hands of the group and I just spoke with Special Agent Derrick Fox who stated that the FBI located the group's headquarters. Three boys were at the house and are being examined by pediatricians. At this time, I cannot release the names of the children as we're working on confirming identities and contacting their families."

Angelica angled the microphone toward herself. "Sheriff, was Ava Truman among the rescued children?"

Bryce's loaded gaze met Ellie's, and she felt her phone vibrating on her hip.

"I'm sorry to report that Ava Truman was not one of the little girls rescued in this operation." Bryce sighed. "She is still missing at this time, and we are doing everything possible to find her. Once again, we implore those with any information regarding her disappearance to call the tip line."

Bryce raised a questioning brow, silently asking if she had anything to add, and Ellie shook her head. He'd already said it all.

Her phone vibrated again, flashing with the Trumans' name. Angry and bottled with frustration over the case, she hurried into her office and shut the door.

The Trumans had most likely seen the news. She'd wanted to spare them that, but once again, Bryce hadn't been able to keep his mouth shut. He'd called Angelica so he could gain the glory for the arrest.

ONE HUNDRED THREE
BLACK GUM AVENUE

Jan's stomach roiled as she watched Angelica Gomez interview the Bluff County sheriff. The police had just busted a child kidnapping ring.

Cold sweat exploded on her neck and her mouth suddenly felt dry. What if that same group had kidnapped her daughter?

Horrified at the thought that Becky had been sold, she turned to the Facebook group and posted, addressing Priscilla.

Jan: *Saw the news about that child kidnapping ring. Makes me wonder if my little girl was taken by them.*

She waited several minutes but Priscilla didn't respond. Anxious, she drummed her fingers on the table, then sent Priscilla a private message.

Jan: *Priscilla, are you there? Did you call that detective or the reporter?*

Another few minutes dragged by, and she decided to call the woman. She'd stored her number when she'd posted it a while back. But the phone rang and rang and then went to voicemail.

"Priscilla, it's Jan Hornsby from Facebook. Please call me," she said, her pulse quickening. "I just saw news about a child kidnapping ring. I think we should call the police. Let them know to ask about Kaylee and Becky."

ONE HUNDRED FOUR

SPRUCE TREE FARMS

Ava was so cold she couldn't stop shaking.

She peered over the haystack and thought she saw an animal outside the shack. Maybe a wolf or coyote. Its beady eyes seemed to be looking for her.

She shivered and rubbed at her arms to try to get warm. But she had to be quiet or he'd find her and eat her alive.

Monsters were hiding between the big trees. Their eyes glowed in the dark like a spooky owl's eyes. The snakes and spiders and other animals were crawling through the forest, too. She had to be still. Quiet.

Cold rainwater beat at her, and balls of sleet banged the wood shack so hard she thought it was going to fall down on her.

For a minute, she thought about running some more. But she was so tired and her feet hurt and she was freezing. And she had no idea which way the road was. If she ran into the woods, she'd get lost and no one would ever find her. The boys at school had told her bad people lived in the caves. Bad men that would cut her head off if she got near them and then feed her to the wolves.

She closed her eyes and pictured her mommy decorating the sugar cookies they always baked together. She saw the little presents her mommy lined up on the mantle, pictured the snow globes and the reindeer and Santas. Last year Mommy had hidden a bright red bicycle outside and they had a scavenger hunt to find it.

Her lip quivered. Swiping at her tears with the back of her hand, she stared into the dark again. There was no way she could find her way tonight. The cold wind whirled loose hay around her. The puddles of water grew bigger.

In the woods, she thought she saw a flicker of light up the hill. She curled into herself and tried to make herself as small as she could, peering between her fingers.

No, it wasn't a light. It was the beady eyes of a monster coming for her...

ONE HUNDRED FIVE

"Ava! Ava where are you?" Silas trudged through the mud, shining his flashlight across the wet grass and weeds. The rain made it impossible to follow the girl's footprints and he had no idea where she'd run.

But he had to find her.

He'd already killed his own daughter. He couldn't let Ava die, too. And then there was Becky... She wasn't doing well. She needed medical attention.

But if he carried her to the hospital, he'd have to explain. Then they'd arrest him and his wife.

And he'd lose everything.

He was starting not to care... everything he'd loved was falling apart anyway. He'd ruined it all. Destroyed everything he'd ever believed in. The nightmares of killing Piper tormented him day and night. He couldn't live with another child's death on his conscience.

But he couldn't betray his wife. Couldn't send her to prison. She'd never survive.

Rain slashed his face and coat as he hurried across the rocky terrain. The wind swirled wet leaves from the trees, sending them in a blinding haze. Sleet pounded the ground at his feet.

His flashlight lit on a patch of weeds, and he spotted a torn piece of fabric caught in it. It was from Ava's shirt.

Damn, she'd run out without a coat or hat or gloves. She could freeze.

He shined the light down the hill and into the woods in the distance. In spite of the frigid temperature, sweat beaded on his neck and trickled down his back. Even if she didn't freeze, she might get lost in the forest or fall and get hurt.

If he found her, his wife would punish her for running away.

Desperation ate at him. He panned the grassy land below the secluded house his wife had bought and saw the trees lined up for picking. All the good ones were gone now, the farm shop having shut down, leaving the area even more isolated. His wife had been careful not to let the girls outside while people combed the farm choosing and cutting down their own tree.

Seeing the families there, laughing, the kids running between the rows of pines, spruces and firs, had tormented him and made his wife cling to the girls even more. He'd been shocked at the lengths she'd resorted to in order to bring them here. When he'd seen the news last year about Kaylee's mother's suicide, he couldn't help wondering...

The sound of the wind howling made him step up his pace and he hurried down the hill, shining the light at the edge of the woods. For several minutes, he searched the trees, pausing to listen for a child crying.

"Ava, it's cold out here. Please let me take you back where it's warm!" he shouted.

Fear bolted through him as he trudged several feet and searched behind trees and stumps and in the bushes. "Ava!"

But his voice sounded muffled in the wind, and she was so tiny that if she did call out, he probably wouldn't hear her.

He spent the next half hour hacking at weeds and drudging through the murky vines. Turning in a wide arc, he looked back at the tree farm again, then decided to search there. Maybe Ava saw the hut and ran to it to escape the rain.

His boots skidded as he hurried along the edge of the woods, then down the hill, the cold biting through his coat. "Ava!"

The rain intensified, making visibility difficult, but he pushed on until he reached the small hut. The farm shop had shut down early this year because the owner had sold out, and it was deserted. The saplings which weren't mature enough for cutting swayed in the harsh wind gusts.

"Ava?" He shined the light across the ground and the sleigh where families enjoyed taking holiday pictures, then walked toward the hut. Hay had been stacked inside, and puddles of water circled the ground. He approached slowly, peering around the hut, then finally spotted Ava curled into a ball on the floor against the hay, her body trembling violently.

ONE HUNDRED SIX

Kaylee hugged her arms around herself as she stared out the window of the upstairs bedroom. After Ava had run off, Mommy had locked her in the room and told her it was her job to help Ava learn to be happy here.

She remembered how mad she'd been when the lady first brought her here too.

"You're mean, I want to go home," Kaylee yelled.

"This is your home now. Your mommy is dead," the lady said. "She's never coming back."

"No, you're lying," Kaylee shouted. "She can't be dead."

"She is." Then the lady showed her a newspaper picture of Mommy's grave.

She stared at it, crying. "That's all wrong. Mommy hated pink carnations. Aunt Prissy would never put them there."

"Well, somebody did," the lady said, her tone mad.

"Where's my aunt Prissy?" Kaylee whispered. "I want to go live with her."

"She doesn't want you. Now be quiet." Then the lady took her arm and dragged her to a room where it was dark and locked her inside. "You can come out when you calm down and can be nice."

She was terrified as she huddled in the dark. She thought Aunt

Prissy loved her. They had fun together making up silly songs and wearing funny hats. Aunt Prissy made funny face pancakes with chocolate chips and reindeer sandwiches at Christmas time. And when she babysat her, Aunt Prissy let her stay up late to watch movies.

Did she really not want her?

She pulled the blanket up to her chin with a shiver. She was terrified now, too. If they found Ava, the lady would be mad. No telling what she'd do to her. She'd already moved Becky into the other room. Kaylee hadn't seen her in days.

Secretly, part of her wanted Ava to get away.

But then she'd be alone again, and she didn't like being alone here. The trees and woods out there looked scary.

But so did her new Mommy.

ONE HUNDRED SEVEN

All she ever wanted was to be a mommy. To have a passel of kids to love and take care of. She remembered the day she'd brought Piper home from the hospital, dressed in a pink dress with that big purple bow around the soft strands of blond hair. Her tiny fingers curling around hers. The low suckling noise she'd made when she latched on and fed from her breast.

Then all her firsts. Her first smile. The day she'd rolled over in her crib. The moment she'd learned to crawl and pull up. The glorious day she'd taken her first step.

Then her first birthday with the smash cake and balloons and presents and she and Silas smiling and laughing as Piper dug her fists into the white frosting then smeared it on her cheeks.

But she'd only had her for six years. Then she'd been robbed of her precious baby.

She wrung her hands together, pacing by the fire, biting her tongue to keep from screaming. How dare Ava run away when she'd given her a nice home to live in and a beautiful family?

How dare she run out in this storm where something bad could happen to her?

Outside, the rain slammed the roof and cold air seeped through the eaves of the old farmhouse. She heard crying from Becky's room, then rushed in to check on her.

"I'm cold," Becky said, her teeth chattering.

"Shh, Mommy's here," she mumbled as she sank onto the bed beside Becky. Tenderly, she brushed her dark red bangs from her eyes and laid her hand over her forehead. It felt clammy and hot, and sweat dotted her forehead. Becky made a little mewling sound.

Worry formed a lump in her throat. Becky had been given her insulin regularly. But she definitely had a fever, maybe an infection.

She patted the little girl's shoulder. "I'll be right back." Rushing into the kitchen, she grabbed some children's painkillers and a damp washcloth and hurried back.

"Here, honey, take this. It'll help with your fever." She slipped her hand beneath Becky's head, then lifted her enough for the child to swallow the medication and a sip of water. Then Becky sank back beneath the covers, her face pale.

She rocked back in fear. Becky had to be all right. So did Ava. Hadn't her husband found her yet?

She sat for what seemed like forever, watching until Becky eased into a deep sleep, then she heard a noise in the kitchen. Tucking the covers over the child, she hurried into the kitchen and saw her husband carrying Ava inside.

The girl was soaking wet and crying, and she ran to her. But Ava curled away from her and into her husband's chest.

Rage shot through her. How could Ava choose him over her when he was a child-killer?

ONE HUNDRED EIGHT

BLACK GUM AVENUE

Tuesday, December 24

The tea kettle on the stove whistled shrilly, blending with the bitter gusts of wind pummeling Jan Hornsby's house. The sleet had sounded like golf balls banging the roof last night, but it wasn't the weather that had kept her tossing and beating her pillow.

Today was Christmas Eve. Every year she and Becky got up early and made waffles with strawberries dipped in powdered sugar, then baked a batch of sugar cookies to leave out for Santa. Before they finished, flour dusted everything in sight and sprinkles speckled the table and floor. With Becky's diabetes, she had to watch Becky's sugar intake. But she could handle one cookie every now and then if she managed her diet and insulin.

For the millionth time, mind-numbing pain gripped her, clutching at her with icy fingers.

Where was her precious little girl? Was she safe? Had those horrid people on the news sold her to someone else?

She checked her phone again, but there was no message or call from Priscilla. Nerves skittering through her, she had a feeling something was wrong. She dialed Priscilla's number again, but it went straight to voicemail.

Grief welled inside her as she glanced at Becky's picture, and she flipped on the morning news. First up was the weather report predicting the sleet might be turning to snow by nightfall.

Then Angelica Gomez reporting the latest on the other missing girl's case. And then the anchor moved on to the next story: *"Yesterday a young woman was found injured at Hangman's Dome and transported to Bluff County Hospital. Police have identified her as thirty-three year-old Priscilla Wilkinson. At this time, they are treating the accident as suspicious and are asking for anyone with information about the young woman to please call the police."*

Panic roared in Jan's ears. *Suspicious accident.*

It was suspicious, Jan thought. Priscilla had called that sheriff in Bluff County, but he'd blown her off. They'd talked about going to the reporter.

And now Priscilla was in the hospital.

She snatched her phone. Forget calling the sheriff.

She'd sent a message to the reporter earlier telling her there were more missing children, not to forget them. She'd hoped that would stir things up. Maybe she hadn't been direct enough.

Time to take the bull by the horns. Her fingers shaking, she dialed the number for the news station.

A woman who identified herself as Roberta answered. "How can I help you?"

"I need to speak to Angelica Gomez about the woman who was injured last night. Tell her to call me as soon as she gets this message. It's urgent." She left her number, then hung up and went to the kitchen.

The ingredients for the sugar cookies ridiculed her from the counter. Last night she'd gotten them out and thought she'd make them to honor Becky.

But this morning, she couldn't bear the thought. Angry and frustrated, she grabbed the flour and sugar and sprinkles and jammed them back in the cabinet. She slammed the door, the empty hollowness of the day mounting.

ONE HUNDRED NINE

CROOKED CREEK

One more day until Christmas.

Another day had passed without putting the Truman family back together again.

Ellie's nearly bare Christmas tree looked as depressing as she felt this morning. Vera had called after she'd seen the news report the night before, asking if she was all right.

Of course, she'd lied and said she was. Although nothing was right in the world when people sold children like objects.

She rubbed her throbbing head, ducked into the shower and let the warm water assuage her aching muscles while a fresh pot of coffee brewed. She quickly dressed in jeans, a denim shirt and thick socks, chilled just looking through the window at the gray skies. Everywhere she looked the bare branches hung heavy with the weight of the hailstorm. More clouds moved in, topping the sharp ridge and cliffs.

She blew her hair dry then pulled it back into a ponytail, hurrying to the kitchen for coffee. Her phone buzzed from the kitchen island, and she snagged it then checked the number, expecting it to be Derrick or Shondra. Her friend had her hands full the night before after the Trumans had seen the news.

Instead, Angelica's name appeared. She answered as she stirred sweetener into her coffee.

"Ellie, I just got a call from a woman named Jan Hornsby. You need to hear what she has to say."

"What's it about?"

"Just meet us at the police station."

The urgency in Angelica's tone made Ellie's heart skip a beat. Adrenaline surged through her. "See you in half an hour."

"We'll be there."

Ellie grabbed a bagel, smeared it with cream cheese then holstered up, dragged on her coat and gloves and poured her coffee to go. Outside, it took a minute for her defroster to warm up and the wipers to clear the frost on her windshield. Driving even the short distance to town meant watching for black ice. At least traffic was minimal. By now, most of the town had finished their Christmas shopping, and after last night's news report on MWC aired, families were probably tucked in their houses out of fear.

By the time she arrived, Angelica was parking. She and a thirty-something brunette climbed out, the woman bundled up, and Angelica in a red wool coat and hat. She always looked like dynamite, professional and ready to take on the world. Today an eagerness lit her eyes as if she knew she was on to something, but the other woman had a wariness in her eyes.

Ellie ushered them inside and Angelica made the introductions. "Let's grab coffee and go to my office," Ellie said leading them first to the coffee machine and then to the sitting area in the corner of her office, hoping the warm drink and more relaxed seating would ease the tension radiating from Jan Hornsby in thick waves.

"How can I help you?" Ellie asked.

Jan rubbed her fingers up and down the coffee mug, and Angelica offered her a tentative smile. "Jan saw the report about the woman who was brought into the hospital yesterday—Priscilla Wilkinson."

Ellie fought disappointment. She'd hoped this was about Ava.

"Do you know her, Jan?"

Jan nodded, her shoulders stiff. "We met on a Facebook support site that I started for mothers of missing children." Her breath gushed out shakily, and Ellie sat up straighter.

"Jan sent me that text about there being other children missing," Angelica explained.

"I was hoping to get your attention," Jan said.

Ellie's interest was piqued. "Go on."

"My daughter Becky was abducted six months ago in Chattanooga," Jan continued. "And Priscilla's niece Kaylee disappeared a year ago."

"I'm so sorry," Ellie said, her heart starting to thunder. "Did the police investigate?"

Jan ran her finger around the edge of her coffee cup. "Yes, but neither Kaylee or Becky have been found. The cop who investigated Kaylee's case arrested her mother and she died in prison."

Angelica pressed a hand to Jan's shoulder. "Tell her the rest. You can trust Detective Reeves. She'll help you."

"Yes, please talk to me," Ellie said softly.

Jan relaxed slightly. "Priscilla was told her sister Renee committed suicide, but she didn't believe it, only nobody would listen."

The hair on the nape of Ellie's neck prickled. "And you think her daughter's disappearance is connected to Ava's kidnapping?"

"Yes. We were both following the story about Ava Truman," she said. "Then Priscilla realized that Kaylee was abducted on the same day last year as Ava disappeared this year."

Ellie's blood ran cold. "Exactly a year apart?"

Jan nodded, her eyes bright with alarm. "We both thought that might mean something and I persuaded her to call the police tip line."

The tip line Bryce was monitoring. "And did she?"

"She did, but the sheriff blew her off."

Anger made Ellie grind her teeth. That was the call Bryce had told her about. "Then what happened?" she asked.

"Priscilla was upset and frustrated, so we decided to call Ms. Gomez. We thought she might take us seriously. I tried to contact Priscilla again and again, but suddenly she wasn't responding. That's not like her. We've gotten pretty close the last three months."

Ellie gave her a sympathetic smile. Their shared pain had obviously brought them together.

"Anyway, then I saw the news that Priscilla was in an accident."

"A suspicious one," Angelica said with a flicker of intrigue in her eyes.

"Yes, the ranger who found her said that there might have been a struggle," Ellie said.

"Don't you see?" Jan said, her tone shrill, desperate. "Whoever took Kaylee and maybe Becky could have found out Priscilla was going to the media and tried to kill her."

Ellie's mind raced to keep up. "I suppose that's possible," she said. "But how would that person know?"

"I don't have the answer to that," Jan said. "But it doesn't feel right."

"No, it certainly seems concerning," Ellie agreed.

"There's more," Angelica interjected. "Tell her more about Priscilla's sister."

"Renee, Kaylee's mother, was accused of criminal negligence the day Kaylee was taken," replied Jan. "According to the police, they thought she'd been drinking and passed out and Kaylee wandered off and drowned. But Priscilla swore that Renee didn't drink, that her sister had been in AA for two years." A fine sheen of perspiration covered Jan's forehead and neck and she dabbed at it with a tissue she pulled from the box on the table.

Ellie waited silently, giving her time to tell the story in her own time. "You mentioned she died in prison?"

Jan nodded. "Just a couple of weeks after the arrest. The police said it was suicide, but Priscilla insisted her sister wouldn't take her own life. That she was determined to find out what happened to her daughter."

Ellie and Angelica traded looks.

Red flags waved frantically in Ellie's mind. A possible murder and attempted murder of two family members related to a child abduction could not be a coincidence. And Jan was right—the fact that Kaylee and Ava disappeared exactly a year apart had to be significant.

ONE HUNDRED TEN

Ellie's mind raced with the implication that these cases were connected. She had to look into Kaylee Wilkinson's disappearance and her mother's death. But Jan Hornsby's daughter had also been abducted. Could the three kidnappings have been carried out by the same person?

The text Jan sent Angelica now made sense.

"I saw the story about that awful child kidnapping ring," Jan continued, her voice a pained sound. "Do you think they took Kaylee and my daughter?"

"I don't know, but I promise you I won't rest until I find out," Ellie said. "Tell me about what happened the day Becky went missing."

"That day is a blur," she said, her eyes cloudy with the memory. "They had a little fair at the park in Chattanooga with a puppet show Becky wanted to see. And there was a petting zoo and an adoption area for rescue dogs and cats. It was crowded with a lot of families." Her voice wavered. "Becky ran over to see the animals and I tried to catch her. I always told her to stay by my side, but she loves cats and dogs, and... she got away from me."

"All it takes is a minute," Ellie said to soothe the woman who she knew had probably blamed herself for months now. "Did you notice anyone paying special attention to Becky those last few weeks or days before she was abducted? Maybe a neighbor or someone at the park where she played?"

Jan shook her head. "I told the police all of this before. I mean there were other mothers and families there, but I kept a close eye on Becky because of her health issues. I was always overprotective."

"What health issues?" Ellie asked, instinct prickling.

"Becky is diabetic," Jan said. "She has to have her insulin." Tears glittered on the woman's long lashes. "I've been so afraid whoever kidnapped her isn't taking care of her."

Ellie barely kept from reacting. Going without her insulin could be deadly, just as not having her immunosuppressive drugs could endanger Ava.

"I'd like to speak to the detective in charge of Becky's case," Ellie said.

"Of course. His name is Manning." She pulled her phone and gave her the man's number. "I call him every week to make sure he hasn't forgotten about Becky."

Angelica patted her shoulder. "Leave that up to me. I'll run a series on missing children and include both Becky and Kaylee in it. I'll call it 'The Forgotten Girls'."

Jan wiped at fresh tears. "I can't tell you how glad I am to hear that. I... Some days it's been hard to go on. The only way I have is to imagine bringing Becky home one day."

"Let me check on Priscilla," Ellie said. "If she's awake, maybe she can shed some light on what happened to her."

She stepped over to her desk and called the hospital.

"She's pretty battered and in and out of consciousness," the nurse told her. "But you can see her for a few minutes."

After hanging up, she told Jan and Angelica. "Jan can ride with me," Angelica said.

Ellie sent her a thankful look. "Thanks. I'll meet you there."

On her way to the hospital, she phoned Detective Manning, the officer in charge of the Hornsby case.

"What can you tell me about the investigation?" Ellie asked.

"The mother doted on the child," Detective Manning said. "Her story checked out. Witnesses saw her with Becky at the park by the river. They seemed happy and were having fun. Becky got her face painted and while Jan paid the artisan, Becky ran toward the petting zoo. Jan went after her but she just disappeared into thin air." He paused. "I questioned everyone at the park, neighbors, friends, school staff, and Becky's mother's employee, who all stated that she was a caring, loving single mother."

Another single mother whose child had disappeared in the blink of an eye.

ONE HUNDRED ELEVEN
BLUFF COUNTY HOSPITAL

On the way to the hospital, Ellie called Derrick, and asked him to meet them to question Priscilla. The sleet had momentarily stopped, but a fog had developed, a strange murky scent in the air. A cloud of air burst from her lungs as she inhaled the freezing wind that screeched through the bare branches of the trees, and she rushed across the hospital lot, carefully avoiding patches of ice and puddles.

Derrick was waiting at the entrance, where Angelica and Jan joined her. She made quick introductions, then they walked to the nurses' station together.

"She is stable," said the nurse, "but has a concussion, multiple contusions and the doc casted her wrist, which was fractured." She dug her hands into the pockets of her uniform. "Frankly, she's lucky she didn't die from the fall. The doctor said only one or two visitors at a time. She needs her rest."

"I understand," Ellie said. "I'll go in first. And maybe you, Jan. It might help if she sees a friendly face."

Jan nodded. "Yes, please. We've been each other's support group for a while. And I feel terrible that she was hurt since I was the one who encouraged her to call the police."

Ellie glanced at Derrick. "Get her clothing and phone and see if the doctors collected any forensics. If they didn't scrape her nails, we will. If she was pushed, we might find her attacker's DNA."

"I was thinking the same," Derrick said. "She also might have seen her attacker."

Ellie's pulse jumped with hope. "Angelica, if you want to start researching the Wilkinson case and Becky's, that would help."

Clearly excited at the prospect of a breaking a big story, Angelica retrieved her pocket notepad and tapped it. "On it."

"Come on, Jan. Let's talk to Priscilla," Ellie told the woman, who eagerly followed her.

Machines beeped, hospital carts clanged, and the scent of antiseptic, medicine and sickness permeated the air as they made their way. Nurses' voices blended with those of the patients and their families, and the Christmas decorations meant to liven up the hospital only accentuated the despair hanging heavy in the air.

When they reached Priscilla's room, Ellie gently knocked, then eased open the door. Jan hovered behind her, her breathing shallow as if she was trying to stay calm in the midst of a storm. She'd probably been struggling with that for the last six months.

"Priscilla," Ellie said softly as she and Jan crossed the room. "I'm Detective Ellie Reeves. And you know Jan Hornsby."

Priscilla's head was bandaged, her tangled hair peeking beneath the dressing. Scrapes and bruises marred her face and arms, her lip was slightly swollen, and she had stitches above her right eye. A cast covered her left wrist and hand, and Ellie imagined other bruises hidden by the covers.

Her eyes looked slightly glassy from the concussion, but she blinked and focused on Jan.

"Jan?" she said in a hoarse whisper.

Jan rushed to her and cradled Priscilla's uninjured hand between hers. "Hey, lady. I was worried when I didn't hear back from you. Then I saw on the news that you'd been hurt."

Pain flashed in Priscilla's eyes. "I... don't know what happened... I went to meet you but... it wasn't you."

Jan's body stiffened. "What are you talking about? We weren't supposed to meet."

Priscilla gaped at her friend. "But you texted me, said we should go to the reporter together."

"No, I'm sorry, but I didn't," Jan said, her eyes rounding.

The women looked confused, and Ellie considered Cord's suspicions that Priscilla's accident wasn't an accident at all. "You received a text?" Ellie asked.

Priscilla nodded, although it looked as if the movement pained her.

"We'll check into that text," Ellie assured her. "Jan was worried and called Angelica Gomez. I'm here to help."

Relieved tears softened the anguish on Priscilla's face.

"Jan told me about her daughter Becky's abduction. And about what happened with your niece." Ellie hoped she wasn't wasting valuable time chasing this when she should be concentrating on Ava, but if the abductions were connected, this might be a true lead.

"Can you tell me what happened with your sister? And who handled her case?"

The covers rustled as Priscilla shifted to get more comfortable. "A Detective Forrester in Savannah. But he arrested Renee instead of looking for whoever took Kaylee."

"Could you please describe what your sister said happened that day?"

Priscilla coughed and Jan handed her the cup of water on her bedside tray, and they waited for her to take a long sip.

Finally, Priscilla pushed the cup away. "Renee took Kaylee to the beach for a picnic. But for some reason she fell asleep and when she came to, Kaylee was gone. The cop accused her of drinking and criminal child negligence."

"Go on," Ellie prodded gently.

Priscilla's breathing sounded ragged with emotions. "He was so hateful to Renee, just blamed her. He didn't even look for anyone else."

"What about Kaylee's father? Is he in the picture?"

"No, he walked out when she was a baby, didn't want to be tied down."

"So Renee was alone with Kaylee?"

"Yes," she said. "Except for a few other people on the beach."

"I don't understand why Forrester was so convinced your sister was negligent. Were there witnesses, someone who said your sister hurt Kaylee or neglected her?"

A tense second passed, Priscilla's eyes glassy. "Some lady on the beach said Renee looked as if she'd been drinking. But she didn't drink anymore, and she never would have had a drop while she was taking care of Kaylee."

Ellie treaded lightly. "Did she have a drinking problem?"

An awkward moment lingered, and Ellie could see Priscilla struggling not to give into her exhaustion. Or maybe she was trying to fabricate an excuse for her sister.

"No," Priscilla finally replied. "She wasn't a serious alcoholic anyway. But when Kaylee was sick, Renee had trouble sleeping so she started having a couple of glasses of wine at night to help her relax. But our father had a real problem, so I talked to her and she joined AA and cut out the habit."

"She could have fallen off the wagon," Ellie said. "It happens."

"No," Priscilla insisted. "She didn't keep alcohol in her house at all. And she never missed one of her meetings. Renee lived and breathed for that little girl. And no one is even looking for her anymore."

Ellie didn't want to make promises she couldn't keep. But under the circumstances she had to explore every possibility. "Tell me what happened to Renee. How did she die?"

"I don't know, I never could get a straight answer," Priscilla murmured. "One day they called me from the jail and said she died of an overdose. I asked questions, but no one seemed to care."

"Was there an investigation into her death?"

Priscilla made a sarcastic sound. "No. I begged the detective to look into it and told him Renee didn't do drugs, not ever. I even tried to reach Renee's sponsor but couldn't find her."

"Did the detective locate her?" Ellie asked.

She shook her head. "No. I don't think he even tried. He wrote Renee off as a bad mother and refused to investigate." Bitterness crept into her voice. "But I think someone murdered her to keep her from looking for Kaylee."

ONE HUNDRED TWELVE

SOMEWHERE ON THE AT

Last night, her husband had slept in the other room after he'd tucked Ava in bed with warm blankets. They'd had words.

"We need to carry Becky to the hospital and take Ava home," he'd said.

"You've been giving Becky her medication," she said stubbornly.

"True," Silas said. "But she has an upper respiratory infection."

"Then give her antibiotics."

"She needs IV fluids and IV antibiotics," Silas stressed. "And tests that I can't run here to make sure her kidney isn't damaged."

"But she needs to be with me for Christmas!" she'd screamed at him.

"This is not their home." Silas had looked at her with such a coldness that she'd feared he'd sneak the girls away during the night.

"If you take them, I'll tell the police this was all your idea," she said.

His face had contorted with anger and hurt, as if she'd driven a knife into him, then he disappeared into the guest room and slammed the door.

Now, the scent of burning bacon wafted to her and she looked down at the frying pan and jerked it off the stove, rattled. She'd have to make something else for breakfast. Maybe eggs-in-a-nest, as she called it. Piper had always liked that.

She set out the eggs, bread and cheese, then Kaylee came into the kitchen leading Ava, who looked up with big sad eyes.

"Good morning, girls," she said with a smile. "I hope you learned your lesson and won't run away again," she said to Ava.

Ava clung to Kaylee's hand, and they obediently sat at the table, sipped their orange juice and took their medications while she cooked breakfast. "I call this eggs-in-a-nest," she said as she set the plates on the table. "Eat up, then we're going to color your hair, Ava. It's going to be so pretty!"

Ava's bow-like mouth pinched, but Kaylee said nothing, just picked up her fork and took a bite of the egg toast. She turned up the holiday music to fill the silence as the girls ate. Ava pretty much just pushed her food around the plate, but she managed to eat the blueberries that she'd put in small bowls for each girl. After all, blueberries provided anti-inflammatories they both needed.

"Grandma Got Run Over by a Reindeer" played on the radio and she sang along, remembering the way Piper would laugh at the silly song. But Kaylee and Ava didn't laugh.

Irritation nudged her away from her cheerful mood, but she tamped it down. Tomorrow was Christmas. Everything would be perfect on Christmas Day. She glanced at the ornament on the tree with Piper's picture on it. Piper was here.

Well, almost.

When the girls finished their meal, she removed the dishes, then wrapped a towel around Ava's shoulders and secured it with a clothespin.

"This won't take long," she told Ava. The little girl stiffened, her pouty face back in place. Then she clenched her hands together as she worked the dye into Ava's hair. "Now it has to sit for twenty minutes, then we'll rinse it," she said. "While we wait, let's make cards for Daddy." She set markers, crayons, glitter, glue, kids' scissors and ribbons on the table along with a stack of tagboard.

"Just fold it in half," she instructed them. "Then you can decorate it any way you want. Daddy will be so excited that you remembered him."

Kaylee sang along to the holiday music, although Ava remained close-lipped and stoic as she drew a Christmas tree on the front of her card and added ornaments and packages beneath it.

Twenty minutes later, she helped Ava crawl onto the kitchen counter, then lie back over the sink so she could rinse out the dye. When she finished, she helped Ava up, smiling as she saw the change happen before her eyes.

"You look so beautiful now, just like Piper!"

Last night Ava's little escapade had ruined her plans. But today she would carry them out. The photo of little Sarah taunted her, and she knew she had to have her next. Then her family would be whole again and everything would be as it should be.

Ellie was reeling from her conversation with Priscilla and Jan. If Renee Wilkinson had been murdered and Priscilla attacked because she'd connected Kaylee's case to Ava Truman's, this case had just gone from felony kidnapping to homicide.

She tasked Derrick with tracing Priscilla's text messages, then continued to probe the young woman. "Priscilla, could you tell us what happened at Hangman's Dome?"

The woman sucked in a breath. "Like I said, I received a text from Jan—at least I thought it was Jan—asking me to meet her there so we could go to the reporter together. But when I got there, I saw a van."

"What color was the van?" Ellie asked.

"Light, I think white."

Ellie breathed out. Could it be the same van Nolan Grueler had mentioned? "Then what happened?"

"It was dark and shadowy and at first I thought it was you, Jan," she said. "But then I knew it wasn't."

"What did the woman look like?" Ellie asked.

Priscilla closed her eyes and rubbed her temple, and Ellie realized her head must be throbbing. "I didn't get a good look at her face, but I think her hair was dark under her hat. In a bob at her chin."

"That's good," Ellie said. "I know this is difficult, but just a few more minutes."

"You're doing great." Jan squeezed Priscilla's hand.

Priscilla released a trembling breath. "She had a gun," she said. "And she ordered me to walk toward my car, next to the ridge. And then..." A strangled cry escaped her. "Then she... pushed me over the edge."

A deafening silence filled the room while Jan blinked in shock.

"Priscilla, did you fight with her? Maybe scratch her?"

She rubbed her temple again. "I... can't remember. It happened so fast."

"That's okay," Ellie said. "But I'll have someone scrape beneath your fingernails in case you got the woman's DNA under there. If you did, we can use it to identify her."

Priscilla gave a weak nod, the trauma of the memory wearing on her.

"Was this the woman you saw?" Ellie asked, showing her a photo of Autumn from her phone.

Priscilla narrowed her eyes, then shook her head. "No. She was... taller."

"This has been a big help," Ellie said, her mind sorting through the information. "Who else knew that the two of you were going to the reporter?"

Priscilla's eyes were drifting shut, but she murmured no one. But Jan answered, "We talked about it on the Facebook support group."

"How many people belong to the group?" Ellie asked.

"A hundred or so," Jan replied. "Although some are more active and share while others lurk. Sometimes it's difficult to talk about a loss like we've all experienced."

"I need the name of the group," Ellie said, adrenalin spiking at the thought of a suspect pool. "It's possible your attacker was following the online activity, that she knew you were getting too close to the truth, so she pretended to be Jan to lure you to that isolated location."

Priscilla's frail hand reached for Ellie. "Then you believe me? You'll find out if she murdered my sister and took Kaylee?"

"Yes, I will. And I'm going to post a guard outside your door." If Priscilla's attacker learned she was still alive, she might come back to finish her.

ONE HUNDRED FOURTEEN

Ellie joined Derrick and Angelia in the waiting room and relayed her conversation with Priscilla. "I'll arrange a guard for Priscilla's room. Landrum's digging into that Facebook group—Jan has admitted him on a dummy profile. It's not ideal, but needs must."

"I sent Priscilla's belongings to the lab," Derrick said. "And I checked her phone. There definitely was a text asking her to meet at Hangman's Dome. It didn't come from Jan Hornsby's phone though. It came from a burner."

"Why am I not surprised?" Ellie muttered. "I'll call the detective who investigated Kaylee's disappearance and the prison warden and find out exactly how Renee Wilkinson died."

Derrick's phone buzzed. "It's my partner. I need to take this. He may have more info on MWC and whether or not they orchestrated these other abductions."

"I've been working on the content for a news broadcast about the forgotten girls," Angelica said. "Maybe bringing more attention to these old cases will spark some tips."

With a plan intact, Derrick walked down the hall to make his call and Angelica left, her eyes buzzing with the anticipation of a hot story.

Ellie phoned the Savannah Police Department and asked to speak to Detective Forrester.

"This is Detective Forrester," he said when he came on the line. "What's this about, Detective Reeves?"

Ellie filled him in. "We're still investigating that group and searching for other children they may have abducted and sold to families," she said. "But I've discovered my case may be linked to one of yours. The disappearance of Kaylee Wilkinson."

"That case is closed," he said curtly.

"Maybe it shouldn't be. It's my understanding that you never found Kaylee or her body."

"That's true. The mother refused to talk then killed herself out of guilt."

"What made you so convinced that she was guilty?" Ellie asked.

"When I first arrived on the scene, she kept saying it was all her fault that Kaylee was gone. I could smell the booze on her breath. Then I learned she had a drinking problem." He grunted. "She was also confused and disoriented. She said she didn't remember what happened, that she wasn't drinking, but that was a lie. Lab work proved her blood-alcohol was high."

Ellie's gut stirred. "Was anyone else around? Were there witnesses?"

"Another woman on the beach said she saw them playing, then she saw Renee chugging a drink and weaving around. Later she heard Renee screaming. She ran over and saw that Renee had been unconscious and the little girl was gone. We searched the beach but by then it was deserted. We believe Kaylee drowned and was swept out to sea."

"Without a body you can't know that," Ellie said. "I've spoken to Renee's sister Priscilla and she insists that Renee hadn't had a drink in two years. Isn't it possible that someone drugged her or slipped something in her drink or food to incapacitate her?"

"You're grasping," Detective Forrester said coldly.

"I don't think so," Ellie said, her anger rising. "You see, Priscilla realized that Kaylee and my victim Ava Truman were abducted exactly one year apart. In my experience, there are no coincidences."

"What are you saying?" Forrester asked, his tone brittle.

"I want a copy of that file," Ellie said. "Because I think that the same woman abducted those two children and possibly a third child named Becky Hornsby."

A long second passed. "You have proof of that?"

"Priscilla Wilkinson and Becky's mother, Jan Hornsby, decided to go to the media with their stories. They discussed it on Facebook. And then someone posing as Jan tried to kill Priscilla."

ONE HUNDRED FIFTEEN
NORTH EAST HOSPITAL

Silas checked the corridor as he slipped down the hall to the hospital pharmacy. Security measures had been instigated to protect supplies from people desperate for drugs, even staff who might sneak some for their own use—or to sell.

Now he had become one of them. If he got caught, his career was over. Everything he'd worked for and stood for would spiral down the drain and he'd be caught up in the sewage of his own weakness.

But he'd already gone too far. Already crossed the line.

In his attempt to atone for his wrongs, he'd stepped onto a landmine that was doomed to explode beneath him.

Still, he loved his wife. Blamed himself for tearing her apart with his mistakes and then his decisions. He deserved whatever happened to him, and he'd accepted it.

He just wanted to give her this last Christmas. And it had to be the last.

His job, his life's work, had been about saving lives. Not destroying them. He had taken a vow when he'd earned his medical license, just as he'd said vows when he'd stood in front of his wife and pledged to love her for better or worse.

He just hadn't expected the worse part to be hell and for him to be walking with the devil.

Now he'd broken his vows to his work and... if he did what he knew he had to do, he would break them to his wife.

For a second, he stood in the shadows of the corridor, his lungs wheezing for air as if he was already half dead and was on a ventilator.

The whir and whistle of the machine screamed in his ears, and even though he told himself it wasn't real, as he dug the keycode for the pharmacy from his pocket, he felt like the life was draining from him second by second.

But, knowing he had to oversee Becky and the other children's care, he paused to listen for voices or footsteps indicating someone was coming. He wasn't even supposed to be at work this morning.

Except for the rumble of the air vents, silence surrounded him.

Holding his breath, he punched in the code, opened the door and grabbed the supplies he needed.

Ellie fought anger as the sheriff met her outside Priscilla's door. "Captain Hale called, told me to come here," Bryce said.

"Did he explain?"

"No, just said it was urgent."

Ellie breathed out to keep from lashing into him. "The woman in that room is Priscilla Wilkinson. She called the tip line about her niece's disappearance. Her name was Kaylee Wilkinson."

She paused, giving Bryce time to absorb what she'd said. A vein pulsed in his neck as his eyes narrowed. "I told you about the mother. She was arrested and killed herself in prison."

"She died in prison," Ellie said. "But I don't think she committed suicide. I've requested the case files for Kaylee's disappearance, talked with the investigating officer and spoken with her sister."

"You knew good and god damn well that this Priscilla is probably in denial. She'd lie to cover for her sister."

"Bryce, that is not what happened. I think Kaylee's disappearance is connected to the abduction of two other kids. One is Ava Truman."

Bryce's beard stubble rustled as he raked his hand across his chin. "Why do you think that?"

"Ava was abducted exactly one year to the day that Kaylee went missing." She fisted her hands on her hips. "And when Priscilla decided to meet Angelica, someone tried to kill her."

Interest sparked in his eyes, but his mouth flattened into a thin line. The stubborn man hated to admit when he was wrong.

"If we're on to something and the girls' kidnapper murdered Renee and then attempted to kill Priscilla, they might come back and try to finish the job." She pinned him with a look that warned him not to argue. "Or if this person is panicked, they might try to flee the state or country. I need you to stay here and protect Priscilla while I find out who hurt her."

"But—"

"No buts, Bryce. If you'd dug into Priscilla's story, she might not be in the hospital now. We could have saved time, and maybe Ava and Kaylee wouldn't still be missing."

Without waiting for a response, she turned and strode away from him. She had three precious little girls to find. And the clock was ticking.

ONE HUNDRED SEVENTEEN

HONEYSUCKLE LANE

Lara's coffee threatened to come up as she flipped off the news. She'd been struggling to hold on to hope that the police would find Ava before Christmas.

But the reporter's story about the forgotten children sent a wave of despair over her. One of those little girls had been missing an entire year and the other six months. How had their parents gone on day after day?

She walked over to the tree, her lungs straining for air as she looked at the reindeer ornament Ava had made with the two different colored eyes. It was her favorite.

How could she survive without Ava?

Jasper's footsteps echoed on the deck outside as he paced back and forth. He'd just talked to that FBI agent and learned that Autumn had been involved in the child kidnapping ring, although they were certain that she hadn't taken Ava. Her head spun with it all.

She hugged her arms around her waist, her fear so mind-numbing she felt as if her legs would give way. *Where are you, baby?*

The twinkling lights of the Christmas tree painted the family room in colors. Tonight, she and Ava would have set out cookies for

Santa and carrots for the reindeer and read *The Night Before Christmas* in their matching holiday pajamas.

And in the morning... Ava would crawl in her bed and wake her and they'd race into the living room to see what Santa had left. In her mind, she could hear Ava's squeal of delight at the wiggling puppy she'd reserved for her.

Now the quiet was unbearable.

She walked back to the kitchen where she'd put the stockings she'd purchased. Today, she'd planned for her and Ava to fill them for the seniors at the nursing home nearby. Stomach churning, she set the bags on the table and laid the stockings across the kitchen bar.

Did she have the heart to do it without Ava?

Her daughter's voice echoed in her head, "Why do we go there?" Ava had asked last year.

Lara closed her eyes as the sweet memory washed over her. Although money had been tight, she scrimped and saved and clipped coupons all year so she could still help the needy. "Because some of those people have no family, honey. They're lonely and we can be their family for a little while."

Ava had nodded, grabbed a stocking and began to stuff it. Together they worked, adding warm socks, hand lotions, body spray, new toothbrushes and toothpaste, and soft warm scarves for winter. Even inside the rooms, the patients got cold and needed the comfort of being wrapped up. Ava had made cards and they added those last.

On the way to the nursing home, they'd picked up cinnamon muffins and peppermint candies. Ava had held her hand, timid, as they went in, but when she saw the excited smiles on the older people's faces, Ava beamed herself. All year, she'd been asking if they could go back this year.

Emotions welled in Lara's throat, but she made a snap decision. Those people were lonely and so was she. They didn't deserve to be let down.

She'd just pretend Ava was with her. And when Ava came home, she'd carry her to visit them.

ONE HUNDRED EIGHTEEN

SOMEWHERE ON THE AT

Ava's eyes widened as she saw herself in the mirror. "It's all wrong. You colored it," she whispered.

"But you look so pretty now, just like my little angel," she said as she brushed the girl's hair and clamped a pretty green barrette on the side to keep it from her eyes. She'd given Kaylee one as well, then handed Ava Piper's favorite reindeer sweatshirt and Kaylee the blue one with the snowman applique.

"Put them on and we'll have a fashion show," she said. "We can take a family photograph once Daddy is back from picking up everyone's special medicine."

Ava frowned again and she felt like shaking her.

She was getting tired of the girl's sullen silent treatment. Thankfully Kaylee had chattered away while they decorated the cards and sang along with the music.

Kaylee was such a sweet girl now. It was a good thing she'd gotten her away from that mother of hers.

"You look perfect!" She clapped and urged the girls to stand in front of the tree.

She heard the garage door open and close, then Silas walked in and murmured a sound of disapproval. "What have you done now?"

"We're taking a family picture," she said. "I need to get Becky to join us."

He caught her arm. "Don't you think you're carrying this too far? You're scaring Ava."

She gave him a hate-filled glare. "No, I'm not. Now let me get Becky."

She pushed past him and down the hall, toward Becky, but when she tried to wake her, the little girl didn't move. She shook her harder then tried to lift her by her shoulders, but Becky sagged back down, limp and still.

"Honey, wake up," she cried.

But the little girl did not respond.

Panicked, she ran back to the door. "Silas, come here! Hurry, something's wrong with Becky!"

Seconds later, he raced into the room, his jaw clenched as he knelt by Becky's bedside. He felt for a pulse, then looked up at her with cold fear darkening his eyes.

"She needs a hospital," he said sharply.

Then he scooped her into his arms, grabbed the blanket from the bed, and headed to the door. She raced after him, pulling at his arm. "You can't take her," she cried. "I can't lose her again."

"Get out of my way," he ordered. "You've gone too far." She tried to stop him by blocking the door, but he shoved her aside. "I said get out of the way! I'm not going to let this child suffer any more."

She chased him down the hall to the garage door, but he rushed to his car and laid Becky in the back seat. She yanked at his arm, but he shoved her backward so hard she stumbled into the wall.

Buckling Becky in, he tucked the blanket around her, then dove into the front seat. Glancing over her shoulder, she saw Kaylee and Ava watching in the doorway, clinging to each other as Silas slammed the car door, started the engine and backed out of the garage.

ONE HUNDRED NINETEEN

Ava felt like she had a big rock in her chest. What was wrong with Becky?

Kaylee's low cry made things even worse.

"Get in the house!" the lady shouted.

Kaylee snatched Ava's hand and dragged her back in the house. The lady ran after them, her eyes wild as she screamed, "Go to your room and stay there. You'd better not come out."

Ava made a little strangled sound and Kaylee shushed her, then pulled her toward the stairs. The lady was shaking her fists in the air and hit the wall, and Ava stumbled on the bottom step.

"Come on, Ava." Kaylee helped her up and they ran up the stairs, slipping on the cool wood and fumbling along the wall until they reached their room.

"I mean it, stay in there!" the lady yelled.

Kaylee slammed the door shut, and Ava snatched one of the chairs and pushed it against the door. Then she and Kaylee climbed on one of the twin beds together. Ava pushed her fist against her mouth to keep from crying.

"What's wrong with Becky?" she whimpered.

"I don't know, but I heard the man say she might die."

Ava buried her head into the pillow and let the tears fall. If Becky died, had the lady and man killed her?

Would they kill her and Kaylee, too?

ONE HUNDRED TWENTY

CROOKED CREEK

Fueled with coffee and donuts that Derrick had brought, Ellie studied the file Detective Forrester had sent over. His handwriting was a mess, but they waded through the scribbled notes of the officers who'd canvassed the beach, questioning guests and families that day.

"This is Renee's statement," Ellie said. "According to Forrester, she seemed confused and disoriented. She and Kaylee collected seashells then made sandcastles and picnicked on sandwiches and brownies, then Kaylee spread out her beach towel and played Barbie going to the beach."

She hesitated, picturing a sweet family scene in her mind. Ellie's stomach plummeted as she realized what could have gone wrong. "Renee cleaned up their trash then stretched out to watch her daughter play. Other families had gone for the day, but Kaylee insisted on staying. Sometime later, Renee woke up and realized she'd fallen asleep, something she never did when she was with Kaylee.

"'I'm always super careful about watching Kaylee,' Renee insisted. 'I was paranoid about something happening to her.'"

Ellie scrunched her nose in thought and continued to read.

"Yet Renee either fell asleep—or passed out—for over two hours, during which Kaylee disappeared."

"She could have drowned," Derrick said, his tone dark.

Ellie nodded. "But Renee refused to accept that. She said a mother would know."

She and Derrick exchanged looks. "I don't know what to think," Ellie said.

She flipped another page and skimmed the interviews with folks on the beach. "An older man walking his dog saw Renee and her daughter playing. He said the mother seemed attentive." She moved onto the next one. "A couple of teenagers were boogie boarding. They saw the mom and little girl carrying water to fill a moat they built around their sandcastle. Another woman told the officer that she saw Renee staggering around yelling for her daughter. She gave the officer her contact information and went home." Ellie chewed the inside of her cheek. "According to Forrester, Renee didn't remember that exchange or the woman."

"That's odd, but could have been the alcohol," Derrick said.

"I want to follow up with her." Ellie skimmed the notes. "Her name was Jordan Jones." She found her phone number listed and called the number. But her senses prickled when she got an out-of-service message.

"The phone number is no longer good," she told Derrick as she flipped further and found a statement filed by Renee's lawyer. "Listen to this. Renee's attorney tried to reach the Jones woman to question her but couldn't locate her."

Derrick's gaze met hers. "That sounds suspicious. Let me see what I can find on her."

A knock sounded at the door, then Captain Hale poked his head inside her office. "Ellie, the hospital just called. Nolan Grueler came to."

Ellie stood, her jaw clenched. "I'm on my way."

Ellie left Derrick searching for Jordan Jones while she went to talk to Grueler. But first she stopped at the nurses' station to check on his mother.

"How is Ms. Grueler?" she asked.

The nurse on duty leaned across the desk. "She's doing better. Since she lives alone, the doctor released her to a rehab facility so she can receive physical and occupational therapy."

Relief filled Ellie. At least there the woman would be safe from angry citizens.

She headed down the hall to Grueler's room and found one of Bryce's deputies standing guard. "Take a break," said Ellie. "I need to talk to Nolan."

"I could use some coffee," the deputy said. "But call me if you need me. I've already fended off two more folks who were furious that we're protecting him."

"Thanks. I think I can handle it." Ellie let his comment roll off her as she entered. She heard the beeping of machines monitoring his heart and saw he was being given oxygen, fluids, pain meds and probably antibiotics via IV.

His eyes fluttered open as she entered, and his fingers curled into the blanket.

"You should have let me die," he said in a raspy voice.

Ellie inhaled a deep breath. "I'm not a killer or judge and jury," she said. "All I want is to find Ava Truman." She moved closer to him. "Did you have anything to do with her disappearance?"

He shook his head, emotions flaring across his face. "I didn't take her. I swear."

Ellie released the breath she'd been holding, then gave a little nod. "You said that a woman was watching her. Tell me about her."

"I saw her in a van. She sat across from the bus stop a lot. At first I thought she was a parent just dropping her kid."

"What made you change your mind?"

"I never saw a kid with her. And one day I saw her get out of the van and follow Ava."

Ellie's pulse quickened. "She followed her?"

He gave a weak nod. "To Ava's house."

"Did she talk to her or approach her?"

He coughed then fiddled with his oxygen. "No, but she looked through the fence at Ava playing."

Goosebumps skittered along Ellie's neck. "You sensed it was wrong, didn't you?"

He nodded.

"Why didn't you report it or tell her mother?"

He made a pained sound. "You know the answer to that."

She didn't like it, but she understood—for him to be watching Ava violated his parole. And anyone he talked to would have seen it as suspicious, just as she had.

"Was there anything distinctive about the van? Any logo? Did you make a note of the license plate?"

"No, it was just a plain white van. I couldn't even tell you the model."

She pulled up Serena's booking photograph on her phone and angled it for him to see. "Nolan, was this the woman you saw?"

He squinted as he studied it, then shook his head. "I've never seen that lady."

"How about this one?" She flashed Autumn's next.

"No, not her. This lady looked like a mama."

"What do you mean?"

"Mom jeans, sweatshirt, not fancy."

Ellie's mind raced. "If I send in a police artist, can you describe her?"

"Am I going to jail for this?" Fear flickered in his eyes.

Ellie balled her hands into fists. "Do you think you should go back to prison?"

"I won't survive in there again," he grumbled. "And out here, it's almost as bad. Everyone watching me and hating me."

"How about an inpatient treatment facility?" Ellie suggested. "You'll be safe there. And if you're really committed to serious therapy, it's the best option."

He dropped his hand from the oxygen tube then gave a little nod.

"And the artist? You'll work with her?"

He gave another nod, and Ellie stepped from the room to call for a police sketch artist. A commotion down the hall drew her eyes and she saw nurses racing into another room with a crash cart.

She turned her back to it so she could hear as she spoke to her captain. Out of the corner of her eye, she noticed a man in scrubs pushing a food cart. Carrying a tray, he entered Grueler's room.

Hopeful for the first time in days, she quickly updated Hale. He hung up so he could call the police artist. The minute she had the sketch, she'd run it on the news.

Pushing open the door, she saw the man's back as he leaned over Grueler. He was tall and lean, maybe five ten, with brown hair streaked with gray. It took her a minute to realize what was happening. Grueler gasped and was struggling to push the man's arms away. Then she spotted a knife in the man's hand as he raised it above Grueler.

This was no doctor or nurse or staff attendant.

"Stop!" Ellie lunged at the man and yanked at his arm. His hand flew up, and she knocked the knife from his grasp. But he shoved her backward so hard she hit the bathroom door, while Grueler groaned.

Stars swam in front of Ellie's eyes, and she choked out a cry then dove toward the assailant again. He bellowed and turned the knife on her, then she saw blood dripping down the knife as he plunged it at her. The blade struck her arm and she felt her own blood run.

Grueler's body jerked, then she saw his gown was ripped and bloody. The machines went crazy, the heart monitor flatlining.

She threw up her arm to deflect the knife, then kicked the man in the balls and pulled her gun. "Drop the weapon!" she shouted.

He was doubled over on the floor, but dark rage flashed in his eyes, and he still had the knife. Then he spat at her. "Why are you protecting that sicko?"

Ellie kept her gun trained on him. "I said drop the knife. Now."

Ignoring the sting of the cut on her arm, she inched forward and pressed the nurse's call button. The man lunged at her, but she punched him in the face and he slumped over again. The knife hit the floor and she grabbed her handcuffs from her jacket, jerked him around and got them on his wrists. A nurse raced in, took one look at the scene, then called for help. Anger suffocated Ellie as she looked back at Grueler's limp body. He was staring dead-eyed at the ceiling, his body unmoving.

Ellie rolled the man over to face her and pushed him against the wall. "Do you have any idea what you've done?"

"Who cares?" he growled. "He took that little girl and probably killed her."

Ellie shot him a laser-sharp look. "He didn't take her," Ellie snapped. "But he saw who did. Now you killed him, we may never find her."

ONE HUNDRED TWENTY-TWO

HONEYSUCKLE LANE

Lara carefully wrapped the little snow globe with the dove inside and placed it on the mantle beside the other gifts she'd wrapped for Ava.

"That was nice what you did," Jasper said. "Carrying stockings to the nursing home."

Lara swallowed against the lump in her throat. "The patients were so excited. It meant a lot to have someone remember them." Some had even asked about Ava. "I hope Ava will be back to take one to Ms. Dottie next door. She dropped off a sweet potato pie this morning. Said her granddaughter isn't coming to see her this year."

Jasper sat down beside her, his bleak expression mirroring hers as he looked at the presents beneath the tree. "You're amazing, Lara. Even now, thinking of others."

Despair threatened to overcome her. "What if Ava never comes home?" she whispered.

Jasper covered her hand with his. "She will. She has to."

"But you hear stories where kids go missing and they're never found," she said brokenly. "There was a story about it on the news earlier. It was called 'The Forgotten Girls'."

Jasper curled his fingers around her arms and forced her to

look at him. "She's not going to be one of them," he said with a strength that surprised her. "We won't let her be. If the cops stop looking, I'll quit my job and spend every minute of my life searching until I find her."

Lara squeezed his hand. He sounded like the man she married, strong and determined and loving.

"I was thinking," he said. "I know Ava wants a puppy."

"I've already chosen one for her." Lara sniffed. "Oh God, I should call the shelter and let them know I can't come to collect him."

Jasper stood. "We just can't sit here. Why don't we go pick him up?"

Before, when she'd mentioned a puppy, he'd balked. "I thought you didn't like dogs."

"I know I was difficult, Lara. But I can change. Right now, all I want is to bring our little girl home."

Lara heard regret and love in his voice. Once again, it reminded her of the Jasper she'd fallen in love with eight years ago before they'd hit hard times financially and Ava's medical issues had brought their world crashing down.

"How about it?" Jasper asked. "Should we get the puppy so we can surprise her when she comes home?"

Lara knew it might be crazy. It had been days already and the police hadn't found her daughter. But she refused to give up hope.

"Yes. It's a little wiener dog," she said. "Ava loves them, and one had been dropped at the shelter just before I visited. I thought it was meant to be."

Jasper smiled. "Then let's go. Ava can name him when she comes home."

Lara latched onto Jasper's hand. If she didn't, she might not be able to go on another minute.

Derrick found Ellie in an ER room being stitched up. When Captain Hale had told him Grueler had been attacked, he'd raced over.

"Are you all right?" Derrick asked.

"Yes," Ellie winced as the doctor finished stitching her arm. "I stepped into the hall for a second and this man dressed in scrubs went in. Then I saw Grueler struggling with him and realized he had a knife. He stabbed him." Self-disgust tinged her voice. "I tried to pull him away, but it was too late."

Dammit, she could have been killed. Derrick fisted his hands by his sides to tamp down his anger.

"The sheriff's department took him into custody," Ellie said. "His name is Tony Studdard. Some kind of vigilante."

"And he killed Grueler for something he didn't do."

"Right." The doctor bandaged her arm, and Ellie slid off the exam table as he left the room. After pulling her torn sleeve over the bandage, she reached for her coat and Derrick helped her into it.

"Nolan did tell me he saw a woman in a white van watching Ava near the bus stop and at her house. The van could be the one Priscilla described. He said she seemed just like any other mom.

She only stood out to him because he realized they were both watching Ava."

"No wonder no one suspected anything," Derrick said thoughtfully.

"I'd already requested a sketch artist to work with him, but now... that lead is gone."

Derrick sighed. "Maybe not. You said there's a lady in the neighborhood who formed a neighborhood watch. She might have seen this woman."

Ellie nodded. "Yes, Dottie Clark. Deputy Landrum talked to her. She was the one who overheard the Trumans arguing. Maybe she can give us a better description."

He indicated her injured arm. "Come on, I'll drive."

ONE HUNDRED TWENTY-FOUR

HONEYSUCKLE LANE

"I'm fine to drive," Ellie said. "Let's drop my Jeep at the station then we'll question Dottie together."

"Stubborn woman," Derrick grumbled.

But he didn't waste time arguing and followed Ellie. At the station, she jumped in his car, then he drove them to Dottie Clark's small ranch house. The storm the night before had blown down tree limbs and twigs, and a fog had settled in, adding a gray cast to the sky, just as Ava's kidnapping had over the town.

Unlike Lara's home, which was welcoming with its festive décor, Dottie's looked bare and void of holiday cheer. Ellie wondered why.

She glanced through the window but spotted no Christmas lights, just a faint glow from what looked to be the kitchen. A gray cat was sprawled on the floor, and two more in chairs near the fireplace. She rang the bell again and finally heard footsteps shuffling.

Ellie had seen the plump gray-haired woman in town and always thought she looked a little sad. When she opened the door, she wore a purple sweatsuit and cat-shaped earrings. A long-haired orange cat curled around her legs, meowing.

Dottie scooped up the cat and nuzzled it to her cheek, and Ellie introduced herself and Derrick.

Dottie's eyes crinkled in confusion. "I already told that deputy everything I know."

"Can we come in for a few minutes?" Ellie asked. "I'm talking to the neighbors again to make certain we didn't miss anything."

The wind picked up, shaking residual raindrops from the trees and splattering the window, but the wood fire added warmth to the house. Although it was so quiet it seemed lonely. Ellie shivered and Dottie stepped aside and motioned for her to enter.

"Do you want some coffee?" Dottie asked.

They both declined, then Dottie led them through a small living room with a chair and couch, and a bookshelf that held kids' toys and games. "You have grandchildren?" Ellie asked.

The woman cut her eyes toward the bookshelf, her knees cracking as she showed them to the kitchen. "One. A granddaughter. But she's not coming this year. That's why I haven't decorated." Sadness flickered in her gray-green eyes. "Don't seem worth it."

Dottie poured herself a cup of coffee then set the cat in her lap where it purred loudly. Two more loped into the room and curled at her feet.

Ellie joined Dottie at the chrome table with orange vinyl chairs. It was the kind of retro style young professionals in Atlanta swooned over, but this set looked as it had been here forty years.

"Dottie, I heard you organized a neighborhood watch. We know that Nolan Grueler watched Ava, but we've cleared him of wrongdoing." Not that it would do him any good now he was dead, but it might bring his mother comfort. "He told me he saw a woman in a white van near the bus stop and by Ava's house. Did you ever notice her or the van?"

Dottie dumped two teaspoons of sugar in her coffee then so much creamer that it looked almost white. As she stirred vigorously, Ellie wondered if she could taste the coffee at all.

"Hmm, now that you mention it, I did. A few times. I figured it was another mother, maybe dropping or picking up kids for a carpool. Sometimes moms sit in their cars near the bus stop until the kids get on."

Derrick walked to the living room window and looked out into the street, before returning to the kitchen. Ellie knew he was judging the view Dottie's front yard offered to the bus stop and the Trumans' house.

"What did this woman look like?" Ellie asked.

Dottie pinched the bridge of her nose. "I just saw her through the window of the van. I think she had straight dark hair, cut to her chin. Didn't see her eyes. She wore a ball cap. I waved to her one time, but she started the car and left in a hurry."

"Did you think that was odd?" Ellie asked.

The woman sipped her coffee. "Didn't think so at the time. Figured she was just in a rush to get somewhere. Everyone's always racing around these days. Don't have time for us old people."

Ellie squeezed the woman's hand. "Do you remember anything else? Did you see the license plate of the van?"

The lines around her mouth bunched. "No, I'm afraid I didn't notice it. But come to think of it, I did see her get out one day, and she was taking pictures of the kids. I didn't think much of it at the time—what with assuming one of them was hers. Do you think that means something?"

Ellie stiffened. She definitely thought it meant something— that the woman was stalking Ava.

She started to shift the pieces in her mind. The woman on the beach with Renee and Kaylee that day had disappeared. What if it was the same woman who'd stalked Ava?

Slivers of sunlight wormed their way through storm clouds as Derrick parked at the police station. The wind had picked up, catching Ellie's ponytail and tearing it from its rubber band as they hustled inside. They grabbed coffee then went to the conference room.

She added Kaylee and Becky's names to the whiteboard.

"I want to look at Renee's statement again," she said, then pulled the print-out of the file Forrester had emailed.

Derrick took the chair opposite her, opening his laptop on the table.

"So we have a woman driving a van who may have stalked Ava and attacked Priscilla Wilkinson," Ellie said. "Renee's sister insists she would not have committed suicide." She ticked off what they knew so far, trying to weave the threads together. "And the woman who claimed that Renee was intoxicated is nowhere to be found."

"We should question the warden at the prison. I want to know more about Renee's alleged suicide," Derrick said.

"I agree." She thumbed open the file and began skimming. "This is what Renee told the police when they interrogated her the day after Kaylee disappeared."

Ellie read out loud: "'Kaylee was so excited about going to the beach. I'd already bought some canvasses for us to do some sand paintings and seashell designs for her room. We chased the waves and built sandcastles and collected seashells. Then we had our picnic.'"

Ellie skimmed further.

"'That morning we packed ham sandwiches, celery and carrot sticks and apple slices. The night before we baked brownies together, so I packed those for dessert. And we took our water bottles and I included a juice box for Kaylee as a treat. She loves the fruit punch ones.'"

Ellie continued. "Detective Forrester asked her if she left the picnic basket alone at any time and she admitted she did for a few minutes while they combed for shells."

Derrick listened intently, his gaze on the whiteboard.

Ellie propped her chin on her hand, thinking. "What if this woman was stalking Kaylee and Renee, just waiting on the right moment to kidnap Kaylee? She could have slipped something in Renee's water while they were hunting shells."

"Sounds feasible," Derrick said. "It would explain the results of the blood tests and the reason Renee was so disoriented. Did the police analyze the water bottle?"

Ellie rummaged through the notes and then checked the crime-scene photos. "I don't see anything about it. And I don't see the water bottle in the photos." She thumped her fingers on the file. "Which means the kidnapper could have tossed it or taken it with her."

ONE HUNDRED TWENTY-SIX

It was unsettling how quickly Forrester closed the case, Ellie thought.

Irritated at his lack of detail, she dug for information on the detective. Either he'd jumped to conclusions and hadn't conducted a thorough investigation, or he was biased against women, as Renee's sister suggested.

"This is interesting," she said, understanding dawning. "No wonder Forrester came after Renee so hard. In one of the interview transcripts when he was pressuring Renee to confess, he admitted his little brother was killed by a drunk driver."

Derrick tunneled his fingers through his hair. "That would make him a hardass on anyone he thought was under the influence when a child was hurt."

She phoned Detective Forrester again and put him on speaker. "I've been studying Renee Wilkinson's statement," Ellie said. "According to her and her sister, she was in AA and was not drinking at the time Kaylee disappeared."

"Jesus Christ, Reeves. It's Christmas Eve. My shift's nearly finished. Like I told you before, her blood-alcohol level told a different story," Forrester said. "Lab results don't lie."

"Whether or not she willingly consumed that substance is the key. We have a theory. The woman you interviewed, Jordan Jones, either disappeared or she used a fake name. So far we haven't found anything on her."

"So? She said she was just passing through and we didn't need her testimony to make the case, not with the lab results."

"Priscilla Wilkinson said she tried to contact Renee's AA sponsor but couldn't find her. Did you look for her?"

"No reason to," he muttered.

"Did you consider that Renee could have been drugged?" Ellie asked, not bothering to hide her frustration. "That that's the reason she was so confused and disoriented?"

"Listen, I tied this case up with a nice red bow," he said, his tone irritated. "The whole story about AA was fabricated to build her case."

"I don't think so," Ellie said. "I think that the woman who sponsored her might have actually been this Jordan Jones woman you talked to. She knew Renee would be at the beach, followed her and somehow drugged her water. When Renee passed out, she took Kaylee."

"You really do have some kind of imagination," the detective said. "But no proof."

"That's why we're calling. According to Renee's statement, she carried water bottles for both her and Kaylee to the beach." Derrick said. "But there's no mention of them or photographs of them in your file."

"Again, she lied," he said.

Ellie was losing her patience. "Did you find a liquor bottle? Wine? Anything in her cooler?"

An awkward pause followed while she waited on his response.

"I take that as a no," Ellie said.

"She could have thrown it away," he muttered.

"Or this woman Jordan Jones threw it away," Ellie replied. "Did you search the area? Trash cans? Her car?"

"We searched her car, and we searched the beach for Kaylee," he said. "But with the witness's account and the lab results, we saw no need to look for her drink container."

His voice wavered slightly, as if he realized that might have been a mistake.

"I want you to work with a sketch artist and come up with a composite of Jordan Jones," Ellie said. "Then send it to my office right away."

"Okay, okay," Forrester said. "There's a sketch artist in the station now, I gotta catch them before they leave for the holiday. Bye." With that, he hung up.

Ellie and Derrick spent some time going over the case file again, but there wasn't much more to take from it for now. They were planning their next move when Captain Hale burst into the room.

"Ellie, Derrick, I just got a report. A little girl was dumped at the hospital in Gainesville. She's in a serious condition."

Ellie's breath caught. "Is it Ava?"

"No," he said. "But she was wearing a diabetic bracelet—the name on that is Becky Hornsby. The hospital found her picture online and say it's her."

Chairs scraped the floor as Ellie and Derrick both pushed away from the table and stood. "Is she okay?"

"Gainesville PD didn't have any medical information except that she's being treated."

Ellie's heart hammered. At least that meant Becky was alive. "Her mother is at the hospital with Priscilla. We'll go get her."

Ten minutes later, Ellie and Derrick rushed into the hospital and straight to Priscilla's room. Jan looked up from the chair by the bed, where Priscilla was sleeping.

"How is she?" Ellie asked.

"Resting, but the doctor says she'll be okay," Jan said.

Ellie approached the bed while Derrick remained by the door. "We have some news," Ellie said softly. "We're highly confident Becky has been found."

A myriad of emotions flashed across Jan's face, and she jumped up from the chair. "Where is she? Is she all right?"

Ellie felt Derrick tense behind her and took Jan's hand. "Someone left a little girl at the hospital in Gainesville. She was wearing Becky's diabetes ID bracelet and the staff there are confident it's her."

Jan swayed slightly, her face turning a pasty yellow. "Please tell me she's okay."

"I don't know her condition yet," Ellie said as gently as she could, "but we'll drive you there now."

"Yes, yes, please," Jan replied, her voice trembling.

"Kaylee?" They spun to face the bed. Priscilla had woken, and was clutching the side of the bed to get up, but fell back against the pillow with a groan.

"I'm sorry, no word yet," Ellie said. "But we've talked to Detective Forrester, and I think you're right about someone drugging your sister."

Forrester hadn't wasted any more time. On the drive, he'd texted Ellie a sketch he'd put together of the woman at the beach, Jordan Jones. Although the woman was wearing a beach hat, Ellie could see that she had brown hair in a chin-length bob, similar to the woman Grueler and Dottie had described. An angular face, square chin and olive skin. She didn't see any other distinguishing marks except a small diagonal scar at the corner of her mouth, which looked like it had come from a cut of some kind. Maybe an accident?

She showed the sketch to Priscilla. "This is a sketch of the woman he spoke to. Does she look familiar?"

Priscilla groaned as she looked at it. "It's hard to tell with her wearing that big hat, but she reminds me of Renee's AA sponsor. I never met her, but one day I saw the two of them outside the church where the group met. Renee waved me over, but the woman dashed away before I could get close."

Ellie's breath came faster. "We think she may have drugged Renee."

"But she was in AA," Priscilla said, clutching the sheets.

"It's possible she joined just to get to know your sister. That she had her eyes on Kaylee all along."

"Oh, my God." Priscilla blinked away tears, her pain raw.

"Could she be the woman who pushed you?"

"I don't know, maybe? It was dark and happened so fast."

Ellie squeezed the woman's shoulder. "That's okay, Priscilla." Ellie didn't want to push Priscilla any more for now, with her concussion, but flipped the phone around to show Jan. "How about you, Jan? Did you ever see her?"

Jan clawed her hands through her hair as she studied the picture. "I... don't know. I don't remember her."

But she could have been at the park that day in Chattanooga, Ellie thought.

"Why would she take Kaylee?" Priscilla asked.

"I don't know yet. But we're going to find out." She angled her head toward Jan. "Come on, we'll drive you to the hospital to see Becky."

"Yes, please." Jan fluttered a hand to her chest. "She has to be okay. She has to be."

Jan gave Priscilla a forlorn look, one filled with hope for her daughter and sympathy for Priscilla. "I have to go."

"I know," Priscilla said softly. "Hug her tight. I'll say a prayer for both of you."

Jan looked as if she was going to burst into tears. "I'll be back. I promise. And we'll find Kaylee, too."

The two women traded the kind of look only a person in the same situation would understand, then Jan grabbed her purse and coat. "Let's go. I need to see my baby."

ONE HUNDRED TWENTY-EIGHT
GAINESVILLE

On the way out of town, Ellie dropped by Jan's to pick up her mother.

"You found her?" the older woman said in a stunned whisper.

"Yes, Mama," Jan said. "Come on, we have to go to her."

The two women huddled together in the back seat, their emotions spilling over as Ellie drove. On the way they had a call from Hale, who had been liaising with Manning at Chattanooga PD. As the lead detective on Becky's disappearance, he'd been all set to drive over to Gainesville too, but had agreed to let Ellie and Derrick run things for now, given the situation. The rain began again, droplets shimmering off the trees and storefronts and trickling off the awning as if the buildings were in mourning. Ellie hoped there would be happy tears when they reached Gainesville and that Becky would be stable.

A half hour later, she parked at the hospital, and the Hornsbys tugged the hoods of their coats up to ward off the deluge, sliding from the vehicle, undaunted by the cold.

Ellie followed, anxious and hoping that not only was Becky alive, but she could tell them where she'd been all this time and if Kaylee and Ava were with her.

Derrick pulled his phone as they entered. "I'm going to call the warden at the prison where Renee was sent. If she had visitors, I want to view that footage."

"Good idea." If their kidnapper's face was on camera, they could run it through facial rec. Grateful he was thinking methodically while her emotions were in a tailspin, Ellie followed Jan and her mother inside. The familiar hospital smells and sounds did nothing but ratchet up her nerves.

"My daughter... Becky Hornsby..." Jan said as she clutched the edge of the nurse's desk. "She was brought in here."

Ellie flashed her badge. "She's been missing for six months. I'll need to speak to the doctor as well."

The nurse waved them toward the waiting area. "Please have a seat and I'll call her."

Jan's mother huddled beside her, her eyes red from crying as she lent her support.

The doctor, a forty-something woman named Dr. Conley, appeared with a frown. "This child was abducted?"

"Yes," Jan said. "How is she?"

Her expression was somber, eyes tired as if she'd been working a long shift. "We're stabilizing her."

"She was kidnapped six months ago. I'm one of the investigating officers." Ellie indicated her badge. "Can you tell us what happened to her? Was she hurt? Injured?"

The doctor glanced at Jan as if to ask permission to discuss Becky's medical condition in front of them, and Jan murmured for her to answer.

"There are no signs of physical abuse that I've found," Dr. Conley said. "But she has a fever and an upper respiratory infection."

"She has diabetes," Jan said, paling. "She needs insulin."

"It appears she was given her medication, and her glucose levels are in good shape, but we've started her on antibiotics for the infection. I saw the surgical scar—did the diabetes develop after the kidney transplant?"

"Yes, that's right," Jan replied. "But it's been a couple of years now, and the pediatrics team in Chattanooga, where she had the surgery, said she doesn't need immunosuppressives anymore. We're hoping the insulin won't be permanent either."

"That's good," said Dr. Conley, and gave Jan a compassionate look. "And so is her prognosis. She's sleeping now."

Jan sagged in relief. "Please, let me see her."

"Certainly. I think you'll probably be the best medicine for her."

Jan gave Ellie a grateful look. "Thank you."

"Of course. I need to talk to her when she wakes up," Ellie said. "But go to her now. She needs her mama."

Jan nodded, clasped her mother's hand and the two of them trailed the doctor down the hall.

But Ellie's thoughts were racing as a new connection formed in her mind. She went to the desk again to check some details, trying to let the thoughts settle. "What time was Becky Hornsby brought to the hospital?"

The nurse consulted her computer. "Early afternoon, around one. Our resident chaplain found her in the chapel on one of the pews, wrapped in a blanket."

"So she wasn't brought in by ambulance?"

"No. We checked with all the medic services we use and 911, and they had no calls involving a child matching her description. We also checked admitting, and she was never technically admitted."

Which meant her abductor had somehow snuck her in and left her.

Just then, Derrick strode back to her. "How is she?"

"Her prognosis is promising," Ellie said. "I need to make a call. Hold on."

Something Priscilla Wilkinson said was thundering through Ellie's mind as the phone rang—she'd said Renee had started drinking more heavily *when Kaylee was sick*. If Priscilla had worried her sister was becoming dependent on alcohol, then the illness must have been longer term than the usual childhood coughs and colds. The call connected.

"Hello *again*, Reeves. I get it—I might have dropped the ball on the Wilkinson case, and I'm going to help put it right. But it's Christmas Eve. What more can I do today beyond that sketch?"

"Just one more question for now, Forrester. I'd ask Priscilla Wilkinson, but as you know she's in the hospital." Ellie let that sink in a moment. "Did Kaylee Wilkinson have any health issues before she disappeared?"

"Errr... yeah, as it happens. It didn't really end up in the files because of the presumed drowning, but the kid had a heart transplant about a year before she disappeared. Why?"

"I'll fill you in later," Ellie said, and cut the call. Her own heart was pounding.

Derrick arched a brow. "What was that about?"

"I've found a common denominator between the girls: Kaylee had a heart transplant, Ava a liver transplant and Becky a kidney transplant."

Suspicion crept into Derrick's eyes. "I've heard of abductions to harvest organs. But why kidnap children who had transplants?"

Good question. Although it had to be an important piece of the puzzle.

She snapped her fingers. "Let's find out where the girls had their surgeries. Maybe someone on staff at one of those hospitals saw something. There might even be a surgeon who treated more than one of them. I'll call Lara and ask about Ava."

"While you do that, I'll look at security footage and see if we can determine who left Becky here at the hospital."

ONE HUNDRED TWENTY-NINE

Grateful to escape the smells and sounds of the hospital corridors, Derrick followed the guard into the main office housing the security cameras for the hospital. "Let's narrow down the time frame," he told the hefty man named Buddy. "She was found in the chapel around one p.m. so let's start looking around noon."

Buddy sank into his seat and found the footage for earlier that day. Quickly, they scrolled through it. There were cameras outside and in various hall areas, more in the nursery wing, so they checked outside entrances and the ER door. Derrick watched the ambulance bring in several patients but no child.

He followed a woman dressed as a nurse enter pushing a wheelchair. "Zoom in on her," Derrick said.

Buddy adjusted the zoom featured, enlarging the footage, and Derrick saw she was pushing an elderly man who was hunched over, his head listing to one side.

They continued scrolling, and at the loading zone for supply deliveries, near the kitchen and laundry area, he spotted a tall, broad-shouldered man dressed in a janitor's uniform and hat enter with his face averted from the camera. He rubbed his chin. All along they were looking for a woman, but this man was carrying something, only he made sure the bundle wasn't visible to the camera.

"That could be him," he said. "Let's follow his movements."

Buddy leaned closer, and they tracked the man leaving the storage area with a rolling cart of laundry. He took the service elevator and pushed the cart down the hall. Checking around each corner and glancing up and down the halls, he wove past a storage closet then down a corridor and ended up at the chapel.

Derrick straightened and watched the guy check over his shoulder again, then ease open the chapel door. Clearly satisfied no one was inside, he lifted the bundle that was wrapped in a blanket and carried it in. He lost the image when the man shut the door, but the blanket slipped as the man maneuvered through the door, and Derrick got a glimpse of dark blond hair. It was Becky.

ONE HUNDRED THIRTY

SOMEWHERE ON THE AT

"Where the hell is Becky?" She clawed at her husband, shaking him. "How could you take her from me?"

He wrapped his arms around her so tightly she could barely breathe, the pain was so intense.

"Her fever had spiked dangerously high. I had to save her life."

She shoved at him until he released her. "You're lying. Get away from me. You did this! You killed her just like you did before!"

He shook his head, his eyes grief-stricken, but she didn't care. It was all his fault. He'd stolen everything from her.

But she'd go after what she wanted.

Sarah. She would get her.

And there was nothing he could do to stop her. She'd kill him if he tried.

She ran for her keys, but he chased after her and grabbed her around the waist. "Wait, this has to stop!" he shouted. "I can't keep letting you do this."

She swung her foot back and kicked his knee and he screamed in pain. He had torn his meniscus a while back and still had trouble with it.

"Let me go! Santa comes tonight!" Desperation made her voice

sound shrill, but she didn't care. It couldn't be happening again...
"She *has* to be here."

"But she's not," he yelled. "And stealing these little girls is not going to bring her back. You're only hurting them and their families."

He tried to yank her back, but she grabbed a lamp from the sideboard. "Don't say that. I'm the mother. I know what's best."

He caught her arm, but she swung the lamp and smashed it against his temple. He staggered sideways, grabbed at the wall to stay upright, but she shoved him with both hands and he collapsed backward, his head bashing the floor.

Breath hissing out, heart roaring like a jackhammer, she watched his eyes roll back in his head and for a moment, fear overwhelmed her. She loved her husband. She didn't want to lose him.

But she wanted her daughter back even more.

Panic assailing her, she looked up and saw Kaylee and Ava watching her with wide scared eyes. "Go to your room," she ordered. "Now."

Kaylee clasped Ava's hand and they turned and ran.

She waited until they were in their room then went and locked it, the click roaring in her ears. Then she returned to the living room where her husband still lay, blood pooling beneath his head.

Terror assailing her, she grabbed his arms and dragged him into their bedroom. He was heavy, dead weight. But adrenaline surged through her, and she knew she had to get Sarah tonight, so she tugged and pulled with all her might until she got him into the closet. She ran to the garage and found rope then hurried back and tied his hands and feet together, closing the door and leaving him inside.

Crazed now, fueled by only one thought, she ran for her keys and purse then jumped in her van, the one they'd bought when Piper was born. They'd planned to convert it into a camper for family trips.

Trips she thought she would never take.

But now she had enough space to fit her whole family inside.

Knowing Kaylee would watch over Ava and telling herself that they would be safe out here, where no one knew where they were, until she returned, she started the engine and sped from the garage. The rain had turned to snow now, flakes fluttering down in a windy white haze.

The trees bled together as she flew down the long winding road and the farm disappeared into the blanket of white behind her.

Ellie snagged a bottle of water and found a table in the cafeteria. Staff wandered in for snacks and meals, low chatter a sign they respected the families also seeking food and quiet time while waiting for news of loved ones.

Hoping they were close to cracking the case, she phoned Lara.

"Did you find Ava?" Lara asked anxiously.

"Not yet, but we may have a lead," Ellie said. "Lara, did you or your family ever have contact with a family named the Wilkinsons or Hornsbys?"

"No, not that I remember. Aren't those the families the reporter said have missing children, too?"

"Yes. They have daughters around Ava's age, and each one of them had been in the hospital," she answered. "Could the girls have met at a camp or something?"

"Ava didn't attend any camps. We kept her close to home to monitor her, due to her illness."

"About that," she said. "Where did Ava have her liver transplant?"

"At Scottish Rite in Atlanta. Is that important?"

"I'm trying to find a connection between the three girls. I'm going to text Deputy Eastwood a photo of a sketch done by a police artist. Take a good look and see if you recognize the woman."

Ellie paused and sent the text, then waited a minute. "Have you seen her before? Perhaps at the hospital."

"No, not at the hospital, although I was pretty stressed then and didn't really pay attention to anyone else in the waiting room," Lara said. "But... she kind of looks like a woman I saw at the pumpkin farm around Halloween. I saw her crying and asked if everything was okay. She said she'd just lost someone close then hurried away." Lara's voice sounded wary. "Do you think she took Ava?"

"I don't know. It's possible. I'll keep you posted."

Ellie hung up then called Bryce. "Everything okay there?" she asked the sheriff when he answered.

"No action here."

"Good," Ellie said. "Listen, I need you to put Priscilla on the phone." Now that she'd confirmed the heart transplant with Forrester, she needed more details from Priscilla.

"All right, just a minute." She heard the swish of air as Bryce walked, then the squeak of a door.

"Ms. Wilkinson," she heard him say, "it's Sheriff Waters. Detective Reeves wants to speak to you for a moment."

Ellie tapped her boot on the floor as she waited.

"Did you find Kaylee?"

"Not yet, but we're working on it."

"How's Becky?"

"She's stable but sleeping now, so I haven't had a chance to talk to her. But I need to ask you another question. Am I right in thinking Kaylee had a heart transplant?"

"Yes, that's right. She had septal defect—a hole in the heart."

"Where did Kaylee have her surgery?"

Ellie heard sheets rustling and imagined Priscilla trying to sit up. "Children's Healthcare in Atlanta."

"Okay thanks. I have to go, Priscilla. I'll keep you posted."

Ellie scratched her head. *Dammit, all the girls had surgeries at different hospitals.*

So why had the kidnapper targeted them? And where were they now?

ONE HUNDRED THIRTY-TWO

SOMEWHERE ON THE AT

"I'm scared," Ava whispered as she huddled on the bed beside Kaylee.

Kaylee looked scared, too. "We have to check on Daddy," she said.

"He's not my daddy," Ava replied stubbornly.

"He's not my real one either," Kaylee said, her voice quivering. "But my mommy is dead, and he's been nice to me..."

Ava hugged her knees to her, wishing she had Bunny. "She said my mommy didn't want me, but she's a liar."

"What was it like when you ran away?" Kaylee asked.

"Scary and cold and dark," Ava admitted.

"I know. I runned away when I first got here. But I got lost and then they found me and I've been too scared to go in the woods again."

"But I don't want to die," Ava whispered.

"Me neither."

Kaylee jumped off the bed, went to the door and tried to open it. Ava ran to help her. "Do you know where we are?" Kaylee asked as they pulled and tugged. But the door was heavy and wouldn't budge.

Ava grabbed the ruler from the shelf where they kept the craft stuff. "Near the Christmas tree farm." Ava jammed the ruler into the space between the door opening and wall just like her daddy did once when she got locked in the bathroom. "My mommy brought me there to pick a tree."

The door was stuck. The stupid ruler wasn't working. "Maybe we can crawl out the window."

Kaylee blew out a breath and they ran to the bed and climbed on it. Ava could see the snow falling outside, swirling and blowing.

They tried to barge the window open, but it was held tight. Kaylee fumbled with the lock, twisting at it until it came unlocked. But when she shoved at the bottom of the window, it still wouldn't come open.

"It's nailed shut," Kaylee said, then slammed her fist against the wood.

Tears dripped down Ava's cheeks and Kaylee sank back onto the bed and began to cry, too.

A noise sounded outside, and she heard a thump from somewhere. She and Kaylee scrambled against the wall, burrowing against each other. Was that the man? Would he come and help them? Or would he take them away like he did Becky?

A car rumbled, and Kaylee clutched Ava's hand. The lady was so mad when she left.

What if she was already back? What would she do to her and Kaylee?

Ellie and Derrick had sandwiches delivered from the Corner Café, then carried them to the conference room. Tonight, Vera had wanted Ellie to join her and Randall for a festive dinner, but Ellie couldn't celebrate when Ava and Kaylee were still not home with their families.

She jotted the latest information they'd gathered regarding the abductions and where the girls lived, then her theory about the woman meeting Renee at the AA meeting.

"The security footage at the hospital showed that a man dressed as a janitor dropped Becky at the chapel," Derrick said.

Ellie stewed over that fact as she ate her roasted turkey sandwich. "Then we may be dealing with more than one person." She snapped her fingers. "A couple maybe."

Derrick's laptop pinged with an email alert, and he scooped up some mashed potatoes and gravy as he opened it. The fork paused halfway to his mouth.

"What is it?" Ellie asked.

"I got the footage from the prison. According to the warden, Renee only had two visitors. Her sister and another woman. She signed in as *Jordan Jones*."

Ellie almost gasped. That name again.

Derrick pulled up the recording of Jordan Jones's visit.

"She wears her hair in a short brown bob," Ellie said as she peered at the footage. "Hard to see her face, though, with the way she keeps looking down at her hands."

But it was clear Renee wasn't meeting a stranger. Their theory that the supposed beach witness and Renee's AA sponsor were one and the same person might be firming up. They watched as the woman handed Renee a soda that she must have purchased from the prison store. Renee uncapped it and took a long slow drink. Her dirty blond hair was disheveled, her blue eyes flat, her movements void of energy, her complexion made even paler by the stark orange jumpsuit. Her hand shook as she drank from the bottle again.

Renee said something, her lip trembling, then dropped her head into her hands and began to sob. The woman reached across and stroked her arm, before a passing guard seemed to admonish her for touching a prisoner.

Renee sat up and wiped at her nose with the back of her hand. Before nodding and mouthing a "thank you" to her visitor.

Ellie had to push her food away. She couldn't swallow for the tears clogging her throat. How tragic that this mother died accused of a crime she hadn't committed and without reuniting with her daughter. *I'm here for you, Renee*, Ellie promised silently.

"I'll send this footage to the lab," Derrick said. He polished off his roast beef while he forwarded the video. "Maybe they can enhance her face, then run it through facial rec."

Ellie checked the time stamp, then the prison report on Renee's death. "The soda," she said. "Renee died a few hours after that visit. The woman must have put something in it."

Giving a nod, Derrick forwarded the video to his Bureau partner. Ellie texted Deputy Landrum: *We think the kidnapper used the alias Jordan Jones. Anyone of that name in Jan Hornsby's Facebook group?*

Ellie imagined poor Renee staring at the dank dirty prison walls each night, wondering where Kaylee was, if she was even still alive, facing life in prison and knowing that people thought she'd caused her own daughter's death. And then knowing she'd be abused by the other prisoners.

She stood, running her hands up and down her arms as she crossed to the whiteboard. "Since Kaylee was the first abduction, she might be significant." Ellie wrote the dates of the abductions. "Kaylee was kidnapped December twentieth last year, Ava December twentieth this year, exactly a year apart." Her mind raced to connect the dots. "But Becky was taken on June 6, a few months after Kaylee went missing."

Ellie wrote the dates and circled them in red. "December twentieth has to be mean something to the kidnapper." She studied it for a minute. "The girls are all around the same age. The other commonality between the three victims is the transplant surgeries."

"Maybe it was someone who worked at the hospital," Derrick said. "Could be someone who blamed the parents for their child's illness and thought they could take better care of the kids."

Ellie contemplated that theory. "That makes sense, but two underwent surgeries in Atlanta hospitals while one was in Chattanooga, so unless the employee worked multiple hospitals in two states, it doesn't fit."

"No," replied Derrick. "But we now know a kidnapping team is working together here, a woman and a man. Becky was also given the medication she needed. Perhaps whoever took her has knowledge of hospital procedures, access to the medications and the children's medical needs."

Ellie's pulse raced.

"It could be someone who hacked into hospital files," Derrick suggested.

Ellie tapped her finger on the board, and suddenly the dots seemed to connect themselves. "Derrick, it's not the *where* of the surgeries—it's the *when*. Lara said Ava's was two years ago, Jan said Becky's was a couple of years back, and didn't Forrester say Kaylee had surgery about a year before she vanished?"

Derrick opened his laptop and scrutinized his notes. "You're right."

Which could mean Ava and Kaylee are still alive. "Transplant organs don't last long outside the body—maybe twenty-four hours —and all the girls had surgery about the same time two years ago. Is it possible to find out who donated the organs to each of the girls?"

He removed his phone from his pocket. "The lists are private to protect donors and recipients. They can both sign agreements if they want their names divulged and then decide if they want to meet. It would not be easy to gain access. I'll have to obtain a subpoena."

While he phoned a judge, her mind sprinted with possibilities. MWC had preyed on people wanting to adopt or find a child to fill a void. If this was a couple working together, that might be their motive. They could have lost a child. She'd considered this at first, but hadn't found anything to support it. Time to analyze the theory from a different angle.

She booted up her own laptop, accessed the state death records, entered the date December 20, then narrowed the search to children between the ages of five and seven. While the program ran, a possible scenario formed in her head. Names appeared on the database and she found a half dozen kids who'd tragically died through accidents or illness.

Working on the fact that Becky had been left in Gainesville, she decided to first focus on children who'd died in the north Georgia area. That cut the list to one.

Piper Gooding. The poor girl had drowned.

She opened another tab and searched for any news reports on the death. She clicked on the first hit: DAWSONVILLE GIRL DROWNS AT LOCAL LANDMARK.

Local girl, six-year-old Piper Gooding, tragically dies after falling through the ice at a frozen pond. Mother, Gayle Gooding, also injured trying to rescue her.

. . .

Ellie lost her breath as she read the names. The image of the tiny graves at White Lilies Cemetery bombarded her. The woman kneeling by the small grave, grieving, looking up at her husband and yelling that he killed their daughter... The caretaker had mentioned the gravestone belonged to a family named Gooding.

Ellie stood, pumped. Something like hope zinged through her. She thought about the puzzle Lara had been putting together and the pieces Jasper had scattered on the floor in a rage and felt as if she'd found the missing piece. A wave of sadness washed over her for Piper's parents. Yet she couldn't ignore the commonality. She shuffled the clues around in her mind.

She raced through to the main station bullpen, where Heath Landrum was hunched in front of his computer. He looked up as she strode towards him.

"Sorry, boss. I was about to reply to your text. No Jordan Jones in the group—I was checking if she was a friend of one of the members but nothing so far."

"What about a Gayle Gooding?"

Landrum's eyes widened. "That name sounds familiar..." He typed rapidly for a few seconds. "Yeah, thought so—she's one of the lurkers. A member of the group who never posts or reacts to other's posts. Looks like her profile's private though."

"See what you can piece together," Ellie said, and rushed back to the conference room. Derrick had finished his call to the judge and was looking at her expectantly.

"How would a child become an organ donor?" Ellie asked.

"Parents would have to give permission," Derrick said. "What are you thinking?"

"Listen to this." Ellie read from the article. *"The terrible accident happened at Cattail Cove on December twentieth. Six-year-old Piper Gooding fell into the pond, which was thought frozen over, and when her mother Gayle raced to save her, she too fell into the icy water. Piper's father, Dr. Silas Gooding, pulled both mother and daughter from the water, but Piper was pronounced dead on arrival at hospital. Mrs. Gooding suffered serious injuries, and has been placed in a drug-induced coma to give her brain time to heal."*

"Jesus," Derrick muttered.

"Find out if Piper was the organ donor for Kaylee, Becky and Ava." Ellie's heart gave a pang, and she ran a search in DMV records for Gayle Gooding. The photo was three years old, and the woman's brown hair was shorter, her face slightly fuller, but it could be the woman in the sketch.

Next, she phoned Shondra. "I'm sending you a photo of a woman who lost a child two years ago. Her name is Gayle Gooding. Ask Lara if she's seen her near the house or near Ava."

"Hang on," Shondra said.

Tense seconds passed, then Shondra returned. "Lara said that's the woman she saw at the pumpkin patch. And Emily Nettles is here. She said Gayle saw her for grief counseling, but she stopped therapy a year ago."

A cold sweat broke out on Ellie's neck. A year ago—right when Kaylee was abducted. "Thanks, I'll keep you posted."

While Derrick answered a phone call from his partner, she searched for an address for the Goodings. She found a listing for a house in Dawsonville and a phone number.

She jangled her keys as Derrick ended the call. "They're working on gathering that information," he said.

They had no time to waste. With news airing about Becky being found, her kidnapper could be panicking and might be planning to move Kaylee and Ava. "Let's go. I have an address for the Goodings."

ONE HUNDRED THIRTY-FOUR

DAWSONVILLE, GEORGIA

Ellie rolled her aching shoulders. With the inclement weather, the drive to Dawnsonville seemed to take forever. From her map, she knew the area where the Goodings lived consisted of acres of farmland. She phoned Cord and explained their theory. "Will you meet us there in case we need to search the property?"

"I'm on my way," Cord agreed.

Ellie thanked him and hung up, hope warring with panic. Night was setting in and Christmas Eve was upon them. Endless farmland and winding mountain roads led deeper into the hills that stretched in all directions. Clapboard houses and rustic cabins were spread out in darkness, yet most were decorated with twinkling lights, Christmas blow ups, and a manger scene glowed on the lawn of a church.

They passed a salvage store, stone yard, and garage and outbuildings erected for a weekly flea market. Yard art crafted from metal in the shape of bears, bobcats, and birds of prey sat in front of a country store boasting boiled peanuts and local honey for sale.

A few scattered snowflakes had started to fall as they passed the sign for Big Daddy's Barbecue. Red and green lights flashed along the awning of the store and a neon sign advertised a Christmas Eve special of pulled pork, black eyed peas and collards.

Ellie remembered coming here with her father for a NASCAR event, and every year hikers began their trek on the AT from the input trail here.

But the serene beauty was lost as she feared the isolated countryside had become a haven for a child kidnapper. All Ellie could think about was Lara and Priscilla and how excruciating each day was for them. The holiday had to accentuate their anguish.

She drove through town, then followed the GPS along a country road that led towards a Christmas tree farm that had been advertised in the town. *ENJOY AN OLD FASHIONED FAMILY HOLIDAY – Cut Down Your Own Tree! Hot chocolate, homemade decorations and sleigh rides!*

But judging from the fact that there were no lights glowing from the Spruce Tree Farms, they'd obviously already closed for business. The hair on her arms rose. Off the road, with no other houses or businesses nearby, the land looked eerie and lonely.

She veered down the drive to the farm to check it out, snowflakes swirling in a blinding haze and dotting her windshield. A brisk wind battered the spruce and fir trees still remaining. One section held saplings not yet mature enough for cutting while a larger section looked as if it had been picked over, only sad trees that needed loving left. Ellie used to beg to take one of them home and nurture it, but Vera insisted on having the perfect ones, just like she'd wanted Ellie to be perfect.

There were no cars or lights, and the sleigh and outbuilding were void of decorations.

Seeing no one was there, she wove to the right and followed the narrow ribbon of road up an incline and over a bend where an older farmhouse was perched on the hill.

The white paint had faded on the wood, black shutters slapped in the gusty breeze, and a wide front porch wrapped around the side of the house. Flowerbeds that probably held an array of colors in the fall and spring were now dusted in white, and icicles dangled from the windowsills.

"Looks like lights are on inside," Derrick said. "One downstairs and another in an upstairs room."

The tiny window at the top suggested an attic room or bedroom. Were the girls being held captive here?

She cut the car lights, eased off the gas and veered onto the shoulder to keep from being seen. Climbing out, she and Derrick crept along the bush-lined drive until they neared the house. The wind whined through the bare branches of the pines and snowflakes spattered her coat and cheeks as they approached.

Ellie pointed to the silver Lexus beneath the carport. "I don't see the van."

"They may not be here," Derrick mouthed.

But there were lights on in the house, so they couldn't assume anything. Pulling their service weapons, they darted along the weeds and bushes until they reached the front porch.

Slowly inching up the steps, Ellie paused every other second to listen for voices or signs someone was inside.

A quick peek and she didn't see anyone. A deadly quiet echoed around her. Derrick motioned that he was going around back, and she indicated that she understood. Slowly, she turned the doorknob and tiptoed inside the house.

The wood floor creaked, the furnace whirring in the silence. The scent of cinnamon hung heavy in the air along with the smell of pine and spruce.

A Christmas tree glittered with lights and ornaments and the kitchen table held signs of Christmas crafts left unfinished. Three angel costumes hung across the doorway, similar to the ones that had been worn in the Angel Pageant. She paused to listen, then went to the back door and waved Derrick inside.

He surveyed the scene, then they began to search the first floor. Somewhere down the hall they heard a noise, and she led the way and found a bathroom then a locked door. Derrick jiggled the doorknob, and she braced her gun as he shouted, "FBI! Anyone here?"

Pushing open the door, Ellie illuminated the space with her flashlight and found an empty bed. Derrick checked the bathroom and she rushed to the closet. It was dark inside and the door was locked, but as she pressed her ear to the door, she thought she heard a moan. Her heart tripped in her chest. Were the girls locked inside?

Shaking with anger at the thought, she slammed her shoulder against the door, but it didn't budge. "Who's there?" she shouted.

Silence mushroomed around her, thick and stagnant. Maybe she'd imagined the moan.

Fueled by the need to save the girls, she raised her foot and kicked the door in. Wood splintered and cracked and it crashed in.

Quickly she shined her light across the interior. The girls weren't inside, but a man lay on the floor half-conscious. She moved forward, shining the beam over his body. Gray slacks and white shirt, both bloody. Teeth gritted, she stooped and focused on his face. Broad jaw, short brown hair, a gash on his forehead.

Silas Gooding. She recognized him from the online article about the accident.

She pressed two fingers to his neck to feel for a pulse and held her own breath as she listened for the sound of his.

ONE HUNDRED THIRTY-FIVE

"Derrick! Dr. Gooding is in here!" She barely felt a pulse, but the man was alive.

Derrick rushed to her side, glanced at the man, then yanked his phone from his belt. "I'll call an ambulance."

"Help is on the way, Dr. Gooding." Ellie stood, adrenaline surging. "I'll look for the girls."

"I'll take the downstairs," Derrick said. "Be careful, Ellie. The wife might still be here."

Ellie clenched her gun and headed into the hall. As Derrick called the ambulance, he rushed back downstairs. With every step she took, she listened for sounds that the woman or the children were home, but only the creak of the wood floors and the wind howling outside broke the silence. Tension coiled inside her as if a rubber band was wound around her lungs, squeezing the air from her.

There were two rooms, one on the left and one on the right.

She stopped at the first one and paused at the door. Except for the whir of the furnace rumbling, it was silent. She twisted the doorknob and the door screeched open. Inside she spotted a single bed, covers rumpled, and a table that held a cup of water, a prescription pill bottle and vials of insulin. This must be where the couple had kept Becky.

Shaking with fear, she stepped back into the hallway and inched to the next room. She jiggled the door and it swung open. Inside, she found twin beds and a play area with an art table, toys and books.

"Ava? Kaylee?" She called the girls' names over and over as she searched the closet and under the bed, but the children were not there.

Dammit, where were they?

Moving back into the hallway, she noted another door at the end of the hall. Senses alert, she opened the door and saw a flight of stairs that led into an attic. That was where she'd seen the light outside.

Shining her flashlight along the rickety steps, she headed upward. The narrow staircase smelled musty and dust motes floated in the air. When she reached the landing, she shined her flashlight around and found another single bed with a thin blanket.

Had Gayle Gooding kept one of the girls up here?

Fingers of disgust danced through her as she walked over and saw scratch marks on the inside of the door. The thought of one of the little girls—or all of them—trying to claw their way out made her knees buckle.

ONE HUNDRED THIRTY-SIX

"Shh, don't cry. We're going to get Sarah and then we'll go see Piper," Gayle told the girls as she sped toward Sarah Lundy's house in Dawsonville. Ava and Kaylee huddled in the back seat, clinging to each other, their little cries reminding her of Piper when she missed her best friend's birthday party when she was five. She'd wanted to ride the ponies. Gayle had felt so helpless that day and rocked Piper and held her while she struggled to breathe, and she'd promised her daughter that one day she'd have pony rides at her own party.

She brushed her tears with the back of her hand. But that would never happen.

Silas was angry and Becky was gone, and she didn't know what she'd do once she got Sarah. But she'd think of something. All that mattered was that she'd have her family together again. They would all be together.

She'd panicked when her husband fell and hit his head. But on the road to Sarah's, she'd decided she couldn't leave the girls alone —what kind of mother would do that?

Then she'd heard the news on the radio about police looking for Ava and that Becky had been found and they thought the children's disappearances might be connected. She'd been terrified they'd figure out where she was.

If they found her and the children, they'd take them away and that would mean losing Piper all over again. She couldn't live like that. Not another year without holding her daughter in her arms.

The girls kept crying, though, and that was making her nervous. Her skin was crawling. But the flashing lights of a police car in the distance reminded her to slow down. She couldn't draw attention to herself. The snow thickened to a white haze, just as it had that awful night two years ago when Silas took them to Cattail Cove.

Vision blurring, she was catapulted back to that night.

"Stop, Piper, stop!" Terror seized her as she raced onto the ice-covered pond. Her feet slid, Piper's ponytail twirling in the wind as she skated over the surface. Then the sound of ice cracking, Silas yelling at both of them, Piper screaming...

Her little arms flailing to keep her from sinking as the thin layer of ice snapped and melted beneath her, shattering like crystal.

"Wait, Gayle!" Silas shouted.

But it was too late. She was almost to her daughter. She had to save her. One more step, another, she reached out her hand to save Piper, but the ice burst open beneath her boots and she was falling and screaming. Freezing cold water dragged her beneath the surface and stung her eyes.

Fighting the force, she blinked and searched the darkness for Piper. Her hat had come off, her blond hair floating around her face like white snakes... Her little arms pumping, struggling to do the crawl stroke she'd learned in her swimming lessons. But she was sinking deeper and deeper.

Her lungs screamed for air. Her clothes felt heavy, dragging her deeper and deeper, but she ordered herself to keep fighting. She pumped her legs and arms, clawing at the frigid water. Her eyes hurt, her skin tingled, and she felt herself moving slower, her limbs weighing her down, the water flooding her nose, her lungs on fire, screaming...

Then Piper disappeared in a cloud of darkness, and her vision turned to black and she felt herself plunging to her death...

Sometime later, the sound of a voice murmured in her ear as if it was far far away. "Hang in there, honey. We're on the way to the hospital."

She tried to open her eyes to find her little girl, but her eyes felt frozen shut, her body was shaking uncontrollably and she felt numb all over. The sound of sirens wailed and bright lights spun into the blinding darkness... "Piper..."

"I've got her," Silas said, although his voice sounded like gravel.

Knowing he was taking care of Piper, she let herself fall back into the abyss. She was going to die, she knew it.

But she didn't care. As long as she'd saved Piper.

ONE HUNDRED THIRTY-SEVEN

Cord called Lola as he raced toward the address Ellie had sent, hoping she found the little girls safe and alive.

"Sorry I have to cancel tonight," he told her. "Ellie has a lead on the missing child. Benji and I are meeting her to search the property."

Lola released a long-winded sigh. "All right. I understand you can't say no to Ellie."

"Not when a child's life is in danger," Cord said, struggling to control his irritation. He felt like he was riding a slippery slope with Lola. He cared about her and they'd grown close, but when Ellie needed him, he would be there for her.

"I'm on the task force Agent Fox is spearheading, Lola. And you want that little girl found, don't you?"

"Of course I do," Lola said. "You know I dropped food at the Truman's earlier."

"That was really caring of you, Lola," he said and meant it. Thankfully, she was finally starting to heal from her ordeal with that damn sick serial killer.

"I just want us to spend Christmas together. But you're right, the Truman girl comes first. I know her parents are worried sick."

"Thanks for understanding," Cord said. "And we'll see each other tomorrow."

He reached the fork in the road to turn to the Gooding property. "I have to go now. It's almost whiteout conditions and I can barely see out here."

"Be careful," she said.

But his reception was breaking up and he could barely hear over the sound of the wipers and defroster. Ahead, the white blended into the night, reminding him of when he'd been lost in the wilderness himself as a kid. When nobody had cared or come looking for him.

Thank God these kids had Ellie.

ONE HUNDRED THIRTY-EIGHT

A car horn blasted the air, jolting Gayle back to the wintry scene in front of her. The storm was gaining momentum, the car skidding as she rounded a corner and fought to maintain control. A deer suddenly bolted across the road, and she swerved toward the shoulder to avoid hitting it.

Calm down. You'll pick up Sarah and find a nice place to have Christmas. She glanced at the girls in the back, hating that she'd scared them.

"Just wait till you see Sarah," she told the girls. "She's going to make our family whole again."

"I'm hungry," Kaylee whined.

"And I gotta go to the bathroom," Ava said in a quivery voice.

She ground her teeth. There was no way she could stop at a store or even a drive-thru right now. Someone might see the girls or one of them—Ava most likely—might start screaming and draw attention to them.

"I don't feel good," Ava cried.

Piper was never whiny like that. She was sweet and obedient, and she did what she was told. She was such a happy little girl, always smiling and singing, her voice like an angel.

"We'll pick up some food after we get Sarah and see Piper," she said. Once they met her, they'd understand everything.

Then they'd be grateful she'd brought them all together. One happy family.

But the haunting memory of that day at the pond still held Gayle in its clutches and wouldn't let go, like a vulture sinking its claws into carrion, devouring it piece by piece.

Pain pounded through her head when she woke up in the hospital. Machines beeped and hummed in a droning sound, and she felt odd, as if she was floating outside her body. She tried to move and opened her eyes, blinking against the bright white lights.

"Gayle? You're awake?"

She blinked again then twisted her aching head to the side. Silas was sitting next to her, head in his hands, his shoulders shaking.

She groaned, disoriented, her mind a black hole of screams and darkness as if she was fighting her way against a river current sweeping her into a vortex. "Where am I?" Her voice sounded raw—barely there.

"The hospital," Silas murmured as he cradled her hand in his and grasped it. "You don't remember?"

She winced, sinking deeper into the warmth of the covers. "A blur... what happened?"

"We were at Cattail Cove with Piper. She ran onto the ice..."

The brittle sound of her daughter's screams reverberated in her head, making her shudder. She saw her blond hair swirling around her face... they were under the water...

The pond... frozen water... ice cracking and giving away...

She tried to sit up with a gasp, but pain ricocheted through her and she collapsed back onto the bed. "You had her... we were in the car... we saved her..."

Silas made a choked sound. "I'm so sorry, Gayle... she didn't make it."

His words sounded as if they were in a wind tunnel. Then denial set in. "No... where is she, Silas?" This time she forced her body up, ignoring the pain as panic took root. Her eyes darted across the room. "Where is she? She has to be here."

"I'm so sorry." Silas's deep moan of pain enveloped her.

Then she looked into her husband's tear-stained face. She'd seen him with that same grave look in his eyes when he'd lost a patient before. But he had to be wrong. He had to be.

"No, you saved her," she whispered. "You do it all the time."

"I tried, but I couldn't," he whispered, his voice filled with anguish. "I did everything, Gayle, but she was under the water too long and... I couldn't revive her."

She shoved at the covers to get off the bed but her legs felt weak. "No, you're lying. I have to see her! Where is she?"

Silas gripped her arms to keep her from falling into a puddle on the floor. "Honey, I had to bury her. You were in a coma. You have been for a month."

Shock immobilized her, and she went bone still. "That can't be true. It was near Christmas. We were getting ready for Santa..."

"Christmas has come and gone," he said in a low voice. "I'm sorry. I had to make the decision..." He lifted her chin with his thumb. "There was no time."

Gayle clawed at his arms. "What are you saying, Silas?"

But in her heart she already knew.

ONE HUNDRED THIRTY-NINE

Cord arrived just as Ellie met the medics at the front door of the Goodings' house and ushered them back to treat the doctor.

"The girls?"

"They're not here," Ellie told Cord. "The husband has been hurt, so Gayle may have driven off with them, although he didn't think she left with them. Do a thorough search of the property and that tree farm down there. Derrick is looking for an outbuilding or tornado shelter."

"I saw him on my way in. I'll spread out further to look," Cord said, his voice determined.

While he led Benji back outside and the medics worked on Silas, she searched the kitchen and desk for a calendar, planning book, or something that might indicate where Gayle Gooding might go next.

Meanwhile, Derrick examined the exterior of the house and Dr. Gooding's car and phone.

She came up empty, then stepped back into the hall as the medics were loading Gooding onto a stretcher. "He needs stitches and probably has a concussion, but should be all right," one of the medics reported.

Gooding moaned and opened his eyes, blinking rapidly, disoriented.

Ellie rushed to his side. "Dr. Gooding, my name is Detective Ellie Reeves."

He made a strangled sound. "My wife... Gayle... the girls..."

"She's not here, and neither are they," Ellie said. "Do you know where she took them?"

"She's not well," he mumbled. "Told her it had to stop."

"I think the girls received organs from your daughter. Is that right?"

He nodded, emotions clouding his eyes. "Did you find Becky?"

"Yes," Ellie replied. "She's going to make it. You carried her to the hospital, didn't you?"

"I had to. She was getting sicker and weaker..."

"That's a good thing. Her mother is with her now. But you have to tell us where your wife was going with Ava and Kaylee."

"To get Sarah," he mumbled weakly.

Ellie's heart thundered. "Sarah?"

"Sarah, she..." his breath wheezed out, "received Piper's lungs."

Ellie clenched his arm. "What is her last name?"

"Lundy," he said. "My wife... Gayle was so depressed, despondent after Piper died. Then she became obsessed with knowing who received her organs."

"And you helped her find them," Ellie filled in. "You work at the children's hospital."

"The transplant team," he rasped. "Gayle blamed me for the accident. I save lives but I couldn't save our daughter's. But after the accident, Gayle was in a coma, and I had to make the choice quickly about what to do."

Ellie's lungs tightened. "I understand. You couldn't save Piper, but you could save other sick children who needed organs."

He nodded miserably. "But Gayle hated me for it. Last year on the anniversary of Piper's death, she took Kaylee."

"I know," Ellie said. "And we can sort it all out later. Right now, though, your wife must be desperate. What kind of car does she drive?"

"A white Ford Econoline," he said, coughing.

Ellie looked up as Derrick walked in. "Mrs. Gooding has gone after another child, a girl named Sarah Lundy. Find out where she lives and issue a bulletin for Gayle's vehicle. A white Ford Econoline."

Derrick charged into action, and he phoned her captain to make the request.

A minute later, he turned to her, "I have the address. We'll call local police on the way."

"You can take him now," Ellie said, motioning to the medics. "But I want him transported to Bluff County." If his wife came after him to silence him, she'd most likely go to Gainesville. He'd also be closer for her own people to guard him until he was well enough to be arraigned.

Gooding reached out his hand, waving for Ellie to listen. "Detective, please find Gayle and the children. And... please... don't hurt Gayle."

Sympathy for his wife's grief, for everything she'd lost, filled Ellie. But what she had done was unforgiveable, and rescuing the girls safely was her priority, so she rushed outside without making any promises. She'd do whatever she had to do in order to save Ava and Kaylee.

ONE HUNDRED FORTY

Ellie and Derrick left Cord searching the property and sped toward the Lundy house. She prayed Silas was wrong and that Gayle hadn't gone after Sarah.

But who knew what kind of mindset the woman was in by now?

The snow had lightened up but was accumulating, traffic slow as she veered onto the street where Sarah Lundy lived with her parents Jo and Harold. The house was a brick ranch which had been painted white, with twinkling Christmas tree lights adorning the windows and the cornflower-blue door. A giant blow-up Santa and reindeer waved in the wind in the front yard, and a sign saying *Santa Stop Here!* stood by the driveway. Fresh snow blanketed the roof, giving it the appearance of a wintry holiday card.

Except the air was charged with pure fear. Ellie was certain now that Gayle had killed Renee and had attempted to kill Priscilla.

On the drive over, Derrick had alerted local police. Ellie spotted Gayle's van on the street and pulled to the curb just as a squad car from the Dawsonville Police Department arrived. The officer emerged but stayed by his car, per their orders to wait for backup.

Ellie cut the engine, then pulled her night binoculars to analyze the scene. Red, green and silver lights sparkled on the Christmas tree visible through the window. Past it, she saw movement, then spotted Gayle and a woman who had to be Sarah's mother. The front door jerked open a second later, and Gayle stepped outside, her arm around the shoulders of a little strawberry-blond girl with freckles. *Dear God.* The woman looked disheveled, eyes flaring with panic, desperation and determination as if she was in another place, another time.

Little Sarah looked terrified, wide-eyed and crying.

Ellie lifted her weapon from her holster, and Derrick did the same, then they both eased from the Jeep.

Gayle was tugging the child onto the stoop, and the little girl screamed as she dragged her down the steps. Sarah's parents ran out, shouting and yelling at Gayle to stop.

Ellie froze as Gayle lifted a pistol and aimed it at the couple. "Stay back or I'll shoot!"

Mrs. Lundy darted down a step anyway, eyes wild with horror. "Please let her go," Mrs. Lundy begged. "It's Christmas..."

Mr. Lundy clutched his wife to prevent her from lunging forward and getting shot. "Don't hurt her," the father shouted.

Ellie sensed the patrol officer moving and heard Derrick order him to hold off.

"Gayle," Ellie said, then motioned for the Lundys to stay where they were. "I'm Detective Reeves. Please put down the gun."

Derrick crept around the back of the Jeep toward the van, where she saw Ava and Kaylee banging on the back window, screaming.

"Please," Ellie said. "You're scaring Sarah."

"Go away and let me leave." Gayle waved the gun around, her expression crazed. "I need my Piper back and these people stole her from me." Her voice warbled. "I can't go another Christmas without her."

Ellie forced a calming voice. "I understand, and am so sorry for your loss," she said, slowly lifting her hand to indicate she didn't intend to shoot. "We talked to your husband and he explained everything."

The Lundys looked confused, and poor Sarah was shaking, her little legs flailing to stand up.

"Silas loves you," Ellie said, striving to deescalate the scene. "He's so sorry for what happened. I know there was a terrible accident at the pond. Tell me what happened that day, Gayle."

The gun bobbed in her hand, but she clutched Sarah tighter. "Silas insisted on taking us to that place, Cattail Cove. I told him it was too cold, but he wouldn't listen." Tears rained down her face. "Then Piper ran onto the ice. She thought the pond was frozen but it was just a thin sheet of ice. I could see the water bubbling and moving below it..." With her free hand, she swiped at the tears on her face that were mingling with snowflakes clinging to her lashes.

"But the ice cracked, didn't it?" Ellie prodded. Behind her, she felt Derrick and the officer slipping toward the van to rescue Ava and Kaylee. She had to keep Gayle talking.

The Lundys were clasping each other, their terror vibrating in the frigid air.

Gayle made a strangled sound. "It cracked and she fell under, and I tried to save her... then I plunged into the water, and I was fighting to get to her, but... it was so cold and dark and I lost her..."

"That must have been so horrible," Ellie said softly. "You trying to save her, the cold water seeping into your lungs... but you did everything you could to save her."

"It wasn't enough," Gayle said shrilly. "It wasn't and then in the car, Silas said he had her, and I thought she was okay..." Hysteria sharpened her cries. "Then I woke up in the hospital..." Her voice trailed off, her eyes pleading with the girl's parents.

"Silas tried to save her, didn't he?" Ellie said, praying she could calm Gayle somehow.

"He said he did, but then he didn't," she shouted. "He let them cut her up and pass her around, give her away piece by piece. Then he buried her while I was in a coma, and I... didn't even get to say goodbye." She pulled Sarah down another step. "But I found her now. I found all of her and I want her back."

Sarah's mother reached out her hand. "I'm so sorry you lost your daughter," she said, hurt and fear heavy in her tone. "We knew when we got the call for Sarah's transplant, that it meant someone lost a child that day, but we didn't know who it was." Her gentle tone implored Gayle to listen. "I can imagine how it felt to lose her. When Sarah was sick and waiting on the transplant list, we thought we were going to lose her, too, and I was terrified."

"But you didn't because of my baby!" Gayle said brokenly.

Sadness filled Mrs. Lundy's eyes. "I am sorry for you, Gayle, and we will forever be grateful for your sacrifice. But Sarah is not your daughter. Just look at her." She hesitated and stepped forward. Her husband released her, obviously hoping his wife could reach Gayle.

Gayle's anger wilted slightly, her hand dipping slightly with the gun, her grip on Sarah loosening slightly.

"I know you were a good mother," Mrs. Lundy continued. "You almost died trying to save Piper. But right now, you're frightening Sarah."

"She's right," Ellie said. "You don't want to scare Sarah or hurt her. If you do, you're hurting part of Piper."

ONE HUNDRED FORTY-ONE

You're hurting Piper. Hurting Piper. Hurting Piper.

No… she would *never* hurt Piper. She lived and breathed for her child. She wanted her back so badly that the fierce hollow void in her chest could never ever be filled. Not unless Piper was with her.

"Please, let Sarah go," the other woman pleaded. "She's just a little girl and she's been through so much already. She fought for her life and is terrified now. I know you don't want to hurt her."

You're hurting Piper. Hurting Piper.

Gayle looked down at the little girl, whose freckled cheeks were soaked in tears, and her stomach rose to her throat. The fear in Sarah's eyes tore at her. She heard her whimpering and glanced around at the detective and the FBI agent and the police officer. She was cornered.

Silas was right. So was this woman. Sarah was not her child. Not her Piper. Neither was Ava or Kaylee or Becky. They had pieces of Piper, but it wasn't the same.

They would never love her as their mommy, just like Piper would never have loved some stranger who'd stolen her.

Closing her eyes for a brief second, the pain ripped at her as if some invisible force was shredding her heart. Then the wind ruffled her hair and a snowflake landed on her nose, and she could see Piper running in the snow, twirling around, catching snowflakes on her tongue then dropping to the ground, waving her arms, making snow angels. Her laughter tinkled in the air. Her bright eyes glittered like Christmas lights.

Then Gayle opened her eyes and realized it was all in her mind. The little girl she was holding wasn't smiling or laughing. She wanted her mommy.

"Gayle," the detective said. "Each of these children's families love their daughters just like you loved Piper. Please don't put them through the same kind of pain you're feeling."

For weeks and months after she'd lost her daughter, Gayle couldn't believe she was gone. She'd searched the faces of every child on the street looking for her. She'd become so depressed that Silas insisted she see a grief counselor. When that didn't seem to help and she insisted on knowing who received Piper's organs, finally Silas relented and learned that Kaylee had received Piper's heart. After all, the heart was the essence of life.

At first she'd just driven to the little girl's house and watched her play. Watched her from afar. She'd thought that would be enough. Seeing her heart breathing life into another child.

Then one day Kaylee had kicked a ball into the street and she'd caught it and handed it back to her. The moment she'd looked into the girl's eyes, she'd felt a connection and knew Kaylee belonged with her. She'd become obsessed with having her.

Now she saw the little girl clinging to the police officer, tears tracking her cheeks, and realized the depth of what she'd done.

"Gayle, please, let's end this," the detective said as she inched toward her.

"Please," Sarah's mother said softly. Compassion softened Mrs. Lundy's eyes and hacked at Gayle's anger. "I'm sorry," she murmured. "I... I'm so sorry."

She stooped down in front of Sarah and wiped at her cheeks with her thumb. "I'm sorry I scared, you, honey." She patted her shoulder then released her. "Go back to your mommy."

Sarah turned and ran, and her mother raced forward, scooped her in her arms and pressed her head against her shoulder. The father wrapped his arm around both of them and ushered them up the drive and onto the porch.

"Gayle?" Detective Reeves said. "Please give me the gun now."

Out of the corner of her eye, she saw the officer and that agent carrying Kaylee and Ava from the van and running over to a police car.

"You killed Renee, didn't you?" the detective asked. "You poisoned her soda at the prison."

Gayle nodded, remembering the day she'd overheard Renee and her sister talking about Renee's drinking.

"I heard the sisters talking about AA one day at the park," she said, the confession pouring out of her. "Then I thought, why does she get to have a daughter when she was drinking and my baby got taken away? It wasn't fair." She swiped at the snowflakes on her face. "She didn't deserve to raise my Piper. So I decided to join AA and get to know Renee."

"But then you kidnapped her daughter and framed her by telling the officer at the beach that Renee was drinking. You drugged her water bottle, didn't you?"

"Yes," she murmured, "while they were collecting seashells."

"I don't understand, though," the detective continued. "She was in jail, why kill her?"

Rage seethed through Gayle. "I had to. She told her sister and the cops about me, and I knew she could recognize me and then someone would figure it all out. I... was so desperate," she said in a low voice. "It was a year since Piper had gone. With every day that passed, I died a little inside."

"And then you pushed Priscilla off the ridge at Hangman's Dome," the detective said.

Gayle nodded, expression crazed. "I found that stupid Facebook group. I saw the two of them making friends. They were going to the reporter, and you were looking for Ava and... I had to do something."

The detective inched forward. "It's over, Gayle. I know you're sorry for frightening the children and that you're in pain, but I know you don't want to hurt anyone else, do you? That's not what Piper would want."

Pure agony overwhelmed Gayle, and she shook her head.

The detective was right. It was over. She knew what would happen next. She'd gone too far. Crossed too many lines. Hurt too many people.

Her husband. The children. Their mothers.

She'd go to jail. Be locked away forever. She deserved it.

Although she'd been a prisoner to her pain for two years now.

She lifted the gun again, then backed to the van, keeping the .22 trained on the detective. Then she dove into the driver's side and started the engine.

Silas was right. This had to stop. But before she really ended it, she had to be with Piper.

ONE HUNDRED FORTY-TWO

Ellie wanted to go after Gayle, but the kids needed her. For once, she had to delegate.

"Take my car and follow the van. I'll have the officer drive me and the girls to the hospital," she told Derrick. "Their families are waiting for them."

Derrick took her keys, jogged to the Jeep and sped off.

Ellie ran to the girls and climbed in the back seat of the squad car with them. "Take us to Bluff County Hospital," she told the officer, then she turned to the girls. "It's okay, Ava, Kaylee," she said. "We're going to carry you back to your families."

She fastened the girls in the back. Ava's tear-stained eyes sparkled, but Kaylee dropped her head forward. "My mommy's dead," Kaylee said in a tiny voice.

That was true. And Ellie couldn't change that. She pulled the child into her arms and brushed her hair from her face. "I'm sorry, honey. But your aunt Priscilla came to me. She's been looking for you. That's why I'm here."

Kaylee's eyes sparked with life again. "She did?"

"She did," Ellie said and gave her a big hug. "And I'm going to take you to her."

Ava's lips formed a pout. "The lady said my mommy didn't want me anymore. That I was too much trouble."

"Oh, honey, that's not true," Ellie said softly, cradling Ava's small face in her hands. "She loves you and has been worried out of her mind. She called me, too, and she hasn't stopped looking for you since that lady took you."

Ava reached across and clasped hands with Kaylee. "I told you she was a liar."

The defroster and wipers worked furiously as the officer drove back toward Bluff County. By the time they reached the main highway, the girls were so exhausted they'd curled into the seat and fallen asleep.

Ellie phoned Shondra. "We have Ava and Kaylee," she said. "They're frightened but okay. I'm on the way to the hospital with them. Tell the Trumans and bring them to meet us."

"That's great news," Shondra said. "Lara's been so despondent, but she and her husband went and picked up a puppy for Ava today." Shondra's voice wavered with emotion. "I think they had to do something, hold on to hope."

"Good. I'm just glad the girls are safe." She explained about Gayle Gooding and her husband. "We issued a bulletin for her car and Derrick is in pursuit. I want to question her husband, see if he knows where she might go. He was transported to Bluff County Hospital earlier."

She imagined Lara and Priscilla's faces when they heard the news and smiled in anticipation.

ONE HUNDRED FORTY-THREE

Derrick sped after Gayle and trailed her onto the highway, grateful Ellie's Jeep had four-wheel drive and snow tires. Still, the wheels chugged through the slushy streets and icy patches, slowing him. A few snowflakes blended with another deluge of rain, and fog blurred his vision. He cranked up the defroster, heat whirring through the vehicle, the windshield wipers scraping furiously to clear the ice.

Traffic was thicker tonight, with people traveling to visit their families and for Christmas Eve church services. Gayle was driving too fast, weaving around slower traffic and in and out of lanes. He tried to keep up, but she swung around another car, clipping its front bumper and sent that car into a spin. Derrick veered sideways to avoid hitting it and attempted to pass and keep up with Gayle, but an oncoming tractor trailer plowed toward him and slammed into the car that had skidded. The car went off the road and the tractor trailer careened toward the ditch then skated sideways and ended up blocking the highway.

He cursed and screeched to a stop. *Dammit to hell.* Gayle disappeared in a thick blur of fog and darkness. Cars skated to a stop on the other side of the tractor trailer, someone honked loudly, and two vehicles roared to a halt behind him, headlights nearly blinding him. Clenching his phone, he got out to see if anyone was hurt in the accident. A man was climbing from the truck and looked to be okay, just annoyed, and Derrick rushed to the car and found a woman trembling and looking shaken. He opened the car door and looked inside.

"Are you all right, ma'am?"

She looked up at him with a stunned expression, then gave a little nod. "Yes, but that car... it almost hit me."

"I know, ma'am. Do you need an ambulance?"

She moved her arms and legs as if to see if they were injured. "I don't think so."

Hands in the pockets of his big winter coat, the man in the truck walked over to join them.

"Are you all right, sir?" Derrick asked.

"Yeah." He indicated the woman. "You?"

She nodded shakily, and the man rubbed a hand over his beard with a weary sigh.

"I'll call it in," Derrick told them.

He pulled his phone, then made the call. Then he'd phone Ellie and tell her he'd lost Gayle, and he had no idea where she was going.

Snow fluttered down, the sea of white almost ethereal as the officer drove Ellie and the children through town. The candles glowing from the prayer vigil for Ava glowed like tiny moonbeams of hope in the night. Signs advertised that they were having a repeat performance of the Angel Pageant tomorrow at 4 p.m. at the children's hospital. Then Santa would pass out the gifts they'd collected at the Angel Tree.

Ellie had never felt such a surge of pride for the town in the way they'd come together to support the Trumans in this holiday season when fear and worry had shattered the joy. Dottie Clark with her neighborhood watch program. Emily Nettles with the Porch Sitters and the prayer vigils and fostering. Even Vera collecting gifts from the Angel Tree in town to pass to the needy.

Her phone buzzed, Derrick calling. "Ellie, dammit, I lost Gayle. She caused an accident and the road is blocked, but she went on."

Ellie clenched her teeth. "Is everyone okay at the accident?"

"Yes, I called it in, and I hear a siren already. Are you at the hospital?"

"Almost. I'll see if Gayle's husband has come to. Maybe he has an idea of where she might go."

"I'll meet you there."

She hung up, but her phone was ringing again. This time, Angelica. "Any word, Ellie?"

"Yes. Meet me at the station in the morning for the full story." She wouldn't trust anyone else to handle it.

"What can you tell me?" Angelica asked.

"We found Ava Truman and Kaylee Wilkinson and I'm about to reunite them with their families. Tomorrow I'll give a full report."

"Let me know the time and I'll be there," Angelica said.

She hung up, and the tires on the police car bounced over the speed bump in the entrance to the ER. Ellie felt as if the girls were healthy, but with their medical conditions, both would need a thorough work up.

"Help me get them in," she told the officer.

He cut the engine, hurried around to the backseat and opened the door then scooped a sleeping Kaylee into his arms. Ellie climbed out and picked Ava up, cradling her little body to her as they hurried inside. The doors swished open and ER workers rushed to greet them.

"What do we have?" a nurse asked.

"Two kidnapped little girls," Ellie said, then she heard a gasp and saw Lara and Jasper Truman running toward them from the waiting area, Shondra close behind.

"Ava!" Lara squealed. Jasper was right behind her, and Ava jerked her head up. Emotions bled through Ellie as Lara ran to her and reached for her daughter. Her eyes silently asked all the questions a mother would.

"She seems okay, just scared," Ellie said softly.

"Thank you," Lara murmured as she pulled Ava against her chest and kissed her hair, then Ava reached for Bunny.

"Mommy! Daddy!" Ava threw her arms around her mother's neck, burrowing into her, and Jasper wrapped his arms around them both.

Jasper looked up at Ellie with tears in his eyes. Regret mingled with relief and an apology in his voice. "Thank you for bringing our baby home."

Ellie gave a little nod. "I'm just glad she's here in time for Christmas."

"Good job," Shondra said warmly.

"I couldn't have done it without a team," Ellie replied, smiling.

Kaylee stirred and glanced up, searching their faces. "Ava?" she whimpered.

"I'm here." Ava reached for Kaylee's hand.

Lara stepped closer and the girls clung to each other for a second. "Kaylee took care of me, Mommy," Ava said in a small voice.

Lara blinked away tears and patted Kaylee. "I'm so glad you made friends."

"Let's take her to her aunt," Ellie said. "Lara, Jasper, you might want to come with and meet Priscilla. If it wasn't for her, we might not have found Ava."

"Yes, let's go," Lara said eagerly.

Ellie took Kaylee from the officer and led Lara and Jasper, clinging to Ava, down the hall to Priscilla's room. Ellie was glad to see Bryce still at the door.

"Thanks for staying, Sheriff," she said. "We found the girls."

"Good work, Ellie."

Had Bryce just given her a compliment?

He touched her elbow. "Mind if I go now? Mandy agreed to have breakfast with me tomorrow."

Ellie gave him a smile. "I'm glad. Just take it slowly, Bryce. Your daughter's lost a lot already."

His jaw tightened but then he slipped something into the palm of her hand. "My one-month chip," he said in a voice only she could hear. "I'm trying, Ellie."

Ellie was so touched she couldn't speak. Kaylee shifted in her arms, and Ellie knocked on Priscilla's door and opened it as Bryce headed down the hall.

Lara and Jasper stood aside and let her head in first. Priscilla was sleeping but lifted her head at the sound of them entering and when she looked up, squealed and reached for her niece. "Oh my goodness. Kaylee, baby, come here!"

"Aunt Prissy!" Kaylee squirmed against Ellie, and she hurried over and lowered the child into Priscilla's waiting arms.

Priscilla hugged and kissed Kaylee, and the girl wrapped her arms around her aunt's neck and laid her head on Priscilla's shoulder.

Ellie's lungs squeezed. Losing Piper had torn the Goodings apart, while almost losing Ava had brought the Trumans closer.

She looked at the clock as it struck midnight. Technically, it was Christmas Day. At least they had done it—the families would share the holiday together.

ONE HUNDRED FORTY-FIVE

Ellie stepped into the hall with Shondra and explained what happened. "Gayle got away. I need to talk to her husband and see if he has any idea where she'd go. Will you stand watch here in case she shows up to retaliate against Priscilla?"

"Of course." Shondra's eyes glittered with emotions.

Ellie breathed out in relief. "I'm supposed to go to Vera's for Christmas dinner tomorrow. Do you want to come?"

Shondra fluttered one hand to her chest. "Thanks for the invite, but I have plans. I... started seeing someone. Her name is Jules."

"Good for you," Ellie said. "You deserve to be happy, Shondra."

Shondra's phone buzzed, and she checked it. "It's her now. Merry Christmas."

"You, too." Shondra disappeared down the hall, and Ellie went to the nurse's station and asked where Gooding's room was.

"Room three-oh-six," the desk nurse said.

Ellie thanked her then rode the elevator to the third floor. There was a sheriff's deputy posted outside room 306. As she entered the room, Dr. Gooding was staring out the window looking desolate, resigned to him and his wife both being in serious trouble.

"Did you find the girls?" he asked as he pivoted to talk to her.

She nodded. "We did. She was at the Lundy house, but we stopped her from taking Sarah."

Tears filled his eyes. "And Gayle?"

"She got away," Ellie said. "We're looking for her and staking out your home. Do you have any idea where she might go?"

"It's all my fault," he said in a tortured voice. "I never should have taken Piper to Cattail Cove."

"It's not your fault," Ellie said softly. "It was a terrible, awful accident. And I'm so sorry for you and Gayle. But right now, she's panicked, and we need to find her before she hurts someone else." Or herself.

He pinched the bridge of his nose, then ran his hand over his bandaged head. "All she kept saying was that she wanted to be with Piper for Christmas. That she couldn't live without her."

A sense of foreboding rippled through Ellie. "Piper's buried at White Lilies, isn't she?"

His eyes sharpened, as he must have read her mind. "Oh, dear God. Yes, beneath the angel statue. That's where she's going."

Of course. Ellie dragged her keys from her pocket.

Ellie spun around, told the deputy where she was going and texted Derrick.

He responded: *Just getting to the hospital.*

She sent a return text: *Pick me up outside the ER entrance. I know where Gayle is going.*

Heart in her throat, Ellie jogged to the elevator, rode it down to the ER floor, then ran outside. The snow had stopped falling, but at least three inches covered the ground and the wind was howling as if crying out Gayle's pain.

Derrick rolled up in the Jeep and she jumped inside. "White Lilies Cemetery, across from Haints."

A grim look darkened Derrick's eyes, but he pressed the accelerator and sped from the parking lot. The cemetery was only a few miles away, but it felt like a hundred as he maneuvered the icy roads and fought to keep the Jeep on the road. The church bells were ringing as they reached the chapel by the graveyard, a few twinkling stars breaking through the pockets of snow clouds as if to offer light to the dreary day.

Derrick veered onto the narrow drive that wound through the graveyard and followed it until she spotted Gayle's van.

Parking behind her, they both drew their guns. Senses honed, Ellie scanned the graveyard for the angel statue. The small snow-covered tombstone markers, cherub and dove statues and the trickling waterfall looked almost surreal, but sadness and grief hovered in the air as if the innocent children lingered, running and playing chase in the gardens.

"Silas said Piper is buried near the angel statue." Ellie pointed it out and she and Derrick rushed toward it, weaving through the rows of graves. As she neared the statue, cold sweat beaded on her skin. She halted, her boots digging into the damp earth. Derrick made a strangled sound behind her as he stopped on her heels.

A profound sense of loss overwhelmed Ellie. They were too late.

Gayle Gooding lay face down, her hand outstretched on the nameplate carved into the small grave marker, bright red blood streaking the snow all around her body.

Gayle had finally found peace and gotten what she wanted— she would be with her daughter for Christmas.

WHITE LILIES CEMETERY

Ellie met the ME, Dr. Whitefeather, and the ERT at the edge of the graveyard and led them over to where Gayle lay in the crimson-stained snow. She and Derrick had already taken photos, but the ERT would conduct a formal investigation to confirm suicide. Although judging from Gayle's mental state, the blood spatter, position of the body and the gun residue on Gayle's hands, she didn't think it would take long for them to conclude the obvious.

"She was so distraught and grief-stricken over losing her daughter two years ago that she never recovered," Ellie explained. "We found the children she abducted, but she pulled a gun. Agent Fox gave chase and lost her. Her husband thought she would be here."

"That is so sad," Laney said. "I can't imagine the pain of losing a child." Laney stooped down to examine the body then gently rolled Gayle to the side. Blood spattered her jacket and clothing and hands and a gaping bloody hole had opened in her chest.

"Looks like the bullet pierced her heart," Laney said.

Laney examined Gayle's face, arms and hands. "No bruising or scratches to suggest anyone else was here or that she fought with an attacker."

"The gun is the same one she brought with her," Ellie said.

The forensic team began searching the area for footprints and evidence that someone else could have been here, but Ellie knew it was simply protocol. More ominous snow clouds rolled in, the temperature dropping as the forensic team worked and Laney arranged for Gayle's body to be transported to the morgue. The church bells struck one, the air shifting, and Ellie knew it was time she and Derrick went to talk to Silas again.

Derrick's phone jangled as they got in her Jeep.

"It's my partner at the Bureau," he said, then connected and put it on speaker.

"Fox, we busted MWC wide open. It wasn't as big an operation as we feared. Serena Morino was definitely running the show. We found three children at the headquarters and have them in foster care until we can locate their families. Two of the boys said they were living on the streets and the third said his parents were dead. That he'd lived with his grandmother but she became ill and couldn't get out of bed so he went out searching for food in the dumpsters near his house. Autumn Juniper saw him and took him. She's facing charges now, just as Ms. Moreno and everyone involved in the organization is."

"Great work," Derrick said. "Hopefully the kids can be adopted through legal means now and be placed with loving stable families."

Ellie's heart ached for the children, and she hoped Derrick was right, that they didn't get lost in a broken system. Thick snowflakes fell in waves as they drove to the hospital again, the cloud of white glowing against the headlights.

"What are you doing for Christmas?" Derrick asked.

"Going to my folks," Ellie said, a tense second passing. She would love to invite Derrick but the tight set of his jaw indicated that would never happen. "How about you?"

"My mother called. She sounded lonely. I'll spend it with her."

Another reminder of the fact his family had suffered because of hers, that they might never be able to cross the divide between them.

Her heart was heavy as she parked, and she and Derrick walked inside. The halls were quiet tonight, the holiday decorations meant to add cheer to the sick and their families, yet Ellie had no good news for Silas. When they reached his room, Ellie knocked and eased open the door.

Derrick squeezed her arm for comfort, and they slipped quietly inside.

Silas jerked his eyes open, searching their faces, and Ellie gave a sad shake of her head. "I'm sorry, Mr. Gooding. We didn't make it in time."

"Where..."

"You were right. She was at White Lilies with Piper."

Pain and sorrow wrenched his eyes, then he squeezed them shut and made a low keening sound.

Ellie's heart broke for him. He'd blamed himself for his daughter's death and ruined his career to try and atone to his wife. But nothing could bring Piper back.

And now he'd lost it all.

ONE HUNDRED FORTY-SEVEN

CROOKED CREEK

Wednesday, December 25

Ellie woke to sunlight streaming through the window and a blanket of white on the ground outside. She imagined all the children in Bluff County rushing to the Christmas tree, excited and squealing as they found toys left by Santa.

And the Trumans, Priscilla Wilkinson and Kaylee, and Jan and Becky Hornsby would be celebrating as families. Ava would finally get her puppy.

Vera was probably already working on her prime rib, peeling tiny new potatoes and baking pies. But before Ellie could join her own family, she had a press conference to address.

Though she hadn't slept much the night before for thinking about Silas, Gayle and their little girl, she crawled from bed and padded to the shower. She quickly cleaned up and dressed in a red holiday sweater and jeans that she would later wear to Vera's.

The mountains looked like a white winter wonderland as she dashed outside to her Jeep. The streets were fairly empty now as she drove, although she noticed lights flickering inside houses, a few kids already out sledding, having snowball fights, pushing new scooters and bicycles in their drives.

Angelica was waiting when she arrived at the station, looking regal in a red dress with her hair in a sophisticated, braided bun.

Her cameraman had already set up, and Captain Hale stood to the side in the press room. She'd texted Cord the night before and asked him to be present, too.

"You ready?" Angelica asked.

Ellie lifted her chin. "Yes, let's do this."

Tom gave the 1-2-3 signal and Angelica began, lifting her microphone. "Angelica Gomez, Channel Five News. This Christmas morning we're happy to report that thanks to the great police work of Detective Ellie Reeves, Ava Truman has been found safe and sound. She is now home with her parents for the holiday." She paused and pushed the mic toward Ellie. "Detective Reeves?"

"During the investigation into Ava Truman's disappearance, we discovered her abduction was linked to two other missing children, Kaylee Wilkinson and Becky Hornsby. All three girls have been reunited with their families. Sadly, a woman named Gayle Gooding abducted the children because she was distraught over the death of her own daughter, six-year-old Piper Gooding, two years ago." Ellie decided to omit the details about the transplants for now. Angelica could cover that in a more detailed report later. After all, this was Christmas and she wanted to focus on the good news today.

"I have some thanks to give. They say it takes a village to raise a child. This time, the residents of Bluff County were that village, and Ava, Kaylee and Becky might not have been found if not for your help, support, and the love that went out for Ava. From those who prayed and lit candles, to those who brought food to the Trumans, to the neighborhood watch, to Ranger Cord McClain and fellow SAR workers and town members who searched and hunted for Ava, and those who phoned in tips, you are the ones who held this town together."

Unexpected emotions teetered to the surface and Ellie worked to keep them from spilling over.

The hard cold details were hard to say out loud, but Ellie

couldn't help but think about them. One woman, Renee, died trying to convince the police to look for her child. Another mother, Jan, claimed she lived each day to find hers.

And Gayle Gooding took her own life to be with her daughter.

She thought of her own birth mother and how she'd suffered. First thing she'd done when she woke up this morning was to call and check on Mabel.

"She's making some progress," the doctor had said. "But I still think it's too soon for you to visit again. We don't want her to have a setback."

Ellie understood the message. Seeing her might thwart Mabel's progress. Her heart felt heavy but she accepted it.

"Detective?" Angelica prodded.

She jerked her attention back to the press conference then cleared her throat. "It's Christmas, folks, a time we are supposed to celebrate. So let's do that today. Hug your children and your families, keep them close and show them you love them."

She thanked everyone again, then stepped away and Angelica tied up the interview. Cord approached her, looking slightly sheepish. "You don't have to thank me for doing my job, Ellie."

She squeezed his arm. "Yes, I do. You're always there when I call."

He shrugged, his eyes flickering with unease. "I always will be."

Their gazes locked for a long minute. "Do you have plans today?"

He gave a tiny nod. "Lola asked me over. She's cooking."

Ellie smiled. "Then you're in for a treat."

A blush colored his bronzed skin. "How about you?" he asked.

"Going to my parents."

Cord nodded, then lingered another minute as if he had more to say. But Angelica approached her, and he headed out. The reporter had commented that she had no family, but that wasn't true. "Angelica, today is for family. Will you come to dinner at the Reeves with me?"

Angelica's brown eyes turned wary. "I don't want to intrude. And I know you haven't told them about me."

Ellie's heart skipped a beat. "No, but it's time I did. I meant what I said. You're my sister and I want the Reeves to know it. Today, families should be together."

Angelica's gaze met hers for a heartbeat, emotions clouding her serious face. "I don't know what to say."

"Just say you'll come," Ellie said, then pulled Angelica into a hug.

"I will," Angelica whispered. "Merry Christmas, Ellie."

"Merry Christmas, Angelica."

A LETTER FROM RITA

Thank you so much for coming back to read more about Detective Ellie Reeves! And if you're new to the series, don't worry—each book continues her journey but is a standalone novel so I'm happy you've found her. If you'd like to keep up with all of my latest releases, you can sign up at the following link. Your email address will never be shared, and you can unsubscribe at any time.

www.bookouture.com/rita-herron

Stolen Angels is the fifth installment in the series and challenges Ellie in new ways, both professionally, personally and emotionally.

The moment my editor suggested the title *Stolen Angels*, I imagined a holiday tree with paper angels that held gift requests for needy families and children, much like the one at my YMCA and church. I saw little girls in angel costumes singing and dancing and the town of Crooked Creek coming together to celebrate.

I saw a child gone missing and the fear and terror that came from it and how it might shatter families and destroy a holiday known for joy and cheer.

I knew Ellie Reeves would fight tooth and nail though to find that child and bring her home safely. I also knew it wouldn't be easy, that one missing child would lead to another and another…

I hope you enjoyed Ellie's determination to solve this case and the twists and turns the story took. If you did, I'd appreciate it if you left a review and share your feedback with others.

I love to hear from readers so you can find me on Facebook, my website and Twitter.

Thanks so much for joining me in cheering Ellie Reeves on!

Happy Reading!

Rita

facebook.com/ritaherron

twitter.com/ritaherron

ACKNOWLEDGMENTS

As always, I have to thank my fabulous editor Christina Demosthenous for literally handing me a great title that spurned the idea for this story. Her insights, patience, advice and suggestions took the basic idea to an entirely new level!

Thanks to the entire team at Bookouture for the amazing cover and support you've shown for the series and to my agent Jenny Bent for her support over the years. And much thanks to the line and copy editors who catch all my bloopers!

Printed in Great Britain
by Amazon